Summer Breeze

FOUR SEASONS

Summer Breeze

CATHERINE PALMER & GARY CHAPMAN

TYNDALE HOUSE PUBLISHERS, INC.
Carol Stream, Illinois

Visit Tyndale's exciting Web site at www.tyndale.com

Check out the latest about Catherine Palmer at www.catherinepalmer.com and about Gary Chapman at www.garychapman.org

TYNDALE and Tyndale's quill logo are registered trademarks of Tyndale House Publishers, Inc.

Summer Breeze

Designed by Jennifer Ghionzoli

Edited by Kathryn S. Olson

Scripture quotations are taken from the *Holy Bible*, New Living Translation, copyright © 1996, 2004. Used by permission of Tyndale House Publishers, Inc., Carol Stream, Illinois 60188. All rights reserved.

Some Scripture quotations are taken from the *Holy Bible*, King James Version.

Library of Congress Cataloging-in-Publication Data
Palmer, Catherine, date.
   Summer breeze / Catherine Palmer and Gary Chapman.
     p. cm.
   ISBN-13: 978-1-4143-1166-1 (pbk. : alk. paper)
   ISBN-10: 1-4143-1166-4 (pbk. : alk. paper)
   1. Marriage—Fiction. 2. Ozarks, Lake of the (Mo.)—Fiction. I. Chapman, Gary D., date.
II. Title.
PS3566.A495S857 2007
813′.54—dc22   2007004158

Printed in the United States of America

13 12 11 10 09 08 07
7   6   5   4   3   2   1

When two people are under the influence
of the most violent, most insane, most delusive, and most transient of passions,
they are required to swear that they will remain in that excited,
abnormal, and exhausting condition continuously until death do them part.

GEORGE BERNARD SHAW
Getting Married

NOTE TO READERS

There's nothing like a good story! I'm excited to be working with Catherine Palmer on a fiction series based on the concepts in my book *The Four Seasons of Marriage*. You hold in your hands the second book in this series.

My experience, both in my own marriage and in counseling couples for more than thirty years, suggests that marriages are always moving from one season to another. Sometimes we find ourselves in winter—discouraged, detached, and dissatisfied; other times we experience springtime, with its openness, hope, and anticipation. On still other occasions we bask in the warmth of summer—comfortable, relaxed, enjoying life. And then comes fall with its uncertainty, negligence, and apprehension. The cycle repeats itself many times throughout the life of a marriage, just as the seasons repeat themselves in nature. These concepts are described in *The Four Seasons of Marriage*, along with seven proven strategies to help couples move away from the unsettledness of fall or the alienation and coldness of winter toward the hopefulness of spring or the warmth and closeness of summer.

Combining what I've learned in my counseling practice with Catherine's excellent writing skills has led to this series of four novels. In the lives of the characters you'll meet in these pages, you will see the choices I have observed people making over and over again through the years, the value of caring friends and neighbors, and the hope of marriages moving to a new and more pleasant season.

In *Summer Breeze* and the other stories in the Four Seasons fiction series, you will meet newlyweds, blended families, couples who are deep in the throes of empty-nest adjustment, and senior couples. Our hope is that you will see yourself or someone you know in these characters. If you are hurting, this book can give you hope—and some ideas for making things better. Be sure to check out the discussion questions at the end of the book for further ideas.

And whatever season you're in, I know you'll enjoy the people and the stories in Deepwater Cove.

Gary D. Chapman, PhD

ACKNOWLEDGMENTS

So many people affect the writing and publication of a novel. For his valuable information about the Missouri Water Patrol, Officer Shannon Bledsoe has earned my admiration and gratitude. Any errors in the manuscript are my own. For inspiration as well as prayer support, the young wives and mothers in Michael Vitelli's Bible study class have my deepest thanks. Frances, Carolynn, Tammara, Liz, and many others, may God bless and reward you for your faithful service. For sharing both laughter and tears, my longtime friends are treasures I cherish. Janice, Mary, Roxie, Kristie, BB, Lucia—I love you. My prayer support team holds me up before God, and I can't thank you enough—Mary, Andrew, Nina, and Marilyn.

I also thank my Tyndale family for all you have meant to me during these past ten years. Ron Beers and Karen Watson, bless you for making this series not only a reality but a pleasure. Kathy Olson, I can't imagine having the courage to write a single word without you. Your careful editing and precious friendship are truly gifts from the Lord. Travis and Keri, Andrea, Babette, Mavis, Victor, the amazing sales team, the wonderful design department—thank you all from the bottom of my heart.

Though I often leave them for last, first on my list of supporters, encouragers, and loved ones are my family. Tim, Geoffrey, and Andrei, I love you so much.

CHAPTER ONE

The crackle of the two-way radio mounted in his boat alerted Officer Derek Finley to a call from Water Patrol headquarters in Jefferson City.

"Boater in distress," the dispatcher said. "Boater in distress at the twenty-mile mark in front of Green Oaks Condominiums. Dan Becker is reporting the incident. Repeat, Dan Becker. He says he's in the path of other boats, and he believes he is creating a possible hazard in navigation."

"Ten-four, Jeff City." Derek began to turn the twenty-nine-foot Donzi the Patrol had assigned him. With its twin outboard motors—each at 250 horsepower—the boat could go sixty-five miles an hour. But he wouldn't push it to that speed on a routine call like this one.

"Okay, Jeff," he told the dispatcher. "I will be en route from the twenty-five-mile mark."

As he increased speed, Derek scanned for other boats in his path. On such a warm, beautiful day, the first day of the long Memorial Day weekend, the water would be busy. Without doubt, several folks would be boating while intoxicated. Though Missouri had many lakes, rivers, and streams, Lake of the Ozarks had the highest number of BWI arrests in the state. Working the night shift, which began at three in the afternoon and wouldn't end until three the next morning, he had already stopped a boat after spotting a woman who had decided to sunbathe on a bow gunwale lacking adequate rails. Later, he had taken a call about a personal watercraft operating in a no-wake zone near someone's dock. Many PWC operators had no idea they were supposed to obey the same rules as a full-size craft.

The Donzi cut through the sparkling water, and as he often did, Derek reflected on how much he enjoyed his job. Though he had graduated from college with a degree in business and had worked behind a desk for almost a year, he'd quit the minute he heard the state was recruiting. Not long after, he'd passed the background check and the physical fitness test. His work with the Water Patrol provided the perfect blend of excitement, enjoyment of nature, public service, and—during the rare criminal investigation—intellectual challenge.

Now approaching the twenty-mile mark, Derek spotted the stranded boat—a twenty-five-foot Challenger bobbing midchannel as other vessels zipped around it. Two middle-aged couples, sunburned and hatless, began waving the moment they saw him.

"Jeff, I am 10-23 with the boater in distress," Derek told the dispatcher. He slowed the Donzi as he approached the stranded vessel. "How're you folks doing today? Is there a Dan Becker on board?"

"That's me," one of the men answered. "It's my boat. I'm the one who called."

"I understand you broke down."

"Yeah, looks that way. We were out all morning fishing. Then we headed home and got this close to our dock, and suddenly the motor died."

"We've tried everything," the other man said. "The boat won't start."

"You got gas?"

"We had a full tank when we left the dock." Dan Becker scratched the rosy bald spot on his head. "We can't have used all that up. Lemme check." In a moment, he groaned. "Empty. Oh, brother. I never even thought of that."

Derek smiled. Though the common boating mishaps that took most of his time could feel a little routine, he enjoyed helping people—whether it was seeing an intoxicated person out of danger to himself or others, guiding someone who'd gotten lost on the lake, or assisting a couple of stalled fishermen. Derek felt a sense of purpose and accomplishment at the end of each day. "Happens all the time," he told Dan. "How about a tow? I can take you to your slip. Or there's a gas dock about a half mile down. Mermaid Marina. You can fill up there."

Fanning themselves, the women begged to be taken to their personal slip near the condominium. But Dan and his buddy prevailed. "Let's get some gas. Might as well take care of it, since we've got you here, Officer."

Expecting that answer, Derek was already gathering the tow rope. "I'm going to throw this across. Hook it to the bow eye."

As the two men worked to clip the rope to their boat, Derek checked the black tow post mounted on his Donzi. When they signaled him, Derek stepped into the shade of the canopy to the operator's position and took the wheel. As his Donzi moved forward, the tow rope tightened, and the Challenger began floating safely behind.

Out of gas, he thought with a chuckle and a shake of his head. How many times had he heard that one? His Donzi and the nineteen other Water Patrol boats that constantly roamed Lake of the Ozarks carried officers to answer complaint calls and emergencies. Success depended on control, wits, courage, and skill. Most of the time, the calls were run-of-the-mill, but he had to stay always alert in case of a real problem.

He mentally recounted the list of reasons people gave for their boats stalling in the water. "Officer, our motor broke." "My boat won't start." "Our outdrive is busted." "We were pullin' a skier and our motor fell off!" But by far the most common was "We ran out of gas."

Towing the Challenger alongside the Mermaid Marina dock, Derek noted the college-aged young women who worked the gas pumps and encouraged people to visit the lake-view restaurant just uphill from the dock. He tipped his cap as a pleasant reminder that he'd be patrolling the area for boaters who might have had too much to drink.

Then he turned to Dan Becker and his companions. "Well, you're here safe and sound," he said as they unhooked the tow rope and tossed it back to him. "You folks have a great day now."

"Say, Officer," Dan called, "what do we owe you for the tow?"

"Part of the job." Derek waved as he pulled away and reported to the dispatcher. "Jeff, I'm 10-24 and 10-8."

With the assignment completed, he was back in service. As Derek steered into open water again, a fellow officer radioed him, and they agreed to meet at the fifteen-mile mark to touch base. With overlapping shifts, the men often met on the water to discuss ongoing investigations and recent incidents. In the past ten years, Derek figured he had seen just about everything. But the recent unusual drowning had him and the other officers puzzled. Five days earlier, Derek had found a body floating in a tangle of fishing line near Deepwater Cove. So far there were no clues as to the victim's identity. And no one had reported a missing person.

Surveying the many boats on the lake as he passed them, Derek knew the unresolved incident was nagging at him. But without more information, there was nothing he could do.

Dark hair flying, the ten-year-old pressed back hard on the pedals of her bicycle. Girl and bike skidded to a stop in the driveway of the gray, wood-framed house with its window boxes full of draping, hot pink petunias. As the bike's front wheel rammed into the post that supported the mailbox, the child's mother gasped aloud.

"Lydia, where is your helmet?" Kim called from the front porch of the lakefront house. "I told you never to ride your bike without a helmet. Go to your room and put it on this instant!"

"I'm done riding for the day," Lydia announced, dropping her bicycle in the driveway and flouncing toward the house. She wore a midriff-revealing, spaghetti-strapped T-shirt; a pair of tight aqua shorts; and sparkly flip-flops. "I called Dad while you and Luke were at the doctor. He wants to talk to you."

A chill of dread swirled through Kim's stomach. "Lydia, you're not supposed to talk to your father unless I'm in the room. That's a court order."

"Court order, court order! I'm sick to death of court orders. Who cares, anyhow?"

Lydia tried to step past her mother, but Kim blocked her way with an outstretched arm.

"What?" the girl snapped. "Let me by! I need to call Tiffany."

"Sit down here on the porch with me a minute," Kim ordered. Seeing the stubborn tilt to her daughter's chin, she added more softly, "Please."

"Mom, I need to find out what Tiffany's wearing to church tomorrow." Lydia, all skinny brown legs and lanky arms, dropped onto a wicker chair. "Her mom's going to let her wear shorts to church, because it's already a week past Memorial Day, and everybody knows Memorial Day is the start of summer."

"You're not wearing shorts to church," Kim declared. Two years older and a grade ahead of Lydia in school, Tiffany had little parental supervision. Lydia's best friend, she often accompanied the Finley family to church and on other outings, but her mother never joined them. In fact, Kim had never met the woman, who seemed to allow her daughter to do whatever she wanted any time of the day or night.

Kim shook her head. "I don't think shorts are appropriate for church, and—"

"They're appropriate if everyone else is wearing them!" Lydia glared at her mother with narrowed eyes. "You don't know anything."

Taking a deep breath, Kim settled onto a wicker love seat beside her daughter. As she studied Lydia, she attempted to pray away her ire while focusing on the lovely young woman emerging from childhood before her eyes.

"Lydia," she began, stifling the urge to scold, "you know all the rules are for your own safety. The helmet is to protect your head, and the court order is to regulate your father's contact with you. He hasn't been abiding by our agreements, and I'm this close to calling my attorney about it. The last thing I need is for *you* to be calling *him*."

"How long is this lecture going to take?" Lydia cut in. "Tiffany wants me to call her right after she gets home from the mall."

"Interrupting me is rude and unacceptable," Kim retorted. "I'd better not see you riding that bike without your helmet again, or I'll ground you from it. And you can forget about wearing shorts to church. The ones you have on are too short. Don't you realize what you look like these days? You're almost a teenager, Lydia. You have to start behaving more maturely, and that includes being aware of the way you dress. And if I hear that you've called your father again, young lady, you're going to have serious consequences. Now go move that bicycle out of the driveway before Derek comes home and runs over it."

"Would you relax?" Lydia asked, her voice just at the edge of a sneer. She pushed up from the chair and started across the porch, headed for her bicycle. "You're so grouchy. You yell at everyone and preach at us all the time. We used to have fun when you were home, but now I can't wait until you go back to work. You're making Luke and me miserable. I'm surprised Derek even bothers to come home. All you do is bite his head off."

"You're exaggerating, Lydia. I don't yell at you and Luke, and I never . . ." Kim's voice faltered as her daughter defiantly swung a leg over the bike, settled onto the saddle, and pedaled off up the road. As Lydia's glossy brown hair vanished around a curve, Kim knotted her fists and battled down a cry of rage. This was not supposed to happen!

The focus of the family ought to be on Luke, not Lydia. Luke was the twin with diabetes. In order to stay alive, Luke needed the right diet, enough exercise, and regular monitoring of his blood glucose level. In the past few weeks, Kim had reexamined everything she knew about nutrition and basic general health. And then she'd had to absorb an enormous amount of new information. Things like syringes, glucose monitors, and lancet needles were part of everyday life now. She easily used new terms such as *beta cells, HLA markers, hypoglycemia, ketones,* and *triglycerides.* Day and night for the month since Luke's first symptoms and then the diagnosis, she had watched over her son. She spent hours praying for his health, worrying over any sign of a possible problem, and phoning to discuss each development with his endocrinologist.

Unwilling to send Luke to the sports and recreational camps the twins usually attended in the summer, Kim had asked permission to take a leave of absence from her work as a hygienist for a dentist in Camdenton. Dr. Groene was sympathetic and kind, and he'd hired temporary help for the short term. But Kim's paychecks had stopped, and the family was finding it hard to make ends meet.

A voice broke into her thoughts. "Where's Lydia?" Luke pushed open the screen door and stepped onto the porch. "I thought I heard her out here. Tiffany just called."

"She's riding her bike," Kim told her son. She signaled for Luke to join her by patting the wicker love seat. "How are you doing, honey? Are you shaky or nauseous like this morning?"

"I'm fine, Mom." He plopped down in the chair where his sister had sat moments before. "I wish I felt like riding my bike."

"Well, why don't you? Do you feel dizzy or anything like that?

Do you have a headache?" She reached toward him. "Let me see if you're sweaty."

"Mom, stop. I'm okay." Luke pulled his knees to his chin and wrapped his arms around them. "You're treating me like a baby! I checked my blood. Nothing's wrong with me. Leave me alone."

"Then get your helmet and go catch up to your sister. I'm sure she'd enjoy the company."

"No." Glaring over his knees, he frowned out at the world. "I don't feel like doing anything. And I'm not wearing that stupid helmet anymore."

Kim sighed. Growing up in a home in which her parents' constant fighting had led to divorce, she had learned to cope with the unexpected. Her alcoholic mother had moved the children from town to town as drinking cost her one job after another. Kim had been determined never to repeat her parents' mistakes. The summer after graduating from high school, she'd gone to work for Dr. Groene as a receptionist and moved into a small apartment. Soon her next-door neighbor had charmed his way into her heart, and she happily married the handsome marine-engine repairman.

It wasn't long before Kim realized she had done exactly what she'd hoped to avoid. Every now and then—seemingly out of the blue—Joe became loud and mean. She was just past her first trimester with the twins the first time he slapped her. After that, her life became a nightmare.

Terrified to leave her husband and terrified to stay with him, she walked on eggshells and prayed that she could safely deliver her babies. Soon after they were born, Kim had started attending the Lake Area Ministry Bible Chapel. At LAMB Chapel, as it was called, she found strength and courage she had never known in her life. With the help and support of several women in the church, especially Patsy Pringle, she had managed to escape her husband and take refuge at an abuse crisis center. After divorcing Joe and winning custody of the twins, she settled into what she hoped could be a normal life.

And then she'd met Derek Finley. Even as she thought of the wonderful man who had stepped into her life and swept her off her feet three years before, Kim saw his truck rolling along the lake road toward their home in Deepwater Cove.

"Hey, here comes Derek!" Luke shouted. "I wonder if he brought me any cherry strings."

"You can't have—" Kim bit off the rest of the words. If Luke wanted to eat a snack now and then, he would simply have to monitor his blood sugar and keep everything in balance. He had learned to do that already. She needed to start trusting him. But a ten-year-old boy? It was so hard not to worry.

"Look, he's got Lydia's bike in the back!" Luke jumped off his chair and raced across the porch and down the steps. "I bet she fell off! I bet she wasn't wearing her helmet!"

"Oh no!" Kim ran toward the approaching truck. "Derek? Is Lydia all right?"

"Of course I am." Lydia opened the door on the passenger side and slid out onto the driveway. "Derek saw me riding near the highway to Tranquility, and he picked me up. Hey, Luke, want some trail mix? It's cheese flavored."

Before Kim could react, Luke had stuck his hand into the bag. She was trying to say something about it being almost suppertime and not good for his glucose level when Derek swept her up in his arms and planted a warm kiss on her lips. She resisted for a moment—fears, worries, and frustration still at the forefront of her mind—and then she smelled his sun-heated skin. Melting into her husband, she wrapped her arms around his neck and slid her hand down the soft hair at the back of his head.

"Surprise," he said, kissing her cheek and then the side of her neck. "I hope you made enough supper for one extra. The captain saw I was getting bleary-eyed and sent me home for a couple of hours to eat and put my feet up."

"Bleary-eyed?" Kim murmured. "Not you. And surely not in Party Cove."

He laughed and swatted her playfully as he followed her to the porch. They both knew that in his ten years on patrol, Derek had become jaded by the skimpily clad twentysomethings who cavorted from boat to boat in the notorious cove.

With more than a little pride, Kim opened the front door to a home filled with the aroma of homemade spaghetti sauce and toasted garlic bread. As it was a Saturday, she had been able to start the morning by tackling the laundry that piled up through the week and scrubbing the master bathroom.

In the midst of tensions converging like a line of thunderstorms capable of producing tornadoes, Kim always tried to keep the house peaceful and clean. She knew she was sometimes discouraged or grumpy, but she hoped her husband and children understood how much she cared by the things she did for them.

"The doctor says Luke is doing very well at monitoring his glucose levels," she told Derek as they stepped into the kitchen. That morning, Kim had fed the twins an early lunch before driving her son to his pediatrician's office. Afterward, she'd had time to finish the laundry and vacuum the living room.

"I knew the boy could conquer this thing," Derek said. "He's tough as nails, that kid. How's Lydia been today?"

"The same." Kim lifted the lid on the spaghetti sauce and gave it a stir. "She wants to wear shorts to church tomorrow."

"Why not? She's a pretty little gal, just like her mom. Both of you look cute in shorts. Besides, it's summer."

"Don't you dare side with her, Derek," Kim warned. "She's already pushing every limit we've set. She called Joe this afternoon when we weren't home. She won't wear her bike helmet. And now she's determined to wear shorts to church just because Tiffany's mother is letting Tiffany wear them."

"Does God have something against shorts?"

Kim pursed her lips to keep from saying something she might regret. The only thing that had caused her to doubt the wisdom of marrying Derek Finley was his disinterest in church. She had read about the importance of sharing a religious faith with your spouse, but she hadn't realized how much it would mean to her until they were already married. Then she saw that Derek slept in on his work-free Sunday mornings, and he never made anything but indifferent comments when Kim tried to talk to him about her beliefs. He certainly didn't try to lead the family in prayer or direct their thoughts toward heaven. Still, in every other way, he had proven himself just about perfect.

"Oh, baby, that is the best-smelling sauce in the world." Derek sighed as he leaned over to savor the scent. "You are the queen of cooks, and I mean that. My mom could make some pretty decent spaghetti, but you have her beat hands down."

Kim smiled as she set an extra place at the table. Derek's mother was exactly opposite to hers. Kim's mom had barely been able to afford the clothes she needed to wear to apply for work, while Derek had been brought up in a lovely home in Clayton, near St. Louis. Before he was killed in an automobile accident, Derek's father had worked as an award-winning freelance photographer for various wildlife and exploration magazines. His mother always dressed in linen and pearls. She belonged to a country club and several volunteer organizations. And she never failed to point out the small flaws in her son's chosen life partner.

"I got my spaghetti recipe from that chef I told you about," Kim said as Derek washed his hands in the kitchen sink. She had asked him a hundred times to wash up in the bathroom. He never noticed the coat of grime he left on her white porcelain sink.

"The guy your mother worked for when you lived in Joplin?" he asked, shedding droplets across the countertop as he reached for the towel. "He taught you a lot. I owe that fellow. If we ever get down south, we'll stop by the restaurant so I can shake his hand and thank him for turning my wife into the best cook ever."

"You would have liked him. His name was Marcel, and he was from France. But he could make just about anything, including spaghetti."

"He let you hang around in his kitchen?"

"Well, not at the restaurant. My mom got fired only a couple of weeks after we moved to Joplin. But she and Marcel had already struck up a thing for each other, so we moved in with him for a while. I can't remember how long that one lasted. Anyway, he used to cook for us after work, and I would watch him."

Derek came up behind Kim and slipped his strong arms around her waist as she checked the pasta. "I don't know how a woman like you could have emerged from that kind of past," he murmured. "But I sure am glad I found you."

Kim turned her head and kissed his cheek. "God brought us together," she told him. "And I have no idea how He feels about shorts in church."

"Go easy on Lydia, Kim. I bet if Luke starts acting more like himself, Lydia will follow."

Kim stepped out of her husband's embrace and took down bowls for the sauce and pasta. She generally respected the way Derek handled the kids, but when they disagreed, it was all she could do to keep from reminding him that they were *her* children, and he ought to just back off. This time, as usual, he was right.

"I'm probably being too hard on both of them," Kim admitted. "I talked it over with Patsy last week, and she thought maybe Lydia's rebellion is her way of responding to all the changes we've had to make because of Luke. It made sense. I know I'm overprotecting him and making both of the kids as afraid as I am."

"Really, Lydia's doing pretty well, considering." Derek sat down at the table as Kim called the twins to dinner. "The shorts, the helmet, even calling Joe . . . none of those things is all that bad. Not like the stuff I see going on with girls just a few years older than Lydia. She's a great kid."

"What do you mean calling Joe is not that bad? You know what kind of a man he is. I can't believe you think Lydia's behavior today is okay."

"Calm down, honey. Joe only contacts the kids because it makes you crazy. There's no way he's getting anywhere near them. Don't get so upset."

"You'd be upset too if you really understood what that man put us through. You may be used to dealing with out-of-control drunks, but I'm not! The kids and I were his victims long enough, and the thought of him being in contact with them still scares me."

"You're a strong woman, Kim."

"Maybe so, but Joe is stronger." She shook her head in frustration. "You know what he's like, Derek, but you're never willing to discuss it with me. You won't do anything about it, either. You just keep telling me it's going to be okay. Sometimes I wonder if you even hear what I'm saying. Where's your concern for me? Where's the protection you ought to be offering the children? Joe is out there, and he scares me to death."

"But he can't hurt any of you, Kim. The law protects you, I'll protect you, and you can stand up for yourself. At some point you need to trust yourself—and the kids."

"They're only children, Derek. They're ten years old." Kim glared at him as she took the chair across the table. "Things have changed. I realize the twins are almost eleven, and I've left them alone in the past. Summers have been filled with camps and clubs and some free time at home. But with Joe making trouble and with Luke's problems, I can't imagine doing that now."

"Listen, I had an idea—"

"Hey, Derek, did you find out who drowned the other day?" Luke skipped into the kitchen, followed closely by his sister. "Did some drunk fall out of a boat again? Or was it a murder? That would be cool!"

"He's not going to say anything about it," Lydia admonished her brother. "I already asked him."

"Your sister's right—I can't talk about an ongoing investigation," Derek told Luke, reaching over to rumple his hair. "You know that, buddy. Besides, who wants to hear that kind of thing at the table? Look at this awesome dinner your mom made."

"I hate spaghetti," Lydia announced. "I'm not eating it. She leaves chunks of tomatoes floating around so you can see them. It's disgusting."

"Lydia," Kim began.

"Are we going to pray?" Luke cut in. "I'm so hungry I feel like I'm going to throw up."

"Hunger and nausea. That's a blood sugar imbalance!" Kim started to leap up from the table, but Derek caught her arm.

Luke scowled. "Mom, just feed me, okay? I'll be fine in a minute."

"Just feed him," Lydia insisted, her face going pale. "Feed him, Mom!" Suddenly bursting into tears, she grabbed her brother's plate and ladled spaghetti sauce onto it. "Eat, Lukey," she said, pressing a spoonful toward his mouth. "Eat! Eat this right now."

"Stop it, you idiot!" Luke knocked the spoon out of his sister's hand, splattering the kitchen floor and wall with red sauce. "I'm not gonna die! Everybody quit freaking out! I hate the way you guys treat me all the time. You make me feel like I'm dying, and I'm not!"

"Whoa there." Derek laid his hand firmly on Luke's shoulder. "Nobody thinks you're dying. You're *not* dying, kiddo; you're living. You're doing great with everything, and your mom and I are so proud of you we could just about bust. So, let's all settle down and have some dinner. Kim, how about if I pray?"

It was the first time in their marriage that Derek had even mentioned prayer, let alone offered to ask a blessing. Kim was so astonished she couldn't speak.

Keeping one hand on Luke's shoulder and the other on his wife's arm, Derek bowed his head. "We're all a little off-balance here," he began, "and we need to settle down and realize that someone bigger than us is in control. Please help Luke get to feeling comfortable managing his diabetes, and help Lydia to accept the change in her brother without getting too upset. And be with Kim, who trusts in You to look out for her family. Amen."

Everyone lifted their heads at the same time. Kim swallowed in grateful amazement that for the first time, her husband had acknowledged the existence of a heavenly power. Maybe Derek hadn't used God's name or mentioned Christ, but at least he had offered up a prayer. It was a beginning—a huge beginning.

A smile softening her heart, Kim lifted the bowl of pasta and passed it to her husband. "Thank you, honey," she said. "That was exactly what we needed."

Derek grinned as he dished out a plateful of noodles. "And here's something else that'll help us all feel better—an answer to my prayer right off the bat. I was about to mention this earlier, but I got interrupted. Kim, you're going to be able to go back to work on Monday, and the twins will be safe and sound right here at home." He looked around the table. "My mother called this afternoon. Kids, your grandma Finley's on her way down here from St. Louis for a nice long visit!"

CHAPTER TWO

Well, howdy-doody," Pete said, waggling his eyebrows as Patsy settled onto the weather-beaten gray bench beside him on the dock. "I've never seen you without all your gear."

"What gear?" She stretched out her legs and drank down a breath of cool air off the lake. "Pete, if you start talking about how I change my hair color all the time or the fact that I enjoy wearing makeup or how many pairs of high heels I own, I'll go home and take a nap."

"All right; I won't say a word." He leaned over and gave her a little peck on the cheek. "But I sure do like the look of those bare toes."

It was the first time Pete had come close to even touching Patsy, let alone kissing her, and she just about fell off the bench into the lake. Instead, she grabbed the iron post that supported the dock's roof. Taking a deep breath, she tried to calm herself.

Under normal circumstances, Sunday afternoon called for a nap. But lately the order of Patsy's Sundays had altered, and she liked the change. Nowadays, she met Pete Roberts in the sanctuary. They sat together on her favorite pew near the front of the chapel, where the music and preaching could keep her awake. After that, she and the owner of Rods-N-Ends dined at Aunt Mamie's Good Food in Camdenton. You couldn't find a better place for fried chicken, roast beef, hot homemade dinner rolls, and mashed potatoes with creamy brown gravy.

Today Pete had persuaded Patsy to accompany him to Deepwater Cove's community dock for a little postlunch fishing. It was the worst time of day for the crappie to bite, but Patsy figured the dock might be a good place to accidentally on purpose run into the Finleys. The twins loved to swim, and Patsy often spotted the family at the lakeshore in the afternoon.

Unwilling to admit that Pete's kiss had startled her, Patsy dipped her toes into the water. "Any sign of the Finleys?" she asked, looking around. "I'd like to ask Kim how things are going with Luke."

Aware of Pete's shoulder next to hers, Patsy kept her focus trained on the lake. For umpteen years, she had shampooed, trimmed, dyed, curled, and styled people's hair. She knew the feel of long hair, short hair, fine hair, coarse hair, limp hair, and overpermed, overbleached, over-blow-dried hair. But Patsy couldn't remember the last time she had felt the brush of a man's mustache and beard against her cheek.

Not that she particularly *liked* it, she told herself as Pete went back to his minnow. Facial hair held no appeal to Patsy. It hid a man's best features—his mouth and jawline—not to mention the crumbs and other junk that could get caught in it.

But that kiss . . .

It had caught her off guard and sent a shiver down her spine. Patsy absently stuck her hand in Pete's minnow bucket and came up with one of the small, wriggling silver bait fish. Did her reaction to a kiss on the cheek mean Patsy's well-barricaded heart was softening to the man?

She poked her hook through the minnow and cast the fishing line out across the open water that surrounded the dock. The afternoon sun glinted off the blue-gray surface, casting spangles of light on the dock's corrugated tin roof. On this weekend, one of the busiest of the year, Lake of the Ozarks bustled with traffic. Runabouts pulled inner tubes, skiers, and wakeboarders. Pontoon boats drifted along, loaded down with families who were barbecuing or fishing. Jet Skis zoomed by, ripping up the water and making conversation difficult.

Despite the hectic activity on the lake, its surroundings remained peaceful. Thick forests of maple, oak, dogwood, redbud, and hickory trees draped with ivy and carpeted with layers of fallen leaves and mushrooms reached down to the water's edge. Red and yellow limestone bluffs formed caves for bats and sanctuaries for all kinds of wildlife. Overhead, in a blue sky dotted with puffs of white clouds, ravens circled, gulls searched for fish, and flocks of geese winged toward secret nests.

Patsy would have enjoyed the scenery if not for that kiss Pete had given her. Boy, oh boy. She could not afford to let her comfortable, well-ordered life get thrown off-kilter by a man. Especially not Pete Roberts. Everything he had told her about his past made her uncomfortable—two divorces, enough DWIs to send him to jail, a stint in a rehabilitation center, and a job that barely let him make ends meet. He had been known to chew tobacco and spit wherever it was convenient, including the flower box outside Patsy's salon. He was pudgy, hairy, and annoying. Other than that, she didn't mind him too much.

"Nice day for fishing," Pete drawled as he turned the crank on his reel. "What did you think of the sermon this morning?"

"I liked it." Truth be told, Patsy had already forgotten the topic of the message, but she admired Pastor Andrew and knew he had probably preached on something she agreed with.

"Fishing for men," Pete said. "Craziest thing I ever heard. Anyone who knows fishing knows that when you pull a fish out of water, it's gonna die. No ifs, ands, or buts. That fish is doomed. So why on earth would Jesus tell the disciples to go fishing for men? Pastor Andrew talked on and on about it, saying we were supposed to be like that and go fishing for men too. I wanted to stand up and ask him if he was missin' a few shingles from his roof."

"It was a *story*, Pete. Jesus didn't mean it to be taken exactly the way it sounds." Patsy reeled in the last of her line, noticed that her minnow was gone, and reached for another. "It was a whatchamacall-it . . . a metaphor or an allegory or something like that."

"A parable?"

"Well, I don't know what it's called, but Jesus was saying that He wants us to go find other people and tell them about Him."

"Yeah, but He shouldn't have told us to be fishers of men. It makes me think of a stringer of dead folks, and what good is that?"

"Oh, Pete." Patsy shook her head. How strange the Bible's teachings must sound to someone who had rarely heard them.

"What I'm saying is that if you fish for men," Pete muttered, "then you're gonna have a problem on your hands. You'd think Jesus would have been smart enough to know that, Him living out by Lake Galilee."

"He was smart, all right," Patsy countered. "The thing is . . . people *do* have to die once they get caught by Jesus. You know how Pastor Andrew always reminds us that we have to die to ourselves?"

"How—like that business about taking up our cross?"

"Yes, and giving up our life in order to save it. All those famous verses from the Bible. If the true Fisher of Men reels you in, Pete, you are going to die to your old self and be born again."

"*Born again.*" With a snort of disgust, Pete laid his rod on the bench and took a round can of snuff from the back pocket of his jeans. "I've heard that one before. I never wanted to be one of those born-again kind of Christians. Holy Rollers is what my dad called them. Crazy-sounding folks, if you ask me."

As Pete reached for a pinch of tobacco, Patsy snatched the can away and flung it out across the lake. It made a couple of skips over the water, then disappeared beneath a wave.

The moment she realized what she'd done, Patsy dropped her pole onto the dock and covered her mouth with her hand. "Oh, Pete, I am *so* sorry," she said. "Sometimes I act without thinking, and it never turns out right. I'll get you another can of snuff. In fact, I'll drive over to the convenience store right this minute—"

"Calm down," he said, patting her bare knee with his minnow-baiting hand. "Don't you worry about it, pudd'n. I need to quit chewing anyhow. Dr. Groene says it's bad for my teeth and gums."

Patsy glanced over at him. "You're not mad?"

"Naw. Hey, look who's coming up the dock. It's Steve and Brenda Hansen. And they've got Cody, too."

He waved at the handsome couple strolling hand in hand. Behind them sauntered the thin, curly-haired young man who had found both residence and employment among the homeowners in Deepwater Cove. Cody was a little slow to figure things out, but he was the hardest worker Patsy had ever employed at her salon. He kept the place spic-and-span, and he was polite to the patrons too.

"Caught anything?" Steve Hansen asked.

"Nothing but this pretty gal here," Pete answered, sticking a thumb in Patsy's direction. "We're just warming up our rods. You going out in your boat?"

"Yeah, we thought we'd look for a quieter cove. Brenda wants to try to teach Cody how to swim."

"I don't want to swim," Cody said. "My daddy always told me that swimming is for fish, and I am not a fish."

"You'll be fine," Brenda assured him. "I taught my three kids, and they love it. Once you learn how, you'll enjoy swimming. It's fun."

"Okay." Cody gave the word a backwoods Missouri twang—*oh-kye.* "Patsy and Pete have minnows in their bucket. You can eat them if you're real hungry, Patsy, but I wouldn't if I was you. They don't taste too good."

"Thanks for the warning, Cody." Patsy smiled at him. "You sure are looking dandy today. I believe we've finally got your hair just the right length."

The young man blushed and clapped his hand on his head. "You always cut my hair good, Patsy Pringle. Especially the first time."

"We'll never forget that big event; will we, Brenda?" Patsy murmured, grinning at Steve's lovely wife. After a difficult adjustment to the empty nest, Brenda and Steve Hansen seemed to be back on track. In fact, today they looked as chipper as a pair of lovebirds perched side by side in the summer sunlight.

"Cody came out from under all that hair and surprised every one of us ladies," Brenda said.

"And you came out from that rocking chair you were always sitting in too." Cody nodded at Brenda. "You did, huh? You were sad all the time, and you didn't want to talk to me. But now you're happy."

"That's right, Cody. I'm feeling lots better." Brenda smiled at Pete and Patsy. "I wanted to tell you we found a roofer whose bid was reasonable. He'll be starting work in a couple of weeks."

"That reminds me," Pete said. "Thanks for patching the leak over my cash register, Steve. I'll be glad when they put a new roof on the whole shebang. I mailed my rent check on Friday, by the way. You ought to have it by Tuesday."

"Mine, too," Patsy echoed.

Steve and Brenda had recently purchased the strip of attached shops in the nearby town of Tranquility. Now they were busy tending to the many repairs neglected by the former owner.

"And did you hear our good news?" Brenda asked, leaning one shoulder against the dock's iron post. "We found a renter for the empty store."

"Who?" Pete and Patsy asked at the same time.

"Her name is Bitty Sondheim," Steve said. "She's new to the area, and she'll be opening a little restaurant called the Pop-In. Just breakfast and lunch."

"There goes my hot dog business," Pete lamented.

"Uh-oh." Cody shook his head.

Everyone knew that Pete's hot dogs were among Cody's favorite foods. Patsy could see that the young man was crestfallen, and to tell the truth, she didn't feel so good about the information herself.

"I doubt you're going to lose much traffic to the new place," Brenda told Pete. "It'll have a different kind of food than yours. The owner wants to serve mostly omelets and sandwiches."

"Sounds too much like my tearoom," Patsy said. "I'm happy you didn't rent the space to that man who wanted to open an adult video store, but I don't know what I'll do if people stop coming by for tea. It's helped so much financially, and I've got those local ladies baking for me. They count on that extra income. I really can't afford the competition."

"Don't worry," Steve said. "This new place is missing the one thing you've got, Patsy: chairs. Tables, too, in fact. There's just a kitchen, a front counter for ordering, and a little bit of standing room. People won't be able to sit around and chew the fat."

"Patsy doesn't serve fat," Cody spoke up. "She serves chocolate cake. It comes in squares, just the way I like it."

"You mean no one can sit down to eat?" Patsy asked. "So this little restaurant is going to serve fast food?"

Brenda nodded. "Basically you're right—only it won't taste like fast food. That's what the owner assured us. Bitty got the idea from a little beachfront restaurant in California. It'll be omelets-to-go and sandwiches-to-go. She wraps everything in parchment paper, warm and easy to hold. Real cute, too, and reasonable prices. She's got a simple menu that one or two cooks can handle—with no need for waitresses or busboys."

Steve slipped his arm around his wife. "Brenda is going to do the interior design for the place. She has some great ideas for a color scheme and decorations."

"Now there's a good idea," Patsy said. "I don't think any house at the lake is as pretty as yours."

"Hey, you haven't seen mine," Pete protested.

"You're my friend, Pete, but I shudder to think what your place looks like."

"Shudder all you want. I'll have you know I'm as neat as a pin, handy with tools, and a fanatic about my yard. I built all those planter boxes for the shops, didn't I? You've never seen flowers as happy as the ones in my garden at home. And how about that soundproof wall I put up between your salon and my store? I can do carpentry with the best of 'em. Not to mention my cooking, which I must say is pretty up-and-walkin' good. I make the tastiest chili anybody ever ate. When I fry up a mess of fish and hush puppies, there's not a soul around that can stay away."

"You're mighty skilled at bragging, too," Patsy added. "Well, one of these days maybe Cody and I will come over and inspect this house and yard you're so proud of, Pete. Meanwhile, I'm glad Brenda is going to put her artistic skills to work on the new shop. If you have any ideas about improving the looks of my salon, honey, I'd be happy to hear them."

"I'll give it some thought," Brenda said. "Well, we'd better head out in the boat if I'm going to begin teaching Cody to swim before sunset."

"I don't want to swim," Cody said. "My daddy always told me that swimming is for fish."

As Brenda and Steve started toward their boat, Cody dawdled behind. When the couple was safely out of earshot, he leaned over and spoke in Patsy's ear.

"I . . . am . . . not . . . a . . . *fish*," he emphatically enunciated.

"I know you're not a fish," she whispered back. "People swim too. Now go get on the boat."

"Okay," Cody said forlornly.

Pete was chuckling as he cast his line out across the water again. "That Cody's got more brains than folks think. He knows he's not a fish, and that's just exactly what I've been trying to tell you. Jesus missed the mark when He told His friends to be fishers of men. That idea is plumb loco, and don't try to explain to me about being born again, Patsy Pringle. I got born once, and that was plenty."

Patsy pinched her lips shut and reeled in her line. Pete sure thought he knew a lot about everything. But he had no idea that the woman on the bench next to him was fishing for more than crappie and bass. She was fishing for *him,* and if she had her way, Pete Roberts would be born again before the summer was out.

As Kim Finley and her twins approached the lakeshore, she waved at the couple on the end of the dock. It was nice to see Pete Roberts and Patsy Pringle sitting so comfortably together, she thought. They made a perfect couple. Though Patsy was reluctant to admit it, everyone else knew Pete had fixed his eye on her the moment he opened his bait shop next to her salon. She enjoyed his company too, even though she complained about him. Kim wondered how long it would take for Patsy to come to her senses. It hadn't taken Derek long to win Kim's heart, she recalled as she watched Luke and Lydia race ahead of her toward the water.

A short distance from the swimming area stood Deepwater Cove's dock—a double row of boat slips with decking in between and a roof overhead. Today, nearly all the boats were out on the water as full-timers and weekenders made the most of the beautiful weather. The place where the neighborhood's families could picnic and swim featured a large parklike patch of green grass, several shady trees, a bench, and a few tables and chairs. A square wooden swim dock floated in the center of a roped-off area of water.

It was a little late in the day for a swim, but Kim had finally given in to her twins' desire to join the neighborhood's other children on the beach. She packed a basket of thick towels, snorkels, masks, flippers, and healthy snacks. Then she added the zippered bag she had put together for Luke to keep with him at all times. Syringes, a monitor, needles, insulin, and glucose pills filled the bag they had come to call his "insulin kit." As the kids raced to the water, Kim spread out a blanket and settled in the shade to watch them paddle around and splash each other.

"Well, that was a major flop." The cheerful voice behind Kim belonged to Brenda Hansen. Hair damp, the slightly older woman sat down cross-legged on the blanket. "I hope you don't mind if I join you, Kim. I could definitely use some female companionship after what I just went through."

"Sure, I'd love your company. Derek's working, and I'm keeping an eye on the twins." Kim could see the outline of Brenda's wet bathing suit beneath her T-shirt. "What happened?"

"I tried to teach Cody how to swim."

"Uh-oh." Kim was sympathetic, but aware of Cody's quirks, she couldn't hold back a smile. "Trouble?"

"First he started yelling, 'I am not a fish! I am not a fish!' over and over."

"Oh, dear."

"When I finally got him off the boat and into the water, he thrashed around so much that he nearly drowned both of us."

"Did he have on a life jacket?"

"Of course, but that made no difference to Cody. He was petrified. The next thing I knew, he had lost his swimsuit."

Kim threw back her head and laughed. "You're kidding! How did that happen?"

"He hadn't tied the string around his waist, and the elastic was too loose. There we were—flailing around, Cody and I hollering at each other, Steve yelling at both of us as we all searched for Cody's trunks. And then here came a Water Patrol boat."

"Was it Derek?"

"I wish. The officer thought we were trying to drown a poor naked man. He jumped into the water and so did Steve. There we all were, churning up waves and struggling to hear each other over Cody's hysterics. It was ridiculous! Cody kept grabbing the ladder on the boat and trying to haul himself out of the lake before we had found his swimsuit."

"Oh, I can't wait to tell Derek!" Kim giggled. "This will rival some of his stories, for sure."

"I finally found the trunks snagged on the propeller, and Steve and the officer got them free while Cody sobbed his heart out. You would have thought we really had been trying to do him in. Poor guy. Then the officer happened to mention the drowning near Deepwater Cove, and that made Cody cry even harder. Finally Steve helped him get dressed, the officer went on his way, and we all got back in the boat and came home."

"Wow, you must be exhausted. Where's Cody now?"

"He and Steve went up to the house. Cody was eager to frost a cake we baked before we left."

"Let me guess—chocolate?" Kim asked, and the two women shared a smile. "I can't picture Steve baking a cake. Does he cook often?"

"He never used to lift a finger in the kitchen, but lately he's been doing a lot of grilling for us. He discovered he likes to bake, too."

"That's fantastic. Derek helps when he can, but his hours are so unreliable that most of the cooking has fallen to me."

"That's how we used to be. But in the last couple of months, things have been a lot better."

"I'm so glad, Brenda. I didn't want to pry, but I've been concerned. You seemed very depressed. It reminded me of how I felt during my divorce. You look so much happier now."

Brenda reached over and gave her a hug. "Thanks for caring, Kim. Now that I think back on what happened, I can see that things hadn't been great between Steve and me for a long time. But we really started to fall apart about the time Jessica and Justin went off to college and Steve got so busy selling real estate. His new agency kept him away from home constantly. I've learned that I need my husband to spend quality time with me. Steve simply didn't have any time to give. That hurt me so much that I withdrew from him into myself, and nothing could make me feel better."

"But you were remodeling your basement—painting it all those wonderful colors and—"

"None of that helped," Brenda interrupted, holding up a hand to stop Kim. "Trust me; things were bad. I got to the point where I was down all the time. I didn't even feel like I could pray. Steve and I . . . well, we were in trouble. But things turned around, thank God. And I mean that literally. You and the other ladies came over to help me. Steve finally began to understand that I missed him and needed time with him. I saw that I had pulled my love and support away right when he needed it most. I hated his job, and I resented the long hours he put into selling houses, but I realized I had to change my attitude if I wanted to hold our marriage together."

"It looks like you sorted everything out."

"Well, we're working on it. We still have a long way to go. Sometimes Steve gets busy and ignores me. Sometimes I still withdraw from him. But we're making a real effort to forgive the past and support each other. I've been joining Steve for dinners with his clients, and he's become very enthusiastic about my interest in interior design. It surprised me that only just now is he beginning to appreciate what I've been doing all these years. Plus, we bought the shops in Tranquility, and we're working to revitalize the strip."

"I'll bet that's drawn you closer together."

"It has, and it's added some stress to our lives. But we're doing pretty well with the problems that crop up. I'm sure there will be more rough spots to come, but I pray we don't let our guard down. Neither of us wants to allow things to get that bad again—ever."

"That's a good way to look at it." Kim watched Lydia cannonball into the water next to her brother and come up laughing. "My first marriage was a nightmare. When Joe started hitting me, I knew I had to get out. He refused to acknowledge the problem, and nothing I tried helped at all. It took a long time—and the help of some good friends—before I accepted the truth, but there was no room to work on a relationship that threatened my life."

"I'm sure things are different with Derek."

"Like night and day," Kim said. "He's the most loving man I ever met. He treats me so well, and the twins adore him. It hasn't been easy on him, either. He'd never been married before or spent much time around kids. As an only child, he had to work pretty hard to get out from under his mother's wing. Miranda is a nice woman, but she kept Derek on a tight rein, so he focused his attention on getting through college and then working with the Water Patrol. Luke and Lydia can be a handful, but Derek is wonderful with them. Last night, he came home for supper, and we were all upset over Luke's health. Brenda, you won't believe this. . . . Derek had us sit down at the table, and he prayed for us."

Brenda's mouth parted in delighted surprise. "Oh, Kim! We've been asking God for this to happen. How wonderful!"

"I was shocked. But he did it as if it was almost natural. You know how Derek has always said he wasn't sure if there even was a God. But last night, he actually acknowledged that there was someone bigger than us, someone in control. It wasn't the all-out change we've been praying for, but I was thrilled."

"Kim, that's great. How are the twins doing? Has Luke's diabetes changed things at home?"

"Everything." Kim studied her children as they paddled around among the others in the swim area. "Sometimes I feel the way I did when they were toddlers—unwilling to take my eyes off them for a second."

"I can't imagine how hard it must be."

"Until the diagnosis, I was comfortable leaving the twins home alone for a few hours after school. I used to let them ride their bikes unaccompanied. And they were free to go down to the lake anytime they wanted."

"They're strong swimmers," Brenda said. "Unlike *some* people we know. Luke and Lydia remind me so much of my three. They stayed tan and healthy every summer from the sunshine and exercise they got living here at Deepwater Cove."

"Derek and I thought it was the perfect place to raise children. Until diabetes." As Kim spoke, she realized she had come to view the disease as a monster that hovered over her family, lurking and watching, waiting for the first slipup before pouncing on Luke.

"The doctor told me to treat it as a normal part of living," Kim told her friend, "but I just can't shrug it off like that. It threatens my son's life."

"I know," Brenda said in a hushed voice.

"And even though I have Derek, I still see myself as Luke's main protector."

"That's understandable." Brenda nodded.

"I dread the thought of going back to work, but I have no choice. Dr. Groene needs me. And . . . well . . . I know I should be grateful but . . . Derek's mother is coming for a visit. Miranda is supposed to get here later this evening. She'll look after the kids while I'm out during the day."

"I can't remember meeting her. What's she like?"

"Perfect."

"You two should get along great then."

"Ha, ha," Kim said dryly.

"I mean it. You're so organized, and the twins always look great. You and Derek love each other. You're supportive of his work. He's happy. You have a nice, tidy home—all the good things. To my way of thinking, you're perfect."

"That's a stretch, Brenda. I'm keeping up with the house, but other than that, I'm just functioning. And since Luke's diagnosis . . . barely. Now I'm adding my job at Dr. Groene's office *and* a guest to my workload."

"How long will your mother-in-law be here?"

"Who knows? It could be a while. With her husband gone, she

doesn't have much to hold her in St. Louis. She worries constantly about Derek. When she finds out about all the extra work the drowning has caused him, she'll be really uptight."

"And she's concerned about the twins, too, of course."

"Luke and Lydia are not really her grandchildren, you know. Stepgrandchildren. Miranda reminds me of that now and then, just in case I forget. I'm sure she cares about them, but in the past I've felt that . . . well, that they get on her nerves."

"What kid doesn't? That's part of their job description."

"I guess so." Kim leaned back on her elbows and pointed her toes out toward the water. If she could just stay calm and relaxed while Derek's mother was visiting, then things would be so much easier. She had to trust Miranda Finley with her children; there was no other option.

"Want some chocolate cake? We brought plates and forks, too."

Kim turned to find Cody and Steve holding out their newly frosted sheet cake. And behind them stood Miranda Finley—blonde, tan, fit—with a paper plate of chocolate cake in her hand.

"Hey, there!" she greeted Kim. "No, don't get up!"

"Miranda!" Kim got to her feet anyway and embraced her mother-in-law. "I'm sorry I didn't hear your car pull up. This is Brenda Hansen, and it looks like you've already met her husband, Steve, and our friend Cody Goss."

"Nice to meet you, Brenda," Miranda said. She was wearing a white sweater set with a pair of white linen shorts and matching sandals. "I stopped at the house, Kim, and when no one answered, I drove around and spotted you down here. I hope you don't mind if I join in."

"No, of course not," Kim told her.

As Steve and Cody put squares of cake on wobbly paper plates, Miranda slipped off her sandals and stepped onto the blanket. She reminded Kim of a vintage Barbie doll. Tall, thin, her hair highlighted and her makeup expertly applied. So ladylike and genteel. The fragrance of expensive perfume drifted from her neck, where two gold chains hung in perfect symmetry.

Steve and Cody joined the women, hunkering down in the grass to eat their cake. The sun hung low in the sky and cast a shimmer of bronze, orange, and red across the lake. A blue heron flapped its huge wings as it swept over the water to find a roost for the night.

The cake was good, and Kim had never minded if the kids snacked occasionally before supper. Now, of course, she had to help Luke watch everything he put into his mouth. He would come home ravenous, as he always did after swimming. She had a large pot of pasta, alfredo sauce, and baked chicken nuggets waiting.

"This is delicious," Miranda told Steve and Cody. "I love chocolate cake."

"Me too," Cody said. "In squares."

"Squares are definitely best," she agreed. Then she glanced expectantly at her daughter-in-law. "The twins will each want a piece. Oh, Kim, I just thought of something. You did remember to put sunscreen on the children, didn't you?"

Kim's stomach knotted. "Not today. It was so late when we came out."

"I just read an article that said ultraviolet rays can reflect off the water no matter how late in the day. Can you imagine? Thank goodness, I always kept Derek coated when we were at the pool. With children, you never can be too careful."

Kim glanced down at the basket she had packed. She was sure she had taken care of everything the twins could possibly need or want. But as always, Miranda Finley had found her Achilles' heel.

"What a sweet picture this is." Miranda sighed. "Parents and children. A sunset and a lake. Good friends and—"

"And chocolate cake," Cody added. "But no more swimming. Not for me, huh, Brenda? That's because what my daddy always said was true. Swimming is for fish. And now we all know the truth about that: I am not a fish."

CHAPTER THREE

Hello?" Derek said into the empty house. "Anyone there? Kim?" He'd just arrived home after working the late shift and had been surprised to spot a light in the living room. Had Kim waited up for him? Or was it his mother? The memory of coming home after a date to find Miranda waiting for him gave Derek a jolt of apprehension. Surely not. He was thirty-four and had been out of the nest for well over a decade.

He'd steeled himself for trouble ever since moving his mother to Deepwater Cove. Not only did his family increase by one, but Miranda Finley had about as hard a head as anyone he'd ever known.

No one answered his greeting, so he stepped into the foyer and loosened the straps on the heavy bulletproof vest he had begun wearing recently.

To be honest, he was glad no one had waited up for him. He was hoping to have a few minutes of privacy to call one of the other officers he'd chatted with on the lake that day. Though Derek thought Jerry had a good head on his shoulders, he was afraid the guy wasn't taking his work seriously enough.

"Derek?" Kim's low voice drifted from the shadows. "Hi, honey. I guess I drifted off to sleep on the couch. Welcome home."

The sound of her voice startled him. "What are you doing up so late, babe?" he asked as Kim approached. "I thought you'd be in bed by now."

"I was waiting for you," she said.

"Is that right? Well, I'm glad." Though he was happy to see his wife, Derek was annoyed at having to wait another day to call Jerry. If the officer was in over his head, Derek wanted to do what he could to help, and the sooner the better.

Instead, Kim was taking his hand and leading him toward the kitchen. "Lydia and I baked you some brownies. Have a seat, and I'll get you one."

"Brownies?" Preoccupied with his friend's situation, Derek tried to readjust his focus on his wife.

"Baking brownies was the only thing I could think of to calm Lydia down," Kim said. "You won't believe what she did. She got on the computer again—without permission. This time she looked up diabetes."

"Uh-oh," he said. With this news, Derek realized he not only couldn't call Jerry, but he had better start paying closer attention to Kim. Though it bothered him to neglect something that was such a concern, he took a closer look at Kim's face and saw that those deep brown eyes he loved so much were puffy from crying. As he settled into a chair, Derek tried to tear his thoughts away from his friend and focus on dessert and a distraught wife.

Kim slid a plate with a brownie on it in front of him, and then she poured him a large glass of milk.

He sighed and took a bite. "Good," he said. "Pecans . . . my favorite. Lydia helped with these? I didn't think she was interested in cooking."

"She's not, but I had to find something for her to do after your mother called me today in a panic."

"Uh-oh," Derek said again. The bite of brownie began to sink like a stone into his gut. "Mom called you at work?"

"Yes, and I was right in the middle of helping Dr. Groene with an extraction. Lydia knows she's not allowed to be on the computer unless one of us is around. But the minute you walked out the door for work, she talked your mother into letting her use it. Then she found . . ." Kim's face crumpled as she tried to force out the words. "She found a Web site. It was about diabetes. And it said . . . it said the life expectancy for a child with type 1 is shortened by fifteen years."

"Aw, Kim, come here, sweetheart," Derek whispered, pulling his wife into his lap and sliding his arms around her. "That's just some stupid statistic. It doesn't mean it will happen to Luke. He's young and healthy, and we're taking good care of him. More important, he's learning how to manage his own symptoms. The kid is bright—a bona fide genius. Both of them are, and they know how to look out for each other."

"That's partly what I'm worried about," she said. "If anything bad happens to Luke, you know Lydia will blame herself. They're twins, Derek! When things began to get so bad with their father—or maybe it was before that—I told them to keep an eye on each other. I shouldn't have done it. You can't expect a child to take on such a heavy responsibility."

"But that's why my mom came down from St. Louis. She's here to help."

Kim's lips shut tight, and she rose from his lap. "Your mother had *no* idea what to do today," she told him as she tucked aluminum foil around the brownie pan with a lot more force than Derek thought necessary. "When she called, she sounded practically hysterical. I was sure Luke had gone into a coma or the house was burning down or something."

"Hysterical?"

"Dr. Groene and I were working on a difficult wisdom tooth extraction when the receptionist opened the door to say I had an emergency call. You know how Dr. Groene feels about interruptions during surgery, but what could I do? When I answered the phone, your mother was so frantic that I couldn't make heads or tails of what had happened. Lydia was crying in the background, and Miranda was babbling, and it was pure bedlam. Guess who finally got on the line? Luke. He told me that Lydia and Grandma Finley were both freaking out. Your mother was trying to turn off the computer in the middle of Lydia's efforts to print the diabetes data. Luke was furious. Just like the other evening, he insisted that we all think he's going to die, and maybe we even want him to die so he won't bug us so much, and—"

"Now hold on, honey," Derek cut in. "I'll set Luke straight on that nonsense in the morning. He's got this crazy notion in his head, and everyone's reinforcing it by pushing the panic button every two minutes. I'll talk to Lydia, too. She violated the house rules by using the computer. Did you ground her?"

"I couldn't. Oh, Derek, I didn't have the heart. I know they fight like cats and dogs sometimes, but Lydia loves her brother so much. That's why she was researching diabetes on the Internet."

"Which is against the rules. What did you say to her about that?"

"What could I say? There wasn't anything I could do. I just left work as soon as I could, drove home, and made brownies with her."

"Kim, you can't do that to Dr. Groene. He relies on you."

"I know. Of course I know! He tells me all the time. He postponed a lot of appointments while I took all that time off. But, Derek, this was about family."

"You can't intervene every time there's a problem at home. Mom and the twins have to learn to manage things. If you come running whenever they have the least bit of trouble, you're going to lose your job."

"Is that what you care about? My job?"

"I care about it, but—"

"Don't you see what's happening, Derek? Everything is falling apart. I need to be here for the kids—"

"*No.* No, you don't." He stood, took her shoulders, and turned her around to face him. "Kim, you're as spooked as Lydia, and it's not doing Luke a bit of good."

"How can you say that? I'm the one who helped him learn to take care of himself. I keep my eye on him constantly in case something happens. I monitor him and check on him—"

"Yeah, you watch him like a hawk. The kid is scared he's going to get pounced on every time he moves. You're too protective, Kim. You've got to let him go a little bit—Lydia, too."

"You're the one who wanted to ground Lydia." She pulled away and set the brownies on top of the microwave. "Sometimes you can be so harsh, Derek. All your rules and regulations! It's like you don't understand how this has affected all of us. You were happy when everything was normal, but now that Luke is sick, you're coming down too hard on us."

Derek gritted his teeth, trying to keep from saying something he might regret. He had been married to Kim for three years, and he certainly did know how the family interacted. He also knew that these so-called rules and regulations were what kept things functioning. Exhausted from hours on the water and frustrated with the drowning case that was drawing so many blanks, he had little energy for an argument with his wife in the middle of the night.

They both needed sleep. They needed a break from the chaos.

"Let's just hit the hay," he said.

"Derek, I waited up for you because I wanted us to talk! We have to *do* something. I'm giving this all I can, and you have to do your part. We have to take some kind of action here. You make these rules, but I'm telling you things feel out of control."

"Whether you like it or not, Kim, rules are important. That's how the world functions—laws and regulations. Everything needs order so the people in charge can have some control."

"But you won't even talk to me about *what* rules and regulations. We need to sit down and make a plan."

"I'll make the rules right now: Computers are still off-limits without you or me around. Helmets and kneepads still have to be worn while biking. Grandma watches the twins if they want to swim. And Luke's kit goes everywhere."

Kim tucked a tendril of her dark brown hair behind one ear. "Yes, Officer Finley." She gave him a mock salute. "Aye aye."

Derek gazed at her long, pretty neck and the soft sweep of her nightgown. He reached for her and took her in his arms. "Will that make it better, baby?" he murmured against her ear. "You know I love you. I'll do everything in my power to make you happy. You are the most beautiful, amazing lady," he said, tracing a finger down her neck. "All these years, and I finally found you. I don't know how I got so lucky."

"It wasn't luck, Derek. God brought us together," she said softly. "We have to trust Him to keep us strong."

Confident that he had solved Kim's latest crisis, Derek began unbuckling his gun belt. He was pulling it from his waist when he heard something slide off a shelf in the living room and land on the floor with a crash. In a split second, Derek had snapped his .40-caliber Glock from its holster and aimed it in the direction of the noise.

"Who's there?" he called out.

"Ow! Ouch!" His mother's voice echoed clearly into the kitchen. "Oh, nuts. Now what? Derek? Derek, honey? Is that you? I heard something . . . people talking . . . arguing. I can't find the light switch, and I've knocked something off the piano, and, well . . . I'm barefoot. Derek?"

Letting out a deep breath, he felt the adrenaline rush begin to subside. He pushed his weapon back into the holster and snapped it shut.

Kim's dark eyes flashed up at him. "We don't have a piano," she whispered.

"But we do have my mother," he muttered back.

Kim laid her head against his shoulder. Derek wrapped one arm around her, flipped on the foyer light, and stepped into the living room to assess the damage.

✤

"The meeting of the Tea Lovers' Club will now come to order," Esther Moore announced as she tapped her china cup with the side of her spoon.

Patsy Pringle watched in amusement as the clusters of tea drinkers ignored poor Esther. The group had been gathering around tables in a sunny corner of Just As I Am every Wednesday afternoon since the club formed. And from day one, Esther Moore had been trying to impose *Robert's Rules of Order* on the others.

Several times Esther had referred to herself as the club's president, only to be reminded that the TLC had no officers. She regularly took meeting minutes and kept them tucked away in her purse. But whenever she brought out her notebook to read, the whole room begged her not to keep any records in case someone had accidentally gossiped the week before. So far as Patsy knew, "no gossiping" was the only rule the group kept, and she had laid down that law herself.

"I have several updates from last week," Esther said, still tapping her teacup. "I think you should all hear the minutes."

Cody Goss, seated beside Patsy, began snickering. "Minutes," he whispered to her. "Minutes are on a clock, not in a notebook. The big hand points to them, because Brenda told me that. . . . Hey, Mrs. Moore," he called out, reaching clear across the table to bump her elbow for attention. Manners were not Cody's strong suit. "Hey, nobody can hear what you're saying, Mrs. Moore. If you want people to listen up, you might as well stop hitting your teacup with that spoon and just whistle."

Before Patsy could react, Cody lifted his fingers to his mouth and blew. The earsplitting screech brought conversation in the salon to an instant halt as everyone clapped their hands over their ears. Everyone, that is, except Opal Jones, who was ninety-four and deaf as a fence post. She owned a pair of hearing aids but hated to wear them. While the echoes of Cody's whistle died down, Opal took a sip of tea and then calmly rearranged her napkin on her lap.

"There," he announced, grinning from ear to ear. "My daddy taught me how to get people to pay attention. Whistling is pretty easy if you practice."

"Gracious sakes alive, Cody Goss!" Esther frowned at him. "You've nearly scared the dickens out of us."

"Okay," Cody said nervously, eyeing Brenda Hansen.

Patsy knew Brenda had been making a valiant attempt to teach Cody some social skills. The look on Esther's face would have withered most people's confidence. But Cody was cut from a different cloth.

He glanced at the ladies gathered around the room and said, "I'll help anyone learn how to whistle. I'm good at it."

"Thank you, Cody," Brenda spoke up. "Maybe after the meeting. *Outside.*"

"Okay." He nodded and poked a bite of chocolate cake into his mouth.

"As I was saying," Esther resumed while she fished around in her purse for her meeting notebook, "I believe we should begin. Kim, would you like to introduce your guest?"

Kim Finley stood and laid a gentle hand on the shoulder of the slender, deeply tanned woman beside her. "This is Derek's mother, Miranda Finley, from St. Louis. She's here to spend time with the twins while I'm at work."

"Well, isn't that nice," Esther commented. "We're pleased you could join us this afternoon. I guess Derek is watching Luke?"

Kim reddened slightly at the obvious reference to her son's medical problems. Patsy hadn't been able to talk to Kim last Sunday at the dock, though she had tried. There were just too many people—Cody, Steve and Brenda Hansen, and Miranda Finley had all clustered around her and the twins. Even with that many people clamoring for Kim's attention, Patsy knew how private her friend was. Kim wouldn't want to discuss her son's diabetes in such a large group.

Acknowledging Esther's question with a nod, Kim sat down beside her mother-in-law. Miranda had been chatting with everyone at their table. Patsy was pleased to note that Miranda's short, spiky hair tipped with pale blonde highlights was going to need regular care at a good beauty salon. Her roots were showing already.

"First I'd like to catch us up on last week's items of discussion," Esther continued. "One of our dear founding members, Ashley Hanes, was kind enough to ask her husband to build a bridge over the Hansens' drainage ditch. Brad completed the project last week, and he did a lovely job. But with the summer construction business heating up, he doesn't have time to paint it. Would some of us like to take on that job?" By now she had her notebook out and was running a pencil down her list.

Patsy decided to check the tea bag supply. These women tended to deplete it in a hurry. Cody could just about gulp a teacupful in one swallow.

Besides, she didn't need to hear the minutes. Patsy knew more about the goings-on in Deepwater Cove than anyone. While she styled hair or painted fingernails, her customers talked. Sometimes she had trouble concentrating on the topic, like when they were explaining how to crochet an afghan or deal with the latest hitches in Social Security or Medicare. But usually she listened.

As Patsy restocked the tea bags and sugar cubes, she noticed Brenda Hansen across the room. The lovely blonde woman reminded Patsy of a golden yellow crocus bud emerging from a deep blanket of snow—the first sign of spring after a long, bleak winter. Hope flourished in her bright green eyes, and joy radiated from her glowing pink cheeks. If Patsy guessed right, Brenda was beginning to fall in love. And the object of her blossoming affection was none other than her good-looking husband himself.

"All right, we've got a painting committee," Esther said, keeping a fragile hold on her authority as the women began to refill their teacups. They had started murmuring again, so Esther raised her voice a little. "Now, Brenda and several others—including me, if I may say so—pitched in and fixed up Patsy Pringle's front flower bed the other day. How do you like it, honey?"

Patsy sat down again and nodded. She wasn't much for speeches. "It was a real nice surprise when I drove up to my house," she said. "I like it just fine. Thank you all for helping me out."

"You're welcome," Cody replied, though Patsy was fairly sure he hadn't been a part of that particular project. In fact, Cody spent most of his time going from the salon to various houses in Deepwater Cove—dusting, mowing, gutter cleaning, window washing, and doing myriad other tasks the neighbors paid him to perform. A couple of weeks ago, Brenda had helped him open a bank account, and Patsy imagined the boy would be close to a zillionaire before—as he liked to put it—he crossed the Jordan and passed on to glory.

"Does anyone else have a project they want help with?" Esther asked. When no one volunteered right away, she continued. "Then let's turn our attention to new business and catch up on our members. Opal, how's your colon?"

Opal was adjusting her pearls as she gazed out the window toward the forest on the other side of the highway. She looked so peaceful sitting there, and Patsy thought how comforting it might be to go deaf.

But Esther was clearly anxious for a report from Opal. Ashley Hanes tapped her shoulder, and Opal looked around in surprise.

"Your colon!" Ashley shouted. "Mrs. Moore wants to know how it's getting along!"

"My colon? Well, mercy." Opal narrowed her eyes at Esther for a moment; then she turned to the others. "If you must know, yesterday I ate some chocolate pie that my sister Mabel brought over. I'm not supposed to, but I did. Boy, oh boy, did I pay for it. You betcha. Besides that, I planted tomatoes again this year, and I'm going to eat 'em, too. I know I shouldn't, but why not?"

"Because you had cancer," Ashley reminded her loudly. "They took out most of your colon!"

"I know what they did. Good gravy." For a moment, Opal pursed her lips and rolled her eyes. Then she spoke up again. "I hear tell somebody drowned in the cove. Who was it?"

At that, everyone turned and looked at Kim Finley. With all the attention suddenly focused on her once again, Kim shrank back into her chair. Patsy's heart went out to her. Kim had been through a lot more than people knew.

Luke and Lydia had been the only bright spot in Kim's desolate life until three years ago, when Officer Derek Finley of the Missouri Water Patrol walked into Dr. Groene's office needing a root canal. Then he came in for a filling. And a good polishing. And some whitening. By the time his teeth were so shiny they could knock you over when he smiled, Derek had won Kim's heart.

The little family was about as happy as they come, but this past spring the warmth of their love had been hit full force by Luke's diabetes diagnosis. And now Kim's mother-in-law had moved into the Finley household. Patsy was no psychologist, but it didn't take much to figure out that could turn into a recipe for disaster.

"The drowning?" Kim asked, as if she wasn't quite sure what Opal had been referring to. "I haven't heard anything new. Derek is working on it, but he can't say anything about an ongoing investigation."

"An investigation!" Esther cried out, as though she had struck gold. "Does that mean there was some kind of crime?"

Kim shifted in her chair. "Most deaths call for an investigation. Accidental or not."

"I haven't read about the drowning in the local paper since the first mention of it," Brenda said. "Do they have any idea who it was, Kim?"

"Yeah, who was it?" Ashley echoed. The young redhead wore a skinny tank top and a necklace of homemade beads. "Brad doesn't like the idea of someone drowning so near us. He says Deepwater Cove is too quiet a part of the lake for people to go around drowning. It's not like Party Cove or the main channel, where they're always drinking and acting crazy. He thinks that because Derek is having to spend so much overtime looking into the death, the drowning might be a murder."

"Murder?" Esther exclaimed. "Now, that doesn't seem possible. Not around here. We're so peaceful. Parents and neighbors are always out watching the kids swim. Kim, could it have been a murder?"

As she sat amid the busy, nosy flock of women, Kim Finley reminded Patsy of a lone, straight oak tree rising above the forest floor. Strong, quiet, faithful, she looked like someone you could rely on, a friend who would never betray or hurt you. But a blast of chilly wind had torn at her leaves, turning them from green and gold into brown, fragile wisps. She wouldn't die, and she wouldn't collapse. But she might be facing a winter that would threaten her to the core.

"Derek and I don't discuss his work," Kim told the women. She squared her shoulders and spoke almost defiantly. "If there's a crime, the press will report it. There are confidentiality laws, of course, but that doesn't stop the television crews and newspaper reporters. I doubt the drowning is anything unusual. Lake of the Ozarks is known for its troubled waters. Last year we had the most BWI arrests in the state. The Water Patrol worked more than a hundred and fifty boating accidents with nearly a dozen fatalities. Derek does his job, and he does it well. But the last thing he wants to talk about when he comes home is drunk boaters and drownings."

"I suppose you're right," Esther said. She appeared slightly put out that Kim hadn't succumbed to the group's pleas for details. While canvassing the neighborhood in his golf cart, Esther's husband usually picked up every snippet of local gossip to be had. Charlie related the news to Esther before he told anyone else, and the Moores took pride in knowing everything about everyone—or as they put it, having a deep concern for the welfare of the Deepwater Cove community.

Charlie, a retired mail carrier, had once told Patsy his intuition was so finely tuned that he could tell what was in a letter just by lifting the envelope. The mere sight of stilted writing on an address or a stamp stuck on sideways had taught him trouble was headed for the recipient. Charlie had six senses, he liked to tell people: sight, smell, hearing, taste, touch . . . and mail. The last, he insisted, was the most dependable. He could read the mood of a family by the glint in their dog's eyes. He knew what was happening in a household by the way the curtains were drawn, the grass mowed, or the sprinklers set. A neighborhood kept no secrets when Charlie Moore was on his rounds. And even though he had retired, Deepwater Cove still benefited from the daily patrols he took in his golf cart.

But Patsy was proud of Kim for sticking to her guns. If Derek wasn't supposed to discuss his work, then so be it. Patsy had done her share of trying to pry information about the drowning out of Officer Finley, and she felt pretty bad about it.

As Kim was obviously not going to say another word, Esther wrote something in her notebook of meeting minutes. "Thank you for that report, Kim," she said. "And now I'd like to find out more about the new shop moving into Tranquility. Brenda, we hear it's a restaurant."

"Was it a man or a woman?" Cody asked in a loud voice before Brenda could respond. "The dead person in the water—was it a him or a her? Because if it was a him, then maybe nobody would come looking. My daddy told me that hims can disappear off the face of the earth and nobody might miss them. But people would look for a her. She might be a mother or daughter or sister, and that means someone loves her and wants her to come home. That's how it is with women, but a man could run off and even take his son with him. And if that man was not someone's favorite person in the world, and if the son didn't know but to do as he was told, then the two of them could leave forever. That's how it could be."

The hush in the tea area was broken only by the whine of a blow-dryer over in the salon. Was that what had happened to Cody? Patsy had heard that a letter found in the young man's pants pocket told how he came to be wandering around the lake homeless, filthy, and hungry. Cody's father wrote that his wife had died. Was that true? Or was it possible that the man had run off with Cody when he was just a little boy? Had no one ever gone looking for the two of them? Could there be a woman somewhere—an aunt, a sister, or even a mother—who might want to know what had happened to that child?

Patsy glanced at Brenda, who had gone pale as a sheet. Then Patsy looked at Esther, whose mouth hung so far open it looked like her teeth might drop into the teacup. Last, Patsy focused on Kim, who wasn't moving a muscle.

She had the most awful feeling that no one would say anything, and then Cody might blurt out something even more shocking.

But Kim, bless her heart, chose that moment to stand up and settle her purse strap on her shoulder. "I don't know if the person who drowned was a man or a woman, Cody," she said. "But I do know that we would all miss you very much if you suddenly disappeared."

Cody beamed. "That's because I'm in the club. And I work hard to keep everything span. And I take showers and wear clean clothes." His face sobered. "Swimming is not for me, though. I am not a fish."

"I won't go near the water either, Cody," Esther sang out as she put her notebook away. "No one cares about that, honey. We love you just the way you are. Say, did you eat all the chocolate cake, Cody? I noticed it was cut into squares, the way I like it."

"Me too! I'll get you a piece, Mrs. Moore. There's lots left."

Cody leaped up and headed for the dessert counter as the women broke into relieved chatter. Patsy leaned back in her chair and watched as Kim Finley crossed the salon and disappeared through the front door.

CHAPTER FOUR

Kim didn't know when she had ever looked forward to a weekend so much. Or dreaded one so intensely. As she gathered up her purse and car keys in the staff room at Dr. Groene's office, she heaved a deep sigh.

"Everything all right?" The dentist's gentle voice drifted in from the doorway. "I hope I haven't overloaded you this first week back in the office, Kim. We had a few cases I just couldn't put off any longer. Old Abe is about to lose his teeth. If we don't take some action, he's going to lose every last one of them."

Kim reflected on the shabbily dressed and slightly odorous man who had come into the office several times lately. Dr. Groene was doing his best to preserve the fellow's few remaining teeth, but one of his molars was just begging to be pulled.

"It's pretty obvious that Abe Fugal hasn't ever been to a doctor—or a dentist, for that matter," Kim agreed. At some point in life, the fellow had broken several fingers, and the bones had fused in such a way as to render his left hand almost useless. His eyesight was poor, and he blinked repeatedly as he asked about the sterilized tools spread out on the tray next to his chair. And as for his mouth . . . well, it was safe to say those teeth hadn't seen a toothbrush in many a long year. "You know," Kim continued, "even though we didn't need to use gas today, I was concerned about him driving. Doesn't he usually have a woman here with him?"

"Yes, June Bixby—long gray hair and brown eyes. She's been here a few times. I was hoping to get a look at her teeth one of these days too." Dr. Groene tugged off his white coat and dropped it into the laundry bin. "Well, anyway, I hope it hasn't been too much for you this week."

Though they worked closely together, Kim rarely spoke to the dentist at any length. She viewed her role as one of support and assistance. Occasionally he chose to consult with her about a perplexing situation, but usually he chatted with the patient and ignored Kim almost completely. She didn't mind. Ben Groene had an excellent reputation in the area, and his office was filled with patients from the moment Kim arrived in the morning until she left each evening. He paid her well, provided excellent health and retirement benefits, and treated her with respect.

"The extra hours are fine," she assured him. "I appreciate your willingness to let me take so much time off for Luke."

"Not a problem," he said. "Seems like one of my six is always into some kind of trouble—a broken arm, a fever, a loose tooth, a skinned knee. The older ones run my poor wife around the bend with their hormone surges. If they aren't in love, they're sobbing their eyes out in the bathroom. The dramatics would do Shakespeare proud."

Kim laughed. "Lydia is almost eleven, and I'm starting to see some of that. She constantly challenges our rules."

"Eleven's about the right age for the rebellion to start. My wife taught me the secret to good discipline. If anyone knows how to manage kids, it's my Mary. When they're little, the occasional timeout or a single swat on the backside will do the trick. About the time the pimples start, be ready to ground them when they misbehave.

No TV, movies, time with friends—that kind of thing. When they hit fifteen, you've *really* got the keys to good behavior."

With a sly grin, he pulled a key ring from his pocket and jangled it to emphasize his point. "Threaten to take away the car keys, and they'll do anything you want," he declared. "You see these? They're Jordan's. He's eighteen and thinks he rules the world. But Dad owns the car. And when Jordan misses his curfew by an hour, Dad takes the keys. You can bet that kid will come home on time from here on out."

Recalling the night Lydia had screamed and Luke had knocked the spoon from his frantic sister's hand, Kim wondered if Dr. Groene's parenting technique was really that simple. And it didn't take into account the fact that her own family now had another authority figure living with them.

What would make Grandma Finley a help rather than a hindrance?

"I guess Luke is getting along pretty well these days," Dr. Groene commented as he took a bottle of cold water from the refrigerator and twisted the cap until the seal broke. "Good thing Derek's mother was able to come down from St. Louis and help out for a while. It shouldn't be long before your boy gets his routine figured out."

"He's managing, but . . . it's hard to be away from him. Even when I'm deep in the middle of a procedure, I realize I'm worrying about Luke."

Dr. Groene nodded. "Yes, I can imagine." He eyed her as he took a sip from his water bottle. "I remember how my wife worried the first few months after I was diagnosed."

"You? Are you . . . are *you* a diabetic?" Kim stammered.

He smiled. "You make it sound like you just found out I'm an alien. Diabetics are not as rare as you think. I was nineteen when my doctor diagnosed me with type 1. Mary and I had been married less than a month."

"I never knew. All these years."

"I don't let the disease own me. I like to be the boss, you know." He winked as he stepped toward the door. "Here's my motto: If you've got to be a diabetic, be a good one. Be disciplined. Monitor yourself. Get a buddy to keep an eye on you for signs of trouble. Mary knows that if I start acting odd, she needs to take charge right away. When my blood sugar gets low, I dislike being compliant, and sometimes I'm even a little combative. But years ago we made a pact, and I've learned to obey my wife. The kids have known about my diabetes all their lives, and we're used to it. In fact, I don't even bother to look for a private room to give myself insulin. We can be watching TV or fooling around in the backyard, and I'll whip out the ol' kit."

Kim stood staring at him, stunned. Never once had Dr. Groene mentioned having diabetes. He acted so normal about it. Even casual. As if it weren't really a factor in his life.

Heading out the back door toward his car, he spoke over his shoulder. "All I'm saying is, Luke will be fine. Don't worry."

The door closed behind him, and Kim walked to the front of the building to lock up. Was it really possible to be a diabetic and still have a full, happy life? Ben and Mary Groene had enjoyed a long marriage. They had six healthy children. They lived on the lakeshore in a large, beautiful home. Their oldest daughter attended Yale University.

As she settled into her car and drove toward Deepwater Cove, Kim reflected on the serenity with which Dr. Groene conducted his life. Everything went like clockwork at the office. She had always thought that was simply a reflection of his tranquil personality and the calm demeanor of the staff he had hired. But maybe he had taught himself to be orderly and careful so he could keep his blood sugar levels regulated. *If you've got to be a diabetic, be a good one,* he had told her. Ben Groene must be among the best.

As she pulled into the driveway of the Finley house, Kim realized that her employer had given her the advice she'd been looking for ever since the endocrinologist had uttered Luke's frightening diagnosis.

Order, she thought. *Serenity. Peace.* Pondering how she could implement this atmosphere at home, Kim was stepping out of the car when the front door flew open. Lydia hurtled through it, with Derek in hot pursuit.

"No way!" Lydia screamed at him as she tore across the porch and into the yard. "I won't! I will not take it off, and you can't make me!"

"Get back here, Lydia!" Derek caught up to the girl in a matter of seconds. With one arm, he snagged her around the waist. His knee gently knocked her feet out from under her, and she slumped backward onto the grass.

"You can't do this!" she shrieked as he stood above her, hands at his waist. "You're not my real father! You have no power over me. Let me go, you jerk!"

"Lydia!" Kim cried out, rushing toward them. "Derek, what's going on?"

"Get up, kid," Derek barked in a tone Kim had never heard. His forehead furrowed, he glanced at his wife. Then he turned back to the skinny girl writhing on the lawn. "I said—*get up*! Now!"

"Ow! He hurt me!" Lydia hollered as she curled into a ball. "I'm calling the police! I'm calling the child-abuse hotline!"

"What on earth—?" Kim dropped her purse and fell to her knees. Memories of her first husband flooded Kim's mind. She had been thrown across a room, knocked onto a couch, slapped on the cheek so hard her ears rang.

"Lydia, are you all right?" she asked, gathering her daughter in her arms. "Sweetie, what are you doing? What happened?"

"*He* did it!" Lydia spat. "He said I had to . . . to . . ."

Fear filling her heart, Kim stared up at Derek. "What did you do to my daughter?"

Wearing his Water Patrol uniform, Derek stood over them. Kim was taken aback by the fury in his eyes. Her husband never got angry. Part of what had drawn her to the man was his composure, his detachment even in the midst of crisis. But now she feared he might whip out his baton or even his gun—as he had the other night when he'd thought there was an intruder in the living room.

"Take a look at *your* daughter," Derek said. "Then ask her what happened."

Kim's focus shifted to Lydia. Dark smudges of mascara streaked toward her temples. Deep blue eye shadow stained her lids. A thick layer of foundation ended at her jawline, as though she were wearing a mask. Two spots of bright pink on her cheeks matched the glossy sheen on her pouting lips.

Stepping out of the painful memory of her own past, Kim was suddenly able to see her daughter's face. Her fear turned to confusion. "Lydia, why are you wearing my makeup?"

"It's not yours. It's mine. I bought it with my allowance, and I have the right to wear it."

"But you're only ten years old, honey," Kim said in dismay. "You don't wear makeup."

"I'm almost eleven, and I can wear it if I want to. I'm going to spend the night at Tiffany's house. She gets to wear makeup. Her mom even helps her with it."

"Well, I don't care what Tiffany and her mother do together," Kim said firmly. "You don't have our permission."

"I don't need Derek's permission," Lydia sneered. "He's not my dad."

Kim fell silent for a moment as she tried to remember what Dr. Groene's life had shown her: order, serenity, peace. She had been raised with so much discord and confusion that she had rarely known what was allowed or what wasn't. Her mother had been sober only part of the time, and rules seemed to ebb and flow with the alcohol.

At a loss, Kim studied the comical looking child in the grass and then turned her attention to her husband. "Derek, what happened?"

"I'll tell you what's happening." The voice came from Miranda Finley, who was crossing the lawn toward the others. She had on a pale pink knit top, matching linen shorts, and a pair of pink beaded sandals. "These children are a mess, Kim. All Luke wants to do the entire day is play games on his little machines. Lydia is either on the phone or the computer. When I try to get them up and outside, they argue with me. I tell them I'll go with them down to the lake to swim, but they refuse. I offered to take them shopping at the outlet mall. Only Lydia agreed, so we had to leave Luke at home."

"You left Luke by himself?" Kim cried.

"Derek was home," Miranda pointed out.

"But you came here for Luke, not Lydia. He's the one who needs to be watched."

"Which is exactly what I was doing the whole time this little imp was upstairs getting carried away with her makeover."

"*You* helped me buy the makeup, Grandma Finley," Lydia retorted. "You even picked out the lip gloss."

"You let her buy this junk?" Derek turned on his mother. "Lydia doesn't have permission to wear makeup! She's ten, for crying out loud."

"Every girl should learn to use a touch of cosmetics," Miranda shot back. "And who better to teach her than me? My mother took me for a professional consultation when I was ready to start doing my face. I don't think Lydia is too young to practice."

"She's too young to go to her friend's house looking like that," Derek said. "Lydia is sweet and innocent. She's pretty, like her mother, and I don't want that to change." His tone had softened as he spoke, but his face went grim again when he touched his gun belt. "I've gotta go. I'm about to be late to work."

"But what about taking me to Tiffany's house?" Lydia whined. "You promised, Derek! You told me you would drive me—"

"Grounded," Kim said, cutting her off. Dr. Groene's wise words formed in her mind as she stood and pulled Lydia up from the grass. Taking her daughter by the shoulders, Kim spoke firmly. "You are not going to Tiffany's house this weekend, and you won't go next weekend either. If you can follow the household rules until then, I'll consider letting you invite her over here for the night. Now walk back inside and take that stuff off your face."

"I'm sick of this stupid, ridiculous family!" Lydia shrieked as she marched across the yard. Fists clenched, she shook her head. "I wish I lived with my real father."

"You do live with your real father!" Kim retorted loudly as she watched her daughter slam the door. Derek had already backed his truck out of the garage, and he drove off without even a glance at his wife. Turning to her mother-in-law, Kim eyed the blonde, spiky hair and the bright blue eyes rimmed in dark liner. Come to think of it, Miranda Finley wore far too much makeup for Kim's taste.

Unable to think what to say to the woman, Kim picked up her purse. "I'd better help Lydia find the cold cream," she murmured.

"I have an exfoliating cleanser that works so much better," Miranda called after her. "Cold cream can really clog young pores!"

❦

As Derek steered his boat toward the mile marker where he and another officer had agreed to meet that afternoon, the recent unusual drowning nagged him. But for some reason, Lydia's unexpected outburst bothered him even more. The child had sassed her stepfather with more venom than most of the belligerent drunk boaters he'd ticketed. Worst of all, her rage seemed to come out of nowhere.

He had been crossing the living room to greet Kim before heading to work when he spotted Lydia on the stairs. At the sight of her heavily made-up face, he had stopped dead in his tracks. All he said was "Whoa," and the kid lit into him. It was almost as if she knew he would forbid her to go out wearing makeup, so she had preplanned her temper tantrum.

But why had that one word triggered such a response? Why had Lydia kept mentioning her *real* father, when she and Luke always dreaded spending time with Joe? And how about the way Kim had rushed to Lydia's side before even stopping to talk to him? That bugged him more than he cared to admit. Then his mother had jumped into the fray.

"Women," he muttered as he pulled up beside Larry Marshall's patrol boat.

"What's that?" the other officer asked.

"Too many women at home," Derek groused. "Mother, wife, daughter. All on my case."

"Yow, that bites." Larry paused. "Speaking of women, did you hear the news? We just got the call from headquarters in Jefferson City. The unidentified Code 4 you found over by Deepwater Cove was a female."

A wash of disbelief ran through Derek. "No kidding? I would have sworn on a stack of Bibles it was a man. The jeans, the boots, the T-shirt."

"Me too. I had it pegged as a male all the way. But you've gotta admit, the decomposition was pretty bad."

Derek frowned at the memory of the body he had found tangled in fishing line not far from the small cove where he and Kim made their home. That afternoon, a light breeze had carried an odor in his direction, and he recognized it immediately. As a patrolman, he had worked deaths on the lake before, but he'd never been the one to locate the remains. It was an image he would just as soon forget.

Trained to treat every death as a homicide, they would have to wait until that scenario was ruled out. All the same, such circumstances were rare at Lake of the Ozarks.

"My guess is she was drinking on a dock or a boat," Larry said. "She sure wouldn't be the first drunk to fall into the lake, and she won't be the last. Probably passed out and drowned."

Derek shrugged. "If you'd seen the way the line was wrapped around her, you might think differently."

"You really believe it could have been a homicide?"

"It's possible. Then again, who would wrap a person in fishing line?"

"Someone who wanted to immobilize her?"

"I can snap that line with my bare hands," Derek said. "I checked."

"Yeah, but this was a woman."

"True, and there was an awful lot of line. I just can't believe that no one has called her in as a missing person."

Derek shook his head at the realization that not only was the woman still unidentified, but she hadn't had a funeral, nor had her body been buried. Whether her death was a homicide or an accident, she had once been a living, breathing human.

"I'd better get on over to Party Cove," he told his friend as he checked his watch. "It's prime drunk-hunting time."

"I reckon we've got five or six hundred boats out there," Larry told him. "People are starting to head home so they can get ready to go barhopping."

"Every weekend they cut the animals free."

Larry chuckled. "It's Sodom and Gomorrah all right."

As Derek parted from his friend, he thought about Larry's reference. Derek knew that Sodom and Gomorrah were bad places, but he had no idea why. He thought it might be from the Bible, but he had grown up in a home where God was rarely mentioned, and his limited knowledge of the Bible came from the few times his grandparents had taken him to church.

In that area, Kim couldn't be more different. On free evenings or weekends, she always had her nose in one of her religious books. She tried to read the Bible every day, and she kept markers in all kinds of how-to manuals, self-help books, and Christian novels.

Not that Kim was overly holy by any means. Derek reflected on his wife as he steered the Donzi toward the Glaize arm of Lake of the Ozarks. The breeze cooled his skin, and the hum of the twin motors soothed his nerves. To Derek, Kim was more attractive than ever.

The way she made him feel sent goose bumps down his arms. It was hard to imagine how her first husband could have been so stupid as to let her get away.

Kim was a great woman. She took good care of her children, she cooked delicious meals, she kept the house tidy, and she satisfied his every need. Even her religious bent appealed to Derek. Kim's Christian faith had given her a gentle and kind spirit that he treasured. She loved him more deeply than he would ever have believed possible. What more could a man want? How big a loser did you have to be to start knocking around a woman that wonderful? And she had been pregnant at the time. With twins!

"Lydia." He uttered the name in frustration. All this time, Derek had done his best to be a good father figure to Luke and Lydia. He had provided for them much better than the worthless alcoholic whose genes they carried. He loved those kids as if they were his own. There was nothing Derek wouldn't do for his family.

But he refused to allow his ten-year-old stepdaughter to be turned into one of those pint-size beauty queens by some friend whose mother was too permissive. As Derek steered into Anderson Hollow, he fumed over the memory of Lydia's mascara-blackened eyelashes and petulant pink lips. Young girls looking provocatively older than their true age could get into trouble so fast they might never know what hit them, he thought as he surveyed the mayhem in Party Cove.

This summer weekend was no different from all the rest. Lines of boats had been anchored to the lake bed and then tethered together. The tangled music from hundreds of sound systems rose in a cacophony of drumbeats, steel guitars, and wailing singers. Crumpled beer cans drifted in the water. An empty foam cooler bobbed past. The distinct smell of burning marijuana mingled with the tobacco smoke that hung in the evening air. Girls in bikinis danced while guys grabbed at them, laughing and teasing. The thought that pretty, dark-haired Lydia might ever become one of these young women turned Derek's stomach.

A couple of his fellow officers were already patrolling the area, but there were never enough to keep the place under complete control. Despite the obvious drunkenness, loud music, and near nudity, it was difficult to make arrests. Though driving a boat while intoxicated was illegal, Missouri had no law against drinking alcohol while boating. Someone sipping from a beer could steer right past a Water Patrol boat without getting a ticket. Catching pot smokers proved nearly impossible. At the first sign of the authorities, a user could easily dispose of his stash. Patrolmen mainly served to deter all-out anarchy and to put a stop to blatant violations.

"Welcome to the cove, Officer Finley," a voice said, communicating by private frequency over the radio in Derek's patrol boat. "You want to take a run by the Gauntlet and see what's going on?"

Derek signaled that he would swing over toward the most notorious section of the inlet. He double-checked his gun belt, a habit that had started years ago. One hand on the steering wheel, he felt his way around the heavy black strap at his waist—two magazines with fifteen rounds each, an extra-bright flashlight, his expandable baton, the radio, a can of pepper spray, a pair of handcuffs, his .40-caliber Glock, a state-issued cell phone, and a pocket recorder. All in place and ready to go.

As Derek headed in the direction of the Gauntlet, he could see a row of houseboats moored along the shoreline, as always. Across a narrow stretch of lake, a second chain of vessels faced the houseboats.

Shaking his head more in resignation than dismay, Derek watched a twenty-five-foot Challenger rumble toward the Gauntlet. As it entered the stretch of water between the houseboats and the chain of vessels, partyers sprayed the Challenger with huge water guns. Mechanical launchers tossed water balloons. Several topless girls stood up on the Challenger's deck and began shimmying around while they got drenched.

"Great," Derek murmured, focusing his attention on the path of open water ahead as he sped up to intercept the Challenger at the other end of the Gauntlet. Though charged with enforcing the state's sexual misconduct law, Derek doubted he'd have to take the situation that far.

He understood the appeal of alcohol, but other questions plagued him. What was the attraction of partying this way weekend after weekend? Why did people bring their children onto the lake and out to this cove? This was fun?

"We've got a 10-38 in Anderson Hollow near the entrance to the cove." The dispatcher on Derek's radio voiced the call for immediate assistance just as he steered the last few feet toward the end of the Gauntlet. "There's a fight in progress with several people involved. . . ."

As the dispatcher at the Water Patrol's general headquarters in Jefferson City gave further information and directions, Derek swung the Donzi away from the Challenger. So much for stopping the boaters for a polite chat about public indecency. Officer Finley was needed elsewhere.

Sodom and Gomorrah, he thought as he navigated past a group of swimmers waving beer bottles to the beat of the music coming from their houseboat. A girl screamed from a nearby vessel, and several people yelled as she yanked up her bikini top and flashed the patrolman speeding by. Derek turned his head away and kept driving. Were people in the Bible ever as crazy as this?

CHAPTER FIVE

Pete Roberts was cleaning a clump of grass from a Weedwhacker's motor when Cody Goss pushed open the front door of Rods-N-Ends. Pete smiled at the young man. The rack of rotisserie hot dogs drew Cody to the tackle shop at least once a week. Now that he had some money of his own, Cody indulged himself once in a while.

"Hey, Pete," he said as he stepped up to the heated case to watch the wieners rotate on the racks. "How are your hot dogs today?"

"Fresh and sizzling, as usual." Pete moved to the sink he had installed near his work area and began washing his hands. "How many you want this time, kiddo? Two or three?"

Cody's tongue slipped out and licked his lips. "Three, please. I'm not fat yet. Not as fat as you anyhow. I think I could have three."

"I reckon you could." Pete grinned at the young man's well-known frankness. Though Cody had offended some with his blunt honesty, Pete enjoyed the fact that the kid said exactly what was on his mind. "You think I'm fat, Cody?"

The blue eyes darted to Pete's face. "I sure do. Don't you?"

"I guess I am, now that you mention it."

"If you looked into a mirror, you would know that you're wider around the middle than anywhere else. Patsy Pringle thinks you're fat. She says you look like a big, shaggy ol' bear."

Pete chuckled as he unwound the wire tie on a bag of buns. "Are you sure she wasn't talking about my beard needing a trim?"

"I don't think so. I'm pretty sure she was talking about your stomach." Cody drummed his fingers on the counter while Pete squirted ketchup and mustard on the three hot dogs. "Hey," he piped up after a moment, "did you hear that the drowned person Officer Finley found in the lake was a lady?"

"I read that in the paper this morning. Where'd you hear it?"

"At Patsy's next door. All the ladies are talking about it, and I was washing windows on the inside, so that's how I heard. It's not polite to listen to other people's conversations. That's what Brenda told me. But if they talk loud, you can't help it. When the blow-dryers are going, those ladies talk loud."

"I'll bet they do." Pete slid the hot dogs into their paper sleeves one by one. "It's kind of unusual to have a female drown, I hear. I reckon she must have been drunk and fell off of a boat or something."

"She was wrapped in fishing line."

"I heard that. Nasty business. Hard to believe she washed up so close to us."

"Officer Finley found her. The women next door said nobody has called to ask about a missing lady. I don't understand why not. My daddy told me that a man could disappear, or even a man and a little boy that nobody wanted, and no one would bother to look for them. But if a woman went missing, people would search for her. Do you think that's true?"

Pete pushed the three hot dogs across the counter toward Cody, who had laid the exact amount of cash—including tax—right next to the register. He couldn't imagine why the boy was so caught up in this drowning incident. As far as Pete was concerned, the less folks talked about it the better. Drownings and such were bad for business.

Tourists liked to think of the lake as a place for sun, water, and lots of fun. Unpleasant news ought to be buried on the back page of the paper, Pete thought. Or left out altogether.

"I reckon people probably have called the police or the Water Patrol about the woman," he told Cody. "No one goes missing without somebody noticing."

"Not even a man? a man and a little boy that nobody wanted?"

Pete frowned as he strolled back to the area of his shop where he repaired small engines. The Weedwhacker would be easy enough to fix. Just getting the moldy old grass out was a good start.

"Cody, who's this man and boy you're talking about?" he asked. "The person who drowned was a woman. Did you know someone who turned up missing?"

The young man wandered across the room, uncharacteristically abandoning his hot dogs on the counter. "That man might be my daddy," he said in a low voice. "And I think that little boy might be me."

Pete looked up in surprise. "You? What makes you say that? Why would your father run off with you, Cody?"

"Hmmm." Cody pushed his hands into the front pockets of his jeans. Then he pushed them into the back pockets. "It might be because nobody wanted me. Not even my mother. Because . . . because I am dumb."

"Dumb, huh?" Pete pointed at Cody with the end of a screwdriver. "You're not dumb, kiddo. I can promise you that. Who ever said you were?"

"Lots of people. One time some men hit me and called me names. They said I was dumb, stupid, idiot, crazy, nuts."

"Good golly, Miss Molly. You mean to tell me you got beat up by a bunch of thugs?"

"They were men, and they hit me because I'm dumb."

"And I'm here to tell you that's a flat-out lie. Did you ever go to school, Cody Goss?"

"No. But I learned my Bible verses real good. Do you want to hear Psalm 139? It's my favorite."

"I don't want to hear no Bible verses. Not right now. I want to know why your daddy didn't put you in school."

"Because the other boys might make fun of me, because I'm dumb."

"Would you quit saying that, kid? You're not dumb! There's not a mother alive who wouldn't be proud to have you for a son and miss you to pieces if your daddy ran off with you."

"Really?"

Cody stared with such intensity that Pete began to wonder if he'd said too much. Flustered, he went back to work cleaning up the Weedwhacker. "Your hot dogs are getting cold," he told the boy. "You better eat them."

Hanging his head, Cody muttered, "Okay."

Pete worked a moment longer on the whacker; then he looked up at the young man, who was still standing there staring at him. "Well, are you going to eat your hot dogs, or not?"

"Do you think I might have a mother?" Cody asked.

"Well, you had a mother once; I know that much. At one time, everyone has a mother. That's how you get born. You grow in her—inside the mother's innards. Then one day, you pop out, and there you are."

"I popped out of a mother?"

"You've got a belly button, ain't you?"

Cody lifted his T-shirt and checked. "Yes, I do."

"Then you were born from some woman just like all the rest of us."

"Where is she?" Cody asked. "Where's my mother?"

Pete swallowed. "Listen, you'd better get over there and eat your hot dogs. You need to go finish washing Patsy's windows. If she finds out we've been jabbering, she'll hang me up by my thumbnails."

"No, she won't," Cody said. "Patsy would never do that. She's nice."

Trying to ignore the kid, Pete studied the Weedwhacker long and hard. It definitely needed oil. And some new line. Probably just a good cleaning would do the trick. People could be pretty ignorant when it came to small engines. They would walk into Rods-N-Ends hauling a perfectly good hand vacuum or chain saw and tell him it was shot. All he had to do was add a belt or work out a kink and the owner was back in business. Good money for not much work. Exactly what Pete liked best.

"I want to see her," Cody said suddenly. "Where is she?"

"Next door. You know Patsy—she never leaves the salon until she's done for the day and ready to lock up."

"Not Patsy. My mother. I want to see my mother. Where is she?"

"Now how would I know that?" Pete asked, wondering how to get the lid back onto *this* can of worms. "Go eat them hot dogs, boy, and let me work."

"I want to see my mother!" Cody said more loudly. As he continued to speak, his voice rose to a wail. "I want her! I want to know where she is! Why did she let me go? Why didn't she find me? Where is my mother?"

"Whoa, kiddo, pipe down!" Pete grabbed his cell phone from the pocket of his overalls and quickly dialed. When a voice answered, he said, "Hey, where's Patsy? This is Pete, next door. Send her over here pronto; you hear me? I got a pack of trouble on my hands, and his name is Cody Goss."

As tears started to roll down Cody's cheeks, Pete lunged for the hot dogs. He snatched them up and waved them in front of the boy's nose. "Looka here. Hot dogs! Yum! How about a bite, okay? Stop your blubbering now, kid. I mean it. Eat your lunch."

"Where is she? Why isn't she looking for me?" Cody's nose was running. "I don't understand. What if she drowned? What if she got wrapped in fishing line and fell off a boat? Maybe my mother is the lady that Officer Finley found! In the water! Dead!"

Pete felt so awful that he was considering ducking out the back of his store and locking the door behind him when he saw Patsy marching, shoulders back and jaw set, toward Rods-N-Ends. Thank the good Lord! There must be a God, Pete thought, and at this moment, he didn't even mind about the fishing-for-men story Jesus had told. He had needed help, and here came Patsy.

"What's going on?" she demanded as she pushed open the door and stepped inside. "Pete Roberts, what have you done to Cody?"

"I didn't do anything!" he protested. "He's got this idea in his head—"

"Cody doesn't make things up out of thin air!" She grabbed a wad of napkins from the stainless steel holder near the hot dog grill. "Poor Cody. What happened, honeybunch? What did Pete say to you?"

"Everyone has a mother, even me," Cody sobbed. "Pete said so."

"Good gravy, Pete! Did you have to go and bring that up?"

"Now wait just a—"

"Blow your nose, Cody," Patsy ordered. "There you go. And again. Good. Now, what's this all about? Tell Patsy."

"I have got a belly button," Cody said, sniffling.

Patsy gave Pete a look that would wither grass. "Yes, so do I. What about belly buttons, Cody?"

"Everyone has a belly button, and everyone has a mother that they popped out of."

"Popped out?" Again she eyed Pete.

He shrugged helplessly. "Well? How else would you describe it?"

"I wouldn't!" Patsy snapped. "I'd let Brenda Hansen do it. You're the last person in the world to be telling this young man about the birds and the bees. What were you thinking?"

"Where is my mother?" Cody asked. "Did she get drunk and wrapped in fishing line and drowned?"

"That's not your mother. That's the woman who washed up in Deepwater Cove. She could be anyone."

"She could be my mother."

"Well, she's not."

"Then where is my mother?"

Patsy sighed. "Cody, do you remember the letter Brenda and Steve found in your pocket? Your father had written it, and he said your mother passed away. I'm very sorry to have to say it, but your mother died."

"I don't want her to be dead."

"Oh, for mercy's sake, let's go call Brenda. Grab your hot dogs, Cody. We'll get Brenda to drive over to the salon and sort everything out. And next time, don't bother asking Mr. Roberts here any questions."

Cody gathered the three hot dogs and held them against his chest as Patsy led him toward the front door of the tackle shop. His eyes focused on Pete. Patsy, too, cast a backward glance. Then she shook her head, grabbed Cody's elbow, and ushered him out onto the sidewalk.

"Hey, Patsy," Pete hollered after her. "Stop telling people I look like a bear!"

Patsy paused a moment, gazing at him through the plate glass window. Then she burst into giggles as she led Cody toward the haven of Just As I Am.

❁

Saturday evening, the telephone rang while Kim was in the kitchen wrapping potatoes in aluminum foil. She reached for the receiver, but when she held it to her ear, she could already hear her mother-in-law's voice on the spare room's extension.

"You've reached the Finley family!" Miranda sang out. "Derek, Kim, Miranda, Luke, and Lydia—all at home and eager to chat. How may I help you?"

Kim winced at the inclusion of their guest's name in the family lineup, but she couldn't deny that Miranda was now definitely a part of the household structure. In the two weeks since her arrival, she had wedged herself firmly into place—like a queen who had arrived to rule an upstart realm from the comfort of her bedroom.

During that short time, the woman had managed to alter just about every routine Kim had established. Miranda's high blood pressure meant less salt in the meals. She hated nuts, so pecans had to be left out of the brownies and walnuts omitted from the Waldorf salad. Peanut-butter sandwiches went straight onto the no-no list. Miranda's clothing added an extra load or two on laundry day. Thank goodness the woman was willing to iron her own linen shorts and slacks and to hand wash her filmy silk blouses. She insisted on a mug of coffee every morning and a cup of chamomile tea at night, and she let it be known if they weren't made just the way she liked them.

Even worse in Kim's mind, Miranda wasn't the least bit interested in church or God, and she often started eating her meal before the blessing had been asked. Her favorite activity was shopping, so the twins had to accompany her on frequent and lengthy trips to the outlet mall. Lydia didn't mind, but Luke deplored being dragged from one store to another. Yet with both parents gone during the daytime in the second week, he was left with no choice. In fact, no matter what the Finleys planned, Miranda had to be figured into the picture.

For the first few days of her mother-in-law's visit, Kim had accommodated the changes. She told herself that Miranda was essentially a kind woman. Nothing would have to be modified all that much.

Though able to ignore the dominating presence for a short while, Kim soon found her patience tested. When she wanted to scream in frustration, she made up her mind to be polite. Her waning goodwill lasted four or five days longer. By the end of the second week, she was downright angry.

Now poised to cut her mother-in-law out of the phone conversation, Kim heard the voice on the other end of the line speak up.

"Oh, is this Miranda Finley?" Kim recognized Brenda Hansen's sweet tone at once. "For a moment I thought you might be Lydia."

"Lydia? Gracious, that would be odd, wouldn't it? We're not even related."

Kim flinched. Derek loved the twins like a father, and Kim had prayed that his own mother would see them as her grandchildren. But Miranda kept the lines clearly drawn between herself and the twins.

"I was hoping to speak to Kim for a minute," Brenda told Miranda over the phone. "Something has come up, and I'd like her advice."

"Oh, dear, I'm all the way down the hall in my room, and Kim is in the kitchen," Miranda said. "She's baking potatoes for dinner, though why, I surely don't know. We've had enough carbohydrates today to sink a ship. She started us out this morning with French toast. Then she fed us sandwiches and chips for lunch. Now it's baked potatoes, and I think I even saw her getting out a box of rice. Can you imagine? I'm afraid I'll outgrow my clothes in no time if she keeps this up."

"I've always thought Kim was a great cook," Brenda said.

"I'm right here," Kim spoke up. "I heard the phone ring. It's okay, Miranda; I'll take the call now."

"Well, I did have something to ask Brenda, if you don't mind, Kim. She has such a way with decor, and I've been eyeing the lace curtains in the living room. I don't mean to be critical, of course, but with the twill sofa and the two leather chairs, I'm wondering if lace is the right texture for the windows. I was thinking maybe a simple sheer fabric would be better in there. You could pick one of the colors from the sofa. Say that soft yellow, for example. Or the muted green. What do you think, Brenda?"

There was a momentary pause. "I . . . uh, I can't really picture the curtains in my mind right at the moment, Miranda."

"They're sort of a thick lace with roses strewn everywhere. Very feminine. Now I don't want to sound the least bit disapproving of Kim's decisions about this lovely home, but I just have a feeling the curtains don't work well with the leather."

By this time, Kim had wandered into the living room and was

studying the beautiful lace curtains she'd found several years ago in an antique shop. The tag said they'd been made in Brussels, and Kim was delighted to discover that they fit her windows perfectly. What was wrong with leather, twill, and lace? To her, they made a perfect combination.

"I'll come over and take a look sometime," Brenda told Miranda.

"Why not now?" Miranda suggested. "Kim's potatoes will take an hour at least, and we're not doing a thing. Come by and see what you think. Then you and Kim can discuss whatever was on your mind."

Kim could think of about fifty things she needed to be doing, but she decided to echo her mother-in-law's invitation. "Miranda's right," she told her friend. "I'd love to see you if you have a minute, Brenda."

"Well, I've got Cody here with me at the house. But I guess we could come over for a little while before Steve gets home. He and I are taking one of his clients to the country club for dinner at seven. Cody's spending the night with Esther and Charlie Moore."

Before Kim could utter another word, Miranda had said good-bye and hung up. Replacing the receiver, Kim watched as her mother-in-law came sashaying down the hall in her spotless white slacks, matching leather belt, and pink-striped tank top.

Miranda clapped her hands when she spotted Kim. "I hope you don't mind that I invited Brenda over, though I wish she didn't have to bring that young man. He strikes me as odd. But she's so sweet, and more my age than yours anyway. I really enjoy Brenda. In fact, I think one day we might be good friends. She knows how it feels to lose your loved ones and be left alone day after day."

"Brenda stays busy," Kim inserted. "There was a time when she felt a little adrift. But she teaches Cody, and she helps Steve manage their rentals in Tranquility. I think she's even been doing some decorating in the homes he has up for sale."

"Now isn't that wonderful?" Miranda had lifted one of the lace curtains, and she began examining it. "What are these flowers anyway?

Roses or peonies? Well, Brenda will know exactly what to do about the windows. Lace is such a feminine fabric, and you've got all this masculine twill and leather in here, Kim. Not to mention the wood floors and coffee table. Don't you think lace is a little jarring to the eye?"

No, Kim wanted to retort. *I love my lace curtains.* But the doorbell was ringing, and it would be Brenda. Kim asked her mother-in-law to let in their visitors, and then she returned to the kitchen to finish up the potatoes.

So what if the Finleys ate carbohydrates now and then? They had fresh fruits and vegetables, meats, and dairy products, too. Kim fumed as she pushed the tray of foil-wrapped potatoes into the hot oven beside the large, onion-coated slab of beef that had already been roasting for several hours. She always checked to make sure Luke carefully counted his carbohydrates. Often they worked together to save up carbs so he could join the rest of the family in treats like an ice cream sundae or a slice of cake. What right did Miranda Finley have to come into her home and criticize the way she cooked? And how dare she disapprove of her beautiful European curtains?

"Hey, Kim! Do you have any chocolate cake in your kitchen?" Cody stood in the doorway, hands pushed down into the front pockets of his blue jeans. "I like chocolate cake, and Esther doesn't make it because of Charlie's diabetes. I'm sleeping at Esther and Charlie's house tonight, and they won't have any chocolate cake. Do you?"

"No, I don't, Cody," Kim told him. The sight of the earnest young man took her frustration level down several notches. "I'm sorry. I've got chocolate-chip cookies, though."

"Those are not my favorite."

"How about if I invite you over the next time I make chocolate cake?"

Cody grinned. "Okay."

"You know, I had forgotten that Charlie has diabetes," Kim said as she checked the pot of green beans on the stove. "So does my Luke."

"I know your Luke. He's a twin to Lydia. That means they popped out of you at the same time."

"Actually, Luke came first and then Lydia arrived about five minutes later. And believe me, Cody, neither one of them popped out."

"Pete Roberts told me that babies pop out of their mothers, and everyone has a mother, even me, because I have a belly button."

Kim blinked for a moment, trying to process the information. "I suppose Pete is right. I'm the mother of Luke and Lydia, and they both have belly buttons."

Cody's eyes crinkled and his nose scrunched up as if he were about to cry. "I don't know what happened to my mother. My daddy wrote in a letter that she was dead, but I want to know why. What happened to her? What if she died from getting drunk and wrapped in fishing line like that woman in the lake?"

"Now, Cody," Brenda said in a warning tone as she stepped into the kitchen and put her arm around the young man. "We've been over this too many times for you to keep repeating it. Your mother died a long time ago. We don't know exactly what happened, but the woman who drowned in the lake was *not* your mother."

"But she might be," he said mournfully, "because nobody knows who the drowned lady was. And I don't know who my mother was. So maybe they're the same person."

"Oh, Cody." Brenda sighed and glanced at Kim as if seeking assistance. "He doesn't seem to understand the passage of time the way we do. Evidently Pete Roberts mentioned to Cody that everyone has a mother, so now we've got this huge issue to deal with."

Kim set the pot holders on the counter. "Cody, did your daddy tell you anything at all about your mother? Ever?"

He shook his head. "He just said when men disappear, no one comes looking."

"Well, I'm sure your father thought he was telling you the truth, but I'm afraid he was wrong. Derek looks for missing men quite often."

"Derek is Officer Finley," Cody stated. "He found the drowned lady."

"Sometimes people do get lost, Cody," Kim said gently. "And then the police, the Highway Patrol, the Water Patrol, and lots of others start looking for them. Men and women get lost. Children too. People search for the lost ones until they're found."

"But does anyone ever get lost and then nobody goes looking for them?"

"Once in a while. No one has mentioned missing a woman near the lake, for example. So that's why this particular drowning case has been in the newspaper a lot."

"I am missing a woman," he said firmly. "I am missing a mother."

"But you have Brenda. And what about Esther and Patsy? Those women look after you and love you just like a mother would. You have me, too, Cody. I care about you very much. So do Ashley Hanes and Opal and all the members of the TLC."

"But you're not my mother. None of those ladies is my mother. Everyone here has a real, true family. Everyone but me. What if I have a sister? Or maybe a brother? Or an aunt or uncle?"

"I don't know. Maybe someone at some point could help search to find out if you have any relatives."

"Which someone at which point?"

"I could do it," Miranda offered. She had been leaning against the kitchen doorway, one of the living room's lace curtains in her arms. "I traced my husband's genealogy all the way back to Ireland in the 1600s. And I've followed my own family to the Civil War. It gets rather complicated there, but I'm not giving up. I'm actually quite good at finding people's relatives."

Kim and Brenda both turned to Miranda and stared at her. Hardly knowing how to respond, Kim watched in astonishment as Cody threw his arms around Miranda.

"Thank you," he said. "I don't know who you are yet, but you must be a Christian, because only a Christian would help somebody find their relatives."

Miranda stiffened and carefully detached Cody from her neck. "I am not a Christian," she told him. "I believe that many paths lead to God—Buddhism, Hinduism, Islam, even paganism. I'm proud to say that I've looked into just about every world religion that is now practiced or ever existed in the past, and I'm convinced there can be any number of roads toward divinity."

Cody looked at Brenda, his eyes blinking in wonderment. "Did you hear that? She's not a Christian. What's her name?"

"My name is Miranda Finley," the woman herself answered. "I'm Officer Derek Finley's mother. We met the day I arrived—by the lake."

Gaping, Cody eyed her in silence for a moment. "Only a Christian would give you chocolate cake," he murmured.

"That's not true, young man. There are plenty of good, caring people in the world, and not all of them are Christians. I would give you chocolate cake."

"Right now?" he asked, brightening.

"No. But if I made some cake, I would share it with you. I'm a very nice person, and I'm not a Christian. I'm not even particularly fond of Christians, truth be told. They're pushy."

Miranda's eyes focused on Kim for an instant; then she trained them on Cody again. "Now then, you need to be quiet while Brenda, Kim, and I chat."

"But what about my relatives?"

"I'll start looking for them on Monday morning. Meanwhile, stand aside, Cody." She stepped between him and the other two women and held up the Belgian lace curtain. "What do you think of this, Brenda? Isn't it a little too flowery to go well with leather and twill?"

CHAPTER SIX

Derek couldn't believe his good fortune at finding Kim awake in bed when he got off work after a twelve-hour shift that Saturday. The twins had been asleep for a while, he knew, and evidently his mother had shut herself into the guest bedroom for the night. This was definitely a positive sign, and he planned to make the most of it. Derek had been out on the lake all day, spending some of it snacking on a bag of nacho cheese–flavored tortilla chips. He would need to take a quick shower and brush his teeth before giving his wife the kind of kiss her eyes were begging from him.

"You look like heaven itself," he told Kim, his voice low as he unbuttoned his shirt. She was wearing one of his favorite night-gowns, a blue scrap that was slinky and silken. "I must have seen a couple dozen half-naked girls in Anderson Hollow today, and not a one of them could hold a candle to you."

"Though I'm sure you didn't spend much time comparing, right?"

"Right," he said with a grin. "Of course not."

Like most of the other officers on the water, Derek was careful about what he looked at in Party Cove. If he spotted some young gal exposing herself, he turned his head quickly. Focusing on contacting the dispatcher and navigating through clusters of swimmers on his way to intercept the woman's boat, he kept his attention in the right place.

A Water Patrolman's hours were long, the sun hot, and the temptation great. Of Derek's entire graduating class, only three officers remained on duty. The job—like most in law enforcement—took a toll on marriages and other relationships. Before committing himself to a wife and children, Derek had made very sure he knew how to handle his assignment and not get into trouble. With a woman like Kim waiting for him at the end of each shift, he didn't have much to worry about.

"I was thankful for my canopy today," he told her. "The sun was blistering. I hope you and the twins stayed inside."

"Most of the time. The three of us drove over to Just As I Am for a cup of tea at about four this afternoon. Luke wanted to go as badly as Lydia."

"Three of you? Didn't my mom tag along?"

"She elected to stay home and wax her legs. Evidently she can't find anyone down here who does it as well as her salon in St. Louis."

Derek made a face. "Wax her legs?"

"Whatever floats your boat."

He shook off the thought and focused on his wife again. "Oh, babe, I can't wait to hold you in my arms. Can you give me five minutes to shower and wash off the day?"

Kim shrugged as she gazed at him. Just the sight of her dark, liquid eyes and bare shoulders sent currents through Derek's stomach.

"Actually, I stayed up because I was hoping we could talk," she said. "There are some things going on that I want to tell you about. I need your opinion."

"Talk?" He froze, his belt halfway out of its loops. "Are you serious?"

"Yes." She swung her legs over the side of the bed. "Listen, Derek, I know what's on your mind, but I'm exhausted tonight. I've spent the whole day on the house, trying to put things back in order after working all week. I must have done fifteen loads of laundry. I made French toast for everyone for breakfast, and then I fixed ham-and-cheese sandwiches for lunch. And then I put in a pot roast and I thought I would bake . . . bake some . . . potatoes. . . ."

"Kim? Are you crying?" He couldn't believe this. He had walked into the bedroom to find his wife looking like a seductress. Setting all his hopes on kissing her sweet lips, he discovered she only wanted to talk about her day . . . it wasn't possible. Laundry and French toast?

"I'm not crying," she said, sniffling and wiping a finger beneath one eye. "I'm fine. It's just that you know I do everything I can to show you and the kids that I love you. I never ask anything of you except to watch the twins when you can. I do all the cleaning, the cooking, and the washing, plus I hold down a full-time job. I'm happy to do it. But then I find out I've hung the wrong curtains in the living room."

"Curtains? Wait a minute. . . . What?" Derek had a bad feeling his wife was upset that he didn't help around the house more. He had been steeling himself to apologize when her train of conversation took a sudden twist, like that last unexpected loop on a roller coaster ride.

Curtains. Derek tried to remember the living room drapes. How could curtains matter after a long, tiring day? What they both needed was to hold each other and ease their stress with some welcome loving.

"I don't know about curtains, baby," he said, stepping toward her and gathering her in his arms. "All I know is that you look delicious in that little blue thing. I could just eat you up."

Usually Kim slipped her hands around him and began drawing circles on his bare back. This time she laid her head on his shoulder and let out a deep sigh.

"The curtains are lace," she murmured. "From Belgium. I think they're wonderful, but even Brenda Hansen said they might look better in the dining room. Can you believe that?"

Derek made a valiant attempt to concentrate on his wife's words instead of on the warm, pliant figure pressed against him. He mumbled in her ear, "So, what was Brenda Hansen doing here?"

"*Your mother* asked her to come!" With that, Kim pushed on his chest until he plopped down on the edge of the bed. She began pacing. "Your mother said she thought our house needed Brenda's decorating expertise. Brenda Hansen is a good friend, but it's not like she knows everything there is about home decor. She doesn't have a degree in interior design. I don't think she even went to college. But everyone around here considers her the expert."

Reaching the wall, Kim made a U-turn. "Well, I happen to like those curtains," she went on. "I love them, in fact. And I think they go perfectly well with the leather chairs and the twill couch. I don't want them hanging in the dining room, because that's where we have the best lake view. Those windows ought to be left bare, just the way I have them."

Another U-turn at the opposite wall. "It's not like I hire Cody Goss to do anything for us. I do it. I do everything myself, because it's the best way I know to show you all how much I love you. I want you to eat a good, hot meal and hear that food whispering that your wife loves you. When you put on your uniform, it should let you know that I care about you, and that's why I take the time to wash it and iron it and fold it so neatly."

Derek began to feel like he was watching a tennis match.

"And I bought those Belgian lace curtains specifically because they were soft and pretty. I keep them washed and bleached and ironed and hung on their rods, because I love my family. Your mother just doesn't get that. All she can think about is rearranging our home and criticizing my baked potatoes."

Derek did his best to concentrate, but he had no idea what she was talking about. All he could see were her long, tanned legs; her graceful neck; that slender waist; and the outlined curves beneath her little blue gown.

But now she turned all of a sudden, hands on her hips and brown eyes boring into him. Like a turtle frozen in the middle of a highway, he held his breath and tried to think clearly. The last thing he recalled Kim saying was something about potatoes, but he couldn't remember what.

"I love your potatoes," he fumbled out.

She let out a muffled cry of exasperation. "Don't you get it? She's sabotaging me with the kids. Now they think we eat too many carbohydrates! Lydia said that very thing, mimicking her exact words right at me. Derek, you know I'm doing everything I can to feed our family a balanced menu. I make sure Luke counts his carbs."

"Of course you do," Derek affirmed. Was Kim upset about Luke's diabetes? Or had Brenda Hansen criticized her cooking? That didn't sound like something Brenda would do.

"And now she's volunteering to help Cody look for his relatives," Kim went on. "Can you believe that? She thinks that because she knows how to trace genealogy, she can find people who've been absent from his life for nearly twenty years. People who might not even exist. Ancestors and missing families are not the same! Besides, it's bound to upset Cody, no matter how it turns out. But she just can't keep her nose out of things."

Derek stood and rubbed his chest. He hadn't seen Kim this upset in a long time, and he couldn't imagine why she was. If Brenda Hansen wanted to look for Cody's relatives, let her. Chances were slim anyone would be found.

"Honey, why has this got you so worked up?" he asked. "You have your own life. Let this other stuff go. Come here and let me hold you."

Kim resumed pacing. "And you know what else? You never tell me anything."

"What? Yes, I do. I tell you I love you. I tell you I think you're beautiful, and I'm crazy about the kids. I love our house, and you're a great cook, and most of all . . . you're beautiful." He shrugged. "And I think you make the best baked potatoes I've ever eaten in my life."

She glared at him from across the room. "I *mean* you don't talk to me about your work! People are constantly asking me about that drowning, and you never even told me it was a woman. I had to find out from someone else. So what do you know about the case? How old was the woman? What color was her hair? How did she die, and why did the body wash up near Deepwater Cove?"

"You know I don't talk about ongoing investigations, Kim."

"Why can't you tell me? Don't you trust me? I'm your wife, and you ought to trust me."

"Why would you even want to know?"

"Because of Cody. He's all confused. He thinks the dead woman might be his mother, but this afternoon I couldn't say, 'No, she's not. I can assure you of that because of the information Derek gave me.' Everyone expected me to know about the body in the cove, but I didn't. You never say anything to me about your day except that I'm prettier than all the half-naked women in Party Cove."

"Well, you are."

"Derek, that's shallow. That's not even real conversation. When you talk to me, you don't say anything. You just toss out compliments like candy at a parade. And I'm supposed to think that's wonderful?"

Whatever flames of passion Derek had been feeling were growing colder by the minute. How could she dismiss his loving words so easily? Nothing communicated love and approval more than a compliment. Not only did Kim rarely return his sentiments; now she was acting like she didn't even appreciate all the kind things he made a point of saying to her.

In three years of marriage, he had never seen his wife this worked up. She was actually wringing her hands. Derek could confront a boater in violation of the law, chase down a jet-skier, or handcuff a belligerent drunk. But this was different. This was an agitated wife in a skimpy gown at the end of a long, hard day.

"Okay," he said, starting for the bathroom. "You made your point, whatever it was, so I'm going to take my shower and get some sleep. If you want to keep talking about all this, we'll try it again in the morning."

"Derek!"

He pushed open the bathroom door and turned to her. "Look, Kim, I'm tired."

"But what about the curtains? And your mom? And Cody? And why won't you tell me about your work?"

"I don't want to fight, babe. Arguing is not my style. You know that. Now get back in bed and try to rest. Things always look better in the morning."

He shut the door behind him and glanced in the mirror. Wow, he'd gotten a lot of sun during the day. His nose was beet red. He would put some lotion on it after his shower.

As he started running the water, he thought about Kim waiting up for him just so she could stalk back and forth across the bedroom floor. Whatever had upset her surely wasn't worth that much energy. Curtains? How trivial could you get? He didn't give a hoot about curtains; that's for sure.

And why all this sudden interest in the drowning case? Kim had never pried into his work, and he didn't ask about hers. They shared highlights once in a while, sure, but he couldn't fake an interest in dental hygiene any more than she could pretend to care how many boaters he had ticketed on a particular day.

Derek stepped into the shower and let the warm water run down his tired body. Why had she put on that blue teddy if all she intended was to rant about Cody Goss and Brenda Hansen? No, the longer he weighed the situation, the more certain he felt that Kim had been preparing for some late-night passion. Maybe these other things had crept into her mind while she waited for him to get home. And maybe . . . just maybe . . . by the time he got out of the shower, she would have remembered her original goal for the evening. As he lifted his face into the spray of water, Derek smiled.

❀

A particularly stubborn head of dark brown curls made Patsy late to the meeting of the Tea Lovers' Club that Wednesday afternoon. The client, a woman from Iowa who had recently bought a house near Camdenton, wanted highlights. Not merely a few gently glowing streaks, either. She insisted on bright gold stripes that Patsy had worried would make her look like she had on a tiger-skin cap.

Not only did the woman's curls have a mind of their own, but that brown color did not want to bleach out. Patsy's first effort wound up auburn, which she thought looked downright pretty. But the new client was newly divorced, and she was out to make a statement. She had on a V-neck top down to here and a miniskirt up to there, and she looked like she was about to spill out everywhere. No matter how much Patsy tried to talk her into a more sensible color combination, the woman was determined that her hair be brown and gold.

By the time Patsy made it to the table with her cup of tea and a buttermilk scone, she was about fried. Tiger Lady had left the salon, pleased at last, but then Patsy'd had to rush through Steve Hansen's trim and Opal Jones's toenails in order to get to the meeting before everyone left. Opal wasn't pleased to be kept waiting either, but she had an appointment that she intended to keep. At ninety-four, she was too stiff to reach her feet and needed Patsy to work on them every once in a while.

"What color did you paint my nails?" Opal asked loudly as she sat down beside Patsy.

"Red!" Patsy shouted into her left ear, which worked better than the right one. "Same as always!"

Opal smiled and took a sip of tea. Patsy knew that no matter how old the widow got, she took great pride in her appearance. She enjoyed wearing high heels to church, and she regularly drove herself to the outlet mall in Osage Beach to shop the sales. Today Opal had on a yellow knit top sprinkled with butterflies and a pair of matching slacks along with her pretty open-toed sandals.

Letting out a deep breath and trying to relax the muscles in her calves and back, Patsy lifted her cup to her lips. Evidently Esther Moore was putting forth her usual effort to impose an agenda on the club. She was jotting down "new business" in her little notebook. This new business included a plan for a Fourth of July decorating spree in which every home in Deepwater Cove and every shop and restaurant in Tranquility would be transformed by members of the TLC.

"The dollar store has red, white, and blue bunting for sale," Esther was saying as Patsy nibbled on her scone. "I think we ought to drape some on the front of each golf cart in the neighborhood. Does anyone know where we can find affordable flags?"

"Our restaurant manager at the country club accidentally ordered too many flags for the tables," Ashley Hanes spoke up. "They're fairly small, but I bet he'd let us have the extras for free. We could put one in every yard."

Patsy noted that the redhead's neck was encircled five-deep in strands of handmade beads, which she fiddled with when she talked. Her skinny tank top and tight shorts bore evidence that the young woman wasn't the least bit pregnant, though Ashley had secretly confided in almost everyone that she and Brad were trying to have a baby. Still starry-eyed about her handsome husband, Ashley took great joy in showing off her engagement ring with its large diamond. It was as though she couldn't quite believe she had actually married the high school's most popular athlete.

Ashley hadn't had her hair trimmed for a while, Patsy realized. The redhead had never been one to sit quietly in the salon chair, and Patsy knew she would always get a full update on how things were going between the newlyweds. Maybe after the club meeting Patsy could schedule Ashley an appointment for a trim. Her ends were getting a bit straggly.

"That is a wonderful idea, Ashley," Esther said, beaming. "If you'll get us those flags, we'll be just about set. Does anyone else have an idea for what we might do to celebrate the independence of our great country?"

"We could put on a fireworks show down at the commons area by the water," Ashley suggested. "Brad loves fireworks. He'd be happy to organize it if people would chip in a little money."

At this, Esther's lips pinched shut. Everyone knew that shooting off fireworks on the commons was against the Deepwater Cove bylaws, and everyone but Brad Hanes was glad. The young man turned into a kid nearly every holiday, blowing up who knew how much money on bottle rockets, Roman candles, and other pyrotechnics. Patsy herself didn't mind fireworks, but she felt sure Ashley's suggestion would be voted down.

"I appreciate the thought," Esther said, "but you know my dog is terrified by fireworks or thunder, or any loud noises. Poor Boofer tries to get behind the sofa, but these days he's too fat. He wedges in as far as he can go, and then he gets stuck. It's all Charlie and I can do to pull him out."

"I'll have to agree with Esther about fireworks," Brenda Hansen spoke up. "My cat feels the same way Boofer does about loud noises. I'll never forget the night lightning struck an electric pole near the house and Ozzie jumped into a pan of pink paint. I thought I'd never get him clean."

Ashley shrugged, her face suddenly forlorn. "Well, if that's how you feel. Most people enjoy watching fireworks on the Fourth. It's traditional, you know."

"How about barbecuing pork steaks on the commons instead?" Patsy put in brightly.

Pork steaks might as well be added to Missouri's official seal. As far as Patsy knew, there had never been a gathering of people in the Show-Me State without someone serving pork steaks.

"Folks could bring their portable grills," she went on, "and we could have a potluck supper with the steaks, casseroles, and different salads."

"Steve will be happy to churn homemade ice cream," Brenda offered. Her husband had kissed her cheek before departing the salon a few minutes ago when Patsy finished his trim.

"I have a great seven-layer dip if people want to contribute bags of chips." Kim Finley hadn't said much till now. As a rule, she was fairly quiet, but when she did have something on her mind, she expressed it well. "And I'll bring the fixings for sundaes, too. There's nothing like hot fudge, pecans, maraschino cherries, and whipped cream on a sundae."

"What's happening on Sunday?" Opal asked, elbowing Patsy.

"We're talking about the Fourth of July!" Patsy disliked yelling, but she didn't have much choice since Opal had left her hearing aids at home. "We plan to barbecue pork steaks on the commons!"

"I didn't realize the Fourth was on a Sunday this year," Opal declared. "I guess I'll bring a couple of my apple pies."

No one could deny that Opal Jones made the best apple pie in the county. As everyone clapped, Esther called the meeting to a close, and the women resumed their chatter. Several rose to refill their cups, while others prepared to leave.

Patsy took delight in the comfortable crowd gathered in her tea area. Since the founding of the TLC, she had come to think of it as a garden—a safe, quiet place set aside for nourishment, growth, and support. As the music of her favorite trio, Color of Mercy, drifted in the air, Patsy studied her patch of blossoms, birds, and butterflies.

Ashley Hanes, still in the springtime blush of marriage, seemed to be settling down a little now, just as flowers sank their roots into the soil in preparation for summer. Orange-red canna lilies blossomed in Patsy's mind when she looked at Ashley. With her flame of long hair and her stacks of beaded necklaces, Ashley came across as tropical and exotic.

Patsy loved canna lilies, and she planted a cluster of them near her mailbox every year. They were tall, showy, and bright all summer, but they didn't last long once the first frost hit. And that was the trouble with cannas—in winter, their raggedy blooms fell off, and their leaves faded from green to brown to black. In Missouri, cannas died out altogether unless you dug them from the ground and hid them in a warm place until the following spring.

Chatting with Esther Moore, Ashley projected a confidence and strength as hardy as a canna's with its thick stem and broad leaves. But Patsy wondered what would happen if winter ever struck the Hanes marriage the way it had Brenda and Steve Hansen's.

Thank goodness, these days Brenda was perking right up. She made Patsy think of another lily that was common all over Missouri. Unlike cannas, surprise lilies could survive the harshest freezes and ice storms. As soon as spring arrived, they sent up long green leaves as a sign that they were still alive. But it wasn't until summer, after the leaves had long since vanished, that these bulbs surprised everyone by bursting out of the ground to show off their prettiest pink ruffles. Leafless, the blossoms danced in the breeze on long stems, nodding as if to welcome everything else in the garden.

Not only was Brenda showing signs of a lovely summertime outlook, but Esther Moore continued to reflect that season too. Calm, comfortable, and satisfied in her long marriage to Charlie, she was a honeysuckle vine. Hardy green foliage and a sweet perfume announced that the honeysuckle, like Esther, was perfectly happy and showing no signs of fading.

"What do you think about bananas?" Brenda asked Kim Finley.

For a second, Patsy feared the others at the table had been reading her mind. Then Brenda finished her thought.

"Steve is crazy about banana splits. He'd rather eat a banana split than a steak dinner. In fact, that's why we bought the ice cream maker."

"I'll bring plenty of bananas," Kim assured her. "Derek likes them too. Lydia won't touch a banana, but Luke might as well be half monkey."

Both Kim and Brenda were seated at the table with Patsy and Opal. While Opal serenely sipped her tea and studied the scene outside the salon, Patsy continued to take account of her tea garden. For some reason Cody hadn't shown up for the TLC meeting, which wasn't like him at all. Some of the women were beginning to leave, and Patsy regretted missing most of the fellowship. She hoped Kim and Brenda would linger awhile, even though she knew they had such busy lives.

"He's doing better each day," Kim was telling her friend when Patsy began listening to them again. "Luke is much more conscientious than I had expected. He's actually pretty good at keeping track of his blood sugar and figuring out his insulin doses."

"That's wonderful. My Justin wouldn't be that responsible. He's still in college, but he barely passes each semester. So unlike Jennifer and Jessica."

Patsy thought Kim looked a little weary today. In the garden of women Patsy nurtured, Kim had never been a summer girl. Life had taken a toll on her, and these days she seemed a bit faded—beautiful but worn, like a cluster of chrysanthemums at the end of the season. Maybe once they had been golden or purple, but now the flowers were losing their color and the leaves were starting to wilt.

"Kim, could we talk about your curtains?" Brenda spoke up all of a sudden.

The way she leaned forward and laid her hand on Kim's arm startled Patsy from her gardening reverie.

"Don't worry about it," Kim said, her lips forming a halfhearted smile. "You're probably right about the lace. I've been thinking about taking them—"

"No!" Brenda's grip tightened on Kim's arm. "Please don't take down those curtains. I mean that seriously. I've done some thinking, and I've looked through my home-decor magazines since I was at our house, and now I realize that lace goes quite well with more masculine furnishings. It provides a balance. Harmony of texture and sensibility. The truth is, those curtains are gorgeous, Kim. Once I got a closer look, I could see they were delicate and unusual—maybe even handmade. I think they should stay exactly where you hung them."

"But you said—"

"I know what I said, and I wish I'd had more time to think it all through before I spoke a single word. The way your mother-in-law was going on about the leather chairs and the twill sofa, I felt overwhelmed. Somehow I thought maybe *you* wanted to replace the curtains. But then as I was leaving, I saw your face, and I realized how much you love them. I think they go perfectly in your living room, Kim. I mean that."

"But lace is a very different texture than leather and twill."

"Exactly. They complement each other. Listen, Kim, I enjoy decorating, and I'm learning more all the time. But I'm no expert. I do what feels natural to me, and that's not always right for everyone else. You've seen my house. Yours is very different, but that doesn't make it wrong. In fact, I've always loved your home and felt totally comfortable there."

"If you think I should leave the curtains, I will. But Miranda won't be happy."

"Well, whose house is it, anyway?" Brenda shot back.

At that, Kim fell silent. She folded her paper napkin into a tiny square. Then she set it on the table and pushed it up against her plate. "I'm not sure," she said finally, glancing at Brenda and then at Patsy with a look of apology in her eyes.

"That house belongs to you and Derek, of course," Patsy blurted out. She had no idea what the big deal was about lace curtains, but she had sat on the Deepwater Cove Association's board of directors long enough to know what belonged to whom. "You own a house, a slip in the community dock, two cars, and a boat."

"But I think . . ." Kim picked up her napkin and unfolded it again. "I think Miranda might be taking over."

Her voice was low when she said the words, and Patsy knew this would be a good time for her to grab Opal by the arm and make an exit. Clearly Kim was burdened, and she had chosen to share her heart with Brenda. But Patsy was sitting right there, and by golly, after being on her feet all day, she didn't feel like getting up. She would do her best to keep her mouth shut and concentrate on the song Color of Mercy was singing. It happened to be one of her favorites, and she might even hum along. Opal, of course, wouldn't hear anything.

"The family unit consists of you, Derek, and the twins," Brenda was saying as Patsy tried not to listen. "Miranda is not part of your immediate family. She can't take over."

"But Derek won't discuss it with me. I tried the other night. I was upset about the curtains—"

"Oh, Kim, I'm so sorry!"

"It's not your fault, Brenda. Miranda instigated the whole issue about the curtains, and then she even had the gall to take one of them down from the window. When Derek got home that night, I did my best to tell him the things that have been on my mind—like how I try to do things for him so that he'll know I love him and how much I want him to tell me about his work. He keeps it all inside and won't share anything with me. Derek actually got upset with me that night. I know he was angry, even though he didn't let on. You know what he did? He walked away and took a shower."

"Who's having a shower?" Opal asked, blinking at Patsy. "I'm not too old to celebrate with everyone else, and I don't want to be left out this time. You make sure my name is on the list, Patsy. I love to shop for babies."

CHAPTER SEVEN

As dearly as Kim loved Patsy Pringle, she was grateful when the salon owner gathered Opal Jones and led the widow away to pay for her pedicure. Kim didn't mind Patsy's knowing about the trouble over her lace curtains. If anyone could be trusted to keep her mouth shut, it was Patsy.

But right now, Kim felt as though Brenda Hansen would truly understand her problems. Like Kim, Brenda had struggled with depression, marital troubles, and the challenges of raising children. Maybe she even had a meddling mother-in-law.

"Men can be so confusing," Brenda commented as she returned to the table with two more cups of tea and a couple of plain butter cookies. "They think *we're* temperamental! At least we know we have feelings, and we're pretty sure what they are. It sounds like Derek is bottling things inside. That's typical, isn't it? Steve used to stare at me while I talked, and I finally realized he wasn't listening at all. If I got the least bit upset, he would walk away."

"Derek told me confrontation wasn't his style," Kim confessed.

"Yeah, right, and he works for the Water Patrol. Officer Derek

Finley confronts people every day. He just doesn't want to argue with *you*."

"But I need to tell him some things he might not want to hear."

"First you have to get him to listen," Brenda said. "Steve is only now catching on to that concept. Somehow you need to get some time alone with Derek, away from his mom and the kids. Make sure he's not too tired or hungry. If Steve is hungry, forget about talking. He's like a grouchy old grizzly, and he won't hear a word. Once you've fed Derek, you can tell him everything."

Kim wished she felt like Brenda's idea would work. "Derek doesn't want to hear anything negative. He focuses on the positive. But for me, life isn't always sunny. Derek throws out compliments and encouragement all day long. That's what I first loved about him. But when things aren't perfect, he wants to run and hide. Brenda, I've been through a lot, and very little of it was good. My life is better right now than it's ever been, but I'm so . . . I'm just so scared. I'm afraid I'll lose him if I can't feel wonderful about everything."

"It's okay that you and Derek are different, isn't it? You don't have to both be Little Merry Sunshine. Let Derek have that role. Someone needs to deal with the fact that Luke has a serious health condition. And someone has to keep the house running and the family fed and the laundry done. If Derek walks around glowing with happiness and showering you with compliments, that's fine. Let him be who he is. You be you. Derek loves you, Kim. He's not going to leave you just because things get rough sometimes."

"I hope you're right."

"Listen, Steve still loves me after all I put him through. And I love him back. Let me tell you; that's a miracle. Based on what we've gone through, I can assure you that Derek will stick it out too. No one's marriage is a fairy tale with a guaranteed happily-ever-after ending. It's hard work."

Kim sighed. "Nobody knows that better than I do."

"You're doing great," Brenda said, squeezing Kim's hand. "I mean that."

"I wish he would tell me more about his job," Kim told her friend. "I'd really like to know—"

"Did we miss the meeting of the TLC?" Cody Goss blurted out as he stepped in front of the table where the two women were talking. "Because I wanted to come, but *she* said we had to go to the library, and that place is full to the brim of books."

"Cody, did you interrupt us?" Brenda asked gently. "Kim and I were talking."

"Yes, I did interrupt, but I don't want to miss the meeting."

"Well, I'm sorry, but it's over. And that's no excuse for bad manners."

Cody hung his head. "Okay. I'm sorry too."

"There you are!" Miranda materialized at Cody's side, while Luke and Lydia made a dash for the counter that held the tea goodies. "Kim, I called home and your cell phone and didn't get you, and I couldn't imagine where you'd gone. Cody kept talking about a meeting, and I had no idea when it was or which day or anything. You know how he is. Of course, if I'd known it was the Little Tea Committee—"

"The Tea Lovers' Club," Cody interrupted, then clapped his hand over his mouth.

"We were at the library, and we got so immersed in our research, and—" Miranda glanced over her shoulder. "Where have those kids gone now? I swear, I could wring their necks. Do you know what they did? They left Cody and me at the library and walked down the street to Lydia's friend's house. I nearly had a panic attack when I couldn't find them."

"Which friend?" Kim asked, rising. "And, Luke, when did you last check your blood?"

"They went to Tiffany's house," Miranda said. "That little tramp in all her eye makeup. I'm going to have to really work with her and Lydia both."

"No makeup, Miranda," Kim said firmly. "We told you that. Luke—what are you eating? Have you saved up enough carbs for that?"

"Lydia is almost eleven and certainly old enough to be taught correctly. You can make cosmetics look natural if you do them right. But how can I be expected to corral both twins when they won't stay where I put them? I had them settled in the children's section when Cody and I went to work on the name *Goss*. It's not a common surname, you know, but that's actually a benefit in situations like this."

Kim barely heard her mother-in-law as she hurried to the display of confections to supervise her children's snack selections. And what was this about leaving the library without telling Miranda? Going to Tiffany's house, of all places!

A touch on Kim's arm startled her as she reached for the brownie in Luke's hand. She turned to find Brenda smiling at her.

"You'll be okay." Brenda leaned close and whispered in her ear. "I promise."

<hr />

When his wife invited him to have lunch with her at the new fast-food restaurant in Tranquility, Derek jumped at the chance. First of all, he liked the meals served at the Pop-In. Other officers called it girl food. They complained that one omelet or a sandwich wrapped in parchment paper couldn't fill a man, but Derek disagreed. He didn't like to eat too much when he was working, and besides, he always carried snacks on his boat in case he got hungry.

Derek also really liked Bitty Sondheim, the owner of the little restaurant. He had grown up in St. Louis, and he felt that the Californian had a certain quality to her that he understood. She had a larger perspective on life. She had gone places and done things. And she wasn't afraid to wear whatever appealed to her, even if it didn't quite fit the local scene. Her long skirts, thick braid, dangly earrings, and sandals added a little sass to go along with her attitude.

"Well, make up your mind, Officer Finley," Bitty commanded from behind the counter that Friday afternoon when Derek and Kim met at the Pop-In. "We don't have all day, you know. Gotta keep the line moving."

At that, Bitty threw back her head and laughed heartily at her joke, because, in fact, Kim and Derek were her only customers. Unfortunately, not too many people knew what to make of eggs wrapped in paper or tortillas wrapped around alfalfa sprouts and wedges of avocado or eggplant. Derek had considered suggesting that Bitty change her menu just a little to accommodate the Missouri appetite for "home-style cookin'." That meant foods like ham, roast beef, and chicken strips. Vegetables cooked until they were good and limp. And sweet, fluffy white bread.

"I'll take the whole wheat fajita wrap, Bitty," Derek said finally. If there was one thing you could always count on for savory taste, it was fajitas.

"The same for me," Kim added.

Derek smiled at his wife. "You sure look pretty this afternoon, Mrs. Finley," he told her. It was true. Kim's brown eyes glowed as she gazed back at him.

"And you, too, Officer Finley." She elbowed him teasingly. "Hey, guess what good news I have. This morning I put the last load of clothes in the dryer. That means I've got the whole weekend free from laundry duty."

"Well, aren't you something else!" Derek chuckled as he leaned against the counter and studied Kim. Sometimes his wife utterly mystified him. Was getting the laundry done really cause for celebration? Laundry was a never-ending chore. But such small victories meant a lot to her, and he wanted to be supportive.

Especially after the trouble they'd had the other night. He didn't even like to think about how upset they had been.

Derek could honestly say he thought he and his wife made the perfect match. He couldn't find a fault in the woman. They rarely had sharp words with each other—in fact, he could count on one hand the times they had disagreed.

Before they married, his biggest fear had been parenting the twins. That turned out to be pretty easy too. Luke enjoyed fishing and swimming with Derek, and until recently, Lydia had been a peach.

"I'm surprised you didn't bring the kids along," he told Kim. "I'd enjoy hearing what they've been up to today."

"I would have needed to drive home and pick them up . . . or ask your mom to meet us here. And I thought it would be nice for just the two of us to have lunch. There are some things I'd like to talk about."

Uh-oh. Derek tried to keep the smile on his face. He did not want to talk about *things.* That could only mean tension. Meeting each other at a restaurant far away from everyone signaled something potentially grim.

"There you go," Bitty said as she returned to the counter with their orders in two to-go sacks. "Fajita wraps, sodas, and tortilla chips. Get your napkins over there by the door, and you two have a good afternoon."

Derek looked at the woman across the counter. Bright blue eyes set off by sunbaked skin bore testimony to many hours on Southern California beaches. He wondered how Bitty was adjusting to small-town Missouri. Had she gotten used to the country ways of folks around Tranquility? Most of all, he wondered if she might sit down with them for lunch to prevent Kim from talking about those *things* she wanted to discuss with her husband.

Too late. Kim looped her arm around Derek's and led him toward the door. "Let's eat in that little clearing down the way," she suggested. "I brought a blanket."

As they strolled past the other shops along the row, Derek wasn't sure whether to enjoy the sudden cool air that had moved in overnight, bringing the promise of rain. If it weren't for Kim's desire to talk, he would be grinning like a skunk in a cabbage patch. Time alone with his wife was rare, and often it occurred only at night, when one or both were on the brink of exhaustion. His fluctuating sched-ule, along with her job and the twins' needs, kept them apart too much for Derek's liking. He had hoped his mother's arrival would ease the situation, but based on the other night's conflict, he was beginning to suspect that Miranda Finley's presence in their home might be part of this discussion Kim wanted to have.

"Here we go," she said, shaking out the blanket she had brought along. "This is shady and out of the path of traffic. Someone ought to put a table and benches in here. Maybe it would help Bitty Sondheim's business."

"A lack of tables and chairs might be part of her problem," Derek said as he hunkered down on the blanket. "But I think she needs to serve something a little more hearty. Blue-collar people work hard, and they want to eat big."

"You may be right," Kim said.

Derek was lifting his fajita wrap to his mouth when he realized that Kim intended for them to pray right out in the open. He quickly bowed his head, hoping against hope that none of the other officers had decided to visit the Pop-In today.

It wasn't that Derek minded his wife's spiritual bent. In fact, he welcomed it. But religion seemed better suited to women. Neither of his parents had embraced any kind of organized church. When he was a child, his mother had read lots of self-help books and gone to weekly therapy, which she had told him was more personally mean-ingful than any sacred creed or ritual. His father's attitude—passed to Derek before the accident that took his life—was that religious people were weak, superstitious, and gullible.

Kim didn't fit that description at all. At the same time, she did rely a lot on God. She had been through plenty of rough water in her life, and her faith seemed to help her deal with the past.

"This is delicious," she murmured when she had finished praying and taken her first bite. "I'm going to spread the word around Dr. Groene's office. Bitty is a fabulous cook."

"She can't hold a candle to you," Derek said, winking at his wife. "I agree, this is good, but I'd rather have a home-cooked meal any day."

Kim took a sip of her soda. She was quiet for a moment, eating and watching people enter and leave the shops along Tranquility's main road. "Is there anything you don't like about me?" she asked, just when he had gotten lulled into a soothing mood.

"Not a thing," he assured her. "You're beautiful. You take great care of the twins and me. People admire you, and you have lots of friends. You're an excellent cook—or did I already say that?"

She smiled. "Yes, you said that. But what about our house? Do you like the way it's decorated?"

Derek could sense trouble coming. It always started small, like the wake from a passing speedboat. And then before you knew what hit you, everything went wobbly and unstable, waves slammed you to the deck, and the boat that had seemed so safe suddenly felt as though it might toss you into the water.

"I don't know anything about decorating a house," Derek said carefully. "But I feel completely comfortable in our home. If I hadn't, I would have said so. And, by the way, I love those living room curtains. Lace . . . nothing better for a living room than lace."

Nodding, Kim took another bite of her wrap. Derek let out a sigh. He felt confident he had passed the worst of it.

"Your mother doesn't like them," Kim said at last.

"Mom has her own ideas about nearly everything. Her own style."

"Yes, she thinks a ten-year-old girl should be taught to wear cosmetics. She thinks I should let her leave a type 1 diabetic all alone, by himself, so she can take the ten-year-old girl on shopping sprees. She doesn't approve of baked potatoes on a day when we have French toast for breakfast and sandwiches for lunch. And she's certain that lace curtains clash with leather and twill."

Derek suddenly felt like he was clinging to the side of a capsized boat. Where had that wave come from? What could he say? How could he make it all go away?

"I don't know how long your mother plans to stay with us," Kim was saying before he could think of a response. "At first it was a couple of weeks. Then she told me she would stay until school started this fall. But these days she never mentions anything about going back to St. Louis. In fact, I'm pretty sure she has moved in with us permanently."

Taking a breath, Derek groped for a lifeline. He hadn't so much as discussed the time of day with his mother, let alone talked about when she might be leaving. To him, she was just part of the Finley household now, participating like one of the family.

"Is that a problem?" he managed.

"What do you think?" Kim returned immediately.

"Uh . . . I think Mom isn't really a problem, is she?" He searched his wife's face. When he didn't get an answer, he continued. "Kim, you grew up with people coming and going all the time. Folks moved in and out of your life on a regular basis. Even in adulthood, things haven't been that different. You met Joe, and then the twins came along, and then Joe left. And after that, I entered the picture. Now my mom is here. So? Is it a big deal?"

"I don't want to model my life after what I saw as a child. I hated all the moving and transition. My mother and her alcohol and all those men . . . it was awful. I'm trying to create a stable home for myself and my children. I already messed up with Joe. And, Derek . . . oh, I don't know."

He was drowning. He could feel it. Tentacles of confusion were dragging him under.

"We have a stable home, babe," he tried. "We're good parents. We love the kids. We love each other."

"Do we? Do we even know each other, Derek? I mean, what is it that you really do all day? Why won't you tell me about your work?"

"Well, what do you want to know? There's nothing that interesting about ticketing someone for carrying too many people on a pontoon boat. If there's a big event, I usually tell you."

"You say you do, but there's been this drowning, and you haven't told me a thing. Did you know your mother is trying to help Cody locate his family? The other day they were in the library most of the afternoon. They missed the TLC meeting completely, even though Cody kept telling her he wanted to leave. She wouldn't listen. She *doesn't* listen. She just says what she thinks. And you know what she thinks? She thinks all religions lead to God. That's what she told our children, Derek. Your mother said she had looked into every kind of faith, including paganism! And she actually had the gall to say that one religion was no more valid than any of the others. She said it right in front of Luke and Lydia! That's not what I want them to hear. Is that what you believe, Derek? What do you really believe about God, and why don't I know?"

He was utterly sunk. No doubt about it. Somehow those lace curtains, his mother, Cody, makeup, religion, and type 1 diabetes had all conspired to drag him to the bottom. He had no idea how to get out of this tangle.

"Religion," he began. He could feel himself beginning to panic, his heart beating just a little too fast. "Uh . . . I don't think about it much. It was never a part of my life before I met you, and it still isn't. That's the truth, Kim. I do my job, and I love you and the twins, and that's about it. I wish I could tell you I was deeper and more complex, but that's all there is."

"You prayed the other day at the table."

"Yeah, but . . ." He wadded up the paper in which his fajita had been wrapped. "Well, I believe in some kind of a Creator. I have trouble thinking that a blue heron or a purple coneflower could have evolved out of a blob of amoebas. I'm sure someone created the world and set it in motion. Some higher being. I don't know what else to tell you about religion, babe. You heard my mother. I wasn't brought up that way."

"Neither was I, but it's important to me."

"Does it have to be important to me, too?"

At that, Kim caught her breath. "Brenda said it was all right for us to be different. You be you. I'll be me." She paused. "But not about God. I think we ought to be united. Would you come to church with the kids and me, Derek?"

Not only was he drowning, but a noose had somehow gotten wrapped around his neck, and it was growing tighter by the second. "Church?" he forced out, his voice quavering like a teenager's. "I'm usually working on Sundays."

"You could request a shift change."

"It would throw everyone else off schedule."

"Please, Derek," she said. "My faith is a huge part of my life. I need for you to understand that. And will you tell me about the drowning?"

He ran a finger around his collar. "We don't know much. I think they're bringing in the Major Case Squad on this one."

"Then it's been ruled a crime?"

"I'm not supposed to talk about it, Kim."

"I'm your wife!"

"I know that, but . . ." He rubbed his eyes. "Okay. We know it was a woman, but we don't know what did her in. The fishing line may be throwing us off track. It was probably an accident, but it could have been a homicide."

"Who would do such a terrible thing?"

"We have no idea. You know how peaceful it is around here most of the time. If we have a crime, it's usually because someone's been drinking. Intoxicated boaters, family feuds, trespassing. We've been seeing more drugs around the lake than usual, but alcohol is still the main issue. I'm not telling you anything you don't already know, am I, Kim?"

She shook her head. "Not really."

"I don't keep things from you. Not if I can help it." He fiddled with the edge of the blanket. "There's just not a whole lot to tell. This morning, I ticketed a kid riding without a life jacket on a personal watercraft. Over the past weekend, we chased down a couple of drunk speeders, and we cited a few females for indecent exposure. Later this month, we'll be setting up a barricade to check for licenses, boating while intoxicated, and things like that. My work is interesting to me, because one day is always a little different from the next. But, Kim, it's not like you're missing a big drama. If you went out on the water with me, you'd be flat bored a good part of the time."

"I wish you'd tell me things, though," she said. "I'd like to know more about your daily life."

"I suppose I can log in with you at the end of the day, but it won't take more than a couple of minutes." He reached for her hand. He wouldn't mind sharing more of his life with her, but there were some things she was just better off not knowing. "Kim, is this really what's got you all worked up? Me not reporting on my day? Me not going to church with you and the kids? This stuff never bothered you before. What's wrong?"

"I didn't say anything about it earlier, but that doesn't mean I didn't care." She sighed, and Derek wondered if she was done. But then she looked up at him again and continued in a softer tone. "Remember I told you about the social worker at the shelter who helped me sort out my feelings after I left Joe? She told me that for a relationship to succeed, both people need to feel safe expressing their needs. Derek, can't you see how scared I am to rock our boat? I want you to be happy, and I live in fear of upsetting you. But I do need for you to talk to me."

"What else do you want to know?"

"Why is it so hard for you to talk openly? Why do you evade me? Why do you walk into another room when someone calls you on your cell phone? Who keeps calling you, anyway?"

"Kim, you know phone calls are a part of my work. I've told you all I can. What more do you want?"

"I desperately want you to go to church."

Here she sucked down a breath that sounded almost like a sob. Derek had thought he was about to reach dry ground, but the quaver in her voice sucked him under again. Didn't Kim realize she had done a lot more than rock their boat? She was drowning him.

He crossed his arms over his chest and focused on the sign over Patsy Pringle's beauty salon in the distance. Just As I Am. That was all he needed from his wife—that she accept him, flaws and all.

Derek didn't mind telling Kim about his day. He might even venture over to her church once in a while to see what was going on inside. One of the other officers, Larry, talked about God all the time. Some of the men kidded Larry about it and tried to get his goat, but Derek respected his friend. If Larry and Kim were good examples of the way Christians lived, then it couldn't be too bad.

Derek glanced surreptitiously at his watch. He needed to be getting back on the water, but he sure didn't want Kim to wind up in tears at the end of their picnic. All the same, he had a bad feeling that she had uncovered the top of a sandbar, and no matter what, their little boat was destined to run aground on it.

"It's your mother," she blurted out suddenly. Covering her eyes with her hands, she shook her head. "Oh, Derek, it's been really hard on me these past few weeks. How long is she going to stay with us? I don't know if I can take much more of her criticism and interference."

He stiffened. His mother might be called a spendthrift or a gossip or even a meddler, but she meant well. At her own suggestion, she had left her home and her busy social life in St. Louis, and she had driven down to the lake to help out with Luke. What right did Kim have to be so hard on her?

"If she's not criticizing my curtains or my cooking," Kim was telling him, "she's dragging the twins off to who knows where. The outlet mall, the library. And then she doesn't even watch them!"

"Let's be grateful we have her help," Derek told his wife firmly, hoping to put an end to the discussion. "Mom's not the world's expert parent, but she's doing her best, Kim. She only had one child to practice on, and that's me. She took on the twins when they were nearly eight years old. You know she would never hurt Luke and Lydia. If anything, the incident at the library was their fault. They skipped out on my mother and ran over to Tiffany's house."

"That never would have happened if your mother hadn't taken them to the library and then left them so she could look for Cody's missing family! Your mom has no idea how to be a real grandmother!"

"Well, she might if you'd ever consider having another baby, like I've asked you a thousand times."

Derek took his sunglasses from his pocket and put them on. He couldn't imagine where that comment had come from, but it was the truth. Ever since they got married, he had been asking Kim to give him more kids. He loved the twins, but he wanted a bigger family. He longed for babies with his genes, his features, his blood. When he asked, Kim always told him she would think about it, but then she never said another word. How many times had he brought up the subject of more children, only to be dismissed with a laugh or a wave of the hand? If she wanted his mother to be a better grandma, Kim ought to be willing to produce a baby or two for her to learn on.

"I've got to get back to work," he told Kim. "I'm late already."

Kim sniffled as Derek got to his feet. More than anything, he wished he could wipe out everything he had said. He wanted to please his wife. He loved her with his whole heart. But what was all this stuff she had suddenly decided to throw at him? How much could a man take before he hurled something back?

As he stood over Kim, he tried to think of something to say to make it all better. Finally he let out a breath, shrugged, and walked to his truck.

CHAPTER EIGHT

Pete Roberts had broken just about every one of the Ten Commandments several times, plus any number of other offenses. Since drying out, taking some college classes, opening Rods-N-Ends, and starting to attend church, he had managed to rid himself of almost all these vices. But there was one he couldn't avoid.

Every time he saw Patsy Pringle, Pete could feel himself heading straight for the devil's workshop. He wanted to hold that woman in his arms. He wanted to kiss those sweet, sweet lips. And he wanted to—

"Pete? Are you coming, or are you just going to stand there looking like a big, hairy goon?" Patsy swung around, her hips aswaying as she sashayed toward the dessert table at the Fourth of July picnic.

Pete stood at the edge of the green, grassy expanse near the lake and stared. Never in his whole life had he seen anything like this Fourth of July celebration. It was better than the Christmas parades his mother had taken him to when he was a kid. It was better than the day his father got out of prison and the whole family went to McDonald's for lunch. And it was a whole lot better than Pete's two weddings, both of which had happened more or less by accident—

being as it was hard to make a clear decision when you were drunk as a skunk.

On this beautiful summer day, everyone in Deepwater Cove had turned out for the festivities. Pete counted eleven grills loaded with pork steaks, sending up an aroma that would make a horsefly dizzy with joy. All fifteen of the neighborhood's golf carts were decked out in red, white, and blue bunting. A giant flag had been strung up on one of the mud poles beside the dock. All that, not to mention the row of tables groaning with salads, chips, dips, sodas, and desserts of every flavor and color. It was enough to make a grown man break right down and cry.

"What're you hanging back for, Pete?" Patsy waited for him to catch up and bumped him with her hip. "Help me carry this watermelon before I fall off my shoes."

The moment Pete laid eyes on Patsy that afternoon, his already high blood pressure had shot up like a bottle rocket. She had bleached her hair until it was almost white, added some long blonde ringlets that must've come out of a package, and pinned sparkling red, white, and blue stars in among the curls. Her red shirt and blue shorts might have been ordinary enough, but her little feet were perched up on a pair of wedgy high-heel sandals pretty enough to make a man's heart stop.

Before Pete could drop dead on the spot, Patsy shoved a watermelon into his midsection and set off ahead of him. Stumbling after her, Pete balanced the watermelon on the cusp of his somewhat substantial paunch. He wished he didn't have that beer belly, and he denied it as much as he could. But truth to tell, once a man had got himself one, it was awful hard to get rid of.

"Where do you want the watermelon to go, Patsy?" Pete asked as he stepped up beside the fount of perfume and hair spray that drew him like a bee to honey.

"Where do you think?" She shot those big blue eyes at him and pointed with a long red fingernail. "Over there under the tree with the other watermelons. I swear, Pete Roberts, are you blind?"

No, he sure wasn't, Pete thought as he made his way to the watermelon cart. He saw those pretty calves and tiny ankles swaying on top of Patsy's high-heel shoes. He saw those red lips that matched her long fingernails. In fact, usually when Pete saw Patsy, he couldn't see much else.

He liked to give her a hard time about her hair, but the truth was plain enough. It didn't matter if she dyed it orange, black, pink, or polka dot, Patsy's hair simply fascinated him. Around Patsy, Pete felt like he had been shot straight through the heart by Cupid's arrow—a sensation he'd never had before in his life. And he wasn't at all sure what to do about it.

"Hey, Pete, how's business at Rods-N-Ends these days?" Steve Hansen was beckoning him over to where a group of men were seated in lawn chairs minding their grills. They wore ball caps and bib aprons with sayings such as *Grill Sergeant* or *Le Chef de BBQ* on the front. Each man held court with a pair of tongs, a bowl of whatever special secret sauce he had concocted, and a flyswatter.

"Didn't I tell you things would pick up during the summer?" Steve asked. "That you'd be so busy you wouldn't know whether you were coming or going?"

"You were right," Pete replied, settling into a chair with frayed webbing. He wasn't real confident it would hold his weight, but he decided if he dropped through, he'd deal with it somehow or other.

"I bet the high gas prices don't hurt," Steve added. "Keeping gas in our cars is about to kill the real estate business."

Pete nodded. "You were smart to buy that hybrid when you did. But I won't accept any blame for my gas prices. They get passed on down the line from the oil wells in Alaska, Oklahoma, or wherever in the world we're buying it from these days. Nope, boys, if you want the honest truth, I make a bigger profit selling minnows."

The other men chuckled.

"At least the minnows are homegrown." Charlie Moore was an avid fisherman. He dropped by Pete's minnow tank nearly every day.

He was waving a flyswatter around his head as he spoke. "If I had my way, Esther and I would buy everything we need right here in the Ozarks. Or grow it ourselves. There's nothing like a fresh tomato right off the vine or a taste of my wife's strawberry jam."

"Who has time to take care of a garden except retired people?" Brad Hanes, a good-looking young fellow who had worked construction so long that his skin was the color of oak, had joined the older men. Pete didn't know Brad too well, though the kid always bought gas for his big new truck at Rods-N-Ends. Brad's favorite thing was to ask when Pete was going to start stocking beer and lottery tickets, and the joke was getting a little old.

"Ashley buys everything at the discount store in Camdenton," Brad was telling the others. "She tries to make our meals unless she can talk me into eating out. But at the rate she's learning how to cook, we'll owe our souls to Bitty Sondheim's place one of these days. I think Ashley has run up a mile-long tab there."

"Kim and I ate at the Pop-In the other day." Now it was Derek Finley's turn to speak. Pete liked the Water Patrol officer as much as any man he'd ever met. Derek was fair, firm, and friendly. He was tending a grill lined with hot dogs for the children.

"Bitty brought sushi appetizers," Derek informed the men as he gestured toward the colorfully clad Californian in the distance. "I'm not sure about eating raw fish on a hot summer day, but I like those omelets Bitty cooks at her restaurant. And her fajita wraps fill a guy up pretty well too."

"Not if he's been hammering shingles onto a roof all morning," Brad observed. "I don't know how many times I've told Bitty she's got to start serving platters with ham, eggs, hash browns, toast, and butter if she expects my crew to eat at the Pop-In. We don't mind her not having chairs and tables. We're used to sitting on the back of a pickup with our sandwiches and water coolers. But I can buy four or five of Pete's hot dogs for what I'd pay for one of Bitty's veggie wraps. Besides, who wants to eat eggplant and alfalfa sprouts for lunch?"

"Might as well go out to graze," Charlie agreed. "In my day, we'd step off the back porch and gather a few turnip greens or plantain leaves. Maybe some spinach if we were lucky. Mother would fry up a mess of greens for us, and we'd eat that along with ham hocks or whatever she happened to have on hand. We didn't pay a nickel for any of it, either. Those were the good old days, and I mean that for a fact."

As the men went on chatting, Pete began a surreptitious survey of the women. He hadn't seen Patsy since he left her for the watermelon wagon. She ought to stand out with her blonde ringlets and those red, white, and blue sparkly stars in her hair, but the whole lakeside was a sea of patriotic clothing. If folks didn't have on a plain red T-shirt, they wore something with the St. Louis Cardinals' red baseball logo. In the Ozarks, rooting for the Cards was considered as patriotic as saluting the U.S. flag. Even the kids had gotten into the spirit of the celebration, waving sparklers as they chased each other back and forth alongside the swimming area just off the shore.

Pete spotted Derek Finley's twins, Luke and Lydia. Cute kids. Too bad about the boy having diabetes, though it didn't appear to be slowing him down any. He was racing after his sister with a red water balloon, and she didn't stand a chance.

On a bench under a tree, the Hansens' two knockout daughters sat watching the kids play. Brenda had brought them with her to Pete's place when she was buying gas the other day. The Hansen girls were blonde, trim, and as sweet as pecan pie. Hard to believe one of them was planning to become a missionary.

What was a missionary, anyhow? Pete wondered as he continued his search for Patsy. Some kind of religious work, Brenda Hansen had told him. Her daughter was going to study at a training center nearby and then head off to live with a remote tribe in the jungle. Pete thought missionarying sounded more like a man's job than something fit for a pretty young lady. Jennifer Hansen had explained that she wanted to tell the natives about Jesus Christ. She hoped to bring them the message of salvation so they could be born again.

Born again. That phrase.

Pete borrowed Charlie's flyswatter and slapped it down on a particularly pesky fellow that had been bothering him ever since he joined the men near the grills. As he handed the flyswatter back to Charlie, Pete had to admit to himself that he'd been doing some thinking ever since Patsy had told him he needed to be born again. And the fact was, he'd botched up his life so bad the first time around that he didn't have the heart to start all over. Oh, sure, he was doing his best not to repeat his previous mistakes. But there was simply not much hope for a man with his past.

"Whoa!" The exclamation escaped Pete's lips the moment he spotted Patsy standing near the salad table. Mercy, that woman looked good in a pair of shorts and high heels.

"Something wrong?" Steve Hansen asked, elbowing Pete. "Or did you just notice Patsy Pringle?"

The other men guffawed as if this were the funniest thing they'd ever heard.

Pete leaned back in the lawn chair and grinned. "As a matter of fact, I believe I do have my eye on the prettiest gal in Deepwater Cove."

"Now, hold on there," Steve spoke up. "Patsy's pretty all right, but I'd have to vote for my beautiful Brenda as the belle of this ball."

All the men focused on the lovely blonde whose smile shone like the summer sun. Brenda was obviously talking to the other women about her daughters as she gestured toward the two young beauties who favored their mother to a tee.

Pete agreed that Brenda Hansen was very attractive, and he was glad to hear her husband speak up for her. But Patsy Pringle—

"Aw, come on, Steve," Brad Hanes said. "My Ashley's the hottest hottie out here. Look at those long legs on my woman."

The men shifted a little uncomfortably as they all made an effort *not* to look at the young redhead's legs. Pete began to wish the topic of women had never come up. Brad shouldn't have drawn the fellows' attention to his wife's legs. Not even Pete was that ignorant, and he decided it was time to steer toward a safer topic than a comparison of one woman's attributes with another's.

"A pretty lady will get my thumbs-up any time and any place," he said. "In fact, I think this little corner of the world has got the pick of the crop. Look at those gals. Esther, Brenda, Ashley, and Patsy—fairest flowers of the land."

"Speaking of pretty women, where's that mother of yours, Derek?" Charlie Moore asked. "And come to think of it, I don't see Kim, either."

Pete glanced over at Derek, who was shifting a little uncomfortably in his lawn chair. "They, uh . . . they had a little problem in the kitchen. Kim's bringing one of those seven-layer dips."

"Got in a fight about which layer went first, huh?" Brad asked with a laugh.

The look on Derek's face told Pete that was exactly what had happened. Charlie gave an awkward harrumph and pretended to search for his wife. Steve reached across his grill with a pair of tongs to turn over his pork steaks. Who would have thought a bunch of good-for-nothings like these fellows sitting around on the Fourth of July could manage to make each other so uncomfortable?

Pete knew women talked nonstop and everyone felt just peachy when they parted company. Before he had built a soundproof wall between his tackle shop and Patsy's salon, Pete had heard the women next door jabbering away day after day. In fact, their constant chit-chat had been partly what prompted him to start up a chain saw every now and then. Anything to drown out that racket.

But men? Men didn't really know how to talk to each other. They couldn't very well admire each other's hairdos or trade chicken soup recipes. What this bunch needed was a woman to sit among them and stir up some cordial conversation. But as it was, the men fanned themselves with their flyswatters or checked their grills until Pete finally brought up what everyone was thinking.

"How about them Cardinals?"

"I couldn't believe the pitcher in yesterday's game," Brad Hanes muttered.

"Did you fellas see that drive down the right-field line?" Charlie Moore asked.

And that was all it took. They discussed the ins and outs of the game, weighed the players' talents, mentioned statistics from the past, and generally talked the subject half to death.

That was okay with Pete. He focused on Patsy Pringle, who was balancing on her high-heel wedges as she picked her way across the grass toward some destination Pete couldn't see. Adjusting her gold ringlets, she began to smile as if she'd just gotten a glimpse of heaven itself. Slightly disturbed at what might have captured Patsy's attention other than himself, Pete leaned forward. The plastic webbing under his backside crackled a little as he scanned the scene, and finally he noticed goofy ol' Cody Goss half skipping and jumping toward Patsy.

"Hey, Patsy," Cody cried, clapping his hands as he greeted her. "You have stars in your hair!"

"It's the Fourth of July, honey!" she exclaimed.

"Happy America!" he said, dancing around her. "Merry Independence! Long live July!"

Patsy laughed and hugged on Cody like he was her long-lost best friend. Then she turned and pointed out the watermelon wagon, the shore where all the kids were playing, the tables lined with salads and desserts, and finally the grills. As her eyes settled on Pete, he decided he'd heard more than enough about baseball. He beckoned Patsy and Cody.

"Look, there's Pete Roberts!" Cody called out. "He makes hot dogs at Rods-N-Ends. Hi, Pete!"

"Hey there, Cody ol' fella; how're you doing today?" Pete pushed himself out of the lawn chair and ambled over to them. "I see you're wearing a flag T-shirt."

"This is the USA flag," Cody explained, laying his hand on his chest to indicate the printed banner. "Brenda and Steve gave me this shirt. The flag has stars like in Patsy's hair. I like those stars. Do you?"

"I sure do," Pete said. "Patsy always looks pretty as a picture."

"A picture? She's prettier than a picture, because this is really her."

"Aw, Cody," Patsy murmured, blushing like some shy schoolgirl. "You are so sweet. And you're handsome, too! Look at that clean-shaven chin. Gracious sakes, young man, who would ever have thought it!"

"Pete should shave, huh, Patsy?" Cody asked. "You told me he looks like a shaggy bear."

Cody glanced from Patsy to Pete, assessed their expressions, and then covered his mouth with his hand. "Oops," he said. "I think I just did bad social skills."

"It's all right," Patsy told Cody, patting his arm. "Pete knows how I feel about that awful beard."

Suddenly grouchy, Pete combed his fingers through the thick mat of dark hair that had been with him since he couldn't remember when. He snorted and hooked his hands in the pockets of his jeans. "A person ought to be able to see beyond a little facial hair, is what I say. Looks aren't everything."

"Oh, really?" Patsy retorted. "Seems you've been doing plenty of looking in my direction today, Mr. Roberts. If you want me looking back, you'd do well to shave off that musty old clump hanging from your chin."

Cody cackled and slapped his thighs. "Musty old clump! At least you don't have mice in your hair like I did when I first got to Deepwater Cove, Pete. Hey, look who's coming now! It's Mrs. Finley and the other Mrs. Finley."

Sure enough, here came Kim and her mother-in-law, Miranda, each carrying a clear glass bowl of seven-layer dip across the lawn toward the gathering. Pete didn't want to make a big deal of it, but he noticed right away that neither woman looked the least bit happy about making an appearance at the Deepwater Cove Fourth of July celebration. As Kim and Miranda set their bowls on the chip-and-dip table, Pete left Patsy's side and wandered over to fetch himself a plate of appetizers. No point just dawdling around when there was good food to be had.

"Afternoon, Miz Finley," he greeted Derek's mother.

Both women looked up at the same time and gave pained smiles.

"Hi, Pete," Kim Finley spoke up first. "Glad you could make it to the celebration."

"Try my seven-layer dip, Pete," Miranda Finley suggested, spooning a dollop onto a paper plate and giving it to him. She dug a handful of tortilla chips from a bag, ran one through her dip, and pushed it between his lips. "I always put the sour cream on top, because that way it's the first flavor to hit your taste buds. Sets the mood, don't you think? With guacamole, cheese, and refried beans all in perfect order under the sour cream, you can almost picture yourself lounging on a Caribbean beach."

Pete tried to talk around the bite of chip and dip Miranda had put into his mouth, but he couldn't manage it. He wanted to say that it didn't matter to him which came first, because eventually the flavors all blended together. But as he started to speak, a sliver of chip flew down the wrong pipe.

As Pete began to cough, he noticed what Kim was doing. Standing beside her mother-in-law, she pursed her lips tight and ladled a large helping of her own seven-layer dip into a bowl. Swigging down some soda to clear his throat, Pete noted that Kim had put the shredded cheese on top, followed by layers of beans, guacamole, olives, and—somewhere down at the bottom—sour cream.

Grabbing a bag of chips under one arm, Kim carried her dip toward the men gathered around their grills. Pete could see the battle unfolding right before his eyes. If anyone declared Kim's appetizer to be delicious, it would undercut Miranda's before she'd even had a chance to show it off. And no doubt those sweaty gents in their barbecue aprons were going to dig into Kim's dip with gusto.

As she realized her daughter-in-law's ploy, Miranda let out a whimper of dismay. She snatched up her bowl of dip, seized a second bag of chips and marched toward the men.

Pete took one look at Derek Finley's face and realized that this unfolding conflict would put the poor man in the hot seat, no matter what. "Hey, Patsy!" he called. "Yo, Patsy!"

If only he could get the blonde in her wedgy sandals and sparkling stars to saunter over to the grills, she might just be able to distract everyone. Then maybe Patsy's kind demeanor and sweet words could defuse the oncoming clash. Determined to keep peace, Pete hurried over to where the salon owner was helping Bitty Sondheim and Opal Jones arrange carrots and sweet pickles in neat rows on a glass tray.

"Patsy," Pete said, sidling up and whispering in her ear. "You've got to come with me right now, and I mean it. No dawdling around, gal. There's trouble afoot."

Before she could respond, Pete took her arm and ushered her toward the battlefront.

"What are you up to now, Pete Roberts?" Patsy challenged him. "Bitty and I were helping Opal fix her relish dish! You know how bad Opal's arthritis gets, and she asked us to—"

"Patsy, get over there and eat some dip," Pete instructed as he propelled the woman across the grass. "Try 'em both, and then talk about something else like hairstyles or whatever comes to mind."

"Pete, let go of my arm this minute! Why, I ought to—"

Patsy caught her breath as Pete pushed her down onto the lawn chair he had recently vacated.

"Look who's here," he said. "It's Patsy."

Pete was turning to scoop dip from the two rival bowls when the unmistakable sound of ripping plastic caught his ears. He looked back in time to see the webbing give way beneath Patsy Pringle's ample backside and drop her right through the aluminum chair frame onto the ground.

Patsy let out a shriek that would curdle milk as her wedge-heeled feet flew into the air, and her sandals sailed over Pete's head.

"Incoming!" someone yelled.

Pete never would have guessed it possible, but the woman folded into that aluminum framework like a hymnbook at the end of a church service. Her legs stuck straight up, her arms waved back and forth over her head, and those sparkly stars went sailing out of her hair.

"Help!" she hollered, bare feet kicking. "Somebody help me! Pete Roberts, I'm gonna kill you!"

Horror-struck, Pete couldn't move for a full second. In fact, it seemed as though the entire Deepwater Cove gathering fell silent and turned to stare at the woman wedged into the frame of the collapsed aluminum folding chair. And then—before Pete could do his part to rectify the situation—Officer Derek Finley bent over and extricated the helpless victim from the jaws of death.

"Are you all right, Patsy?" Derek asked as he pulled Patsy to her feet.

Her blue eyes shot straight to Pete. "No, I am not all right, thank you very much! I am furious! Pete Roberts, what on earth was that all about? I ought to string you up by your thumbnails!"

"Good gravy!" Charlie Moore exclaimed. "For a minute there, I thought we'd been hit by mortar fire!"

Brad Hanes burst out laughing. "It was a blonde bombshell, all right!"

"Did you see those shoes go airborne?" someone else cried.

"I saw shooting stars right before my eyes!"

By now, all the men were grinning as they grabbed the bags of chips and dug into the identical bowls of dip. Feud obviously forgotten, Kim and Miranda Finley circled around Patsy, helping to fix her hair and find her sandals. Somehow a long curlicue had come unpinned, and Pete picked it up.

"Uh, I think you lost this," he said, holding out the blonde ringlet like a peace offering.

Patsy snatched it from his hand. "You'd better explain yourself this minute, Pete Roberts. What did you mean by jerking me away from helping Opal with her relish tray and slinging me into that broken chair?"

"Well, I was . . ." Pete gulped. "I thought maybe—"

"You made me the laughingstock of the whole place! Everyone saw me make an idiot of myself."

To Pete's horror, the feisty woman's blue eyes suddenly filled with tears. He reached out to her. "Aw, now, Patsy—"

"Don't you dare touch me, Pete Roberts!" she said, knocking his hand away. "You're pushy and mean and forward. You're just a bully is what you are! Ever since you moved to the lake, you've done everything in your power to make my life miserable. But this is the last straw. You intended to make me out to be a fool, and you succeeded—and that's the last you'll be hearing from me till the cows come home!"

"Now, listen here, Patsy," he began again.

But the sound of a child's scream drowned out his words. As Pete focused in the direction of the cry, he saw Kim and Derek Finley's young daughter sprinting toward them.

"Mommy, Mommy!" she was hollering as she ran. "Come quick! Luke fell down, and he's not moving!"

CHAPTER NINE

Kim knelt in the damp, rocky sand beside her son. Luke's brown eyes fluttered as she pressed the emergency number on her cell phone. Next to her, Derek was checking the boy's pulse and airway.

"I need a clean towel—his head is bleeding. I'm guessing he gashed it on that big rock." Derek glanced at Lydia. "What were you kids doing?"

"Just playing around, I swear!" Lydia was jumping up and down, shaking her hands, crying, and elbowing away all attempts to comfort her. "Luke told me he was dizzy and he felt like he was going to throw up. Then he started staggering down the beach, but he only got this far before he fell and his head hit that rock. Do something, Derek! Fix him! Fix my brother!"

"Nausea, dizziness, and staggering. Sounds like intoxication. Listen, Lydia, I need to know if Luke drank any alcohol," Derek barked at the girl as someone handed him a towel. "You'd better tell me the truth. What did you kids get into? Was it beer?"

"Luke's not drunk," Kim cut in. "It's his diabetes! His blood sugar must be off. I don't know what to do! I can't think! Where's his kit?"

She looked at Lydia, who shrieked, "I don't have it! Was I supposed to bring it? It's Luke's kit, and—"

Lydia caught her breath as her brother suddenly began to convulse. Kim let out an involuntary wail and tried to gather her son in her arms. Pressing the towel against the gash on the side of the boy's head, Derek urged everyone to calm down. And suddenly the insulin kit appeared in Miranda's hand.

"I found it in his bedroom," she huffed, out of breath. "In all the excitement of the day, he might have forgotten to take his insulin."

"Lukey's bleeding to death!" Lydia screamed. "He's going to die!"

"Someone get the girl under control," Derek shouted at the crowd as he snatched the kit and handed it to Kim. "Mom, take Lydia to the house."

"I'm not leaving my brother!" Lydia cried out. "Make him stop shaking! You have to help him!"

Kim tried to block out her daughter's hysteria as she fumbled with the insulin kit. People had crowded around, edging closer, cutting off the afternoon sunlight. She pushed at Lydia's skinny arms as the girl tried to grab her brother.

"Don't let him die!" Lydia sobbed. "He's all I have. He's my only brother. He's my best friend."

"Scoot over, Lydia," Kim ordered. Luke's convulsions had eased, but he was groggy and unfocused. "I have to test his blood."

"He didn't eat lunch, Mom!" Lydia was down on her stomach, arms around her brother. "We forgot about the snacks you sent with us. Why won't his head stop bleeding, Derek? What are you doing to him? Wake up, Lukey! Please don't die!"

"Please, God, please," Kim whispered as she tested her son's blood and read the indicator. "His glucose is low—but he shouldn't have had a seizure. Why isn't he more alert?"

"Probably the head injury," Derek said. "I'm on it."

Kim could hear a siren in the distance as she filled a syringe with insulin. "Please help my son, Lord. Please help us."

"He'll be all right," Derek was saying. "We've got him under control, honey. He'll be fine."

While Kim injected the insulin, Derek checked Luke's pulse again. "We need to get a saline IV going. He probably needs potassium, too. Hang in there, Luke. You're doing good, kiddo. Lydia, for pete's sake, will you let your brother have some air?"

"You shut up!" Lydia shouted suddenly at Derek. "You don't know anything! You're supposed to be an officer and smart about helping people, but you're just wiping Lukey's blood and letting my mom do all the work. You can't make me—"

"Put a muzzle on that mouth, girl, or I will!"

As the emergency medical personnel clustered around Luke, Kim sensed Derek leaving her side, pressing people back, dragging Lydia away. The EMTs began asking questions, checking Luke's vital signs, starting an IV drip. Kim told them everything she knew. She watched helplessly as they lifted her son into the back of the ambulance. And then, before she could clear her head, she was inside the vehicle speeding toward Lake Regional hospital in Osage Beach.

The EMT team worked over Luke while Kim brushed back tears and tried to make sense of what they were saying. She heard words that had passed through her mind a thousand times since her son's diagnosis—*diabetic ketoacidosis, counterregulatory hormones, electrolytes, ketones.*

She struggled to answer their questions. When had Luke's blood last been tested? By the shore, she told them, ten minutes ago—or was it five?

Had he experienced a recent infection—strep throat, pneumonia, an intestinal virus, or a urinary tract infection? A cough and runny nose, she said. Oh, why hadn't she paid closer attention to her son?

Had he undergone any trauma other than the head injury in the past twenty-four hours? Nothing. Nothing she could recall, but he had been outside with Lydia since breakfast.

Kim told the team everything she knew, and it seemed not nearly enough. That morning, she and her mother-in-law had argued over the right way to make a seven-layer dip. At the sound of their bickering, Luke and Lydia fled the house and began swimming in the cove and playing with the other children. As everyone slowly gathered in the commons area and waited for the pork steaks to cook, the meal had been delayed. So what had Luke eaten that day? When had he last given himself a dose of insulin? What had he done while she was busy in the kitchen?

"I can't believe it," Kim murmured as the ambulance stopped in front of the hospital's emergency room and the EMT team transferred Luke to the waiting medical staff. "I can't believe it. I didn't watch him. And Lydia! Where is—oh, thank God!"

Kim's breath hung in her throat as Derek and Lydia burst through the ER door and ran toward her. Miranda was right behind them, her sandals clattering on the hard floor and her blonde hair sticking out in all directions.

Still wearing her wet bathing suit, Lydia grabbed her mother and began weeping all over again. "Where's Lukey?" she sobbed. "Where did they take my brother? I hate Derek! He made me ride in the car instead of the ambulance, and he doesn't even know what ketones are!"

Kim glanced at her husband, who had leaned one shoulder against the corridor wall as he caught his breath. Obviously fighting for control, he crossed his arms over his chest and stared at Kim. And then a doctor hurried toward them. More questions. Lydia crying and raging. Miranda wringing her hands, sandals clacking along the floor as she paced. Derek, jaw clenched, staring.

The doctor vanished, and someone ushered them all to the ER waiting area. Kim had barely sat down when Lydia curled into her lap.

"It's Derek's fault," the girl whimpered. "He's supposed to know how to help people in trouble, and he didn't do anything."

"Stop that, Lydia," Miranda spoke up firmly. "You can't hold your stepfather responsible. We all played a part. This morning it crossed my mind that Luke might have forgotten to check his blood, and then I got busy with the seven-layer dip. Your mother was so insistent on doing it her way—"

"Wait—you're blaming *me* for the problem in the kitchen?" Kim stared in disbelief. "You were the one who made an issue of the dip, Miranda. In fact, you criticize everything I do. I could have put that dip together in five minutes, but I spent half the morning trying to convince you that I knew what I was doing! And you . . . you . . ." Hearing her own senseless rant, Kim burst into tears and buried her face in her daughter's shoulder.

Lydia wrapped her arms around her mother. "You should just go back to St. Louis, Grandma Finley," she said. "And take Derek with you. We don't need either of you. It's always been Luke and Mommy and me, ever since I can remember, and we were doing just fine till you people came along."

"Lydia, no," Kim cried.

"*You*, young lady, should have been watching your brother." Miranda pointed an accusing finger at the girl. "If I didn't know about the diabetes, I wouldn't have any trouble believing you two had gotten into someone's liquor cabinet! You're both just looking for trouble, aren't you? Like the day you ran away from me at the library. How did you expect me to find you at your friend's house two streets over? The fact is, you were both raised to be wild little things. If my son hadn't married your mother and brought some order and control into your lives, you'd probably be headed for juvenile court by now!"

"That's enough, Mom," Derek growled. "Everyone be quiet for two seconds."

"How can you expect us to be detached and unemotional like you, Derek?" Kim demanded. "We don't even know what's happening to Luke! They've shut us away here in the waiting room, and the least you could do is tell them you're with the Water Patrol."

"Why would I do that?"

"So you could go in there and check on him! You're an officer. You're trained for emergencies."

"Not diabetic emergencies," Lydia tossed out. "Derek doesn't know anything about diabetes, and you know why? Because he doesn't care. I bet he never even read the printout I made. He only cares about his work. He's not our real father. Luke could die, and Derek would be glad, Mom, because that would be one less person to take you away from him. That's all he wants. Just you and his dumb job."

"Lydia." Kim tried to push her daughter off her lap, but the girl clung on tight with fingers like steel bands. "Lydia, stop being disrespectful to Derek. He loves you and Luke, and he takes good care of us—"

"No, he doesn't! He doesn't know what ketones are! All he does is ride around in his stupid speedboat looking at girls in Party Cove. Big deal! Officer Finley, Officer Finley, la-di-da! Who cares?"

"Is that the way you let your children speak to adults, Kim?" Miranda cried. "You should take that girl outside and—"

"I will deal with my daughter when this crisis is over," Kim snapped. "At the moment, all I care about is my son's health! Derek, don't just stand there like a concrete block. Go in there and make them tell us what's going on!"

As Derek roused himself from the wall he'd been leaning against, the emergency room door burst open and in marched half of Deepwater Cove. Patsy Pringle and Cody Goss led the pack as Steve and Brenda Hansen, Charlie and Esther Moore, Brad and Ashley Hanes, Opal Jones, Bitty Sondheim, and a number of others flooded into the waiting area. Pete Roberts brought up the rear, his beefy arms wrapped around a watermelon.

The throng had nearly reached Kim when the door at the opposite end of the room opened and a nurse beckoned the family. Lydia leaped out of her mother's arms and began to run. Kim cast a backward glance at Derek, saw he was speaking to Miranda, and headed after her daughter.

❈

"Ketones," Derek told Steve Hansen as the two men stood in the hospital room's doorway. Two days had passed since the Fourth of July fiasco, and Derek had finally succeeded in sending his wife home to bed. Luke was holding his own now. The diabetic crisis was safely behind them, and the doctor planned to release the boy the next morning. The stitches meant Luke's head would be sore, but the mild concussion should have no lasting impact. Working the late shift gave Derek the opportunity to relieve Kim, who hadn't left her son's side since his arrival at the emergency room.

"What are ketones?" Steve asked. The real estate agent had dropped by the hospital after dinner with a client at his country club. They had sealed a lucrative land deal, and Steve was in a good mood despite the late hour.

"Ketones are chemical by-products," Derek explained. Recalling Lydia's shouted accusations, he had made sure to ask the doctor everything about Luke's condition.

"Are they good or bad?" Steve asked.

Derek rubbed his temples with his thumb and forefinger. "They're bad. They affect the kidneys. Luke forgot his insulin on the morning of the Fourth. He told his mother that he'd been popping in and out of the basement bathroom all day, but he didn't think anything about it. When he got dehydrated, he felt dizzy and fell and hit his head."

"I guess I hadn't realized it could get that serious so quickly." Steve studied the sleeping boy. "Charlie Moore told us he has diabetes, but I guess his is not the same kind as Luke's."

"Charlie has type 2. That can be serious too, but it's different."

Steve clapped a hand on Derek's shoulder. "Brenda mentioned some of the things Lydia was saying to you out there on the commons. Kids can be pretty tough to handle at times, and you took on the twins sort of late in the game."

Derek shrugged. "Being a stepfather is harder than I thought. Kim says I live in my own little world."

"What man doesn't? We see our role as a job, and we do the best we can with it. For years I thought I was a good husband and dad— doing my part, playing my role. And then Brenda accused me of abandoning her."

Surprised at the frank revelation, Derek glanced at Steve. Derek liked Steve Hansen well enough, and he respected the man's dedication to his wife and children. Steve had built a good reputation as a businessman with his real estate agency. He had always seemed cheerful and his family successful.

"You abandoned Brenda?" Derek asked. "That doesn't sound like the Hansens of Deepwater Cove."

"Well, I was gone a lot, especially when the new agency had just started to build up steam. Brenda started missing the kids and struggling over some things, and I was never around. We had a rough time, and I wouldn't ever want to go through anything like that again. But we learned a lot. Brenda and I are working hard to pull our marriage back together. I'd sure hate to see you and Kim fall into the same kind of trouble."

Derek frowned. "I don't think we have any big problems. Kim and I are crazy about each other. It's this diabetes thing . . . and my mother being around all the time. And I do have to work a lot of hours, especially in the summer. But I try."

The men fell silent, watching the lights on Luke's monitors blink on and off. Derek reflected on the arguing and shouting that had taken place at home in the past few weeks. Lydia had become a real pain in the neck, and Luke's diabetes was stressing everyone out. Kim clearly didn't like having Derek's mother in their home, but he couldn't understand why. Miranda looked after the twins so Kim could go back to work. Kim enjoyed her job, and that income was something the family couldn't surrender.

"Maybe the real problem is not you at all," Steve suggested.

"Brenda had focused her whole life around our children before they left home. I'll bet Kim is frustrated over her inability to be with the twins more—especially with one of them sick. But I know Dr. Groene counts on Kim. So what do you do?"

"Turns out he's diabetic too. Type 1, like Luke. He's been great."

"Could Kim stay home with the twins permanently? That way, your mother could go back to St. Louis. Maybe then you could all get back to normal."

Derek shook his head, realizing there was so much more to the financial situation than anyone understood.

"Have you and Kim ever thought of talking to Pastor Andrew? I wish I'd listened better to his advice when Brenda and I were having trouble. He might have some ideas that could see you through this rough patch."

"The guy's been in and out of here every day visiting with Luke and Kim, but I don't feel that comfortable around him, to tell you the truth. I'm not a churchgoer, you know. I don't mind Kim and the kids attending. I just haven't felt the need."

Steve's eyebrows lifted. "Maybe not yet."

Derek glanced over at him. "I've always handled things my way, pal."

"Well, you've got our prayers whether you want them or not." Steve gave Derek a nod. "I'd better head home. Brenda and Cody baked a chocolate cake this evening, and they're waiting up for me."

At the thought of Cody's wide blue eyes, Derek smiled and his shoulders relaxed. "Eat a piece for me," he said. "Desserts are few and far between at our house these days."

"You've got a deal."

"Thanks for dropping by," Derek said. "I'll tell Kim you were here to check on Luke."

"Actually, I came to see you. I called Kim before I left the club, and she told me you were at the hospital. I wanted to visit with you awhile."

"Thanks."

Steve shook Derek's hand and headed down the hall.

❈

Lydia settled into the soft, black vinyl chair at Patsy's station inside the Just As I Am beauty salon. Closing her eyes, she took a deep breath and said, "Cut it off."

"All of it?" Patsy lifted a hank of the girl's thick, dark brown hair. "Honeybunch, are you sure about this?"

"I'm positive. Luke and I are turning eleven in three weeks, and we're tired of being treated like little kids. We're going into the sixth grade this fall. That's middle school, in case you didn't know."

"I know how old eleven is, and I also know that you have some of the prettiest hair in Camden County. I'd put you in the running to wear Jessica Hansen's homecoming queen crown one of these days. You've got your mother's big brown eyes and your own sweet smile. You don't want to cut off your hair so close to school starting up again, do you?"

"Yes," Lydia said firmly. "Up to my ears. I want it short and sassy, like Tiffany's."

Lydia opened her purse and pulled out a school photograph of a girl who didn't have half her beauty. What had gotten into that giggly little pumpkin who used to hold her twin brother's hand as they selected goodies with their mother in the tea area?

When Lydia called the salon to make an appointment, one of the other stylists had taken the message. Now Patsy was beginning to wonder if Kim Finley even knew what her daughter was up to.

"Tiffany's got some natural wave, see?" Patsy said, pointing to the photo. "Your hair wouldn't look the same even if we did give it that style. Does your mother want me to cut it so short, honey? Or did she drop you off here just for a trim?"

As Lydia's pretty lips pinched shut, Patsy noted the film of pink lip gloss coating them. She also saw a dusting of frosted eye shadow on the girl's eyelids and some clumpy mascara stuck to her lashes. Hmmm. This was beginning to spell trouble with a capital *T*.

"I've got an idea," Patsy said. "You sit tight while I call your mom at Dr. Groene's office. She can tell me exactly what the two of you discussed."

"No, wait!" Lydia caught Patsy's arm. "I rode my bike over here by myself, and I'm spending my *own* money for this haircut. My mother has nothing to do with it."

"Really? Don't you still live at home?" Patsy swung the chair toward the mirror and snapped a plastic cape around Lydia's neck. "My parents always said I could make my own decisions when I lived in my own house and paid my own bills and ate my own cooking. Until then, I was under their thumb."

"I'm not under anyone's thumb. My real dad doesn't live with us, so Luke and I don't even have parents like yours. We live with Derek and our fake grandma, who doesn't even like us. She told us we were nothing but a gigantic pain."

"Really? Miranda said that?" Patsy began combing out Lydia's long hair. "Oh, maybe she said it that time you two ran off from her and Cody at the library and she couldn't find you. I guess she must have been pretty upset. People sometimes say and do things they don't mean when they get angry. You know what I did one time when I got mad?"

Lydia's brown eyes swiveled from gazing at herself in the mirror to focusing on Patsy. "Yes. You refused to eat a single slice of the watermelon Pete Roberts brought over to the hospital the night Luke went into the emergency room. You told Pete he could stick that watermelon in his ear."

Suddenly going warm, Patsy fanned herself with her hand. "Did I say that?"

"Uh-huh. Pete brought your watermelon from the wagon under the tree. He cut it up for everyone to eat while they waited to find out about Luke. Mom and I ate some, and even Grandma Finley said it was good—and she never likes anything she didn't do herself. But you wouldn't touch it. You said you didn't ever want to talk to Pete again."

"Oh, dear."

More than a week had passed since the Independence Day chair incident, and Patsy had kept to her word. Once, she and Pete had passed each other in the hospital corridor while visiting Luke. Patsy had turned her head and pretended to be talking to Opal Jones, who didn't even have her hearing aids in. And Patsy had refused to speak to Pete at church last Sunday. They didn't sit together or go out to eat at Aunt Mamie's Good Food in Camdenton after the service. She hadn't thanked him for the pretty antique teacup he had left on her doorstep the previous morning. In fact, she hadn't even read the accompanying note.

"Well, it isn't every day that a man makes a spectacle of you in front of your friends," Patsy told Lydia. "I *was* mad at Pete, and I still am. But what I was going to tell you about was the time I got mad at my father for telling me I was fat. Just like you, I decided to cut my hair off so I could be a whole different person. I wasn't much older than you, and I went into my bedroom, got my scissors, and snipped off every long curl on my head."

"But you change your hair all the time, Patsy." Lydia took the comb and began parting her hair in different places. "I don't see why it's such a big deal. You style it and color it and put in extensions whenever you want. That's what you do whether you're mad at someone or not."

"But you're missing my point, honey. Cutting your pretty hair off isn't going to change anything. All it'll do is give you short hair. It won't fix your brother's diabetes or bring your first daddy home or make your grandma friendlier."

"I never said it would." Lydia's voice rose. "I'm almost in sixth grade, and I want to look older. I want people to stop treating me like a little girl. I'm nearly eleven!"

"Eleven." Patsy shook her head. "I'll tell you what I tell all my clients. You should never make a big change when you're in the middle of a crisis. And you sure shouldn't cut your hair just because you're mad."

"I'm not mad."

"Yes, you are."

"Well, so are you, and look what you did. You got rid of those blonde curls you had at the Fourth of July picnic, and now it's straight and brown. So, cut my hair—" she reached for the scissors—"or I will!"

"Give me those!" Patsy snatched her shears away and crossed her arms. But when she glanced in the mirror, she saw that she and Lydia had the exact same expressions on their faces.

"Everyone keeps telling me that nothing can fix Luke." The girl's eyes welled. "But I just want things to be different, Patsy. Starting with me."

"Real changes start inside a person. You know that, don't you, Lydia?" Patsy asked gently. "God looks at the heart, because that's what matters most to Him. And . . . well, you've helped me see that my heart is hard and cold toward my neighbor. Pete embarrassed me, and I don't know how to forgive him. But I have to change my way of thinking. And you do too. You've got to accept your brother's diabetes. You've got to realize what a good dad Derek is to you and Luke, even though he's not your birth father. You've got to accept Grandma Finley, too. She's trying to help. Everyone is doing their best."

As she spoke, Patsy had begun snipping at Lydia's hair, but it was hard to see through the tears in her own eyes. When Pete Roberts had pushed her into that lawn chair the other day, she had felt so humiliated she wanted to die right then and there. It was as if all the sensitivity and humiliation she had felt during adolescence came rushing back. In those days, her weight had gone up and down as she tried one diet after another. The time her father criticized her, she had retaliated by attacking herself—butchering her hair before she knew anything about style and color. A small voice sometimes still taunted her about it. At the barbecue, everyone had laughed at her, and she sensed that if Luke Finley hadn't collapsed on the beach, her pratfall would still be the talk of Deepwater Cove.

She had blamed Pete, but it was the Lord who had chosen to give Patsy a generous bosom and more than sufficient hips. God made her who she was, body and soul. Was she angry with Him? herself? Or Pete?

"Are you crying?" Lydia's voice was high and hollow. "I didn't mean to upset you, Patsy."

"You didn't, sweetie. You helped me take a look at my own failings, which are many. Refusing to forgive Pete is just one, but I need to deal with it."

Lydia sniffled. "What are you gonna do?"

"I guess I'll have to go next door and talk to him, won't I?" She sighed. "I have to forgive him, even though he makes me madder than a wet hen. And you? How about some wispy bangs, a couple inches off the bottom, and a few layers? You won't look like Tiffany, but why should you? You're Lydia, and I'm proud to know you."

The girl's face brightened, and she nodded. "Okay, bangs and layers. That's a good start, Patsy."

"It sure is."

CHAPTER TEN

Kim slipped into a pair of sandals and grabbed her Bible off the bedside table. If she didn't get the twins out the door in the next five minutes, they were going to be late for church again. It never failed—a last-minute hullabaloo as everyone searched for purses, Bibles, tithe money, matching shoes, jackets, you name it. The fuss often continued all the way to church, but by the time the service was over and the family gathered for lunch, everyone was reasonably cheerful.

After running a brush through her hair, Kim misted it with a little spray, gave one last glance through her jewelry box for her favorite pair of gold earrings, and then gave up. There was no time to keep looking. She must have laid them down somewhere else.

"Luke! Lydia!" she called into the twins' rooms as she hurried down the hall toward the living room. "Are you guys ready to go?"

As she entered the foyer, Kim was surprised to find Derek standing there in a pair of khaki slacks and a polo shirt. The last thing she had seen before heading for the shower was Derek and his mother eating blueberry muffins and drinking coffee out on the deck.

"I didn't know you were going to play golf this morning," she said. Derek rarely went out on the course unless some of the other officers needed a fourth. When he had a rare Sunday off, he usually rested most of the day.

She called down the hall again. "Lydia, Luke, you'd better get out to the car this minute." And then back to her husband. "I hope you won't play more than nine holes, honey. I've got a chicken in the oven, and I was hoping we could have a nice lunch together. I put in onions, potatoes, carrots—everything you like. And your mom promised she'd slide my bread into the oven before we get home. I hope she doesn't forget like last time. Would you please remind her?"

Luke dashed into the foyer, his shirttail hanging out and a dollop of toothpaste on his chin. "I can't find my insulin kit!"

"I've got it in my purse. I told you at breakfast." She huffed out a breath as she wiped her son's chin. "Tuck in your shirt, Luke. You're almost eleven; you should know that by now. Where's your sister?"

"She's scared to come out."

"Scared? Why?"

"She borrowed your favorite earrings without telling you, and she's afraid you'll notice and make her take them off."

"Lydia took my—" Kim shook her head as she pushed her son toward the door. "Oh, for pete's sake, Lydia, come on out. You can wear my earrings today, but in the future please ask before borrowing my things."

At the sight of Derek in his slacks and shirt, Luke let out a grumble of annoyance. "You promised to take me with you the next time you went golfing, Derek," he said. "Mom, I don't want to go to church. I want to go with—"

"We're *all* going to church," Derek announced. "All except Grandma Finley, who's in her bedroom lighting incense to her 'inner deity.'"

Kim realized she was standing there with her mouth open, but she suddenly couldn't move. Had Derek just said he was going to church? With the family?

"Can I wear your blue sweater, Mom? It matches my outfit."

Lydia came down the hall carrying the delicate cashmere cardigan Derek had bought for Kim on their first Christmas. She had admired it in one of the shops in Osage Beach, but it had been way too expensive. Yet there it had lain—wrapped in gold and tied with a red bow—under the tree that perfect, snowy morning.

When Kim didn't respond to her daughter's query, Derek did. "Ask *first*," he said, holding out a hand for the sweater. "You heard your mother."

"But it matches!" Lydia stamped her foot. "You can't tell me what to—"

"Get in the car!" Derek barked. As they left the house, he called back through the door. "We're going to church, Mother. Don't stink up the place too bad." Guiding Kim with a hand on her back, he muttered, "Man, I hate that stuff she burns. Smells like a gas station bathroom."

Kim still hadn't spoken when the car rolled backward out of the drive and started toward the entrance to the Deepwater Cove subdivision. She didn't know what to think, and she certainly couldn't figure out what to say.

Derek was going to church! But why? What had happened? Was God really answering her prayers with a resounding *yes*? Or was this just a whim of Derek's? Or did he have some ulterior purpose?

"You told on me, didn't you?" Lydia accused her brother in the backseat. "I knew you'd tell her I was wearing them. You can't ever keep a secret, you blabbermouth."

"Do you think she's blind?" Luke asked. "First you sneaked off to get your hair cut. Then you went and got Mom's sweater. You think she was gonna look right past her own earrings? You're dumb."

"Don't touch me. Mom, Luke punched me in the shoulder."

"Tattletale," Luke said.

"Luke, don't you dare tell what I said about Tiffany. You promised."

"What, that she's got a boyfriend who's sixteen?"

At that, Kim's brain snapped into gear. She turned around in time to see Lydia haul off and slap her brother across the cheek. Luke snarled and drew back a fist.

Kim caught his arm just in time. "Stop it, both of you!" she cried. "Luke, don't even think about hitting your sister. And, Lydia, you're grounded. Give me those earrings."

"Told you!" Luke taunted his sister.

"You can't ground me any more than you already have," Lydia said. "I'm already up to three weeks, and that's almost the start of school."

Luke chimed in, "Besides, Grandma Finley lets her do anything she wants while you're at work, Mom. Grounding is dumb."

As she put on the gold earrings, Kim glanced at Derek. The small muscle in his jaw flickered as he drove, eyes focused on the road. She swallowed. They could *not* have an argument now—not with Derek on the way to church. This was a miracle, an obvious answer to prayer, and if the twins did anything to jeopardize it . . .

"No more arguing in the car," Kim said, "or you won't get dessert after lunch. I made sugar-free chocolate pie, so that goes for you, too, Luke."

For a few blessed moments, the two hellions in the backseat fell quiet. Kim clutched her purse, trying to think what to say to fill the silence. They were passing the row of shops in Tranquility, and she could see the church steeple in the distance.

How could she make herself sound casual when she was so excited to have Derek joining the family for church? This was no ordinary outing. This was the potential start to a whole new life. If she and Derek were united in their faith, nothing could come between them. They could pray as one, discuss problems in light of God's will, maybe even read the Bible together. They would be like Brenda and Steve or Charlie and Esther. An ideal family.

"So, was I supposed to wear a tie?" Derek asked. "I wasn't sure."

"You look fine."

He smiled. "You're gorgeous. Love those earrings, by the way."

Kim couldn't hide her grin. "I'm so glad you're going with us."

"Thought I'd better see what the fuss was about every Sunday morning. I invited Mom, too, but . . ." He shrugged.

Kim stiffened at the mention of Miranda. "Does she still have an altar in her bedroom? I specifically asked her to put that away. I know it's part of her religion, but I'm not comfortable with it."

"Just ignore my mother," Derek said. "She means well, and is she really hurting anyone with her little statues and incense?"

"All paths lead to God," Lydia intoned from the backseat. "That's what Grandma Finley says. Every religion has some truth in it. And it's smart to know about each of them and use the parts that help you find your inner holiness."

"Whatever," Derek said. "The main thing is that your mother chose Christianity, and until you move out of the house, kids, that's your religion. Then you can choose whatever you want to be. Go burn incense with Grandma Finley if it toots your horn."

Luke laughed. "I'm a Christian, and I'm not changing my mind."

"You don't have any choice except to be a Christian," Lydia said. "We have to do whatever Mom and Derek say, remember?"

"Yeah, so why'd you call Dad the other day, Lydia? You know we're not supposed to talk to him except on his weekends."

"You phoned your father again?" Kim asked, turning to eye her daughter. *Great.* This was just what they needed in the middle of so much friction—Lydia bringing Joe into the mix again.

"I wanted to tell him about Luke being in the hospital. Dad should know. He's our real father."

"I told him," Derek said. "I phoned him that afternoon."

Kim glanced at Derek in time to see his hands tighten on the steering wheel.

"Dad wasn't home when Lydia called anyway," Luke said, his voice low. "She left him a message and he never called back. Both of you told Dad that I was sick, and he didn't come to the hospital."

"He might have," Lydia said. "You were asleep lots of the time. Maybe he came at night after work."

"He doesn't work at night. He goes to bars."

"Stop telling lies about our father," Lydia snapped. "We hardly even know him, because Mom and Derek won't let him near us without a big fuss."

"There are rules, Lydia—and Derek had nothing to do with them. Your father earned his reputation with the court. I've told you the situation in as nice a way as possible, but since you keep bringing it up, I'll give it to you straight. The judge took one look at your father's rap sheet, and the custody hearing went in my favor. I'm not denying him access to you. I'm protecting you from him."

Why had Lydia become so emotional about her father all of a sudden? Kim wondered as the car neared the church building. Her ex-husband made little effort to contact his children, and whenever they returned from one of their rare visits with Joe, they were always upset and off-kilter for days. But suddenly Lydia seemed taken with the man who had fathered her, and she was determined to rub his connection to the twins in Derek's face.

"What makes Derek any better than our real father?" Lydia asked. "And now—because of Derek—we have to live with Grandma Finley, too. Luke and I don't have anyone but each other, Mom, because you're too busy with everyone else. I remember when it was just the three of us, and we were happy."

"Yeah," Luke chimed in. "I like Derek, but he's too strict. He never lets us do anything."

"Derek is sitting right here," Kim said. "If you want to discuss something with him, he can hear you just fine. And for your information, Derek is a wonderful man. He's always fair. If he's strict with you kids, it's for your own good."

"What did we do to deserve Grandma Finley?" Luke asked. "We think she's a witch!"

At this, both twins burst into giggles. Kim found herself searching helplessly for a reason to defend her mother-in-law. Miranda truly had made things difficult in the Finley household. She not only criticized Kim, but she insisted on changing meal plans, moving furniture around, rearranging kitchen cupboards, and worst of all, burning incense before the little statues in her bedroom. Miranda had even told the children she believed paganism was a path to God—and if that didn't put her in the witchy realm, what did?

"Derek, why don't you answer that?" Kim said finally. "Tell the children why you asked Grandma Finley to come to Deepwater Cove."

Derek pulled the car to a stop in one of the parking spaces near the side of Lake Area Ministry Bible Chapel. "My mother is here to help us," he said. "You know that. But all you three do is complain about her. She's done a lot more for us than you realize, and I don't appreciate the griping. Neither does she—and believe me, she knows how you feel about her. As for your *real* father, Luke and Lydia, last week one of the other officers ticketed him for boating while intoxicated in Party Cove. So, if that's the guy you want to admire, fine. Don't expect me to haul either of your little fannies out of jail if you decide to take after him, though, because I'm a man who believes you make your own life. You control your destiny—not your mom or me, and certainly not your dad. I've made my choices, and I'll stand by them. Now, hop out of the car, all of you. I'll be back to pick you up at noon."

Kim froze as she stared at her husband's hardened features. In the backseat, neither twin moved a muscle. Derek rarely expressed negative feelings, but when he did, it had an impact.

For so long Kim and her children had basked in this man's gentle kindness and words of support. How many times a day did Derek tell Kim she was beautiful and whisper that he loved her? How often did he go out of his way to play with the kids, to let them know he was proud of them, to compliment their schoolwork or art projects? Quietly, he had surrounded the family with protection, adoration, and encouragement. And look how they repaid him.

Her eyes filling with tears, Kim reached out to lay a hand on her husband's arm. "I'm so sorry, honey," she said. "Please come to church with us. Please don't let—"

"To tell you the truth," he interrupted, moving his arm away from her touch, "I've decided I like my mother's brand of religion better than yours. If Christianity causes people to act like this, I don't want any part of it. Maybe I'll give ol' Buddha a try."

He reached across her and pushed open the passenger door. Frantic, she brushed at her cheeks, but the tears wouldn't stop. How had things come to this?

"You kids go on inside," Kim ordered, leaning over the seat and brushing them out the door. "Meet us in the parking lot after Bible study time."

"But what about you, Derek?" Luke asked. "I thought you were coming with us."

"Not today," Derek said. As the twins raced for the church, he studied his wife. "I wish you'd go with them, Kim. I need some time to think."

"Derek, we have to talk about this," she told him, shutting the car door. "The kids, your mother, religion. You mentioned wanting a baby, and we need to discuss that. There's the whole issue of Joe and his relationship to the twins. And now we find out that Lydia's best friend is dating a teenager! Please—let's drive over to Bitty's and get some coffee."

"I've had my coffee, and I'm not interested in talking. Everything's abundantly clear to me. I'm sure it is for you, too."

"Maybe our problems are obvious, but we need to figure out how to solve them."

"You know how I solve problems, Kim? I lock them up. That's just the way I handle things."

"Sure, if you're a patrolman dealing with a—" A pounding on the car's window cut off her words. Kim turned to find Luke staring in with a pained expression. She lowered the window. "What is it, Luke? Derek and I are talking."

"My insulin kit. It's in your purse, remember?" His big brown eyes filled suddenly with tears as he glanced at the man in the driver's seat. "I'm sorry, Derek. I didn't mean what I said about you. I hope I grow up to be like you and not my other dad. I don't want to go to jail or become an alcoholic. And I like Grandma Finley. Lydia does too. It's just that we don't think she likes us. She's always reminding us that she's not our grandmother by blood, only by marriage. And when we saw those weird religious things in her bedroom, we started thinking that maybe she was a witch even though we know she's really not. But if she is a witch, it's okay, because we're not scared of her. So please don't divorce us, okay? Lydia feels the same as me; I promise."

Derek blew out a breath and leaned his head on the seat back. "Just go on to church, Luke. It's all right."

"Are you going to divorce us?"

"No, I'm not going to divorce anyone. Get going, now. You'll be late."

Luke gave his mother a final pleading glance; then he slipped his kit into his pocket and ran toward the church. Kim opened her purse and pulled out a tissue. This was a nightmare. For a few precious moments, she had cherished such hope. A fragile hope, but a real one. Now it had vanished like flower petals in a harsh winter wind. And she wasn't even sure why.

Derek put the car into gear and backed out of the lot. Kim blew her nose and tried to blot her cheeks, but the sight of her son's face had just about killed her.

Luke was right in being fearful about the future—look what she had put her children through already. Though they had been young at the time, Kim knew the twins recalled the scenes of drunken rage and cowering fear that had occurred between their parents. When they escaped that life, Kim and the twins had lived in a women's shelter for a time. Things had been so difficult as she struggled to clothe and feed her little ones. Then she had married Derek and forced yet another adjustment on the children. Until now, she had believed their life was finally better. But Derek's angry words had sent a frightening chill clear through to her bones.

She couldn't stop shivering as she dabbed at the tears streaming down her cheeks. Derek had told Luke he wouldn't divorce Kim, but what must he think of her now? He had gone from a peaceful, independent life, in which the only thing he had to think about was maintaining order on the water. Now she had brought all kinds of turmoil and chaos into his life. His words were always kind, but did he really mean them?

"Kim, please stop crying," Derek said evenly. He had driven back to Tranquility and was parking in front of the pumps outside Rods-N-Ends. "We're running a little low on gas. I'm going to fill the tank. Try to cheer up."

Cheer up? Impossible. Nodding mutely, she held a tissue under her nose as Derek got out of the car. Pete Roberts had hired part-time help for Sunday mornings and a couple of evenings a week, but Kim noticed that today Pete was inside the store. To her dismay, he ambled outside as Derek began pumping gas.

"Howdy, Officer," Pete greeted his customer. "Playing golf this morning?"

Kim could hear Derek's deep voice. "Just out for a drive."

"I'll wash the windows for you. Nice day, ain't it? Not too hot. People are heading for the lake like bees to honey. I'm surprised you're not on the water this morning."

"Working the late shift."

"That's when the party gets going." Pete's bearded face and blue eyes appeared in the side window. "Hey there, Kim. How's the kiddos?"

"Fine," she managed. She pulled her appointment book out of her purse and studied it, hoping he wouldn't notice her swollen eyes and damp cheeks.

"I figured you'd be at church by now."

"We dropped off the twins."

"Takin' a break from religion. Sounds good to me. I thought I'd sit by a spell too. Me and Patsy used to see each other at church and go out to lunch afterward, but she won't even look me in the eye since the Fourth of July incident."

Kim frowned. "But that incident turned out fine. Luke is feeling much better now."

"Aw, it's not Luke. Patsy blames me for setting her down in that wobbly lawn chair. I mean . . . well, it *was* kind of funny when she fell through, but Patsy didn't see the humor in it. That one little thing riled her worse than all the chain saws and Weedwhackers I had revved up next door to her salon."

"She'll get over it," Derek spoke up. "Just give her time."

"I hope you're right. I couldn't take another minute of sitting on that hard pew and looking at the back of Patsy's head. You know, if you're going to claim to be holy and righteous and walk around with all that sanctification oozing out, well, it seems to me you ought to be able to forgive a fellow for accidentally dropping you into a loosey-goosey lawn chair."

"I couldn't agree more," Derek said with a dry chuckle as he paid for the gas. He slid back into the driver's seat and looked across at Kim. As he put the car in gear and pulled onto the highway, he spoke gently but firmly. "I'm going to the house. I have some paperwork that I've put off too long. Why don't you drive back to church and pick up the kids? We'll eat lunch, and then I'll go to work."

"But what about Lydia's horrible attitude? . . . And all this tension between us? . . . And your mother?"

As she spoke the final words, a fog lifted momentarily and Kim suddenly saw the crux of their problems. It was Miranda. She had upset the twins. She had destroyed the balance of love and mutual support between Kim and Derek. The longer Miranda had stayed, the worse things got, until now Kim had even begun to wonder if her marriage could survive. Only one solution became clear: Miranda had to go. And Kim had to convince Derek to make that happen.

"Derek, we need to talk about your mother."

"Kim, it's like I told Pete. Let this stuff go. Give it time. It'll pass."

"But it won't. I know we've had a lot of different things come up this summer, but one problem is affecting all of it. Your mother needs to move out of our house. We have to get back to normal, and that means she has to go. I want you to tell her that it's time to leave."

Derek groaned.

"I mean it, Derek. There's no other solution."

"You're looking at this from one angle. Don't overreact. We can handle it."

"Can we? If you really believe that, then we had better start talking. We need to figure out a way to make things better."

"You like to talk. I don't. We're different, okay?"

"No, it's not okay," she said. "We can't be different. Not with this. We have to be united. You want to lock our problems away like prisoners, but what happens when the prisoners get released or break out? And they always do."

"They get out, cause a little trouble, so we round them up and put them back in jail."

She reached for another tissue. "If you won't talk, will you at least listen to me?"

"I heard you already. You and the kids."

"Did you hear me say I want your mother to leave? Did you listen to Luke when he came back for his kit? That's how they *really* feel, honey. They love you. It's not like Lydia said."

"Kim, I'm trained to listen to people. I carry a recorder when I'm on duty so I don't miss a word. It's my job to hear things exactly as spoken."

"But you can't listen just to the words! You have to hear what's beneath them. You have to listen to people's feelings and behaviors and attitudes."

He gave her a long look. "I'm not like you, Kim. I hear what people say, and I take them at their word."

"And then you lock them up behind bars of silence."

The mute hostility continued until they finally arrived back at the house. Miranda was outside in her nightgown and slippers, snipping blooms off the tea roses that Kim had worked so hard and with such patience to grow.

Spotting the car, Miranda lifted a hand and waved. "You both came back!" she said as Derek switched off the engine and opened the door. "How nice! I'm cutting a bouquet for our luncheon table. It's so drab and dreary in the dining room—all those bare windows! I thought we needed a lovely centerpiece to draw everyone's focus and brighten things up. Oh, Derek, will you fetch one of those vases from the garage? Kim has put them up so high I can't reach them."

Feeling as though her last hope had been snipped off like a rose that had just begun to bloom, Kim stepped out of the car. She clutched her Bible and fought tears once again.

"Kim, you'll be happy to hear my news!" Miranda strolled over, a large cluster of red blossoms in her basket—and the rosebush behind her completely bare. "After hearing those awful comments Derek made about my incense, I decided I should make some changes. So I've set up my altar out on the deck. That way I'll have plenty of room to perform my yoga and tai chi movements, I can meditate to the sound of the birds in the trees, and no one will be bothered by the fragrance of my patchouli incense—though I have to say, I like it better than the potpourri you've put in those little baskets around the house. See? Things just have a wonderful way of working out, don't they?"

With that she swung away and hurried over to Kim's patch of newly opened daylilies.

CHAPTER ELEVEN

Patsy was putting the final strokes of topcoat on Ashley Hanes's fingernails when she noticed Cody sweeping up under another stylist's station. The curly-haired young man focused on his work with all the concentration of a brain surgeon. Ever since he had started helping out at Just As I Am, she noted, the salon looked fresh, clean, and tidy.

"I hear Cody's turning out to be quite an artist," Ashley said.

"It sure took me by surprise," Patsy replied. "The first thing I realized was that he had a kind of flair for organizing the styling tools. He wound their cords just so and placed gel, spray, mousse, and shampoo in neat rows."

"Didn't he work on the curtains, too?"

"Yes, Brenda Hansen taught him how to use the washing machine, and the next thing I knew, he had washed every curtain in the salon and then hung them up again. He found a long piece of ribbon, snipped it up, and used it to pull them back."

"I thought he could barely tie his shoes," Ashley said. "And now he's making beautiful bows?"

"Not only that. See those flowers on the checkout desk? I never could get them to look right. But Cody went to work on them, and now they get so many compliments that I bought more flowers for him to put into garlands and posies."

"I didn't know Cody made those! I saw they were for sale, so I bought one and hung it over our bed. Brad hasn't noticed, but I think it looks really pretty." Ashley reflected for a moment. "What got him started on painting the walls?"

"I noticed he was always looking at the hairdo magazines. He told me he would like to paint those pretty ladies, if only he could. So I bought him a watercolor pad, some brushes, and some paper—and lo and behold if Cody didn't knock the socks off everyone with his portraits. So I just decided to give him the whole wall. He works on it every day and night whenever he has a spare moment."

Both women studied the large mural. Then Ashley said, "There's something kind of weird about it. Do you know who those women remind me of?"

"Jennifer Hansen?" Patsy asked.

"Yeah. What's the deal with that? Does Cody have a crush on her or something?"

"Oh, I think he sees her when he's over at the Hansen house working with Brenda on his social skills and his reading."

"I hope he's not getting too attached to Jennifer. I heard she's going to be a missionary."

Patsy nodded. Steve and Brenda's older daughter had returned to Deepwater Cove after a mission trip to Africa. Jennifer had her heart set on living in a jungle somewhere and teaching people about God. She was beautiful, smart as a whip, and sweeter than molasses. But she hadn't even noticed the moon-eyed young man who dawdled nearby every time she came in for a trim. One of these days that girl was going to recognize herself on the wall of Just As I Am, and Patsy feared that her reaction might hurt poor Cody.

"I've made every station span," Cody announced just then, broom in hand as he walked toward Patsy. "I'll mop tonight. Would it be okay if I painted for a while?"

"It's almost time for the TLC meeting," she told him. "Don't you want to join us?"

"No thanks. But thank you anyway."

Patsy smiled. "Ashley, I'm going to go check the appointment book. You keep your nails under the dryer for a few minutes; then you're done."

Cody accompanied her across the room. "You did a great job today, as always, Cody. This place looks so good I hardly recognize it."

"Yes, you do. This is Just As I Am. It's your beauty salon."

"It sure is." She reached out and ruffled his curls. "You might be due for a trim one of these days, sugar pie. We don't want your hair getting all matted up again."

Cody gazed down at the floor for a moment as if searching for words. Then he lifted his head. "I want to tell you something, Patsy Pringle. Here it is. I want to say thank you for shaving off my hair a long time ago when I first came to Deepwater Cove. And thank you for giving me a job. And for paying me real money. And for buying me watercolors and paper. And for letting me paint your walls. And for—"

"Good gravy, that's about enough!" She laughed and gave him a warm hug. "Just seeing your smile is all the thanks I need."

"But here's the last thing I want to say. Even though you never gave me chocolate cake, I think you're a real Christian. My daddy taught me lots of Bible verses, and when I say them in my mind, I think of you because you're like the good people in the Bible. And that tells me you're a Christian."

Patsy swallowed. "Well, that's so nice."

As she had at least a hundred times a day, Patsy gave a guilty glance across the salon at the wall dividing her shop from Pete's Rods-N-Ends. She knew she ought to go over there and make peace with the man. Not only had Lydia Finley challenged her, but every Scripture she read and each whispered word in her heart told her to forgive him.

"Pete says you are an apple." Cody nodded as he spoke. "That's what he told me yesterday. He said you're mad at him, because you fell through the chair and everyone laughed, including me. We were laughing because your bare feet were sticking up in the air. It was very funny. I still laugh about it when I remember how you looked, Patsy. But Pete said you're upset, because you believe people laughed because they think you're fat. But you are *not* fat. You're an apple. That's what. An apple."

Patsy stared at the earnest blue eyes. All she could picture was a big, round, red apple, and if that's what Pete thought of her, well, she ought to just wring his neck. But Cody was standing there looking at her, watching to see what she would do.

She set her hands on her hips. "Did you come over here and talk to me about being a Christian because you know I'm upset with Pete?"

"*Are* you mad at him?"

Was Cody really as innocent as he sounded? Or was this all an elaborate ploy to prod her into doing what she'd been putting off for days?

"I wish you and Pete would be friends again."

"All right then. Enough is enough!" Patsy shook her head. "Are you sure Pete Roberts called me an *apple*?"

"Yes, and of all the fruits, that's my favorite one. Except for oranges. And watermelons. And also peaches."

Sighing, Patsy walked over to the tea area, where the women were already gathering for the meeting. She took down one of the two antique teacup sets that Pete had given her to replace those he'd broken when he first moved in next door. After filling the cup with tea, milk, and sugar, she selected two chocolate-chip cookies and put them on the saucer. Cody had followed her, nearly stepping on her heels the whole way.

Patsy swung around and poked him in the chest with a long, pink, acrylic fingernail. "You stay here." She frowned to emphasize her point. "I will do this myself."

"And it's about time you did."

Rolling her eyes, Patsy carried the teacup across the salon and out the front door. Leave it to Cody to push her into something she didn't want to do. It might be the Christian thing to do, but forgiving a person who had wounded you deeply was just plain hard.

Worse, Pete hadn't asked for forgiveness. That made things doubly difficult. If a person got down on bended knees and apologized and said how wrong he was and how bad he felt, then pardoning him would be a lot easier. But that shaggy ol' bear of a man wasn't the type to say he was sorry. No, he just told Cody and everyone how spiteful Patsy was being toward him, and then he stopped going to church just to rub it in even more. Now he was going around comparing her figure to an apple, of all things.

Well, she was woman enough to handle a man like Pete Roberts. No doubt about that.

Pushing open the door to Rods-N-Ends, Patsy noted that the store was empty. She groaned. If she could have left the teacup and cookies on the counter and made a speedy getaway, that would have been easier. Now she would have no choice but to speak to the man. Especially since he was coming straight toward her.

"Hello, Pete," she said, trying not to sound snippy. "I brought you a peace offering."

He looked her up and down and then grinned sheepishly. "This is the teacup I left for you outside your salon. I guess you read my note."

"As a matter of fact, I did not. I was too upset. But now that I've had time to calm down and consider the situation, I've made up my mind to do what the Bible teaches. I am here to speak plainly about the problem between us and get it over with. Now, as I recall the situation last Fourth of July, I was helping Opal Jones arrange her relish tray when you marched over, grabbed my arm, dragged me across the grass to where the men were grilling pork steaks, and pushed me down into a lawn chair that immediately broke. I was mortified and humiliated and even a little bit hurt, but thank goodness for Derek Finley, who helped me out like a gentleman should. I don't know why you treated me like you did, Pete Roberts, but I have decided to forgive you. So I do. I forgive you. There."

Pete stared at her for a moment. "Is that in the Bible too? The forgiving part?"

"It certainly is. It's all over the place."

"Huh." He scratched his chin for a minute, his fingers disappearing into that awful beard.

Patsy finally figured she'd done her part, and she'd had about enough of his dawdling. "Well, I'm heading back to the salon for the TLC meeting. See you later."

"Hold on, now, woman. I'm from Halfway, Missouri, and I've only got this thing halfway figured out. You need to give a fellow time."

She stood at the counter, tapping her nails on the glass and studying the window display, where Pete had neatly arranged a collection of wading boots, fishing nets, rods, reels, and water skis. He wasn't dumb, so why was this confusing? If he wanted to say something, he should just get to it and let her go to the meeting.

So far, Pete hadn't taken a sip of tea, and the chocolate chips in the cookies were melting from the heated cup. Maybe she would just pick one up and eat it while he continued the second half of his thought process.

As she lifted the cookie, Pete reached for the cup. Their hands brushed for just a second, and Patsy jerked hers away as though she'd been shocked. And in fact, she almost felt she had been. Pete Roberts was ornery, bullheaded, somewhat hard on the eyes, and maybe even a little bit mean. So why did she feel that shiver every time she got near him? The very idea that he affected her in such a way bothered Patsy half to death.

"Good tea," Pete said, setting the cup back in the saucer after taking a sip. "Earl Grey. My favorite, of an afternoon. I prefer Irish break-fast in the morning."

Patsy felt a smile tickle the corners of her lips. "I guess a man can learn some things after all."

"Yep, and here's what I have learned today. First of all, circum-stances are not always what they seem. You see, on the Fourth of July, I was trying to prevent major fireworks between the two Finley women—Kim and Miranda. I figured you, being the prettiest and kindest-hearted of all the ladies in Deepwater Cove, would be the best person to intervene. Seeing as the fuses on those two women are mighty short, I was in a hurry to get you over to where they were facing off with their bowls of dip. So I hightailed it across to where you were arranging Opal's relish dish, fetched you, dragged you back to the grills, where it was high noon between the Finley women, and set you down in the lawn chair I had recently vacated, which had already demonstrated its cracked and frayed webbing beneath my own personal backside. At which time, that chair up and tried to swallow you—an event that took away any need for defusing the conflict between the Finleys."

Blinking in astonishment, Patsy hadn't even managed to take a bite of the cookie as she listened to Pete. "You mean . . . you didn't push me into that chair to poke fun at me?"

"Now why would I do that?"

"Why would you start up a chain saw next to my tearoom?"

"Patsy, I might tease and pester you till kingdom come, but I will never, ever do anything to embarrass you. I would swear on my honor as a gentleman, but I don't think I qualify."

"Well—" she considered for a moment—"that's not what I thought happened."

"So here's another thing I learned today. Christians sure are dif-ferent from what I first believed about them when I moved to town and started going to church."

Feeling about as low as she'd ever been, Patsy put the uneaten cookie back on the saucer. "I don't know what you thought, but now it's my turn to apologize. I'm sorry for the way I've treated you lately, Pete. I shouldn't have quit talking to you, and I wish you would come back to church so we could go out to Aunt Mamie's Good Food for lunch on Sundays."

"Are you sure it's not so you can be a fisher of men and lure me into getting born again?"

"I won't deny that I would be very happy for you to be born again, Pete. But I really have missed talking to you and sitting with you in church. I feel awful that I ruined your good opinion of Christians."

"Well, you did. I used to think Christians were perfect—like you. You always look all gussied up, and you're so nice to everyone, and even when you used to take offense at my chain saws, you were always a lady about it."

"But I'm not perfect. I never was."

"I see that. And now I understand that Christians are just like everyone else."

Patsy started to worry that she might cry. She had marched into Rods-N-Ends as high and mighty as a queen determined to absolve a lowly peasant for his dishonorable deed. As it turned out, she was the one in the wrong, and she felt just awful. Worse than awful.

"Christians are flawed like everyone else," Pete said. "Except for one difference. And here's the third thing I learned today. Christians are different because they try harder than most folks. They read their Bible and go to church and pray and do their dead-level best to be as perfect as God wants them to be. And then when they mess up, they try to make right whatever they did wrong."

"We do try, but we fail a lot. If you want a good example, you'd better look at Jesus and not at Christians. I love Him, but there's a few of us I can barely tolerate."

Pete chuckled. "I reckon you're right on that one."

"In this situation, you behaved better than I did, Pete. You gave me a china cup and saucer."

"And you filled it with tea and brought it over here."

Patsy smiled. "You'd better drink it before it gets cold."

"You gonna sit with me in church next Sunday?"

"Only if you promise to take me to Aunt Mamie's for chicken-fried steak afterward."

"All right. You've got yourself a deal," he said, holding out his hand.

Patsy reached out and gave it a firm shake. But before she could move away, he turned her hand over and kissed it. Beard, mustache, and warm lips brushed against her soft skin. The zing went right up Patsy's arm and shot straight down to the tips of her toes. She gasped as Pete lifted his head and grinned.

"See you later, Patsy Pringle, the sweetest gal in eleventy-seven counties."

Unable to speak a word, Patsy turned and fled straight back to the salon. Barely breathing, she threw open the door, stepped inside, and sank into a chair in the waiting area. This was a very bad situation for a woman who knew her mind and always spoke it. For once in her life, Patsy felt completely bamboozled.

"Did you talk to Pete?" Cody asked. He had a smudge of black paint on his cheek and a brush in his hand as he sat down beside her. "I hope you apologized for getting mad about the chair even though Pete thinks you're as beautiful as an apple."

"I forgave Pete, and he forgave me," she said. "So it's all okay now, Cody."

"That's good. Pete would never do anything to hurt you, because he loves you, Patsy. Everyone loves you. I think you're the best person in the whole world . . . along with Brenda and Steve. And also Esther and Charlie. And Kim and Derek. And maybe some others."

Patsy glanced across to where the young man had been working on the latest version of Jennifer Hansen. "What about that pretty girl you've been painting on the wall?" she asked. "That young lady must be very special to you."

Cody studied his work. "That is a picture, Patsy," he said. "Pictures can't be special. They're made out of paint, and that's all there is to it."

Slightly more relaxed and able to breathe again, Patsy decided it was time to make her way to the TLC meeting. Wanting to make double sure her appointment book was still clear, she stood and crossed to the front desk.

"I realize what's on the wall is only a picture," she told Cody as he shuffled along behind her. "But whose picture did you paint? I think she must be someone awfully important to you, because you've painted her at least four times. In fact, I'm pretty sure I recognize her. That young lady comes in here to get her hair trimmed."

Cody leaned across the desk. "Don't tell," he whispered.

"I won't," Patsy whispered back. "But you're such a good painter that one day someone besides me is going to figure out who it is."

"Okay," Cody said. "That's when I'll tell her that I love her, and I want to get married with her."

Patsy drew closer and whispered in his ear. "She's going to be a missionary in Africa. Even if she likes you a lot, I don't think she'll want to live in Deepwater Cove."

"I don't have to worry about that," Cody said. "God will figure it out."

Patsy sighed as she shut the appointment book. Why couldn't her own faith be as simple as Cody's? Things were always so complicated, and she got herself into such tangles. Look at how much time and energy she had wasted being furious with Pete Roberts. And his opinion of Christianity had suffered as a result.

Disappointed in herself, Patsy tidied the pamphlets she kept by the cash register. All the religious tracts and Christian music and Scriptures painted on the salon's walls didn't amount to a hill of beans if a person was as hard-hearted and unkind as Patsy had been.

As she turned toward the tea area, she spotted the envelope Pete had enclosed with the teacup set he'd given her during their spat. At the time, she'd been too angry to read it. She had tossed the card onto an open shelf under the desk along with some stray curlers and a can of hair spray. But now Patsy knew she had no choice but to find out what Pete had written to her. This would certainly put the icing on the cake of her own humiliation and shame.

Patsy opened the envelope and slid out a greeting card she had seen in a turning wire rack in Pete's store. It was a photograph of a fisherman holding up a bass as long as he was—one of those silly "fixed" pictures made to look real but clearly fake. She opened the card and read the inscription: "Just wishin' we was fishin'! I MISS YOU."

Down at the bottom, Pete had scrawled a message. "Dear Patsy, I'm sorry you think I humiliated you on purpose at the July 4th BBQ. I didn't mean for that chair to break, and I hope you didn't think folks was laughing at you. Surely you know that everyone admires you, including me most of all. In fact, I think you are sweet and kind, and let me just go ahead and say that I very much admire your—"

Here Patsy had to turn the card over to continue reading.

"—ample figure. I looked it up in the dictionary, and *ample* means 'generous, full, and abundant.' To tell you the truth, in every way I think you are ample. Love, Pete Roberts."

Patsy lifted her head and gazed into Cody Goss's blue eyes. "*Ample*," she said.

He nodded. "I told you before. That's what Pete called you."

"You said *apple*."

"Yes, I did. And now I've decided to change my mind about tea. Let's go have some."

Solemnly taking her hand, Cody started across the room. Patsy began to chuckle. When she caught sight of herself in a mirror at a nearby station, she paused a moment, studied her generous bosom, slightly smaller waist, and abundant hips. She decided Pete was exactly right. She was ample. Or apple. Whichever.

By the time she and Cody had filled their teacups, Patsy was giggling as she settled into the empty chair between Kim Finley and her mother-in-law.

"Well, you certainly are in a good mood," Miranda Finley observed. "Maybe it's because you missed Esther's recitation of 'old business,' which included the lawn chair incident at the Fourth of July barbecue."

Kim reached out and laid her hand on Patsy's. "Esther confessed that Charlie had hauled that chair and a couple of others out of their attic. She said those lawn chairs must have been at least twenty years old."

Patsy smiled. "Well, it gave everyone a laugh, and we all need that now and then. Pete and I talked it over. There are no hard feelings between us."

"I doubt that I could ever forgive a man who had made a fool of me," Miranda said. "You were lucky Luke's diabetic crisis came right on the heels of your calamity."

Patsy drew down a breath for fortification. She could see what Kim was up against. A tongue like Miranda's sure could spit barbs. No wonder Pete had felt compelled to come between the two women when he saw a fight about to break out.

"I wouldn't call my son's crisis *lucky*," Kim was saying, her voice stilted. "Luke's condition was very serious. That wasn't *lucky*. I don't see how you can even think such a thing, Miranda."

"Oh, I don't believe in luck," Patsy spoke up, leaning between them to take a sip of tea. "I think the good Lord permits everything that happens to us—and even the bad things can turn out all right in the end if we use them for His glory. Luke made it through his problem, and we all learned a lesson about how to be more watchful. And as for Pete Roberts and me, well, I would call our friendship . . . ample."

●

CHAPTER TWELVE

"Here's the tomato sauce," Luke said, pushing the jar down the counter toward his grandmother. "Mr. Moore grows tarragon in his garden, and he gives us some every summer. We always put extra in our pizza sauce."

"And we don't buy the sauce with tomato chunks." Lydia was unwrapping a package of pepperoni. "I hate tomato chunks."

"We *know*," Luke retorted.

"You won't have to worry about that tonight," Miranda told the twins. "My pizza doesn't have tomato sauce."

Kim turned from the refrigerator in surprise. She had been searching for the mozzarella cheese, but now she saw that Miranda had produced a shopping bag and was setting out ingredients she must have purchased earlier in the day.

Every Friday night, Kim and the twins baked homemade pizza. Since she'd been staying with them, Miranda had participated in the process of building the pizzas, and then she ate with the family. But this evening, Grandma Finley had asked to treat Kim and the twins to something special. She was going to teach them how to make Derek's favorite meal—her unique *gourmet* pizza.

Miranda had spent most of the afternoon outside on the deck, meditating near the collection of items that she believed fostered spiritual enrichment—crystals, a small brass Buddha, a length of sandalwood beads, and a Native American dream catcher. When her stick of incense had burned down to ash, she came inside. Still smelling vaguely of patchouli, she wore an ankle-length turquoise cotton tunic and several silver bangles, which clanged as she began measuring ingredients into a saucepan on the stove.

"To make a good white sauce," she was telling the twins, "you must have whole milk. And here we have cornstarch, salt, pepper, three cloves of garlic—"

"Wait a second," Lydia cut in. "Did you say *white* sauce? Where do you put that?"

"Right onto the pizza crust." Miranda waved her hand over the other ingredients, as if flourishing a magic wand. "Garlic salt, onion powder, oregano, and basil."

"Where's the tarragon?" Luke asked. Staring at the collection of containers on the counter, he was frowning. "I don't get it. How can you have pizza without tomato sauce and tarragon?"

"This is not just any old pizza. This is my specialty—spinach-Parmesan pizza."

"Spinach!" Lydia cried. "Huh-uh. No way. I'm not eating pizza with spinach. I hate that stuff."

"I don't like it either," Luke said, looking at his mother with imploring eyes. "Can't we have regular pizza, Mom? Grandma Finley can make her kind, but I want our usual."

"You won't even recognize the spinach," Miranda informed him before Kim could answer. "It melds right in with the cheese." She paused in stirring her sauce to unwrap a chunk of white cheese and hold it out before the twins. "Now take a whiff of this, kids. This is heaven itself."

Luke sniffed, made a gagging noise, and grabbed his nose.

Lydia took three steps backward, then began flapping her hands in distress. "It smells like vomit!" she wailed. "I'm gonna puke! What is it?"

"This is true Parmesan cheese." Miranda glared at the twins, who were now entertaining each other by pretending to throw up. Turning her focus on Kim, she stared in silence a moment before speaking. "Do your children always have to be so histrionic?"

"Well, they—"

"The production of real Parmesan cheese comes from a restricted area in Italy," Miranda said loudly enough to cover the twins' theatrics. "It's really quite distinctive. The structure of the cheese is remarkable too. See? A true Parmesan will break into slivers. And I happen to love its delicate and fragrant aroma."

"Fragrant aroma?" Lydia was holding her nose and fanning her face. "Puke-o-roma is what you mean!"

"Puke aroma!" Luke said, doubling over in laughter. "Get it, Lyd? Puke aroma!"

Kim stood by helplessly as Lydia joined in her brother's amusement. The cheese really did smell awful, and she could hardly blame the kids for their dramatics. In fact, she was thinking of opening a window to let in some fresh air.

Clearly having decided to ignore the twins, Miranda had resumed her preparations. Between stirring the sauce, she began to coat the three circles of pizza dough with olive oil.

"Wait," Luke said suddenly. "Grandma, you're not making *all three* pizzas with that white sauce, are you?"

"I most certainly am. And if you'd like, you may begin grating this mozzarella cheese. Here's the grater. I'll need six cups. Lydia, take this knife and cut that tomato into paper-thin slices. Kim, if you would wash the spinach—"

"Mom!" Luke cried, brandishing the grater. "Not all three! We want pizza the way we have it every Friday night."

"Luke, you agreed to this," Kim reminded him. "We're going to give Grandma Finley's pizza a try."

"I don't want it! It stinks, Mom. I don't want spinach pizza that smells like vomit!"

"Luke, please."

Kim headed toward her son, but Lydia stepped between them. "Leave him alone, Mom. Lukey doesn't want to eat it. What if it makes him sick? What if his blood sugar goofs up?"

"Lydia, you know that's not going to happen."

"It might! We've never had white sauce before. It could kill him!"

"Ricotta!" Miranda sang out. "If anyone's listening to Grandma Finley, I'm ready for the ricotta."

Kim turned to find that the woman had already ladled thick, cheesy sauce onto all three pizzas. "Miranda, could you hold off for a moment? Spinach really isn't a favorite with the twins, and—"

"I'm not eating that junk!" Luke shouted. "I won't eat it, and my glucose won't be right, and I'll get sick."

"Mom, do something!" Lydia's eyes filled with tears. "Grandma Finley, stop putting on cottage cheese! We hate cottage cheese."

"This is *ricotta*, for your information. Wait until you see how the spinach and basil will blend into the white sauce. In fact, with the mozzarella and ricotta, you won't even notice them."

"But they're green!" Luke hollered. "The only green we have on pizza is tarragon. Mom, make her stop. She's ruining our supper."

"What can Lukey eat tonight, Mom?" Lydia demanded to know, tears streaming. She stamped her foot. "He has to eat the right food, or he'll get sick!"

Kim reached for her daughter. "Now, Lydia—"

"No, Mom! You have to help Luke. He's your son. You can't let Grandma Finley do this!" Sobbing, she shook her head at her mother and then turned and ran from the kitchen. "I hate you! I hate everything!"

"*Now* look what happened!" Luke snarled. "Grandma Finley, don't you even care about Lydia?"

Miranda set her hand on her hip. "I'll have you know I am famous for this pizza. It's delicious. It's made of the finest ingredients. And if you and your sister would stop carrying on like a pair of maniacs, you would find out how good something new can be."

"I don't want something new! I want our same old pizza with tomato sauce and tarragon! I want everything to be normal!" With that, Luke hurled the cheese grater across the room. It slammed into a cabinet and fell to the floor, aluminum clattering on tile.

"Luke!" Kim cried as her son stormed out of the kitchen. "Luke, come back here this instant!"

"Hopeless," Miranda announced as she began washing the spinach. "Your ineffectiveness as a mother astonishes me, Kim. Those two are completely out of control."

Her temper flaring, Kim pointed a finger at her mother-in-law. "*You* are the problem here, not me. You could see right away that the Parmesan cheese was going to be an issue, but you just kept on grating. No matter what anyone says, you insist on having your way."

"We had an agreement, Kim. If you give in to children, you lose all control." She lifted her chin as she stared at her daughter-in-law. "Do you have any idea how easily a child can slip out of your hands? Do you know what it means to lose parental authority? Of course not. You've never had any power over those two. A good mother watches her young the way a hawk guards her nest. She never lets up for a moment. One wrong move and they're out of her control forever."

"For heaven's sake, Miranda, we're talking about pizza here. It's not as though my entire influence over the children rides on this one issue. I'm a good mother, and I happen to believe that it's okay to bend a little. Do you have to make all three pizzas your way? Can't you give the twins one or two crusts for themselves?"

"Give an inch, and you lose them." Miranda swung around and began to put spinach and cheese on the pizzas. "Believe me, Kim, without proper parental direction and control, a child can go off in the wrong direction. Maybe it's pizza today, but you never know what tomorrow will bring."

Kim threw up her hands in disbelief. "Oh, this is ridiculous." She didn't know whether to start making fresh pizzas or go comfort her children. Deciding a decent supper would soothe the twins, she elected to let them console each other for now. "I'm going to make more dough," she told Miranda, "so if you'll please move your Parmesan, I'd appreciate it."

In silence, the women moved around the kitchen. As Kim began spreading tomato sauce on her newly made crusts, Miranda slid her pizzas into the oven one by one, then brushed by without a word on her way out of the kitchen.

Kim pressed the fan button on the oven hood. Maybe she could diffuse some of the Parmesan aroma and at the same time drown out the memory of her mother-in-law's insidious voice. As Kim worked, she gazed through the kitchen window at the lake. Gleaming gold and indigo, the water was as motionless as a sheet of glass. But when a fish leaped nearby, she instantly envisioned the magnificent and satisfying splash that would echo across Deepwater Cove if someone just happened to toss Miranda off the deck.

Shaking her head at the thought, Kim knew it wasn't funny. Still, imagining the expression on Miranda's face gave her such satisfaction that she was still savoring it when she took Miranda's pizzas out of the oven and put her own in to bake.

❖

When Charlie Moore pulled his golf cart to a stop in the Finley driveway that Friday evening, Derek was chopping weeds along his ditch. Though Derek liked his retired neighbor well enough, he had no desire to make small talk.

All day he had been out on the water patrolling Party Cove and cruising the hundreds of inlets that rimmed Lake of the Ozarks. That didn't take into account the several hours spent talking to investigators about the drowning of the as-yet-unclaimed and unnamed female. Her fingerprints hadn't turned up any clues, nor had her dental information. Detectives were now discussing the possibility of hiring a forensic artist to create a facial reconstruction of the woman in order to help identify her. Derek found it hard to believe that there were no records of a missing person who fit the victim's description. He had been working with other law enforcement agencies from the start, but they had made little progress.

As if all that weren't exhausting and frustrating enough, Derek had come home that afternoon to the bleak battleground of yet another family feud—a quarrel over pizza that had left Lydia in tears, Luke furious, Kim in steely silence, and his mother out on the deck lighting incense. The combatants had told him four versions of the same event, none of which registered in his tired brain, and that's when he'd decided it might be a good time to attack the weeds in the yard.

"Things are looking mighty fine around the Finley place," Charlie drawled. He patted his dog's head as he spoke. The two went everywhere together. "Glad we had that rain the other day. Greened up all the yards."

"Brought in a little cool weather, too. I sure didn't mind that." Derek studied the cutting end of his Weedwhacker. "Well, I guess this job's done for now. I'll need more line before next time."

"Isn't that the way things are? It's always something. The trimmer runs out of line. The lawn mower needs oil. The golf cart's battery up and dies. The gutters get clogged with leaves. Spiders start to take over the eaves. A man's work is never done."

Derek nodded. "Yep, and I'd better head back inside to check my honey-do list. It's a mile long."

"How about taking a spin with Boofer and me first, Officer Finley? Couple of things I'd like to talk over. Would you mind?"

Yes, he would, Derek thought. Listening to Charlie Moore—who had all the time in the world to do whatever he wanted and then drone on and on about it—was not Derek's idea of fun. And no matter what Charlie wanted to discuss, Derek knew he wouldn't be interested. The Moores were good people—helpful, kind, and considerate. But they put their noses in other folks' business way too often for Derek's comfort, and he wanted no part of that.

"I'll need to step inside and let Kim know," he told Charlie, "and I have a feeling she's got my evening pretty well planned out."

"Aw, we won't take long. Just a turn or two around the neighborhood. Kim won't even know you're gone."

Derek frowned. He wasn't going to get out of this. He could already see Charlie edging his dog onto the floor, dusting off the seat, and moving his flashlight to a compartment in the back. Well, maybe a trip in the golf cart would be better than heading back into the war zone his house had become.

"Settle yourself right there," Charlie said as Derek stepped into the cart. "I'll tell you what—there's nothing like a quiet ride around the lake of an evening. Boofer would tell you the same thing; wouldn't you, boy? This dog and I take a sunset ride nearly every day. It's gotten to be kind of habitual, if you know what I mean. A mail carrier establishes a routine, and it becomes a way of life. Not even retirement can put an end to that."

Derek leaned back as the cart began its excruciatingly slow journey along the narrow road that served the Deepwater Cove neighborhood. After a day in his Donzi—chasing reckless boaters and zipping from one mile marker to the next—the ride felt interminable. But Charlie wasn't in the mood to push the cart for more speed, so Derek did his best to force his muscles to relax.

"Moon's already up," Charlie intoned, pointing at the silver wedge that hung over the lake. "No sir, you just can't beat a sunset on the water. Nothing prettier, to my way of thinking. Wouldn't you agree?"

"Yep," Derek said, stifling a groan. Depending on his shift, he watched the sun settle over the lake nearly every day. Long ago the array of pink, gold, and blue had ceased to fascinate him. Late afternoon to early evening was the time that parties could turn ugly.

"The Hansen house sure looks nice," Charlie commented as the golf cart cruised by. "That Brenda sure has a way with decorations. She put on the best Independence Day display of anyone in the neighborhood. Flags, bunting, wreaths made out of shiny stars. I never saw the like. Esther pointed out that Brenda had even planted her flower beds in shades of red, white, and blue. Sure enough, she was right. Esther usually is, of course."

He elbowed his companion, who mustered a chuckle. "Sounds like a woman," Derek said. "Kim sure knows her own mind."

"Your mother does too. That must be interesting—living with two women. How're you holding up?"

This time Derek couldn't suppress his sigh. "Things are a little tense, to tell you the truth. But we're managing."

"Miranda takes good care of the twins. I see the three of them down by the lake swimming or loaded into her car heading to town. Miranda tells me they go to the library or the outlet mall, and she enjoys stopping by Bitty's place at lunchtime for some of those California-style wraps. I guess the twins have a fondness for the fajitas, but Miranda prefers the vegetarian ones, since she's watching her weight."

This was all news to Derek, and he found himself warming to the idea that his mother had embraced her new role so well. If "Grandma Finley" was doing a good job with the kids, why did she and Kim have so many problems? Both women were well liked, friendly, kind, and generous. Why couldn't they figure out how to get along?

"Those exercises she does on the deck have sure stirred up talk in the neighborhood," Charlie told Derek. "Esther thinks Miranda is doing stretching drills to get out the kinks. But Kim tells me she's performing some sort of Oriental ritual."

"I don't pay much attention," Derek said. "My mother was always a free thinker, willing to try just about anything. That goes back to her youth—the way she was brought up. Her parents were liberal-minded too. Not much concerned about rules. They never understood why I went into law enforcement."

"Beatniks, huh?" Charlie said. "Miranda's a little younger than Esther and I. She must have fallen under that sixties influence—hippies, war protests, flower children. I was a mail carrier with a young family at the time, so I missed out on all that. Not to say I regret it, of course."

He was silent a moment as the cart rounded the western end of the subdivision and started back the other way. When he spoke again, it was with a tone of amusement. "I guess that would explain the incense."

"Is it bothering people?" Derek asked.

"It's no trouble. Folks were just wondering. It's not every day you see a lovely woman swaying around, listening to flute music, and burning incense. Or maybe it's the fact that most days Miranda exercises in her bathing suit."

"Her bathing suit?"

"Well, she starts out in a robe." Charlie glanced over at Derek and winked. "Mighty attractive lady, in my opinion. But some of the widows were getting a little nervous about the whole thing, especially after Lydia told Esther that her grandmother worships idols."

"Idols?" This time Derek sat bolt upright. "My mother does not worship idols."

"No need to worry. Esther has calmed the widows down, and now that you and I have cleared the air, well, it's not going to be anything to sweat about." Charlie steered the golf cart past an oncoming truck. "The real problem may be just around the bend here. I thought I ought to mention it to you—seeing how you're an officer of the law and you might know about such situations. Of course, it doesn't pertain to water, but all the same . . ."

Derek was still picturing his mother worshipping idols in a bathing suit when Charlie braked the cart a short distance from the smallest house in Deepwater Cove. Next door to a home that was up for sale, it sat at the far end of the cove, some distance from the docks, the commons, and most of the activity. It had probably been constructed as a fisherman's retreat before the area was platted and built into a nice neighborhood. The covered deck was no longer quite level, and the shutters needed paint.

"This house belongs to Brad and Ashley Hanes." Charlie spoke in a low voice through the side of his mouth, as if confiding a deep, dark secret. "I know for a fact that they haven't been paying their subdivision dues. And I hear they're behind on their loan payments. That's their business, of course. But what has come to be of some concern is the activity going on over there to the side of the house."

In the fading light, Derek could barely make out what appeared to be a poured foundation and a couple of framed walls. "Are they building something?" he asked.

"Young Brad works construction, you know," Charlie said. "He told some folks that he's putting up a garage for his new truck. The vehicle isn't here right now. You know, Brad spends his evenings over at that watering hole, Larry's Lake Lounge, waiting for Ashley to get home from her job at the country club. But again, that's their business. Trouble is, Ashley told Esther that they're building this addition to hold a nursery for the baby. She's not expecting yet, but she sure is hoping. That part is a secret, of course. Nobody knows but Esther."

Derek nodded. If the Hanes kids wanted to start a family, what did he care? For that matter, what was Charlie all fired up about?

"You'll notice they don't have a building permit posted anywhere on the premises," the older man continued in hushed tones. "Nobody wants to rain on their parade, but you can't add or tear down anything in Deepwater Cove without a permit. It's in the bylaws."

"Well, you're chairman of the neighborhood bylaws committee, Charlie. You'd better tell Brad before he gets too far along with the garage or baby nursery—or whatever it's supposed to be."

"Problem is, we don't know if we can really enforce our bylaws. They don't carry much weight with the county, and no one knows what the rules are way out here. Do you have any idea?"

"There are zoning laws; I'm sure of that."

"But do they apply this far out of the Camdenton city limits?"

Vaguely irritated, Derek raked a hand back through his hair. "The Water Patrol enforces state statutes, Charlie. We don't have authority where municipal or county laws are concerned. But I'm sure if anyone can find out the rules for construction in Deepwater Cove, it's you. You've got the time and the know-how."

The golf cart moved forward again. "I was hoping you'd have the answer for us. But Esther kept telling me that your jurisdiction was the lake and you might not know. A man ought to listen to his wife."

They rode along in silence with Derek slapping at the occasional mosquito. Listening to his wife was apparently his biggest failing, he thought irritably. When he got home, he would have to explain to Kim where he'd been, and she was upset already. Though he had been trying harder to communicate with her about his work and the other issues she had spelled out, he found it difficult. Derek wasn't used to talking about anything beyond whatever was happening at the time. If he was ticketing someone for a violation, he explained lake laws. If he was meeting with the Major Case Squad, he discussed homicides. If he was eating dinner, he complimented the meal. What was so wrong with that?

"Speaking of the lake," said Charlie, who didn't seem to have any problem talking about anything at any time, "Esther came up with the craziest notion this morning. Not too long after breakfast, I was trying to tell her what I was planning to do about servicing the golf cart, and all the while she was putting together one of those Jell-O salads with the marshmallows and fruit. You know the kind I mean?"

Derek nodded. He'd eaten Esther's gelled salad more times than he could count.

"Well, she wasn't paying a bit of attention to me. When I grumbled about it, she turned around and said, 'Charlie, a woman is like a fish. If you want to capture her, you've got to find the right bait, dangle it in front of her, and then reel in nice and slow.' Can you believe that? Esther—talking about fishing! The woman hasn't tossed out a line in twenty years. But this afternoon while I was working on the golf cart, I thought about it, and sure enough, Esther was right."

"You say that a lot," Derek commented.

"Because she usually is." Charlie chuckled. "I've lived nearly a lifetime with the woman, and she rarely lets me win an argument. So I've learned to pay attention when she tells me something. That fishing idea of hers, for example. Not too long after she told me about it, I had a hankering to go to Aunt Mamie's Good Food for supper. On Friday nights, Mamie's features an all-you-care-to-eat shrimp special. Sautéed, breaded, peel-and-eat—you name it. But when I suggested eating out, Esther got all upset with me—fuss, fuss, fuss. So that's when I decided to go fishing . . . for my wife."

"For Esther?"

"That's right. I wanted to catch her and get what I wanted from her—a trip to Mamie's for the shrimp special. So I sat down on the chair right across from Esther, and I looked her right in the eye—just the way you study a fishing hole before you cast your line. Then I threw out the bait. 'What's wrong, Esther, honey?' I asked, sweet as you please. Right away, she bit. She started telling me everything that was bothering her, and I shut my mouth tight. You can't talk if you want to catch a fish, you know."

Derek did know. He also knew that when Kim started talking about everything that was bothering her, the last thing he wanted to do was sit there gazing at her. He wanted to bolt in the opposite direction—as fast as he could. But Charlie was continuing his tale as he drove the golf cart along the moonlit road.

"The whole time Esther talked," he told Derek, "I kept on looking at her, studying her, not saying a word, just nodding my head. I was itching to pick up the remote and see if the ball game was on TV, but I wanted to eat at Mamie's even more. So I kept my hands still, just the way you do when you're reeling in a big ol' bass. And Esther kept talking. She said she had made that salad, and her feelings were hurt that I would prefer to eat out. She confessed that she had always been insecure about her cooking. She told me she thought Mamie's could fix shrimp better than she could, and she figured that was why I wanted to eat there."

Derek was trying to listen, but he was getting kind of drowsy. All this talk of Jell-O salad and shrimp had made him hungry, and the slow pace of the golf cart was about to put him into a trance. The more Charlie talked, the more Derek envisioned Esther Moore as a largemouth bass. He could almost see her swimming closer and closer to Charlie's goal of eating out at Mamie's as she talked and he reeled her in.

"I didn't move a muscle," Charlie went on. "I just leaned forward and listened. She was talking about her salad, but when she pulled a tissue out of her pocket and went to dabbing her eyes, I started to realize what she was really feeling. Her fussing at me didn't have a thing to do with Mamie's. It was all about the fact that Esther's mother had never taught her how to cook, and that made her insecure about her culinary skills all her life. So you know what I said? I said, 'Esther, you are the finest woman the good Lord ever made. You learned how to be a better cook than your mother ever was—and you taught yourself. Furthermore, I prefer your Jell-O salad to all the salads in the entire universe. And I feel exactly the same about your shrimp.' You know what Esther said to that? She said, 'I love you, Charlie. Put on your shoes, and let's go eat supper at Mamie's.' And that's exactly what we did."

Derek felt as though he had just been handed that largemouth bass in a frying pan with a pat of butter and a sliced-up lemon. Charlie hadn't reeled in a trip to Mamie's. He had landed his wife's heart—hook, line, and sinker.

❋

When Kim heard Derek's footsteps on the porch, she decided to try to intercept him before his mother did. Somehow, Kim *had* to convince Derek to send Miranda back to St. Louis if they wanted any hope of peace in their family. Tensions were strained to the bursting point, yet the man at the center of the hurricane seemed blissfully unaware. And that infuriated Kim.

She was almost at the front door when she heard Derek's voice on the porch. Through the screened window, she could see his silhouette. He had hunkered down and was talking to Lydia, who had stretched out on the swing, one arm thrown dramatically over her eyes. Kim reached for the doorknob, but she paused as she heard Derek speaking.

"What's wrong, Lydia, honey?" he asked, laying a hand on the arm of the swing.

It had been so long since Kim had heard a gentle tone in her husband's voice that she stood unable to move in the darkened foyer. For a moment, no one spoke.

Then Lydia sniffled. "I hate this family," she said.

Derek moved over and sat down on the wicker rocking chair near the swing. "You hate this family?" he repeated. "You mean me, Luke, your mom, and Grandma Finley? Or do you still like some of us?"

"I like Luke," Lydia said. "I like Mom, too, but it makes me sick the way she's been acting. She's such a grouch."

"Hmm." The chair squeaked a little as Derek began to rock back and forth.

Kim eased down onto a chair near the door. She watched the silhouetted shapes and listened through the open window as her husband and daughter talked. For some reason, it felt almost magical to hear their voices. His was deep and manly; hers was small and almost timid. Though Lydia spoke with belligerence, she often sounded fragile and even afraid. Kim wondered if Derek had any idea how delicate the girl was, hovering on the brink of her teens, wondering who she was, unsure of her future. She remembered feeling so much like Lydia, and yet Kim knew Derek must have no idea what to make of such a tightly wound ball of confusion, fear, and hope.

"Grandma Finley is okay," Lydia told him. "She's just weird. You know what I mean? She's got that altar on the deck. People can smell the incense—and she wears her bathing suit to do her tai chi."

"I thought she wore a robe too."

"She takes it off!" Lydia groaned. "It's so embarrassing. I could die. If Mom ever did anything like that, I would just kill her."

"*Die. Kill.* Strong words. You thinking a lot about death, kiddo?"

"Well, wouldn't you? I mean, she's your mother, Derek. Aren't you creeped out by her? You should have seen the pizza she tried to make tonight. It was all Parmesan and spinach and weird herbs. She's just strange. I don't know how you even turned out normal." Lydia fell silent for a moment. "But I don't want her to leave us. I mean, like, I wouldn't want her to really *die*. Or you either. Or Luke."

"Oh yeah. Sure, I know." Derek rocked some more.

"That's how it feels around here. Like everything's breaking apart and about to die. We already went through that, Luke and me, when Mom and Dad got divorced. It's not that I mind having you for a stepdad. But I hated it when they broke up. Even though he wasn't the best father, he was all we had. And then we had to live in that stupid shelter. And then that crummy little house with the leaky roof. Then we got you."

"Yeah, that was next."

Kim realized Derek was saying almost nothing, yet for some reason Lydia had decided to talk to him. Calmly. She was sitting up now, her feet curled under her and her arms wrapped around the chain that held up the swing. In the rocking chair, Derek had leaned forward, elbows on his knees. He was looking at Lydia, nodding as she spoke. The intensity of his concentration almost frightened Kim. She had never seen her husband so purposefully focused.

"You're all right for a stepdad," Lydia admitted. "But why did you have to go and invite Grandma Finley here? We were doing okay without her. Every time I look at her, I remember that she's staying with us to make sure Luke doesn't die. And that just bugs me. Luke can take care of himself, and if he messes up, then I'm there to watch out for him. I mean, I do remember what happened on the Fourth of July, and I'm glad Grandma Finley was able to find Luke's insulin kit so fast. But it's always confusing around here. Who's in charge? I mean, is Grandma Finley living with us forever, or is she going back to St. Louis? It's like things never feel normal. First we lost Dad, then we got you, and now we have Grandma Finley—but we might lose Luke, or Grandma Finley might leave. Or stay. And I've heard you and Mom fighting. You guys might get divorced like she did with Dad, and then you would leave. You can't trust anyone in this family. I just hate it."

"Wow." Derek had stopped rocking. "You really do hate this family."

"No, I don't *hate* it. You're so dumb, Derek. I love this family, but how can you love something that you can't count on? It could all just shrivel up and die and blow away. It's awful. I can't stand it."

At this, Lydia began crying softly, and Kim could hardly bear to watch her daughter struggling. But as she rose to step out onto the porch, she saw Derek stretch his hands toward Lydia.

"Come here, kiddo," he beckoned. "Come sit with me a minute."

Even as he spoke, Lydia was already leaving the swing and curling into his lap as she had when she was younger.

Derek wrapped his arms around her and began rocking. "Listen up, tater tot," he said in a quiet voice. "I am not leaving this family. Not divorcing your mother. Not running out on you and Luke. No way. No how. You got that?"

"Uh-huh," Lydia sobbed, suddenly a baby again. "But what if Mom divorces you?"

"She won't. I'm not going to let her. So that's all there is to it. As for Grandma Finley . . . well, now that you mention it, she is pretty weird. But I'm used to her, because that's how she's always been. You'll get used to her too. Your grandma and your mother are going to have to figure out how to get along, because neither one of them is going away. I haven't gotten around to telling your mom that, so don't spill the beans."

What? Kim couldn't believe what she'd just heard. Hadn't they discussed it? Hadn't she made herself perfectly clear? Miranda had to leave! Now Derek was saying she was going to stay. Not only that, but he was asking Lydia to keep a secret from her mother.

Even as her anger mounted, she saw Lydia snuggle closer to Derek. "I won't tell anyone," Lydia said.

"As for Luke, you're right," Derek told her. "He's smart, and he's getting this diabetes thing figured out. Plus, he's got you to keep an eye on him. So there you go. One family—kind of stressed out, a little bit weird, sometimes sick or angry, but together. That's us."

Lydia sniffled. Kim could see her skinny arms snake around Derek's neck as her dark head nestled against his shoulder.

"You promise?" Lydia asked.

"Cross my heart."

"Hope to—" She caught her breath.

"No, I don't hope to die. I intend to live a long life, watch you and Luke grow up, be a good husband to your mother, and rock your babies just the way I'm rocking you. How's that?"

"Good," Lydia said.

Inside the foyer, Kim leaned her head against the wall and nodded. Not perfect. Not even truly acceptable. Yet in this moment, it was good enough.

CHAPTER THIRTEEN

August came in hot, just as it always did in mid-Missouri. Patsy stayed busy cutting hair short against the heat and humidity. Clients entered the salon wearing shorts and tank tops. Everyone wanted pedicures, because you couldn't go outside in anything but sandals or flip-flops. People smelled like suntan lotion or baby oil. Some of the drop-in customers were sweaty and damp, but by the time they walked out, Patsy had their hair soft, clean, and bouncy. She added three flavors of iced tea to the menu in the tea area, and they were a hit. She could hardly keep up with the demand.

In fact, things seemed pretty good all over. Next door, Bitty Sondheim's Pop-In was hopping with vacationers buying her California-style omelets and wraps to take out on the lake. Now that Pete and Patsy had patched things up, Patsy again frequented Rods-N-Ends for root beer floats and the occasional rotisserie hot dog, which she enjoyed while chatting with Pete over the counter.

His business was booming as people bought gas for their cars, RVs, boats, and Jet Skis. He kept tackle moving in and out of the shop too. His worms and minnows were said to be the healthiest and fattest around, and of course, Pete was generous in counting them out. If you asked for a dozen, you were more likely to get fifteen or twenty.

The chiropractor and tattoo places down the street both saw an upswing in their trade. People were forever flipping or flopping the wrong way in the water, and they'd come to the chiropractor for an adjustment. And the young crowd had a carefree and often reckless attitude that took them to the tattoo parlor in groups of three and four. Patsy knew they would select words or pictures they'd later regret and have them tattooed in places that would one day sag something awful. But she understood. On a dare from a group of her girlfriends, she'd had a small ladybug put on the back of her shoulder one afternoon when she was sixteen. Nowadays, she would sometimes wear a skinny-strapped top to show it off if the mood hit her.

As members of the Tea Lovers' Club began slipping into the salon one Wednesday afternoon, Patsy realized she couldn't think of a single thing for Esther Moore to put on the agenda. Maybe for once the group would be allowed to chat in peace. Not only that, but Patsy had ushered her last customer away in plenty of time to join the TLC at the start of the gathering.

"I think we should fix some hot water," Cody suggested. He was already filling the stainless steel urn as Patsy checked on the dessert supply. "Maybe someone would want real tea," he explained. "With milk and sugar. And maybe that someone would be me."

"You don't like iced tea, Cody?" Patsy asked.

"My daddy never had a refrigerator or a cooler or anything like that. So I prefer my . . . my *beverages* . . . warm. Did I get that right?"

"Sure did. *Beverages.* That's a big word."

"I am increasing my vocabulary. Brenda thought it was a good idea, and so did I. Just so you know, I'm already up to fifth grade reading skills. Phonics and comprehension—both."

Patsy gave him a big hug. "I'm so proud of you, Cody."

It hadn't been so long ago that Cody couldn't read at all. Brenda

Hansen had told Patsy she was terribly frustrated with trying to teach him and had been about to give up. But suddenly everything clicked, and Cody began to understand letters and how they formed words. Recently Patsy had noticed him studying the magazines in the waiting area. Before, he had been looking at the pictures in order to get ideas for his wall mural. Now she realized he was probably reading the text as well.

"Fifth grade?" she said. "No joke?"

"Why would I make a joke about my reading level?" Cody asked her. "Reading skills are not funny. I'm working really hard on them, and right now, I'm reading *My Side of the Mountain*, which is a book written by Jean Craighead George. And do you know what? The boy in that book is sort of like me. He lives in the forest, and so did I. And that's why reading is good. It makes you think about yourself and figure things out. I never had a falcon named Frightful. That part is different. Also, I got beat up by some men who didn't like me. That hasn't happened to Sam. He likes living by himself in the woods, but I'm glad I live in Deepwater Cove with people around."

"We're glad you live here too." Patsy studied Cody's plugged-in water urn. "And as a matter of fact, I believe I'll have a cup of hot tea myself."

"Earl Grey or Darjeeling?" he asked.

"The latter."

Cody stared at her. "There's no ladder in here, Patsy. I'm tall enough to paint near the top of the wall without one."

She opened her mouth to explain, then decided to leave that job to Brenda. "Darjeeling, please, Cody. And I believe I'll have a lemon bar with that. It's a little more sugar than I ought to eat, but you know Pete likes me looking ample."

"I know," Cody said. "You and Pete are friends." He leaned over. "I think Jennifer Hansen is beautiful. Brenda told me she's coming to the TLC today. Do I look handsome as all get-out?"

Patsy smiled. "You sure do, honey. Ever since we cleaned you up, you get handsomer by the day. But Brenda said Jennifer is already starting her missionary studies over at Hidden Tribes Learning Center near Camdenton. I hope you're not still counting on marrying her."

"Yes, I am." Cody solemnly stirred his tea. "I'm counting on it a lot. But don't tell Jennifer when she comes to the meeting. She thinks we're just friends like you and Pete, and she doesn't know that I love her in a wife kind of way. She also doesn't know she's going to marry me. That comes later."

"I see."

As she absorbed this information, Patsy's notion of a glorious gabfest with the other ladies in the club transformed into a knot at the bottom of her stomach. This childlike puppy love Cody had developed for Jennifer Hansen could grow into a real problem. Everyone in the community understood that the young man was unusual—in an endearing sort of way. He was always helpful, kind, cheerful, and sincere.

But Cody simply didn't understand life the way most people did. He looked at the world from a different angle, almost as though his eyes and brain had been borrowed from some other creature. Often it required patience to spend time around Cody. And people didn't always have patience to spare. Patsy herself had snapped at him a few times. Though she felt bad about it, she just couldn't help herself. But Cody always forgave her immediately.

"You took the last lemon bar," he informed her now. "That's bad social skills, Patsy. But it's okay, because no one knows but me, and I won't tell on you. Hey, here comes Kim Finley and Miranda Finley. They don't look mad at each other today. You can tell because they're both smiling. And here comes Esther Moore. She should bring Charlie. Then there would be two men in the TLC. Oh, boy, here's Brenda's car! Look, there she is! Isn't she beautiful?"

Patsy nodded as she settled into a chair. She knew Cody wasn't talking about Brenda, though the older woman was certainly lovely.

Cody's focus was on Brenda's daughter. When Jennifer Hansen stepped into the salon, Patsy could see she had left her long blonde hair hanging loose around her shoulders, and she wore a simple T-shirt, a pair of khaki shorts, and plain sandals. Unlike her younger sister, Jennifer had never been the homecoming queen or the center of the social whirl at Camdenton High School. She was quiet, studious, and as sweet and wholesome as apple pie.

With a sinking feeling, Patsy watched the young woman's face light up when she spotted Cody. He gave an eager wave as he pointed to the empty chair beside him. Jennifer said something in a low voice to her mother, confiding woman-to-woman in a way that unsettled Patsy even more. Even if she genuinely liked him—which Patsy dearly hoped—he would be crestfallen when his romantic aspirations weren't returned.

"Hey there, Cody," Jennifer said brightly. She slipped into the seat he had saved as he fumbled to rise and pull it back for her. "Hey, Patsy. The salon looks great. You're really packing people in this summer."

"Just don't tell me you want to cut off that beautiful long hair," Patsy said. "I couldn't do it."

Jennifer chuckled. "Oh, don't worry. I just pin it up if I get too hot. It's easy."

Unfortunately, this comment caused her to demonstrate, which in turn drew Cody's attention like a moth to a bug zapper. He positively gaped as Jennifer flipped her hair over her shoulder, twirled it around her index finger, pulled a clip from her pocket, and secured the roll on the back of her head. It was deftly done, but Patsy knew Cody wasn't admiring the young woman's dexterity. Those bright blue eyes were glued to Jennifer's face and neck . . . and right on down.

"Wow," he said.

Jennifer shrugged. "It's easy, Cody. I've been putting it up since I was a kid. Patsy's the one who taught me how to braid. I used to do my little sister's hair all the time."

"I remember that," Patsy said. "And now you're all grown up and studying to be a missionary."

"A missionary?" Miranda Finley had somehow finagled a pair of chairs for herself and Kim at the table. "A lovely young woman like you? Oh, dear. But I suppose you're determined."

Jennifer smiled. "I certainly am. I've been praying about where to serve. I loved my mission trip to Africa so much, but I'm thinking more and more about going to New Guinea."

"Not to dash your spirits, dear, but has it occurred to you that the people in New Guinea probably have a perfectly good religion already?"

"Some of them know Christ, but there are still lots of unreached tribes."

"I have never understood why Christians are so determined to impose their religion on others," Miranda said. "I realize you're enthusiastic about your beliefs, Jennifer, but I can assure you that Hindus are very happy as they are. So are Muslims, for that matter. You'll find a great deal of zeal for Islam in the Arab world, of course. No doubt those tribes you're going to visit have a way of worshipping that's comfortable to them too. In my opinion, all paths lead to God."

Kim sighed. "Yes, Miranda, we know what you think. I'm sure everyone here has seen you and Buddha on the deck."

At that, Miranda clamped her mouth shut. But not for long. "Well, at least I'm tolerant of letting people worship however they please. I don't go around trying to convert people to my faith system. I accept *all* teachings of *all* religions."

"All except Christianity," Jennifer pointed out.

Everyone at the table turned to stare at the young woman who had spoken up. Brenda Hansen's face sobered, and she glanced across at Kim. Clearly the two women were realizing they had a couple of firecrackers at the table and there was likely to be trouble.

"What do you mean by that, Jennifer?" Miranda asked with a

sweet expression. "Of course I accept Christianity. It's a perfectly valid path to God. Along with all the others. How can you say I don't accept Christ's teachings?"

"Christ insisted that there is only one way to God. He said, 'No one can come to the Father except through me.'"

"John 14:6," Cody cut in. "It's in the Bible. I've got that whole chapter by memory."

"Really?" Jennifer studied the young man for a moment, as if absorbing and filing away this information. Then she returned to Miranda. "Anyway, if you agree with Jesus that He is the only way to God, you can't accept all the other religions, too."

Miranda shook her head and let out a sigh. She took a sip of iced tea, commented on the delicious flavor, and then turned back to Jennifer. "I must assure you that I do accept all the teachings of Jesus as valid. Of course He believed He was the path to God. So did Muhammad and Buddha. These three men had experienced profound spiritual revelations, and they taught valuable truths that can enlighten us on our own personal journey of self-discovery. I choose to accept them all."

"All *except* Jesus."

Brenda laid a hand on her daughter's arm. "Jennifer. Let's talk about something else. Why don't you tell everyone our news. You know . . . about your sister."

"Jessica's getting married," Jennifer muttered, and in the next breath, "Mrs. Finley, Jesus instructed His followers to go out into the world and make disciples of everyone. When you or anyone else wants to deny Christians the right to try to convert people, then you deny us the practice of our religion. And that's discrimination."

"Well, but I—"

"If you truly accepted Christianity, Mrs. Finley, you wouldn't object to my desire to teach tribal people in New Guinea about my faith, because you would understand that evangelism is an essential part of Christianity. Christ was very clear about that."

For a moment, everyone at the table sat in silence. And then Cody began to clap. "Yay, Jennifer," he said. "That was a long speech about Jesus. I liked it. I thought it was good. You're the best Christian I ever met."

All the time Cody was speaking, Patsy was frantically trying to think of something to say that would divert the conversation away from religion. She briefly thought of asking about Jessica's upcoming wedding. But the truth was, Patsy liked what Jennifer had said, and she admired the way the girl had spoken without the least bit of hesitation. So instead of inquiring about the Hansen engagement, she heard herself echoing Cody.

"You sure are going to make a good missionary, honey," she told Jennifer. "I don't know the last time I heard such conviction from anyone but a preacher. No wonder you're going out into the world. I doubt that wild horses could keep you here in Deepwater Cove."

"But Deepwater Cove has plenty of people who need missionaries," Cody spoke up. "People like Mrs. Finley, who dances on the deck in her bathing suit. She worships idols, and that's against the Ten Commandments, so she definitely needs a missionary." He turned to Miranda. "You should come to church with us and find out what it's like there. If you did, you would know that one day idols shall be utterly abolished. 'And they shall go into the holes of the rocks, and into the caves of the earth, for fear of the Lord, and for the glory of his majesty, when he ariseth to shake terribly the earth. In that day a man shall cast his idols of silver, and his idols of gold, which they made each one for himself to worship, to the moles and to the bats; to go into the clefts of the rocks, and into the tops of the ragged rocks, for fear of the Lord, and for the glory of his majesty.' Isaiah 2:19-21. Right, Jennifer?"

All eyes at the table turned to the young woman, who was gazing across the room with an odd expression on her face.

"Patsy, why are there five pictures of me on your wall?" she asked, pointing at Cody's mural. "Right over there. Five of them. That's me, isn't it?"

Cody grinned. "I painted them," he said. "I put beautiful ladies on the wall to show off lots of hairstyles."

Jennifer looked at him. "But the faces all look like mine. Don't they? Does anyone else see that?"

Thank goodness, at just this particular moment, Esther got up and began tapping the side of her tea glass with a spoon. "Ladies, ladies," she said loudly before Cody could whistle them into silence. Then she beamed at the young man. "Ladies *and gentleman,* welcome to today's gathering of the Tea Lovers' Club. We're thrilled to have so many in attendance on a hot afternoon. Before we return to our tea and conversation, let me just recap our old business and mention one thing new."

Esther reached into her purse for her little notebook, and Patsy took the opportunity for a quick glance around the table. It was not a comforting sight. Jennifer was staring at the paintings of herself on the salon wall. Miranda was glaring at Jennifer. Kim was frowning at Miranda. Brenda was eyeing Cody. And Cody was downing the last of Patsy's lemon bar.

"There isn't much old business to report," Esther said. "It's been a glorious summer so far. All the yards look lovely, and we ought to especially recognize Brenda Hansen, who planted red, white, and blue annuals in a tribute to our great country. As we've said before, the Fourth of July barbecue was a stellar event. The commons area and the streets were lined with nearly a hundred small flags generously donated by Ashley Hanes, courtesy of the country club. Opal provided a relish tray and several apple pies, which delighted everyone. We had more salads and side dishes than we could eat. The pork steaks were delicious, and a good time was had by all. Well . . . it looks like that's about it. Is there any other old business to report?"

When no one spoke, Esther charged on. "Then let's get down to new business. I propose we have another Deepwater Cove gathering for Labor Day weekend. How about Sunday after church? It'll still be warm enough for the kids to swim, but we could add a fishing contest at the docks. I was thinking about a hayride, but Charlie says it's too early for that. We definitely want to honor the working men and women among us, so I was thinking about a parade."

"Brad wouldn't march in a parade to save his life," Ashley said. "I'm not too crazy about it either. Would you and Steve march in a parade, Brenda?"

"I doubt that's exactly Steve's idea of fun," Brenda said of her real estate agent husband. "Maybe the barbecue, fishing contest, and swimming would be enough, Esther."

The self-elected chairwoman of the TLC folded her hands and looked down at her notebook. "Well, if that's how you feel about it . . . ," she said, her voice trailing off. "I always loved a parade."

"A raid?" Opal spoke up. "When? I never heard any sirens."

Patsy knew everyone was thinking the same thing—Opal wouldn't hear sirens if they *did* start wailing.

"I have something to share," Brenda said. "My youngest child, Jessica, has just gotten engaged. They haven't set the wedding date, but I'm sure you'll all be welcome."

"Congratulations," several women said.

"That Jessica is so pretty," someone said. "Just like her sister."

"I'm not a bit surprised some boy snapped her up," another commented.

"I'd like to introduce some new business," Miranda said, standing so suddenly that the table jiggled and tea sloshed out of the china cups. "Esther, may I please have the floor?"

"Why, certainly, Miranda. We'd love to hear what you have to say."

For several hammering heartbeats, Patsy was afraid Miranda intended to expound on her theory that all paths led to God. Or maybe she wanted to defend her decision to put Buddha out on the Finleys' deck. But then she smiled warmly and turned to the table where she'd been sitting.

"Cody," she said gently, "I want to announce that I have found your aunt."

A gasp went up from the entire gathering. And then everyone fell silent. Cody stared straight ahead, looking at no one, blinking rapidly.

Finally, Miranda spoke again. "Marylou Annette Goss lives in western Kansas. She's your father's sister. I have spoken with her by phone, Cody. A long time ago, before you were born, your father became estranged from his family, and they never spoke or had any contact after that. Your aunt Marylou had no idea what had become of your father."

Patsy reached under the table, found Cody's hand, and wrapped hers around it. He still wasn't moving, so she gave his hand a little squeeze. "It's a big shocker, isn't it, sweetie pie?" she murmured. "How about that? Mrs. Finley found your aunt, just like you wanted."

"I know," he said. "I heard what she said."

Miranda smiled. "I propose that the members of the Tea Lovers' Club take up a collection to buy a bus ticket for Cody. In fact, I've already looked into it. I can put him on the bus in St. Louis, and his aunt will pick him up in Garden City, Kansas. From there, she'll drive him toward the Colorado border to the town where she lives." Miranda beamed at everyone as she seated herself again.

Patsy slipped her arm around Cody's shoulders. "Sounds like you turned up a lot of stuff when you were looking for Cody's family. I guess his aunt must be pretty excited to see him."

Miranda took a sip of tea. "Well, of course," she said. "She didn't even know he existed. I'm sure she'll enjoy him as much as we all do."

"Maybe not, if she finds out I'm kind of dumb," Cody said.

Jennifer leaned against him. "No way, Cody! You just quoted more Scripture than most of us have ever memorized."

"Your aunt Marylou didn't know your mother and father had passed away," Miranda said. "Mr. Goss didn't contact his family after Cody's mother died. He must have simply decided to take Cody and leave."

"We went a lot of places," Cody put in.

"Marylou told me she's always wondered what became of her brother."

Deciding it was time to change the subject, Patsy gave Cody a little hug. "Oh, my stars, my cup is dry as a bone. Cody, honey, would you mind getting me some more tea?"

He looked around the table, his blue eyes settling on Jennifer for a moment before he rose and headed for the hot-water urn.

As Miranda turned to Esther, Patsy noticed that the older woman's eyes had filled with tears.

Esther slipped her agenda notebook into her purse and pulled out a tissue. Dabbing her eyes, she nodded. "I think that's a wonderful idea," she said, sniffling loudly. "If Cody's aunt wants him to come . . . and if Cody wants to be with family . . . well then . . ." She gulped. "Well, let's all pitch in and make this farewell a send-off to remember."

CHAPTER FOURTEEN

Where are the candles?" Frowning, Kim rummaged through a drawer in the kitchen. "I always keep plenty of birthday candles on hand."

"In the pantry!" Miranda sang out as she hurried through the kitchen bearing a bowl of cheesy popcorn. "I reorganized the baking supplies for you, Kim. I hope you don't mind, but that drawer you had them in was a shambles. I put everything in a lovely wicker basket on the top shelf."

Kim gritted her teeth and hurried to the pantry. No, she would not get angry. Not on this special day. A party day. A day of celebration, thankfulness, and sweet good-byes. Kim had every reason to smile. The twins were turning eleven, Cody was going to meet his long-lost aunt in Kansas, and Kim was determined to focus on her blessings instead of her woes.

True, Miranda was still staying in the Finley house and evidently would be forever. Derek had not uttered a word about the plan he had confided to Lydia that evening on the porch. So Kim told herself she still did not "officially" know that her mother-in-law wouldn't be leaving with the start of school. But she had decided to try to keep her thoughts to herself in order to keep peace in the home. She had suppressed the hurt and anger that Derek's decision—and his refusal to communicate with her—had caused.

In looking back on her own childhood, Kim could recall few good things to be thankful for—but adaptability was one. She couldn't count the times her mother had moved the family from town to town, house to apartment, man to man. People had come and gone from their lives all the time, and Kim understood the anguish Lydia had expressed to Derek on the porch. A fragmented, constantly shifting family group unsettled and frightened children. Kim knew that too well, and she was not about to put her twins through any more upheaval than they'd experienced already. But her own difficult life had taught her to adjust, to make the most of each situation, to search for blessings. And that's what she would do in order to protect her precious family.

Just when Kim heard the twins' feet pounding toward the kitchen, she found the birthday candles in a basket in the pantry. Ten minutes earlier, she had sent Luke and Lydia running to Charlie and Esther Moore's house to fetch Cody—anything to keep the rambunctious pair out of the kitchen—and they were already back.

"Eleven!" she said, poking candles into the cake as the twins breathlessly burst into the room. "Eleven years old. Yay, Luke and Lydia!"

Lydia danced around the room while her brother bounced up and down on his toes.

"I hope I get a skateboard; I hope I get a skateboard," Luke chanted.

"How soon till everyone else gets here?" Lydia asked. "I can't wait!"

"Any time now. Where's Cody?"

"On the deck with Mr. and Mrs. Moore. They followed us in their golf cart."

"Good job. Luke, I know you saved up all your carbs. Have you checked your blood sugar recently?"

"Yeah, and it's just right so I can eat cake and ice cream."

Kim smiled proudly. "I knew you'd figure it out. Okay, kids, run and open the front door for the rest of the guests."

"You made an eleven cake, Mom!" Lydia crowed before racing away after her brother. "Did you see it, Lukey? We're eleven! We're eleven!"

Kim couldn't deny how pleased she was about the large *11* she had crafted out of a pair of chocolate cake mixes. Each year since the twins' birth, she had created a cake in the shape of their age. This year, the double *1*'s iced in chocolate fudge and sprinkled with nuts were large enough to feed all the kids' friends and Cody's well-wishers, too. It would be a big group, but Kim was prepared.

"The deck table is set and ready for company," Miranda announced as she breezed back into the kitchen. "And just look at the cars pulling up along the street. Where is that son of mine? He should be home by now."

"Derek often has last-minute phone calls or paperwork. He'll be here soon."

"Paperwork? How can that be more important than his family? Especially on birthdays! I used to tell his father the same thing—family first. Eric was always off on some photographic safari, you know. But when he came home, I made it clear that his wife and son got top priority."

Kim took two cartons of ice cream out of the freezer—one sugar-free—and carried them to the counter. "I hadn't realized Eric was gone so much."

"Oh yes. The Himalayan mountains in Tibet, a volcano in Hawaii, the Rift Valley in eastern Africa. Weeks at a time. Sometimes months. It's a wonder Derek recognized his father when he came home. If I'd had any idea that marrying an internationally renowned photographer would turn me into a single mother, well . . . well, I would have married him anyway."

To her surprise, Kim laughed. The giggle was natural for once, not the forced chuckle that she so often coughed out for her mother-in-law's benefit. Miranda rarely spoke about Derek's father, and neither did her son. It was refreshing to see the woman in such high spirits and eager to chat.

"You know how you marry people for the silliest reasons?" Miranda was saying as she opened a potato chip bag and poured the contents into a large bowl. "Oh, that Eric Finley was handsome! Curly hair, blue-gray eyes, and a wonderful physique. If I'd given it two thoughts, I would have realized that his tan and all those muscles came from trekking up and down mountains or wandering through deserts. But I thought he was gorgeous. So romantic! And a photographer, too!"

"He does sound handsome," Kim said.

"To die for. In my fairy-tale vision, Eric and I were going to travel the world together, hitchhiking from one adventure to another. Then we got married, and I got pregnant—well, actually the other way around—and off he went without me. It turned out the magazines he freelanced for didn't pay for wives and babies to tag along. Worse, he didn't want company on his assignments, especially not a child. But he came from a wealthy family, and so we didn't lack for money. A handsome, absentee husband; a darling little boy; and enough to live on comfortably forever."

Kim had found spoons for the ice cream and was trying to figure out how to get the double cakes out the sliding glass door to the deck. But at the same time, she wanted to listen to Miranda. Instead of harping about Kim's choice of curtains or hinting at her failures as a mother, the woman was actually conversing.

"Derek works long hours, but he's never gone overnight," Kim said as she arranged the birthday things on a tray. "Weren't you lonely?"

"Of course I was. In those early days of marriage, it was always Eric and Derek. Derek and Eric. And then just Derek. And finally no one at all. But money can do a lot to make up for loneliness." She shrugged. "Until I came down here, I thought that's how my existence had to be. But look—it turned out all right in the end."

"This is not the end," Kim said. "You have so much life still ahead."

Miranda paused for a moment. "Don't start me thinking about that," she said softly. "I'm focused on waiting until I can pass through this life into a new form of being."

"You're waiting to die?"

"To be reincarnated." Miranda seemed to sag as she leaned against the kitchen counter. "And please don't attack me the way that Hansen girl did at the TLC meeting the other day. If I were a Christian, all I'd have to look forward to is an eternity playing a harp and wearing a pair of angel wings. No thanks. I'll hedge my bets and keep the doors open. If I'm right about reincarnation, there's hope for a better future for me. Maybe I'll be a . . . a cat!"

At that, she winked at Kim and began to laugh. Sweeping up the cartons of ice cream Kim had just opened, Miranda headed for the door. "Oh, wouldn't I love to lie in the sun all day and bask away the hours! How lovely to be a cat!"

As Kim picked up the cake tray, she wondered how that existence would be so different from the one Miranda already enjoyed. Money. Leisure. Even a family to keep you busy—or ignore— at your whim.

But there was no time to work up any frustration toward Miranda, whose concept of heaven was so far off the biblical mark as to be laughable. Instead of resenting her mother-in-law, Kim would find compassion for her.

Despite her privileged life, Miranda obviously regretted some of her choices. She had been lonely and self-absorbed for many years. No wonder she was hard to live with. Without the Bible as a guide and the church to provide a support system in good times and bad, Miranda had learned to rely on herself and her own philosophies.

"Did I hear Miranda say something about a cat?" Esther Moore asked as she stepped into the kitchen. "I ought to warn you—your house is already very full, dear. Though Boofer is a joy, that dog takes up so much of our time. I hope you haven't gone and gotten a pet for the twins' birthday."

Kim laughed. "No pets—but we do have Miranda, who's hoping to be reincarnated as a cat."

"A cat?" Esther picked up two bowls of chips. "Goodness, not me. I'm looking forward to heaven. In fact, I can hardly wait. I won't have all these aches and pains, and I'll be able to hold my sister's hand and skip through the grass like we did when we were kids. Charlie says he's planning to sing in the heavenly choir, but I have too many people I want to visit."

At the thought of Charlie raising his voice in praise to the Lord and Esther chatting with friends and family, Kim smiled. She lifted her focus toward the sky as she stepped onto the deck with the cake. How comforting it was to know she didn't need to fear being reincarnated as a cat or a bug or even another human.

When she set the cake down on the table, Kim's eyes fell on her husband, who had just arrived. Still in uniform, Derek was speaking with his mother and obviously getting a tongue-lashing for showing up nearly an hour after the end of his shift. Kim sighed. Well, if Derek could put up with Miranda, why couldn't she?

"I'm going home."

The words were spoken so near Kim's ear that she jumped in surprise. She looked around to find Cody Goss leaning over her shoulder as she straightened the candles on the two cakes.

"Eleven," he said, reading the numerals. "Luke and Lydia are eleven years old, and that's why you made them an *eleven* cake. I never had a birthday cake. I don't know how old I am except more than twenty-one. Do you think my aunt will make me a *more than twenty-one* cake?"

"Maybe she will, Cody. Just ask her when you get there."

"I've missed a lot of cakes. If today was my birthday, I would have chocolate cake cut into squares. These cakes will be easy to cut into squares."

Kim straightened and gazed into the earnest blue eyes. "Cody, would you like to share these cakes with Luke and Lydia? They're so used to sharing everything, I know they wouldn't mind."

"Does that mean I'm eleven too?"

"No … but it does mean you get to eat chocolate cake in squares."

Cody's lips parted over his white teeth as he smiled. "I like that. I hope my aunt is just like you."

"No matter what she's like, she'll be so proud of you. I know that for certain. You've become such a smart, capable young man."

"Excuse me there, Cody," Derek said, tapping him on the shoulder. "Mind if I cut in? I need to talk to Kim for a minute."

"Okay," Cody mumbled, his shoulders sagging. "But I was hoping we could cut those two cakes. I want to eat some, because they're partly mine."

"No, they're not!" Miranda Finley sashayed up to the table bearing a third cake in her hands. "This is *your* cake, Cody! I ordered it especially for your going-away party. It's an ice cream cake. I've had it hidden in Esther's freezer for several days now. A secret surprise, just for you!"

She set the elaborately decorated round cake next to the fudge frosted cakes that Kim had proudly created for her twins. Miranda's cake flaunted gleaming white icing in professional scallops and swirls, a road drawn in gray icing with a yellow stripe down the center, and a miniature toy bus traveling along it. Elaborately scripted letters read *Farewell, Cody!*

The young man gaped at the cake for a moment; then he read the inscription out loud. "*Farewell, Cody!* That means me, because I'm Cody. This is my first birthday cake ever in my whole life."

Miranda touched his arm. "Honey, it's not a—"

"I wonder how old I am," Cody continued. He studied the table for a moment. Then pointing to the three cakes, he said, "One-one-zero. I am 110 years old. Wow!"

As the crowd laughed, Charlie Moore slung his arm around Cody's shoulders. "Come on, then, you old turkey buzzard. Step back and let the twins blow out their candles so we can dig in. That ice cream's already melting, and I'm hungry."

Kim's heart welled with emotion as Derek lit the candles. Luke and Lydia grinned happily while everyone sang "Happy Birthday." And then—with Cody joining in—they blew out the flames. Esther and Miranda moved in to cut cake and dip ice cream while Brenda Hansen poured glasses of punch.

"Kim?" Derek slipped a hand around his wife's elbow. "Can we step over here to the side for just a minute? I need to talk to you."

Concerned, she nodded and accompanied him to a bench at the far corner of the deck away from the hubbub of cake, candles, and gifts. "What's wrong, Derek?" she asked. "Did something happen at work?"

"No, it's not that." He laced his fingers together and rested his elbows on his thighs, his focus on the deck between his boots. "Well . . . it's about my mother."

"You know she's hoping to be reincarnated as a cat," Kim teased.

Derek glanced up, and for a moment his sober expression softened. "With our luck, she'll come back as a tiger—claws and all." He shook his head. "Listen, I've been meaning to talk to you about this, and Mom knows I'm putting it off. She asked me to talk to you today, before the party. I planned to come home right after work, but this morning, we finally got the facial reconstruction on our drowning victim. We've been printing flyers, talking to the media, and trying to get the word out so if anyone has seen her—"

"Derek," Kim cut in, "I know your mother isn't planning to go back to St. Louis when school starts. If that's what you wanted to tell me, I already know. I heard what Lydia—"

"She wasn't supposed to tell you," he ground out. "That ornery kid."

"It's not Lydia's fault. I was on my way out to the porch that evening when you were talking with her. I overheard you tell her about Miranda."

"You knew? All this time?"

"Yes, and I've been pretty upset that you told our daughter before you told me. Why did you do that? Are you afraid to talk to me? Do you see me as a tiger too?"

He fell silent.

"I guess that answers my question," she said, a mixture of hurt and frustration bubbling inside her. "No matter what you think about me, I deserved to hear the truth, Derek."

"I'm telling you right now."

"Here? In the middle of the twins' birthday party?"

"I've kept it from you as long as I could, but it's now or never. You know Mom is leaving for St. Louis tomorrow—taking Cody to the bus station. While she's there, she plans to hire packers, rent a storage unit, and put her house on the market. She wants to stay here permanently."

Despite her best intentions, Kim felt her anger flare. "*She* wants to stay? I thought it was your idea."

"It is. Partly." His head dropped lower. "There are things you don't know, Kim. Things I should have told you a long time ago."

"Derek, this is the twins' birthday party! What's wrong with you? You have no idea how to talk or listen or anything! How can you do this?"

She could see the muscle in his jaw flickering. "I'm sorry I'm not exactly like you, Kim. I don't talk easily. I prefer to take care of today, handle situations as they arise. It's one day at a time with me, okay?"

"No, it's not okay. Not when it affects your family. You'd better start talking—and I mean *now*."

"I'd rather wait until after the party."

"*Now*," she repeated.

"All right," he groused. "Here's the deal. You know I love my mother, and I want to take care of her. But I never planned to have her live with us. *She* decided that, and I can't say no."

"Why not? Miranda has caused so much tension in the house. Of course she's been helpful with the kids, but she's also upset our whole family structure. It's all I can do to keep my spirits up when she's always on me about things. She's given both of the kids a hard time with her crazy ideas, and she's horribly permissive. She flaunts our rules—the computer, the bicycles, swimming, you name it. She criticizes almost everything about me—from my curtain fabric to the way I cook. Worst of all, she mocks our faith. You know how hard this summer has been for all of us, and I can't believe you would let her have her way in this. Especially if it's not what you really want."

"I have to, Kim. That's what I'm trying to tell you."

"Why? You're a grown man. You're the strongest, bravest human being I've ever met. How can you let your mother walk all over you?"

"She's not walking on me. She holds me by a leash."

"What kind of a leash? What are you saying, Derek?"

"Money." He spat out the word. "It's all about money, okay?"

"What do you mean?"

He covered his eyes with a hand and rubbed his temples. "We should wait to talk about this."

"Derek, please."

He let out a hot breath. "Look, there's a part of my life I never told you about. I didn't want to believe it mattered. It happened in the past, and I decided I couldn't let it affect us. Affect *you*."

Kim's heart sank. "Oh no," she whispered. "What happened?"

"It started when I was in college. I racked up a fair amount of debt for tuition, housing, and all that. But there's more. I used to . . . to gamble, okay? The riverboat casinos. You know they line the river in St. Louis, and I'd go there with friends—just for fun. Then I began going by myself. Every day. Every night."

"Derek." She wanted to reach out to him, but she couldn't move.

"I don't know how to explain this, but sitting at the poker table was the only place I felt comfortable. No one demanded anything of me there. I didn't have to be the son of the late, great, world-renowned photographer, Eric Finley. I didn't have to live up to my mother's dreams and expectations for me. I knew I was destroying myself, but for some reason gambling gave me a feeling of security. False security. I figured if I won, I could have the good things in life without having to work for it or inherit it. The bottom line was that I didn't want to grow up, and I thought I could escape responsibility—to the point that it became an obsession."

"This is impossible," Kim murmured.

"It's not impossible. It's true. I barely graduated from college. I spent money hand over fist—always sure I was going to strike it rich. The next big jackpot was just waiting for me. I told myself I had a safeguard. My father's dough would bail me out, and it did. But it came with a price. I ended up owing my mother so much money I'll never be able to pay it back. She holds my debt over my head because she believes that keeps me from relapsing. She's wrong, but I can't convince her of that. My senior year of college, I started going to Gamblers Anonymous. Went to meetings more often than you've ever been to church. You want to talk about a higher power? I've got one, and her name is Miranda Finley."

As Derek spoke, Kim's entire body had stiffened. Every muscle went hard and tense; her teeth clenched; her hands knotted into fists. How could this be happening?

This wasn't true. It couldn't be. Derek would have told her if he'd had a gambling problem. He knew she was the child of one alcoholic and had married another. She had sworn she would never, ever marry anyone with an addiction.

But she had. Somehow the horrible pattern had repeated itself again. Not only was Derek an addict, but he had hidden it from her. Denied and buried his dark secret for three years!

"Sometimes I've told you I had to work late," he was saying now, "but I lied. I was at GA meetings. I have to attend, Kim. It's still hard to resist the urge. I've been away from the boats for years now, but I fight the battle every day. The guys at work will put together a football pool. Or someone's wife is having a baby, and they want me to bet on the birth date. You wonder why I never spend time on the computer? why I'm so hard on the kids about it? Now you know. There's too much opportunity to get into gambling again. Every convenience store and most restaurants have lottery machines. Scratchers. Lotto. That's why I always go to Pete's Rods-N-Ends. He doesn't sell those things, so I won't buy my gas anywhere else."

Kim couldn't speak. She could hardly breathe.

At some far distance, she could see her children tearing open birthday presents, hugging people, laughing, high-fiving each other.

And then there was this man at her side. This gambler. This addict. This nightmare.

"I survive by acting as though I don't owe the money," he continued. "You and I live off our joint income, and we make it every month. Barely. We have this nice house, food to eat, clothes for the kids, cars. But that money you think we've been saving isn't going into an account. It goes to St. Louis. To my mother. It goes to pay off my debt. When my mother dies, which isn't likely to be soon, we'll be free. In the meantime, I'm honor bound to make amends. I have to restore what I took."

Kim swallowed hard, fighting tears. "You should have told me, Derek."

"You wouldn't have married me. I knew that. I'm an addict, just like Joe."

"You're nothing like Joe." But even as she said the words, Kim realized she was kidding herself. In many ways, Derek was very much like her first husband—not only an addict but emotionally stunted, living in denial, hiding secrets. Even Derek's job with the Water Patrol revealed how important control was to him. Joe had demanded ultimate authority, and eventually he became abusive. Though Derek never lifted a finger against Kim or the twins, he had chosen a job and a life in which he could exert power and influence.

Derek had fallen silent, and Kim couldn't make herself move. So they sat on the bench, watching the children laugh and the adults eat cake and ice cream. Brenda and Steve Hansen had presented Cody with a suitcase on wheels for his trip. The Hansens looked happy together, as attractive and cheerful as a spring bouquet. Esther and Charlie were seated side by side in deck chairs, eating ice cream and laughing about something. The summer sun radiated joy from their faces. Patsy and Pete had shut down business early just for the party. He was teasing her, making her blush and swat his shoulder. The twins sat bunched in a group with their friends, examining and admiring their gifts.

Only two in the gathered group seemed less than elated. Lydia's closest friend, Tiffany, had moved a little apart, as if she sensed she was older and somehow different from these happy-go-lucky kids. And then there was Cody. He held a plate with chocolate cake cut into a perfect square by Esther, but he stood at the edge of the deck and gazed at the lake. Kim wondered if his turmoil was anything like hers.

"I'm sorry," Derek said in a low voice. "I should have told you, Kim. I should have known it would come out one way or another. But I've tried so hard to keep this in the past."

"It's not in the past, Derek," Kim heard herself snap back at him. "Not if you're going to Gamblers Anonymous meetings all the time. Not if you're still battling addiction. Not if you lie to me on a regular basis. You're telling me that Miranda controls our future. She holds you by a money leash, as though you're a puppy bound to her will. That means everything I thought about us—all that I trusted and believed in when we married—has been a sham. We're a fraud sitting here."

Derek rubbed his face and then stood quickly. "I'm going for a drive. If the kids ask, tell them I've gone to get something special for them."

"Another lie?" Kim shot out.

"It's not a lie." He looked at her, his eyes red rimmed. "I have presents for them. I'll be back."

Before she could stop him, Derek strode to the sliding door, let himself into the house, and vanished. In moments, she heard his truck starting up in the driveway.

CHAPTER FIFTEEN

I guess they trust him completely now. Letting him ride around on that skateboard the way they do."

Esther was shucking corn on the front porch with Charlie. They had purchased several bushels at the farmers' market in town, and they planned to cut off the kernels and freeze them in plastic zipper bags. In years past, Esther had enjoyed canning the fruits and vegetables Charlie grew in their garden. She made jellies, apple butter, and even salsa once or twice. They still had rows of filled Mason jars lining their pantry shelves, but she didn't bother with the canning anymore. It was just as easy to freeze most of their produce, and it turned out nearly as tasty.

"You couldn't pay me to get on one of those things." Charlie watched young Luke fly down the sloping roadway, his arms outstretched and his knees bent. He wore a helmet, but his big smile was clearly visible. "Can't say I wouldn't have tried it a few years back, though. Looks like fun. But I reckon I've got too many twinges in my hinges now."

Esther chuckled. "I wouldn't put it past you, Charlie. If that boy came up here and offered you a ride, you'd take him up on it. There's no fool like an old fool, my daddy used to say."

Charlie laid the ear of corn in his lap and rocked awhile as he watched Luke enjoying his birthday present. If the truth be known, Charlie didn't feel nearly as old as Esther made him out to be. He still took Boofer around the neighborhood on foot and in the golf cart several times a day. He worked the vegetable garden. He fooled with his tools in the garage, and he even built something useful now and then.

More significant, he was beginning to get an itch to go somewhere. Esther never wanted to wander far from home and her favorite destinations—the beauty salon, the church, the grocery store. But Charlie had been a mail carrier, and he liked to move around a little more. He wouldn't mind visiting the grandkids in California or taking a trip to Florida to see their daughter. But he knew if he mentioned it, Esther would turn him down right away. If the family wanted to get together, she said, let them come to the lake. Why make the old folks run all over the country?

It frustrated Charlie a little. He felt like he had one foot in the grave and was already starting to molder.

"I don't know when I've seen a boy so excited as Luke was when Derek brought that skateboard to the party." Esther tossed an ear of corn into the basket and brushed strands of corn silk from her lap. "And that purse he bought for Lydia! I have no doubt Miranda picked it out. Did you see the thing? Pink leather. I never would have sent it to school with a child the way Kim did. If you ask me, that was a church purse. But I guess Miranda's influence is getting stronger by the day."

"Speaking of Miranda . . . ," Charlie said, and then his words faded as the ritual began.

The thin blonde woman stepped onto the Finleys' deck, which was just visible from the angle of Charlie's rocking chair. Within moments, a gentle tinkling music—panpipes and brass bells—drifted through the air as Miranda slipped out of her long white robe.

For the first few weeks, Charlie had resisted watching the regular evening exhibition, but he finally gave in to temptation. Miranda Finley wasn't too many years younger than Esther, but land sakes, what a few stretching exercises could do for a woman! Lithe, tanned, fit as a fiddle, his neighbor began moving around on the deck— bending this way and that, rolling her head, waving her arms—all to the intoxicating aroma of some kind of incense.

"Charlie, what are you making calf eyes at?" Esther lifted up out of her chair and leaned over in his direction. "Oh, for pete's sake! Is Miranda Finley doing her nightly belly dance? Let me see. Scoot over."

They watched the theatrics for several minutes. Charlie thought this was one of Miranda's better nights. She managed to bend over backward so far she could almost touch the deck with the tips of her fingers. But Esther kept clucking and shaking her head as if the entire performance disgusted her.

"I don't know why Kim and Derek put up with that nonsense," she said as the music tapered off. "You wouldn't want me out dancing on the porch in my bathing suit every night, would you?"

Charlie could think of several responses to that—none of which would be well received. So he picked up an ear of corn and started pulling off the husks.

"Well?" Esther demanded. "Would you?"

"I wouldn't mind you belly dancing in our bedroom now and then," he said. He waggled his eyebrows at her. "If you catch my drift."

"Oh, Charlie!" Esther giggled. "You are such a nut."

Rocking and shucking, Charlie thought he might be a nut, but he sure wasn't dead. As far as Esther was concerned, he might as well be among the dearly departed for all the attention she paid him—at least in that particular room of their house. Still, she'd been a good wife all these years, and he couldn't complain. At least not out loud.

"Here comes Ashley!" Esther said, elbowing her husband as a

small car pulled into their driveway. "She's bringing me some of her handmade beads. I'm going to order necklaces for everyone I know. How about that? All the Christmas presents taken care of in one fell swoop."

"Yahoo," Charlie said.

Ashley Hanes stepped out of her car and gave her long red hair a toss. "Hey, Mr. and Mrs. Moore," she called. "What's up?"

"Not much," Charlie said, watching Miranda Finley pull her robe back on and leave the deck. "Not much at all."

"I brought my whole collection of beads for you to look at." Without being asked, Ashley settled into the third chair on the porch. She pushed a stack of corn husks off the table onto the floor. Then she set out several plastic trays with countless tiny compartments, each bearing a different type of bead.

This was Charlie's signal to head for cover, but Esther was having none of that. She caught his arm just as he tried to rise. "You sit right there, Charles Moore, and help me choose these beads."

Obedient as ever, Charlie slumped back into his rocker. Truth to tell, sometimes he felt like retirement wasn't all it was cracked up to be. Maybe if a fellow could get out and about once in a while. Or kick it up with the little woman. But here he and Esther sat, shucking corn, waiting to croak.

"I like these swirls," Esther commented. "What do you think, Charlie? Can you picture these beads on May?"

He could barely remember his wife's niece, let alone know which beads she ought to wear. He mumbled, "Sure," and turned to their visitor. "Say, Ashley," he drawled as Esther resumed hunting through the plastic containers. "How's Brad coming along with his building project?"

The young woman looked up, flushed a bright pink, and dipped her head again. "He hasn't done anything on it for a while."

"It'll make a nice garage for that new truck of his."

Esther lifted her head and frowned. "Or whatever they decide to use it for," she said, tipping her head and flashing her eyes toward Ashley, apparently to remind Charlie about the young couple's dispute over the purpose of the room.

"I guess Brad got a building permit downtown and cleared his plans with the Deepwater Cove Association," Charlie speculated. "He'd know all about that sort of thing—him working for a contractor."

"I guess so," Ashley said. "How do you like these orange ones, Mrs. Moore?"

"Not for Christmas gifts, dear. Orange is a little much; don't you think?"

Esther had laid a line of beads across the table, and Ashley was jotting who would get which necklace in a little notebook. The women discussed names, ages, hair color, and other such foolishness for females Charlie hadn't thought about in years. Clearly this was great fun for Esther, but he felt a strong urge to go inside and turn on the TV.

"Anyway, we might not finish that room," Ashley said suddenly. "At least not right away."

The idea of an unfinished construction project in the neighborhood didn't sit well with Charlie—especially when the house next door was for sale. "Brad running out of time?"

"Money," Ashley informed him. "Do you like these green stripes, Mrs. Moore? I think they go really well with the purple glass beads. Maybe with some small gold ones as separators."

Charlie studied the green, purple, and gold combo and thought it was the craziest mishmash of colors he'd ever seen. But lo and behold, Esther starting cooing like a lovebird. Said she might even want a strand for herself.

Charlie thought he'd move the conversation back a ways. "Money's always tight when you're just starting out," he commented. "Maybe you and Brad could take out a second mortgage. We did that one time when the kids were little. Wasn't easy making two house payments, but we managed."

Ashley's pretty eyes settled on him for a moment. "I'm thinking about getting another job. I could work during the day and keep my position at the country club too. I never wanted to live like my parents—with the ice cream store always on the verge of shutting down. But if these beads don't start selling better, I'll have to look around for more work."

Charlie appreciated the young woman's frankness, and he understood about financial worries. Still, it would help if Brad Hanes didn't park himself at the bar every night. And what had he been thinking when he bought that big truck? Not to mention having a mortgage and starting to add on to the house. Kids these days didn't seem to have the ability to think ahead very far.

"Pick out a nice set of beads for me, Ashley," Charlie requested. "Let's make it three strands and dip one of them down kind of long."

Esther gave a little squawk. "Oh, Charlie, are you getting me an early Christmas present, you silly goose? Don't you know better than to order a gift right in front of me?"

"Indeed I do," he intoned. "You have taught me well, woman. This necklace isn't for you. I thought I'd have Ashley create something that Cody can give his aunt for Christmas. That way, in case he forgets to buy her something, he'll be covered."

At the mention of Cody's name, all three people on the porch fell silent. Esther messed around with the beads while Ashley wrote in her notebook. Charlie thought about the young man who had helped clean their house throughout the summer. Cody hadn't been gone long, but already the spiderwebs were starting to build up and get messy along the eaves, and the windows could use a washing.

But doing chores wasn't the main reason Charlie missed Cody. There was something special about the boy. The way he always smiled and greeted people with a wave of the hand. The way he would suddenly start spouting Bible verses or discussing his favorite subjects—chocolate cake and hot dogs. Deepwater Cove didn't seem the same without the familiar sight of a slender, carefree figure strolling along the roads from one house to another.

"I miss Cody," Ashley spoke up finally. "It's hard to believe he just up and left us."

"He wanted to go see his aunt," Esther said. "That's understandable."

"Did you get a letter, Mrs. Moore?"

"Yes, but he gave the same information to all of us. Must've just written one letter and then copied it over and over again for each person in the neighborhood."

Charlie grunted. "He ought to have told us what he thought about his new life. The whole letter was nothing but an account of the bus ride and then a long description of his aunt's house. Moldings around the window frames and brass doorknobs. Who cares about that? I want to know if he likes the woman and if he's happy there."

"He assumes we know that," Esther said, patting her husband's knee. "Marylou Goss is his aunt. She wanted to reunite what's left of her family. Of course he likes her. You know Cody. He likes everyone."

"Well, that's true—unfortunately for us. If he could live out in the woods and eat bugs, he can survive anywhere. So I guess we might as well start getting used to it."

At the thought of never seeing Cody's curly hair and bright blue eyes again, Charlie had an awful feeling he might choke up. So he pushed himself out of his rocker and headed for the house. "Corn husks, beads, and belly dancers," he muttered. "I've had about all the fun I can stand. See you two ladies later."

Inside, he settled into his recliner and pressed the Power button on the TV remote control. Through an open window, he could hear his wife giving Ashley all the details of Miranda Finley's most recent exhibition. Thank goodness the game shows were on. Charlie raised the volume just a tad higher than usual; then he leaned back in his chair and shut his eyes.

✿

Working the day shift gave Derek the opportunity to share the evening meal with his family that week. He had made a valiant effort to enjoy the time with his loved ones, but Kim's long silences had erected a definite barrier between them. After his confession on the deck during the twins' birthday party, he had returned to the house bearing birthday gifts he had picked out earlier for them. Despite the kids' joy over the purse and the skateboard, Kim wouldn't even look at her husband.

The rest of the week, they barely spoke each morning, and dinners were taken up with the twins' usual banter. Miranda's quick trip to St. Louis had also impacted mealtimes. Upon her return, Derek's mother felt compelled to describe Cody's departure on the bus, her trouble with the moving and storage company, and her efforts to select a real estate agent and put her house on the market. Kim hardly said a word except to respond to questions.

That Friday's pizza night was proceeding as usual, but Derek sensed that most of the fun was missing as the family picked out ingredients and layered them onto the dough. He knew things with Kim were bad, but he had no intention of reopening that topic. Instead, he wanted to act as normal as possible. Kim and the kids had somehow worked things out with Miranda, so they had an interesting array of toppings to choose from. After the pizzas had baked, Derek tried to liven up the meal as everyone sat around the dining room table.

"Now, what is this green stuff, Mom?" he asked, pointing to a sprig on a slice of pizza. "You know how I feel about green stuff."

"That is basil, for your information." Miranda smiled at her son. "You know exactly what that *green stuff* is, young man, because I grew basil in the backyard herb garden every summer. And you used to pick it for me."

"Which kind do you like better, Derek?" Lydia asked. "Grandma Finley's pizza or ours?"

Derek could see that bullet headed his way, and he quickly dodged it. "Aren't all these pizzas ours?" He pointed to the slices on his plate. "This kind with the pepperoni and this one with the sausage and this one here with the green stuff?"

"But which one tastes best?" Lydia was swinging her legs under the table, which made her bounce up and down on the seat. "I like ours best, because it has tomato sauce. Grandma Finley's doesn't."

"Hers stinks," Luke declared.

"Hey, bud, that's no way to talk about our dinner."

"Oh, Derek, you used to the say the same thing," Miranda reminded him. "I don't know why I bothered."

"Tiffany broke up with her boyfriend," Lydia announced. "She hates him now. She burned all his letters."

"What does Tiffany have to do with pizza?" Luke asked.

"The last time I ate pizza was at Tiffany's house. Her mother's a waitress at the pizza place in Camdenton, so they have it almost every night. And that's when Tiffany told me she broke up with her boyfriend, so we burned the letters."

"You're not supposed to play with fire."

"We weren't. We burned them on the barbecue grill in the back-yard. Then we burned the letters she wrote to him but hadn't given him yet. Did you know that glitter ink sparkles and crackles when you burn it? It's cool."

Derek kept an ear on the conversation and an eye on his wife. Kim was performing her usual mealtime rituals. But not once did she look at her husband.

How long was this going to continue? They had always enjoyed each other's company whenever they were together. He teased her, and she giggled. He complimented her, and she blushed. These days Derek felt like he was living with an ice cube. The chill extended from the moment he opened his eyes in the morning until the last sight of Kim's back turned toward him at night.

As the meal ended and everyone began clearing the table, the twins announced that they had decided to watch a movie together. Miranda declared that she was going to her bedroom to work. Derek wasn't certain how it had happened, but his mother had found a way to spend her free time. It seemed Esther Moore and his mother had formed a partnership that had some sort of connection to Ashley Hanes. Jewelry, he thought, but he wasn't sure.

As Kim started the dishwasher, Derek reflected on the negative changes in their marriage. Had the problems between them begun with the arrival of his mother? Or had Derek's failure to be totally honest with Kim caused this widening rift? Or could it be a combination of the things that life had tossed their way?

While he didn't know what had started them down this wintry path, Derek had no doubt what he wanted to happen. He wanted the arctic winds to cease and a summer breeze to return to his life. He longed to hold his wife in his arms again. Where had she gone? And how could he get her back?

If there was a real God and not just the invisible power Derek trusted to keep himself from gambling, why didn't He step into the lives of good people?

For that matter, Derek wondered, what kept God from feeling real? He wanted to be a part of Kim's whole world, but he couldn't figure out how. They were so different. As hard as he'd tried to convince her that those differences could be worked out, now he wasn't so sure.

As Kim walked past him toward the living room, Derek considered reaching out and taking her hand. But he didn't want to risk another confrontation.

Show me what to do. He ground out the words deep in his heart. *God, if You're there, help me. I need her. I want my wife to love me again. I need to get her love back, and I don't know how. Please make it happen.*

But of course, nothing did happen. Derek didn't know why he had even hoped it might. Whatever changes had occurred in his life were the ones forged by attending GA meetings and constantly working the steps that kept him clean. Now his participation in the organization was routine, so much a part of him that he never mentioned it to anyone and hardly gave it a second thought. In the same way, his loyalty to a higher power had been part of the process he had used to break free, and he still acknowledged it in his effort to stay that way.

With a sigh of frustration, he wandered into the living room. As usual, Kim was nowhere to be seen. Anything to avoid him.

As he settled into a recliner and flipped on the television, he heard one of the twins dashing up the stairs and into the room. It was Lydia.

"Where's our movie?" she sang out. "We can't find our movie! Where is it, Derek? Have you seen it?"

"Check the shelf under the TV," he told her.

Crazy kid. Always trailing bits and pieces of everything she touched. As she knelt in front of the bookshelf, he sat forward and flipped through a stack of movie cases on the table beside his chair.

"Here it is, tater tot," he called. He tossed the case to her.

Lydia leaped up and caught the movie; then she headed for the basement again. As she passed his chair, she paused middash. "Thanks, Dad-o." Throwing her arms around his neck, she gave him a kiss on the cheek. "That's what Lukey and I are calling you now. Dad-o. Hope you like it!"

Before Derek could respond, Lydia had skipped off and was pounding back down the stairs to the basement. *Dad-o.* He thought about the word for a moment. Well, it wasn't bad. Through the years, he had given the twins dozens of nicknames. Nice to have one of his own. Especially one with that treasured syllable—*Dad.*

Slightly encouraged, Derek clicked through the channels. A news show. A foul-mouthed comedian. A sitcom. Maybe his talk with Lydia had actually made a difference, he speculated. Come to think of it, she had been nicer to him since that night on the front porch.

Neither twin had been spewing the "I hate this family" refrain lately. He pressed the channel-change button again. A ball game. A crime serial. A fishing show.

Fishing.

The word hit Derek like a bolt of lightning. His finger paused on the remote. What had Charlie told him about communicating with women? *You've got to know what you want and then fish until you catch it.* Charlie had wanted to eat shrimp at Aunt Mamie's.

Not long ago, Derek had wanted Lydia's trust. He had won it by "fishing" for it that night on the porch. He knew exactly what he wanted from Kim, too. He wanted her love.

What could he use for bait?

Charlie had used a simple query. "What's wrong, Esther, honey?"

It had worked on Lydia and Esther. But would it succeed with Kim? Something so light and obvious? And if it did—if she took the bait—what would Derek pull out of the sea of their marital discord? His wife's love . . . or an ill-tempered shark?

The very idea of trying Charlie's technique on Kim made Derek's palms sweat. Could he do it? Should he? He tried to recall the things the older man had told him. *It's just like fishing, just like fishing. . . .*

"Okay," Derek murmured out loud as he stood and squared his shoulders. It might not work, but what was the alternative? Living with a silent, angry wife for the rest of his life? Or worse—losing the marriage he had sabotaged in his determination to make it work?

After trudging back and forth through the house, even checking the garage to see if her car was there, Derek finally found Kim sitting inside the screened area of their deck. She had taken her file box out to the table and was paying bills—a chore she hated.

Bad timing, Derek thought. Better head back into the house. He swallowed, frozen for a moment; then he lifted his chin. No, he could do this. He would—but not on his own. *God, if You're there, please help me.* He said the words inside his head. But he knew the request wasn't simply a thought. It was a prayer.

CHAPTER SIXTEEN

Kim could feel Derek's eyes on her as she wrote the check for their auto insurance. He had stepped onto the deck and was standing nearby, staring at her. When she left the house earlier, she had switched on the overhead light and pulled the chain to activate the fan. That meant he could see her clearly, but she could only sense his lurking presence.

Obviously Derek wanted something from her, but Kim didn't have any intention of granting it—no matter what it was.

Who did he think he was, anyway, expecting her to acknowledge him? She knew who he was—that stranger in the shadows. He was a liar. Cheat. Gambler. Addict. Manipulator. He was selfish and egotistic. A user. A traitor. A con artist. Indifferent to religion. Unable to express emotion. Hopeless at communication. He was everything she despised and abhorred.

Trembling with anger at the thought of the man she had so foolishly married, Kim tore off the check and stuffed it into the envelope. She could hear Derek's footsteps on the deck. Moving closer, edging toward her. It didn't matter to her if he stood there all night. He might speak, but she wouldn't answer. She couldn't trust anything he would say. He was a liar.

Liar, liar, liar.

She picked up the next bill. Electricity. With the twins and Miranda home all summer, the amount was sky-high. Now she understood that all the money she and Derek earned went to pay bills and to his mother. Not a penny of it became their own. She had trusted her husband when he promised he would add what little was left each month to a savings account he had started when he lived in St. Louis. Little did she know it had instead gone into repaying Miranda for bailing him out of his gambling debts.

Now he was opening the door and stepping into the small screened area where she sat. She didn't look up.

"Hey there," he said.

Kim began to write another check. It was easier this way. Living with him in silence. Not even bothering to try to talk. She had wasted so much energy trying to plumb her husband's emotional depths—only to learn he was nothing more than a stagnant pond.

Derek pulled out one of the green metal chairs that surrounded the table. Sitting down, he let out a deep sigh. At least she didn't have to smell beer on his breath. With Joe, she'd had that constant issue to manage. Of course, Kim knew that no addiction could be managed by anyone but the addict. She had discovered that long ago in her childhood.

Clearing his throat, Derek folded his hands and set them on the table. Then he spoke. "What's wrong, Kim, honey?"

She looked up at him. "*What's wrong? Did you just ask me what's wrong?*"

"Yes," he confirmed in a voice that was barely audible. His eyes met hers. "That's what I said. What's wrong, Kim, honey?"

For a moment, she almost couldn't breathe as the rage rose inside her, bubbled up to the top of her throat, stung the insides of her nostrils, blistered like steam in her ears. The man was an idiot! A total idiot! This college-educated, ten-year veteran of the state Water Patrol was a complete idiot!

"Well," she said evenly. "Let's see. Hmmm. It's so hard to choose just one thing."

He leaned forward. "Okay. I understand that."

"Really? Amazing." She could hear the sarcasm dripping from her words, but she had no idea if her lamebrain husband had the ability to decipher verbal intonations.

Still staring at her, Derek nodded. She hardly knew what to make of it. He was actually looking right at her. Usually he stared at the television. At the kids or his mother. At the lake, a tree, a soaring bird. Or at the message screen on his cell phone. Now he was gazing directly at her.

"You want to know what's wrong," she stated. It wasn't a question. Just a repetition of his words to make sure she'd heard him right. "You want to know what's wrong with me."

"Yes," he repeated, nodding. His eyes were still focused on her face, and he wasn't moving even a finger.

Kim leaned back in her chair. "Why not begin with your gambling confession?" she asked airily. "Unless that was just a bad dream I had."

"It wasn't."

She straightened and pointed a finger at him. "You, Derek Finley, are a liar. The worst kind of liar—habitual and deliberate. You kept the truth from me. When you put a lie into a relationship, I don't think we call that a relationship anymore."

"You're right. I lied to you."

"You never once mentioned that you had a gambling addiction and were deeply in debt."

"You're right. I kept that from you."

"You never said you were sending all our savings to your mother."

"No, Kim, I didn't."

"You never told me that Miranda held power over you by keeping you on a leash like a little puppy. You're not the brave, strong, wonderful man I thought I'd married. You're nothing but a puppet. A mama's boy."

She could see him swallow, and she knew her angry words had hit home. At any moment, he would strike back. He would argue with her, tell her she was wrong, rationalize everything. Or maybe he would hit her, like Joe had done. She was ready for that. She could take it.

Derek knotted his fingers together, squeezing them so hard that the blood stopped and his knuckles turned white. "You . . . feel . . . betrayed by me," he said slowly. "You took a brave step in remarrying, and now you think it was a mistake."

"*You* were the mistake," she said, jabbing her index finger at him. "You, you, you. Don't you get it? I'm repeating my own mistakes over and over again! I'm as big an idiot as you are. In fact, I'm a gambler, too. I took a foolish risk, and I never should have done that. I knew the Bible warned against marrying a nonbeliever, but I thought you were so different and amazing. I thought it wouldn't matter. But I was wrong. Your character is flawed. And so is mine. We're just a couple of stupid . . . dumb . . ."

Kim's eyes filled with tears as she continued. "We're both fools. We never should have married each other. I'm not the right kind of person to be a wife. I don't even know what it takes to make a good marriage. I have too much baggage. And now you're just one more filthy, damaged suitcase I have to lug around. Another mistake. Another terrible, awful blunder."

As the tears rolled down her cheeks, Kim pushed away her husband's reaching hands. No, she wouldn't let him comfort her. No compliments scattered like candy. No gentle hands soothing the pain. She deserved to hurt. She had given control of her life to God and then taken it back the moment she married Derek Finley.

"Kim," he was saying now, pressing his palms flat on his thighs.

"You're right. I am an addict and a liar. I wanted to marry you so much that I deceived you. I am flawed. And I'm powerless. I acknowledge those facts every time I step through the door at a GA meeting or fight the urge to hand over my money for a scratch-off lottery ticket. When I call you up and tell you I'm working late and then go to a meeting, I know I'm a liar. You're right to be angry with me."

Wiping her cheeks with her fingers, Kim sniffled. She couldn't believe he was admitting it. Staring at him through blurred vision, she felt she was seeing yet another side of this man she was determined to despise. Once he had been her knight in shining armor, her dream lover, her best friend. Then he had become her worst nightmare—so horribly fallen from the ivory pedestal on which she had placed him that she was sure he was broken to pieces. And now here he was . . . the broken man . . . crawling toward her . . . holding up the shards of himself. . . .

"How long?" she asked him. "How long have you been clean?"

"I got my eleven-year pin last month. Here. And here's my Combo Book." He took the pin and a yellow pamphlet from his hip pocket and dropped them onto the table. He chuckled without humor. "In Gamblers Anonymous, I'm what we call a 'trusted servant.' Like a sponsor for alcoholics. People phone me, and I help them get through a bad time. There's a guy right now I'm especially worried about. I'm afraid he might be getting in too deep, and I've been talking to him a lot."

"Is that who the mysterious phone calls have been from? Why couldn't you just tell me?"

Derek sighed. "I was afraid you would leave me. GA work takes a lot of patience, and most of us are fairly unrealistic, insecure, and immature. Despite all my years, I still fit the mold pretty well." He paused and looked at the floor. "I guess you've figured that out."

Kim set her fingertips on the well-worn booklet. He must have read it every day. It must have been with him constantly. How could she not have known? Was she blind?

"You told me your mother was your higher power," she whispered.

"I shouldn't have said that. I do acknowledge an authority outside myself—and it sure isn't my mom. Having her around makes it hard to keep things in perspective. She's convinced that forcing me to repay the debt keeps me clean. I've tried to explain, but she has no idea how GA works. She doesn't want to understand."

"Then who is your higher power?"

Derek shrugged. "Something bigger and stronger than I am. Someone. I don't know, Kim. I don't have a name for it."

She dropped her head on her arms. "Oh, why did I marry you? You're not even close to sharing my faith in God. Now here I am stuck with you and your mother. Both the same."

"My mother and I are *not* the—" As if suddenly aware of the vehemence in his voice, Derek cut himself off. He tightened his hands into fists again. "You feel like my mother and I are alike," he said. "And that makes you angry."

Kim sniffled, knowing her tears were dripping onto the utility bill. But she couldn't lift her head. "You know what's worse? The twins now love her. The other day they told me they're glad she's moved in with us permanently. I can't believe I'll have to put up with Miranda and her criticisms, her weird pizza, her tai chi, her incense. I'm faced with this wicked presence infecting me and my children for the rest of my life. Grandma Finley, spouting her phony spirituality and influencing the family in ways that terrify me. And you . . . you just sit there."

This time his exhaled breath was shaky. "Okay, I hear you," he whispered.

"What do you hear?" she fired back at him, lifting her head. "What do you even think I'm saying, Derek?"

He was quiet for a long moment. Kim was about to deride his silence when he spoke.

"You're saying you want a stronger, more influential male in the house. And you're right to expect that. I'm so used to my mother's ways that when she came here, I didn't see how she was affecting us. I didn't challenge her or stand up to her, because her presence felt normal to me, and I hoped the trouble with you would blow over. But I don't want her to dominate our family. I don't want her manipulating anyone—especially you or the kids. Or me." He stood suddenly, scraping back the chair. "And I don't want her bizarre . . ."

Before he could finish his own sentence, Derek turned and pushed through the screen door, slamming it against the side of the house. He strode onto the deck and wrenched his mother's small wooden altar from the corner under the eave where she had nailed it.

Half frightened and half in shock, Kim hurried after her husband as he snatched up Miranda's CD player, her incense burner, and her little statuettes. Cradling those objects in one arm, he reared back like a baseball pitcher and hurled the altar off the deck. The CD player and incense burner went next. Finally the statues and other items sailed one by one through the moonlight into the darkness beyond the deck.

Kim leaned against the railing as she heard a series of splashes from the lake. Gripping the wood beam, she held her breath. What had just happened? What did this mean?

"There," Derek announced, dusting off his palms. His voice was almost jaunty when he spoke again. "Now, what else? What's wrong, Kim, honey? Can you tell me that?"

She searched her mind. Suddenly all the things she had piled up against him didn't seem so huge. The gambling, the bank account, the twins, the family rules, even Miranda . . . they were crumbling, fragmenting into grains of sand as her broken husband mended and stood tall again.

"Nothing," she managed to whisper.

"Then may I have your permission to spell out the list?"

"Yes."

"*Gambling*," he stated. "Can I tell you about that?"

"Of course. I wish you would."

"I have to go to GA meetings. So, from now on, I'll call and tell you what I'm doing, and then I'll go. I'm eleven years clean, and I don't expect to fall off the wagon. But GA is a part of my world, and I should have shared it with you. I'll try to start doing that."

"Okay."

"*Debt*. There's no way I can erase it. I made mistakes, and now I have to pay for them—literally. But I promise I'll stop putting your money toward paying it down. Maybe one day we'll inherit my mother's estate, but until then—"

"Use my money too, Derek," she said suddenly. "If we can let this be a decision we make together, I won't mind."

He eyed her for a moment. Then he nodded. "*Church*," he said. "Another issue. From next Sunday forward, every time I'm working the late shift or have a free day, I'll go with you. In fact, I'll request Sundays off. I can't promise to be good at doing church. I won't say I know God the way you do. But . . . but I do believe He's here . . . and He . . ." Suddenly Derek laughed. "Well, come to think of it, He came through for me tonight when I couldn't think what else to do but pray."

"You prayed?"

Spreading his arms, Derek looked into Kim's eyes. "I love you, honey. I love you so much. I'm sorry I hurt you and lied to you. I don't have any excuses. Just know that I'll do my best . . . that I already am doing my best to be the man you want. The husband you deserve. Can you try to start trusting me again? Can you love me too? Even just a little?"

Before she knew it, Kim had slipped into her husband's embrace. His arms came around her, wrapping her tightly against him. She laid her cheek on his shoulder and let the tears fall. It wasn't perfect, this marriage they had cobbled together. She saw the flimsy construction of their hastily built foundation all too clearly now. So the cracks had begun to show. Would the walls cave in next? Would the roof collapse?

"What can *I* do, Derek?" she asked him as he rocked her gently. "How can I help make us better?"

He fell quiet, and she trailed her fingers up and down his spine as he considered her question. Finally, when he spoke, his voice was low and throaty. "You could let me out of my shining armor. I'm a lot better at patrolling Party Cove than slaying dragons."

Kim nearly said something about his mother, but she decided against it. She would forever remember those distant splashes in the night—the definite sounds of a dragon's death throes.

"You might go to a Gam-Anon meeting," he continued. "Gam-Anon is for families. Maybe if you met with other wives and husbands of gamblers, you could understand me a little better."

"Okay. I'll go. What else?"

"Try to accept our differences. Is it so bad that I'm a quiet man? that I don't have a lot to tell you about my work each day? that my inner thoughts aren't all that deep and profound? And isn't it okay that I like to show I love you by telling you how beautiful you are? My compliments aren't candy at a parade, Kim. They're the truth. Maybe I don't do loads of laundry or cook great meals to express my feelings. That's your way. My way is to say that I think you're the most wonderful, amazing, gorgeous creature on God's green earth. And I mean that."

"Oh, Derek," she said, feeling the heat rise in her cheeks. Then she spoke the words she had been pondering for months now. "How about a baby? Would that help us?"

To her surprise, he shook his head. "Let's wait, Kim. You know how much I want another child. But we need some time right here. With my mother, Luke's diabetes, this new honesty . . . we need to rebuild. I need to become a better fisherman."

"What does this have to do with fishing?" she asked, puzzled.

"Talk to Charlie Moore sometime. Maybe he'll let you in on the secret."

Kim tightened her arms around her husband's chest. "I'm in the mood for rebuilding," she told him. "Or fishing. Or whatever."

At that, she felt Derek's biceps suddenly tighten. "Whatever?" he asked.

"Sure," she murmured.

With a deep chuckle, he lowered his head and kissed her. "*Whatever* sounds *great* to me."

❊

As Patsy finished spraying Esther Moore's weekly set-and-style, she realized she did not have a good feeling about things in Deepwater Cove. Summer was winding to a close, and too many troublesome situations had been left hanging. Patsy wanted all her problems—and everyone else's—tied up with neat little bows. But that just wasn't happening.

The most recent meeting of the Tea Lovers' Club had confirmed that not a single woman had received a second letter from Cody Goss. Shortly after arriving in Kansas, he had written to nearly everyone in the neighborhood—with the exact same news in each letter. But that was it. Not another word. Patsy had considered asking Miranda Finley if she still had a phone number for Cody's aunt.

But the thought of Miranda brought up yet another issue. A big one. Derek's mother was no longer a happy camper at the Finley house. She had moved in. Permanently. To complicate matters, Derek had decided that if his mother was moving in, some other things were moving out. Permanently.

Charlie Moore had discovered one of those things washed up on the lakeshore a few mornings ago. He had taken the former altar home to Esther, who had placed the entire problem in Patsy's lap.

"Well, what do you think we should do?" Esther asked her for the fifteenth time that afternoon. "Should we return it? Or keep it? Or should we throw it away ourselves?"

Patsy covered one of Esther's ears and plastered a curlicue into place with megahold spray. She knew she'd hear no end of complaining if a single strand of that snowy halo wandered from its assigned position. A tornado could land on Esther Moore's head and not a hair would budge.

"The question is," Patsy said, "how did the thing end up in the lake? Are you positive Derek is the culprit? Or could it have been Kim?"

"Or maybe it was Jennifer Hansen," Esther suggested with a little gasp. "You recall how she and Miranda argued about religion a few weeks back? Maybe she crept over to the Finley house under cover of darkness and threw everything over the side of their deck. She referred to the statues as idols, you'll remember. At least, that's what Brenda told me when she related the whole argument. I wasn't a personal observer. Were you?"

"I heard the two of them discussing matters of faith," Patsy said. She used the end of a rat-tail comb to lift and define a few more of Esther's silver curls. "But I don't think that's the sort of thing Jennifer would do. She's such a sweet young woman."

"Oh, don't we know it? Every time I come in here, I see her staring down at me from those portraits Cody painted. That boy was in love, Patsy. I'm telling you, he was truly besotted. How could he just go off and leave us the way he did?"

Patsy gave the answer she had told herself over and over. "His aunt wanted him."

"I surely do miss him. In fact, I can see why Jennifer Hansen is so kind to him. He was a handsome fellow once we got him cleaned up. And he was learning so much with Brenda's help. Did you see how clear and perfect his penmanship was in those letters he wrote us? Not to mention what a fine young Christian man he turned out to be. Well, to tell you the truth, Patsy, I was halfway to loving that boy like a son."

"Cody had us all wrapped around his little finger; that's for sure." To keep from crying, Patsy turned her thoughts to the other problem weighing on her heart. Esther's use of the word *halfway* had reminded Patsy of her next-door neighbor in the strip of shops.

Pete Roberts had been back to church since their spat over the Fourth of July lawn chair incident, but he didn't seem to be one iota closer to the Lord than he'd ever been. He trudged to Bible study and worship service every Sunday morning, same as before. Then he and Patsy ate lunch at Aunt Mamie's Good Food, and that appeared to be all Pete cared to do. In fact, she had a sneaking suspicion that he had figured out a way to sleep with his eyes open during the sermon. One time he even let out a thunderous snore that startled everyone for two rows around them.

"I have to tell you that they did look like idols," Esther was saying as she preened in front of the mirror. Once Patsy finished with the do, Esther liked to take a hand mirror and check all the way around to the back to make sure each curl was cemented into position.

"During the party for Cody and the twins, I went over and took a closer look," she continued, poking a finger at a stray wisp near her neck. "You know, the big one was made out of brass. But she also had a clay one, some pink silk flowers, a few sticks of incense, and some other things. The altar floated in and got caught on a piece of driftwood near the shore. Charlie thinks the brass statue is ten feet underwater, but we both saw it at the party. Which reminds me of Cody all over again. Oh, Patsy, how are we going to get that boy out of our hearts?"

"Do we have a choice, Esther?"

The older woman stood from the chair and removed the cape from her shoulders. "I do try to count my blessings, but right now, it's all I can do to think of any. I guess we have the Labor Day barbecue to look forward to. And we can be grateful that young Luke is doing so much better managing his diabetes. I don't suppose we'll have another crisis like we did on the Fourth of July. I guess you heard that Ashley Hanes is going to have a necklace sale at the next event. That was Miranda's idea, of course. She's behind most of the strategy for selling Ashley's beadwork. Or she was until her little religious items ended up in the lake. Charlie says he never sees her out on the deck doing her exercises, and you know how Charlie keeps an eye on things in the neighborhood."

"Yes, I certainly do," Patsy said. She led Esther toward the cash register. "I hope Miranda is happy there at home despite losing her spiritual doodads. You know how one person's mood can affect everyone else. When my mother had Alzheimer's, sometimes it was all I could do to keep my spirits up."

"Bless your heart, sweetie pie. You did have a rough time taking care of her, didn't you? Well, you're on your own now, though I don't know for how long. You and Pete look awfully cozy together on Sunday mornings."

"We're just friends," Patsy said.

"Sure you are." Esther gave a coy smile as she patted the back of her hair. "Oh, honey, nothing would make me happier than to see you get married. You have the biggest, best heart in all Missouri. And if Pete can win it, I say good for him!"

Patsy slipped Esther's usual tip into her pocket and walked with her to the door. "I don't think Pete is trying to win my heart," she said. "And I'm not at all confident that Miranda is doing the Finley family much good. But you know what upsets me the most?"

Esther nodded. "Yes, I do."

At the same moment, the women hugged and whispered the word in each other's ear.

"Cody."

CHAPTER SEVENTEEN

Kim placed a pitcher of lemonade and two ice-filled glasses on a tray. She reached into the cookie jar and set a couple of vanilla wafers on a plate for good measure. Through the sliding glass door, she could see Miranda sunning herself on the deck.

Feeling like she was headed for the execution block, Kim lifted the tray and started toward the deck. The twins had gone boating with their stepfather that afternoon—a plot Kim and Derek had concocted together—and now it was time to do the dreaded deed. Ever since the night they had discussed their problems, Kim and Derek had felt better about their marriage. Not perfect, but better. At least they were speaking as they tried to work out the issues that had come between them.

Miranda, on the other hand, had not taken the loss of her altar lightly. In fact, she was furious. She had stopped speaking to all of them and refused to leave her bedroom except for her daily sunbathing sessions.

So it was now or never.

Tray balanced on one arm, Kim opened the sliding glass door

with her free hand and stepped onto the deck. While speaking with Charlie Moore the past Sunday after church, Kim had learned the significance of Derek's "fishing" system. But in her mind, the technique could be boiled down to the simple word *listening*. She actually did it all the time.

Kim believed that most women were pretty good at paying attention. Of course, she knew there was going to be one hard part—keeping her own mouth shut. That wouldn't be easy, especially if Miranda began to criticize her. But Kim had promised Derek she would try fishing for her mother-in-law's acceptance.

"I brought us a pitcher of lemonade," Kim began, setting the tray on a small, glass-topped table between the two reclining deck chairs. "Derek just phoned to say they'll be home in about an hour. Luke has caught three crappie, and Lydia hooked into a catfish that nearly pulled her overboard."

Eyes closed, Miranda continued basking in utter silence.

Kim sat down, stretched out on the deck chair, and tried to imagine enduring the humidity for more than a few minutes. She poured lemonade into the glasses and offered one to her mother-in-law. "Something cold to drink, Miranda?"

Not a word of response.

Kim set the glass down on the tray again and took a sip of her own drink. The lake was quiet today, glassy and bright, a green-gray color that reminded her of polished steel. Not a single bird flew in the cloudless sky. Even the trees seemed exhausted by the heat, their leaves withered at the edges and their branches saggy.

Recalling Derek's repeated insistence that Kim begin her fishing session by using the right "bait," she moistened her lips. Then she spoke the words her husband had told her to say. "What's wrong, Miranda?"

No answer.

"Miranda? What's bothering you?"

Nothing.

Forget that kind of bait, Kim thought. She already knew what was wrong. Miranda had made her feelings abundantly clear the other night. Kim decided that what might be best was a guaranteed "fishing" technique she liked to use in Dr. Groene's office to locate the exact source of a problem. When a patient came in complaining about something aching and sore—jaw, tooth, gum, lip, tongue, even throat—she listened carefully. Then she repeated exactly what she believed the person had told her.

She was often wrong.

When people were in pain, Kim had learned, they mumbled and fumbled, pointed here and there, tried to describe the indescribable. Often they babbled about things that weren't important—like where they had been when the trouble started, or how their cousin had diagnosed the problem as something he'd had years ago. It took lots of back and forth, with Kim doing her own poking, rephrasing, and echoing her patient's words, before the real problem finally came to light.

Maybe Miranda's pain and anger would emerge the same way. Kim took another sip of lemonade and cast out her own form of bait.

"Miranda, I can understand why you're upset about Derek throwing your altar into the lake," she began, reciting almost verbatim the words her mother-in-law had used a few days ago after she discovered the items missing. "You believe he did it because he was trying to please me."

Miranda finally responded, her tone icy. "Well? Am I wrong?"

Kim decided not to answer. Instead, she kept repeating her mother-in-law's own words. "I realize you think that no one in the family cares about you or is sensitive to your individuality. You believe we don't appreciate what you've done for us, and we take you for granted."

"That's exactly right," Miranda snapped. Eyes still closed, she reached for her sunglasses and slipped them on. "I might as well be a cockroach the way you treat me."

Stung, Kim thought of all the meals she had cooked, all the laundry she had done, all the times she had purposely included Miranda in family activities—not only trying to make her feel welcome and comfortable but actually providing for the ungrateful woman's basic needs. How dare Miranda say they treated her like a cockroach? That was ridiculous!

Fighting the urge to lash out or retreat into the air-conditioned house, Kim took another long drink of her cold lemonade.

"I see that you really believe we resent your presence in the house," she said. "You must think that Derek's decision to throw away your religious items is evidence of that."

"It most certainly is!" Miranda barked. "My son is an intelligent man, and he knew very well how much those things meant to me. That altar was my place to meditate and reflect on my life. It was the only way I had found to reach out and touch my inner divinity."

"Your soul?" Kim queried, hoping she had chosen the right word.

"Well, that shows just how much you understand! The soul is a Christian concept—something that lets you believe in an afterlife instead of reincarnation. The spirit of divinity, the essence of the Creator, a spark of holiness lies within every thing and every person in this world. My collection of crystals and my dream catcher were ways to receive and conserve that celestial energy. Now the box where I kept my most precious crystals is at the bottom of the lake. Buddha and my other images helped me to meditate on the things they stood for and the truths they taught. Now they're in the lake too. You think it's all about Jesus, Jesus, Jesus, but let me assure you that your narrow-mindedness keeps you from the self-actualization and self-completion available to you through other spiritual paths."

Though Kim was trying her best to hear Miranda out, she couldn't come anywhere near agreement. Countless arguments filtered through her mind. But Kim knew that if she was ever to gain her mother-in-law's trust, she had to begin with a relationship of mutual respect. Shouting their opposing beliefs back and forth at each other would get them nowhere. So Kim swallowed hard and cast out her fishing line one more time.

"I can see how hurt you are," she said as gently as she could. "Some of the things we've said have really wounded you. What Derek did the other night must have felt as though your own son had purposely injured you."

To Kim's surprise, she noticed that Miranda's lower lip was trembling. It wasn't much of a sign, but it showed that Kim's words had found their mark. And maybe, just maybe, she was close to hooking and reeling in the object of this fishing expedition: her mother-in-law's acceptance.

"Miranda, may I please tell you how sorry I am?" Kim murmured. "You came here at a time when Derek and I had run out of options, and you've done a great job with the twins. I apologize that you haven't felt our appreciation."

"No, I definitely have not."

"And you're right to be upset about what Derek did the other night. He shouldn't have thrown away your possessions. If I can explain . . ." Kim paused and took a deep breath. "You see, just a few days ago, Derek finally told me about his problems from the past. I had no idea he belonged to Gamblers Anonymous or that he owed you such a large sum of money. We've been trying to work our way through that issue, and during an intense moment, he reacted strongly. I bear as much of the blame as he does, because I didn't stop him. I should have. I wouldn't want my Bible thrown into the lake, and I ought to have considered how you would feel. Please forgive me, Miranda. And the twins, too. We've been insensitive. I know Derek would say the same thing if he were here."

When she had finished speaking, Kim leaned back in her chair and pressed the cool glass of lemonade to her cheeks and forehead. This had been an awful experience, she realized. She had hurt Miranda, and her words hadn't helped the situation a bit. She ought to just go inside and start fixing dinner. Maybe something would eventually come of the effort she had made, but clearly her mother-in-law had lapsed into angry silence again.

As Kim prepared to stand, she glanced at Miranda. And that's when she realized the trickle running down the woman's bronze cheek wasn't perspiration. It was a tear.

"I didn't want to come, you know," Miranda said in a quavering voice. "When Derek told me about Luke, I didn't even consider doing anything about it. I felt sorry for him, of course, but he wasn't my *real* grandson, and I didn't believe that I had any responsibility toward him. But then I thought about it some more—about how deeply Luke's diagnosis had distressed Derek and how hard my poor son was having to work to make ends meet and how you might have to quit your job to take care of Luke—which would put an even greater burden on Derek. So one day I called and offered to help. I expected to stay only a couple of weeks. At the most I would be here until school started. But then . . . then Luke and Lydia became . . . they somehow became important to me. I enjoyed shopping with Lydia. Since I'd never had a daughter, I didn't know what to expect of her. But we've had so much fun together. And Luke, well, he's such a sweet little guy. When he had that crisis on the Fourth of July . . ."

At this, Miranda stopped speaking and began to sob softly. Kim stared at the sleek, suntanned creature in her white bikini. For a moment, she simply couldn't reconcile her image of Miranda—that vile, heathenish dragon worthy of nothing better than to be slain with the sword of truth—with this weeping, tenderhearted woman.

Before Kim could speak, Miranda held up a hand and continued. "I realized that I truly love those two children. I enjoy being a part of a family again too. It's been so many years since Eric died. And since Derek left me. I sincerely believed I was helping my son's family. I tried to offer ideas for improving things around the house and making life easier. I brought in bouquets of roses, because I know every home needs fresh flowers, and you certainly don't have the time or the interest to decorate things properly. I tried to introduce new foods—like my spinach-Parmesan pizza and my seven-layer dip. I even thought of suggesting a different curtain fabric to bring harmony into the living area and make it more comforting for all of us. But everything I offered was rejected. Thrown back in my face, as though I'd done something terribly offensive."

By now Miranda was blotting her cheeks with her beach towel. Kim sat stone still, appalled at how her own behavior had so deeply hurt her mother-in-law. All this time, she had been looking at her children, her marriage, and her life from her own perspective. She had resented Miranda's presence and had made that obvious from the first day. Was that how a Christian was supposed to act? Would Jesus have done the same?

"You know, I gave up my friends," Miranda was saying now, gulping out the words between sobs, "and the country club and all the high-end stores I loved and the good restaurants. . . . Well, I gave up everything. I even put my house on the market. And then I found out that no one cares at all about my sacrifices. It's worse than that. . . . Not even my son . . . my beloved Derek . . . cares enough about me to respect my beliefs. I see now that I've lost everything, including my only child."

"Oh, Miranda—" Kim began to speak, but an upturned hand silenced her again.

"You think I'm cruel to keep him in my debt. I can see the resentment in your eyes. But you weren't there when he came home drunk and desperate and frightened for his life. You have no idea what I went through—trying to get him into treatment, pay off his creditors, keep him clean, get him through college. Do you know that your husband can't ever invest in the stock market? He can't buy commodities or options. He can never play the lottery. He shouldn't even flip a coin! You think I'm exaggerating, but I went to Gam-Anon meetings. For years I thought I had to keep him locked up or he'd fall right back into it. Do you see that? Do you get it at all?"

"I'm trying," Kim said. "But now?"

"Now I'm not sure. I'm just getting to know him all over again."

"I can understand that."

"I know how deeply I'm resented here," Miranda said. "But I want you to realize that I've done my best to become a part of this community. I helped Cody find his aunt, and I joined the TLC in planning the Fourth of July barbecue, and I've even started a little business to sell Ashley Hanes's beadwork. Luke helped me on the computer, and we made business cards and order forms. Lydia and I bought sample boxes for the beads. I've contacted my friends in St. Louis, and they're buying necklaces left and right. But does anyone in this family really notice me or think I matter? No, it's all been for nothing. No one cares about me. No one loves me or values me. You might as well just throw *me* into the lake."

At the very image that Kim had repeatedly—and gleefully—envisioned, she felt her own tears well. She couldn't deny that everything Miranda said or thought seemed to be about herself, but what woman hadn't indulged in a pity party now and then?

Without hesitation, she slipped out of her chair, knelt on the deck, and slid her arms around Miranda's shoulders. "No one wants you to be thrown into the lake," she said, resting her cheek against her mother-in-law's damp hair for a moment before drawing back.

"Despite what you think, Miranda, we do love you," Kim insisted. "The twins adore you, and they're excited that you want to stay permanently. Derek told me he feels so comfortable around you that he hardly even noticed when you moved in. I realize that you and I have had conflict, but I want to try to change that. I had a difficult childhood and a bad first marriage. It takes me a while to get relationships right, Miranda. But I love your son so much, and I love his mother, too. Can you ever find a way to accept me?"

Taking off her sunglasses, Miranda wiped at her eyes again and took the first sip from her lemonade. "Well," she said, sniffling a little, "when you put it that way, I suppose I can try, too. After all, Derek isn't about to part with you. He's made that clear to me again and again. And I do love the twins. I suppose . . . yes, I suppose you and I should try to do better. For Derek's sake. And the children's."

"Good," Kim said, standing. "We'll make this afternoon our new beginning. Now, if you want some more lemonade, just let me know. I'll be in the kitchen fixing dinner."

She started for the sliding glass door, but in its reflection, she saw her mother-in-law rise from the chair.

"Kim?" Miranda called. She crossed the deck, extended her arms, and drew Kim into a damp embrace. "I do accept you, dear. And I think we're all going to be just fine."

❊

"She's at it again," Charlie observed. "Didn't I tell you?"

Esther nodded. "You were right, sweetie. I never should have doubted you."

Charlie and Esther were sitting on the front porch stringing beads onto clear monofilament. As it turned out, Ashley Hanes's necklace business had taken off like a rocket out of Cape Canaveral, and the next thing Charlie knew, he had been commissioned as an official beader.

This was not his idea of a good time. For one thing, his eyes had trouble focusing on the tiny hole through each bead. For another, his slightly arthritic fingers didn't particularly like working the line through that little bitty opening.

Oh, Charlie was plenty good with his hands—as long as the work involved running a circular saw, a router, a plane, or a drill. He could build just about anything he set his mind to, and the finely crafted shed out back of the house proved he not only knew his tools, but he was skilled at almost any kind of construction. This business of beading necklaces, though, felt too much like woman's work.

On the other hand, creating jewelry for Ashley helped fill the daylight hours, and it afforded the opportunity to sit outside and view the comings and goings in the neighborhood. This afternoon, Boofer lay sprawled at Charlie's feet while Esther sorted the beads into rows on the table at her husband's side. To her dismay, Esther had discovered that beading was not her cup of tea. She couldn't see through her trifocals well enough to thread the necklaces, and sometimes she got the colors mixed up. This meant that unless Charlie was paying close attention, he often had to start a project all over again.

"I wonder what she's using these days," Esther said. "Do you suppose she went out and bought some more?"

Sometimes they spoke this way, Charlie and Esther. It was a kind of code they had developed over the years. From his short, grunted comments, Esther knew right away that her husband had spotted Miranda Finley doing exercises on the deck. And from Esther's mishmash of a question, Charlie knew his wife was asking about the tools of Miranda's religious rituals—an altar and some rocks and statues.

"I guess she could have driven down to Springfield and bought another Buddha or two. You've gone over to orange, honeybunch, and we're still working on red. The polka-dot ones."

"Oh, for pete's sake." Esther picked up the orange beads and put them back into their compartment. "These necklaces are driving me batty. I wouldn't have joined Miranda's project, but I know it's to help keep Ashley from having to take on a second job. I'm just wondering if she will ever have that baby she wants, poor thing. I keep studying her stomach, but there's no sign of a pooch at all."

"Flat as a pancake."

"You shouldn't be looking at a woman's midriff, Charlie Moore."

"She wears those skimpy tops. What's a man supposed to do?"

Esther shook her head. "That nursery of theirs isn't coming along too well either. Last time I went over to visit Ashley, I noticed an electric saw sitting smack-dab in the middle of their living room. There's a lot of construction mess lying around in the yard too. Brad should pick up the wood he bought before the termites get it. Did you notice that the house for sale next to the Haneses' hasn't had any lookers in a while?"

"Oh, that house had a looker all right. I saw Miranda over there the other day. She was peeking in the windows, trying the doorknobs, and tromping around on the porch testing the floorboards."

"Really! Now that's interesting news. I wonder if she's thinking of buying it." Suddenly Esther let out a groan of frustration. "Are we doing orange or red, sugar bear? I can't keep it straight."

"Red. With polka dots."

"Who would wear a necklace with red polka-dot beads anyhow?"

"Some lady in St. Louis."

They worked awhile in silence.

"I think we've about got the Labor Day barbecue in order," Esther said. "Nobody liked my parade idea."

"You told me."

"Did I? Anyhow, the reaction of the TLC sure surprised me; I can tell you that. I always wanted to be in a parade. But no one in the neighborhood would give my idea the time of day. Jennifer Hansen would have made a lovely Deepwater Cove queen; don't you think?"

"I don't reckon missionaries can be beauty queens, sweet pea. How about if you dress up in that old formal of yours, and I'll wheel you around the cove in my golf cart a couple of times?"

Esther laughed—the tinkling, airy sound that Charlie had fallen in love with so many years ago. She looked at him and smiled. "I couldn't fit into that formal with a shoehorn. But it's sure pretty—all that orchid organza. I know I ought to give it to some lovely younger lady, but for the life of me, I just can't part with it."

As Charlie recalled, the gown had so much prickly netting and stiff lace that he'd barely been able to get close to Esther on the night of their high school prom—a situation that had frustrated him no end. In fact, he didn't think he'd even managed to win himself a kiss. Too many petticoats. The dress was up in the attic somewhere, probably eaten up by moths, but in Esther's mind it was still a confection worthy of a queen.

"Are we doing orange beads, honey?" Esther asked. "Or pink? I can't keep it straight."

"Red," he said, watching Miranda Finley finish her exercises, slip a robe over her white bathing suit, and leave the deck for the evening. "With polka dots."

"Oh, good gravy, of course," Esther said. "How could I forget that?"

CHAPTER EIGHTEEN

Kim was so ready to go home for the Labor Day weekend that she could hardly bear to wait another minute. With her husband and mother-in-law joining her in a supreme effort to be cooperative and friendly, the Finley household was happier than it had been in months. In anticipation of the neighborhood barbecue, Derek had bought enough hot dogs to feed two armies, and Miranda was making her special macaroni-and-tofu confetti salad. The whole family had ordered Kim not to do a single thing except relax, rest, and enjoy the time off. Derek had been right that his wife expressed her love best by serving those she cared about most deeply. Still, Kim couldn't deny that the idea of putting her feet up for an entire weekend seemed positively magical.

But the last week in August wasn't over yet, and Kim pulled on her gloves in preparation for the final patient of the day.

"You're givin' me gas, Miz Kim. Ain't that right?"

A tooth extraction on a mouth like Abe Fugal's wouldn't be fun on a Friday afternoon, but there was no way around it. It would really go more easily with the patient unconscious, but Mr. Fugal had come alone to his appointment and didn't have anyone to drive him home.

"Are you sure you want gas, Mr. Fugal?" Kim asked, laying a hand on his shoulder. "Dr. Groene can numb the area without it, but if you'd prefer—"

"I don't want no needles comin' my direction! Not in my mouth nor anywhere near it. I know the doc means well, but the thought of him lungin' at me with one of them syringes gives me the heebie-jeebies."

"We can administer some gas to help you relax, but I'm afraid Dr. Groene is going to have to deaden that nerve before he pulls the tooth."

"Aw, rats. That just burns my toast. I'm sixty-two years old and never been to a doctor once in my whole life. I was born at home, and I never set foot in a hospital except for the time my wife took sick. Cancer, you know. She had to have something for the pain, right until the end. But me, I'm healthy as a horse. I never took no drugs. Not even an aspirin. And here you go wanting to let the doc put a needle in my gums."

Kim patted her patient on the shoulder.

"All right, start up the gas, honey," Abe said. "Hit me good before the doc gets in here with his needle. I don't want no part of that thing!"

Kim smiled as she prepared the small mask that would cover Abe's nostrils. "Breathe through your nose, and you'll start to calm down. When Dr. Groene comes in, I'll tell you to shut your eyes. I bet you won't even know what he's doing."

"Okay, I believe you, but only because you're so purty. Put it on me now, and crank up the knob as far as you can. Get me through this, Miz Kim, and I'll love you till the end of time."

"Please tell me if you start to feel the least bit dizzy," Kim urged him gently as he began to inhale the gas. "We don't want you getting nauseous, Mr. Fugal. If the room starts to spin, squeeze my hand." She slipped her palm over the gnarled fingers.

Abe tightened his hand around hers. Closing his eyes, he breathed in deeply. "I think you're the sweetest young thing I ever saw," he murmured.

"Thank you, Mr. Fugal." Kim was accustomed to the slightly silly, sometimes emotional expressions the dental gas unleashed. She had dealt with giggly patients, groggy patients, weeping patients, and those who professed their undying and eternal love for Ben Groene even as he drilled straight into a cavity.

"How are you feeling now, Mr. Fugal?" she asked after Abe had been lying in silence for a few moments. "Are you dizzy at all?"

"Naw, I'm just a-layin' here thinkin' about my gal. My darlin'. Her and me sure had some good times together."

"I bet you did." As Kim adjusted the dial on the gas, she pictured Abe's darling as the wife who had passed away from cancer some years before. As Dr. Groene's assistant, she had often listened to patients who wanted to share their memories.

"I can't believe she's gone," Abe told her mournfully. "Gone, just like that. Without even a word of farewell. She hollered, 'Hep! . . . Hep me, Abe,' and that was it. I tried. I done all I could to fetch her back onto the dock, but no sooner did I reach out for her, and she was gone."

"The dock?" Kim asked. A prickle ran up her spine and lifted the hair on the back of her neck. "Your wife fell off a dock? When was this?"

A tear trickled down Abe's cheek. "Not my wife. My darlin' June bug. Weren't but a couple months ago. We was havin' ourselves a little party, you know. Just a beer or two. Catchin' some fish off the dock by our trailer. And then I went back inside to fetch us another twelve-pack. It was a party, like I said. My little June bug and me used to party thataway nearly ever night."

Kim swallowed as Dr. Groene stepped into the cubicle. Against all she had been taught about keeping the patient comfortable, moving ahead with procedures, warding off unforeseen problems, she held her index finger to her lip. Pointing at Abe Fugal, she shook her head fervently at Dr. Groene.

He frowned and took a step closer.

"Abe, how did June fall off the dock?" Kim asked, making frantic, senseless gestures at Dr. Groene.

"Awww . . . she was leanin' over to pull our basket of fish out of the water, and in she went. Headfirst. She come up a-hollerin'. She yelled out that she'd got herself tangled up in fishin' line and couldn't move her arms. The line must've been driftin' around underwater—you know how it does when you hook your lure onto a snag that snaps it right off the rod? All that flailin' around probably knotted June up, and she wasn't able to get free. I could hear her yellin', but I couldn't hardly see her no more. It was dark by that time, you know. The lake was nothin' but a big black hole. And it just swallowed up my darlin' June bug quick as a wink. She never was a strong swimmer, and with the fishin' line . . . aw, rats, I hate to think about that. I can't hardly bear it."

"Kim?" Dr. Groene asked, his brow furrowed. "What's going on here?"

Without thinking twice, Kim began to turn down the gas. "Mr. Fugal," she said, "I'm bringing you back."

"Are we done?" His rheumy eyes blinked. "Hey, you was right, Miz Kim! I didn't feel a thing. 'Cept my tooth sure does hurt. Oops, Doc, I think you missed your target. I can still feel that tooth right there where it always was."

"We haven't done the extraction yet, Mr. Fugal," Kim explained as she leaned in to where he could see her face. "I need to talk to Dr. Groene for a minute. You were telling me about June, and I don't want you to keep talking until I'm sure how to proceed."

"Aw, shucks." Abe shook his head. "You turned off that gas, didn't you?"

"Yes. You should be able to think more clearly now."

"Clear as I ever could," he said with a wry chuckle. "Which weren't much."

"Do you remember what you told me about June?"

His expression sobered. "Yeah, I do. I didn't come in here aimin' to talk about it, but you're so purty and sweet that I decided I might as well 'fess up."

"'Fess up to what?" Dr. Groene asked. "Abe, what have you been telling Mrs. Finley?"

"Well, I went ahead and told her about my sweet lil' June bug fallin' into the lake that night after we'd been partyin'."

"Are you talking about the woman who used to come with you to your appointments? I met her once or twice."

"Yep, you did. June done most of our drivin', bein' as I'd lost my license a while back on account of too many DWI tickets. I was in so much pain with that tooth that June convinced me to let you have a look at my chompers."

"I didn't realize she had passed away."

Kim spoke up. "Dr. Groene or I might have wanted to go to the funeral, Mr. Fugal. When was it?"

The corners of Abe's mouth turned down. "It weren't."

"You had a memorial service for her?" Dr. Groene asked.

"Naw. I decided not to spill the beans. Didn't tell nobody June was gone, because . . . well, if you want to know the truth, I didn't have the guts. See, we'd been drinkin' and maybe doin' a few other things we shouldn't of that night—if you catch my drift. I didn't want to get neither of us into trouble. Besides, she don't have no family other than me, and *we* wasn't even married."

"So . . . she drowned?" Dr. Groene asked.

"Didn't you hear about it on the TV? It was on the news for a while after they found her. They couldn't figure out who she was, but I knew. I knew it was poor June."

"I think it would have been better if you'd reported this to the authorities, Abe," Dr. Groene told him.

"Maybe so, but my daddy used to say, 'Dead is dead.' I figured that's the way it was with my darlin' June bug, and not a thing I could do about it. Like I told you, I was flat-out scared to own up to what had happened that night, because of the drinkin' and so forth. June used to watch them detective shows on TV, and these days they can pretty much tell whatever you've been doin' or even might have did a long time ago. Not to mention that I been in the clink a time or two already, and there's somewhat of a record on my name over to the police station."

"I need to call my husband," Kim said quietly.

"Use my office," Dr. Groene said. "Abe, since you've told Mrs. Finley and me about June already, I guess you're willing to tell the police what happened now, aren't you?"

"I know I should. Yeah, I'll do it. They'll probably lock me up and throw away the key for the rest of my life. I reckon I deserve it too."

"I doubt they'll be that harsh under the circumstances."

"Well, like I said—I've done time before, so I know I can bear it. In fact, I'm glad I told you the truth. The grief was about to kill me."

Walking toward the dentist's private office, Kim could hear the two men continue to talk as she keyed in Derek's number. He would still be out on the water, but she knew it wouldn't take him long to get to Dr. Groene's office.

"Hey, beautiful," Derek said when he answered. "Is Dr. Groene letting you off early today? I was hoping—"

"Derek," Kim cut in, almost breathless with excitement. "I'm still at work. You have to get here right away."

"What's wrong, honey? Is this is an emergency?"

"No, but it's urgent. Derek, I need your help. I don't know what to do. One of our patients is here—Abe Fugal—and he confessed something to me while he was being sedated. I turned off the gas as quickly as I could, and I think he's still willing to talk about it."

"What did he tell you, Kim?"

"He was with a woman the night she fell off a dock. He knows she died, because he saw reports about it on the news. But he never told anyone what had happened, and there was no funeral or memorial service. Derek, I don't think anyone else knows about this woman's death."

"Are you telling me the man didn't report a possible drowning?"

"That's right. They had been drinking all evening. He said she was reaching off the dock for a basket of fish when she tumbled into the water. He told me that she wasn't a good swimmer, and she yelled out that she had gotten tangled in fishing line. He tried to reach out for her, but he couldn't find her in the dark. Then he lost sight of her. He thinks she drowned."

"I'm on my way," he said. "I'll be there in fifteen minutes. Calling the police to put a stop-and-hold until I can get to you. Stay with me, Kim."

A moment later, Derek's voice became muffled as he spoke by radio first to municipal authorities and then to the Water Patrol dispatcher in Jefferson City. Kim heard him give his badge number and then say, "Jeff, I'll be off the water . . . 10-6 at the dental office of Dr. Ben Groene on Highway 5, Camdenton."

He returned to the cell phone. "Honey, are you in any danger that you know of?"

"I'm sure Mr. Fugal is harmless. He can barely see, and only one of his hands works right. But please hurry, Derek. He may change his mind and try to leave. He told us he does have a criminal record."

"Can you get me his date of birth, Kim?"

"No, his health data is confidential."

Derek spoke on the radio again. "The subject will be a possible 10-99 out of Camden County," he said, informing the office of the man's checkered past. "The name is Abe—as in Abraham—Fugal. No date of birth available. Can you run a 27, 28, and 29 on him?"

The dispatcher confirmed that Mr. Fugal's name would be checked for possible warrants as well as records on whether he might be dangerous. In moments, the dispatcher asked Derek, "Are you 10-12?"

Kim knew the code well enough to understand that Water Patrol wanted to know if he was already at the scene. That indicated they had turned up something suspicious in Mr. Fugal's documentation. Cell phone still pressed against her ear, she walked back down the hall and glanced into the cubicle to find that Dr. Groene and Abe Fugal were discussing baseball standings, particularly the St. Louis Cardinals and whether they had another shot at the World Series this year.

"Derek," Kim said as she stepped back into the hall, "I think this is it—the clue you've been looking for to identify the body you found at the start of summer. I think the woman who died lived with Abe Fugal in an old trailer around the bend not too far from Deepwater Cove. You know the one that lost part of its roof in last year's big storm? I'm pretty sure I know who she was. I used to see her here when she came in with Abe. Her name is June Bixby."

"June Bixby," he repeated. "Good. I'm on my way. Listen, I want you to know that when I get there, we may be separated. I'll need to work with the Major Case Squad, and I'm sure the police will want to question you. I doubt I'll make it home for dinner tonight."

"It's okay, Derek."

"Kim, you might not think the old guy is dangerous, but he does have a record. Be careful, honey. I don't want anything to happen to you."

"I'm fine," she murmured. "It's all right."

"I just want to make sure you know I love you. We've been through a lot lately, and I need to tell you—"

"Derek, I hear you. I understand what you're telling me." Kim paused. "And I love you, too."

CHAPTER NINETEEN

With a fair amount of trepidation, Patsy eyed the lawn chairs as she carried her plate of appetizers toward the group of men gathered near their grills. She spotted a sturdy plastic chaise lounge that would easily bear her ample figure, so she sat down on it and stretched out her legs.

"Hey, fellas," she said.

The men interrupted their discussion for a moment to greet her. "Hey, Patsy," they offered in a chorus of tenors and basses. Then they went back to talking.

It didn't bother Patsy that the men ignored her. On the Fourth of July, she'd drawn enough attention to last a lifetime. Not only had she endured that awful lawn chair collapse, but her slightly over-the-top patriotic outfit and star-spangled hairdo had only added to the spectacle.

For the Labor Day barbecue, Patsy had decided to go for a more sedate look with an autumn influence. She had returned her hair to the color closest to the one she remembered from childhood. Unfortunately, that particular hue might best be termed dishwater blonde or mousy brown or something in between. So Patsy had added a few golden highlights and then some auburn ones to brighten it up a bit.

As it was still hotter than blazes outside, she had chosen to wear a short-sleeved top with a taupe, brick red, and black leaf print. In order to give it a little more autumn flavor, she had pinned on a brooch that had belonged to her mother—a real maple leaf dipped in acrylic. Its lovely red-orange color perfectly matched the knee-length shorts Patsy wore. And the whole outfit coordinated well with the black platform sandals she had chosen from her closet.

She dipped a corn chip into the puddle of black bean salsa on her plate and chewed thoughtfully. Too bad Pete Roberts wasn't going to make it to the barbecue. He had decided to keep Rods-N-Ends open for the last of the summer gas-guzzlers passing through. She couldn't blame him. The end of the season meant a lull that nearly put the Lake of the Ozarks community to sleep. This was the time when the weakest businesses began failing left and right. Only the locals and a few off-and-on visitors kept stores and restaurants alive through the down season. Pete's first year had been rough, Patsy knew, but he thought he was going to make it.

Bitty Sondheim's Pop-In, however, appeared to be doomed. Two weeks ago, a Closed sign had appeared on the front door, and the inside of the little restaurant remained dark day and night. Patsy hadn't seen her neighbor in several days, so she was happy to spot the Californian with her long hair and swoopy, ankle-length skirts arriving at the barbecue. Bitty was in the parking area, and she seemed to be wrestling with something large in the back of her van.

"Hey, Brad," Patsy called, drawing the attention of Ashley Hanes's handsome young husband, who sat nearby. "How about you, Derek, and Steve helping Bitty out over there? Looks like she brought half her restaurant."

"Probably trying to unload her leftovers on us," Brad said. He glanced at his wife, who was selling beaded necklaces from a table set up under a tree. "Ashley keeps dragging me to the Pop-In. If I never eat another eggplant wrap it won't bother me a bit."

With that, he and several of the other men pushed themselves out of their lawn chairs, checked the pork steaks on their grills, and then lumbered over to see if they could carry anything for Bitty. Patsy had hardly had time to sample the pimento cheese–filled celery sticks on her plate before Brad was back, more animated than she'd ever seen him.

"Charlie!" he hollered. "Patsy! All you guys, come see what Bitty's done. You won't believe this!"

Not wanting to miss out on any excitement, Patsy scrambled to her feet and hurried across the lawn to the long foldout table where Bitty was opening boxes and spreading her wares. The bad news was that she looked close to tears as she set down rows of plates and began laying one or two parchment-wrapped packages on each. The good news was that Brad Hanes had tasted one of these wraps and was about to go berserk with joy.

"Chicken-fried steak!" he exclaimed, displaying the innards of the rolled item he'd just bitten into. "It's covered in mashed potatoes and gravy—with buttered Texas toast on the outside! And she grilled it! It's good. It's delicious. You gotta try one."

"Chicken-fried steak in a wrap?" Patsy murmured, picking up a plate.

"That's not all," Bitty said in a wounded, snippy voice. She pointed to one item after another. "Right here, you've got your batter-crusted catfish. It's coated in tartar sauce and covered with a deep-fried hush puppy batter. This one is your chicken wrap. It's a large fried-chicken tender, rolled in a mixture of mashed potatoes and green beans, and then covered with baked homemade dinner roll dough. And finally, here's your ham wrap. It's got a big chunk of canned pineapple on it, along with a thick layer of applesauce, and it's been baked inside a coating of corn bread dressing."

For a moment, the men stared at the plates in stunned silence.

"Where are the fajita wraps?" Derek asked. "I always enjoyed those."

"And what about that Greek salad wrap my wife liked so much?" Steve asked.

"Discontinued," Bitty said as the men began picking up the plates and biting into the strange-looking food. "Discontinued along with the eggplant wraps, the onion-and-feta-cheese wraps, the baked-lamb-and-hummus wraps, the avocado-and-shrimp wraps. In fact, all the wraps are discontinued. So are the omelets. And so is Bitty Sondheim's Pop-In."

"Now, just a minute," Patsy said. "You're not leaving us, are you, Bitty? You've hardly given us a fair shot. One summer isn't nearly enough time to let us get used to your California cooking."

"It's long enough for me." She looked from man to man. "My out-of-town visitors liked my food pretty well, but I've heard your comments. I've seen the faces you locals make when you read my menu. I know how you feel about my California wraps. So here!" She spread out her hands to indicate the array of food she had brought. "Here's your Missouri-hearty-homemade-just-like-Grandma's-deep-fried-heart-attack *junk*. You kept telling me you wanted chicken-fried steak and mashed potatoes, so here it is. Take all you want. It's on the house."

At that, Bitty burst into tears, turned on her heel, and headed for her van.

Dismayed, Patsy set off after her. "Now, Bitty," she called, regretting her high platform black sandals with every step. "Bitty, please wait. Don't leave us like this, honeybunch!"

"I'm going back to California where I belong. Missouri is just too weird for me."

"Missouri is weird?" Patsy caught up to Bitty, who was pushing boxes and baskets into the back of her van. "We're not weird, sweetie; we're just home folks. We've been doing the same old things for years. We eat what we've always eaten, and we pretty much wear what we've always worn. Change doesn't come easy to us, but it's not impossible.

Please don't run off, Bitty. Give us another chance. I was really beginning to like that humus."

"*Humus* is dirt enriched with cow manure!" Bitty wailed, turning on Patsy. Her voice rose as she spoke until she was practically screeching. "I was serving *hummus*! Hummus is a creamy puree of chickpeas and sesame seed paste seasoned with lemon juice and garlic! Everyone eats it in Greece and the Middle East! Hummus is served with bread for dipping or as a pita filling!"

"Well, all right," Patsy said, holding up both hands to try to calm Bitty. The last thing she needed was to make another big show. "Simmer down, now. I'm sorry; I didn't know the difference, Bitty. I'm sort of ignorant about these kinds of things. Most folks around here are—but that doesn't mean we can't be educated. If you'd put on your menu that you were serving chickpea paste, well . . . well—"

"You see? No one wants to eat my kind of food. You know who my best customer was? Miranda Finley—and that's because she's from St. Louis. She knows about international cuisine. She knows about healthy eating. She understands what I was trying to do. I thought I could come to the lake and set up a little restaurant and just live out the rest of my life right here where the cost of living is low and the pace is slow. But all my dreams are ruined. *I'm* ruined, Patsy! I put everything I had into the Pop-In!"

"Oh, Bitty, come here and let me give you a hug." As Patsy wrapped her arms around the woman, she suddenly realized that most of the men who'd been tending their grills were headed toward Bitty's van like soldiers on a mission. She swished her hand at them to try to ward them off, but they wouldn't be deterred.

"Bitty, we want to talk to you," Steve Hansen said. "These men have just voted me chairman of the Pop-In Revitalization Board."

Snuffling, Bitty lifted her head from Patsy's shoulder. "I already turned in my final rent check, Steve. I'm sorry to let you down, but I just couldn't make a go of it. You'll have to find a new tenant for the space."

"I'm going to have to prevent that," Derek Finley said, stepping forward and leading Bitty back toward the table, where a crowd had gathered to sample her new wraps. "I'm afraid I can't allow you to shut down the Pop-In, Bitty. We don't dare risk the riot that might cause."

"What?" she asked, her voice tremulous. "What do you mean?"

Now Brad Hanes spoke as he held up what was left inside his parchment paper. "We want you to stay open and keep making these Missouri-deep-fried-heart-attack wraps. They're delicious. I mean that. I could eat one for lunch and actually get full. I'm gonna have to go swimming just to work off the one I ate, so I can be ready when the pork steaks are done."

"But they're so . . . awful," Bitty said.

"Awful *good*," Brad declared. "If you'll keep the Pop-In open, Bitty, I'll tell the other guys I work with, and we'll be there every day. I ate the chicken-fried steak wrap, but I'm a big catfish man. Charlie told me his was fantastic."

"Don't ever let on to Esther," Charlie Moore said, leaning in close, "but that catfish wrap has her batter-fried crappie beat by a mile."

"Are you serious?" Bitty asked.

"Serious as a hearty-homemade-deep-fried heart attack!" Brad said with a laugh.

Everyone was still chuckling when Charlie suddenly elbowed Patsy. "Hey, who's that? Over yonder near the edge of the parking lot?"

Patsy's heart lurched as she searched the thick brush at the edge of the clearing. Emerging from the shadows came a tall, broad-shouldered man bearing a large box. For an instant, she thought by some miracle it might be Cody. But this was someone new. A good-looking stranger who must have noticed the gathering and decided to check it out.

"I had to park halfway to Tranquility," the man called as he sauntered toward Bitty's van. "'Course, that's pretty much to be expected, seeing as I'm from Halfway, Missouri."

At that, Patsy gasped so loudly that everyone turned to stare at her. "Pete?" she whispered. "Is that Pete Roberts?"

It was. But it couldn't be. Where was the shaggy sheepdog? the old grizzly bear? the lumbering goof in overalls and a plaid flannel shirt?

"Hey, Patsy." He smiled, and suddenly she realized she was definitely looking at Pete Roberts's teeth. But had she ever seen those lips? that chin? the squared jawline?

"Aren't you going to speak to me?" He paused, grinning. "I brought my homemade pecan pie—a recipe of which I am most particularly proud. I hope I haven't missed the pork steaks."

"You missed Bitty's new Missouri wraps," Luke Finley said. "They're good."

"No problem, Pete," Brad assured him. "You can drop by the Pop-In anytime you want. Hey, did you lose weight or something?"

"He shaved," Patsy said, breathing out the words with a deep sigh. "Pete shaved. You shaved off your beard."

"And got myself a haircut. I should have let you do it, Patsy, but I wanted to surprise you. I closed up early to show off my new do. So, what do you think?"

When she couldn't answer, he handed the box containing his pie to Derek Finley, took Patsy by the arm and planted a kiss right on her lips. "How's them apples, sugar?" he asked.

Patsy nearly fell right off her platform sandals. All around her, the men began to cheer. The Finley twins chanted, "Pete and Patsy sitting in a tree, k-i-s-s-i-n-g! First comes love, then comes marriage—"

"Hold it right there!" Patsy said, snapping out of her trance. "If you all will excuse me, I've got to go and sit down."

As she stepped away, trying to stay balanced on her sandals, Patsy could hear the crowd laughing and murmuring behind her. Well, she'd managed to be the focus of yet another spectacle—and once again Pete Roberts had caused it. Only this time, Patsy wasn't angry. Far from it. In fact, she was so flustered, so dizzied, so downright discombobulated that she didn't know if she could make it back to the plastic chaise.

Just when she feared she might have to slump down into the grass and take off her shoes, Pete slipped his arm under hers. "Are you mad at me again?" he asked, leaning way too close for comfort.

Patsy couldn't believe it, but he smelled like heaven itself. He'd splashed on some kind of aftershave that had hints of lemon and spice, and his breath was sweet, and it was all she could do to keep from turning him around and giving him a smooch to end all smooches.

"Patsy?" he said. "Please don't get upset. I thought you'd be glad I shaved after all this time. Especially right before winter. That's when I usually let the ol' beard grow as bushy as it can. But you kept telling me I ought to shave and get a haircut, so I finally listened. In fact, I did it for you. I'd given you a few teacups, and I couldn't think of another thing that might please you. I really did want to make you happy."

Patsy paused and turned to look into his amazing blue eyes. "You did, Pete," she said. "I'm happy, but . . . but I'm kind of scared, too."

"Scared? Of what? It's just me."

"But you look so different. You're . . . well, you're handsome."

He burst out laughing. "Handsome! First time anyone ever said that about Pete Roberts. But if that's how you feel, you'll never see another whisker on my face as long as I live."

Patsy practically tumbled onto the plastic chaise, and Pete sat down beside her on the grass. She stretched out her legs, closed her eyes, and tried to make herself think straight. Pete could *not* be that handsome. It simply wasn't possible. How many beards had she shaved off men in her lifetime? At least a dozen, and what was underneath never looked as good as that. And how many men had she seen with brand-new haircuts? Thousands? But they were never as handsome as Pete Roberts.

"You'll like my pecan pie," he said, taking her hand. "I shelled the nuts myself, and I made the crust, too. It was my grandma's recipe.

You wouldn't think a fellow like me could bake up a pecan pie, but if there was a fair anywhere near here, I bet I'd win first prize."

You sure would, Patsy thought. *But not for your pecan pie.* She opened her eyes a little and peeked over at him. No doubt about it. Pete was handsome. Oh, he wasn't rippling with muscles or sporting a deep golden tan. He didn't have gleaming white teeth and dimples. But that craggy face could just about stop a woman's heart.

"Before the men get back here, Patsy," he spoke up, "I want to tell you something. It's about fishing."

"Oh, Kim already told me," she said. "Charlie thought up the idea when he was trying to get Esther to go out to Aunt Mamie's. It worked so well that Charlie told Derek, and now all the Finleys are fishing left and right."

"They are?"

Patsy hesitated. "By fishing, do you mean that special way of talking to someone so you get what you want from them? Like Derek winning back Kim's admiration, and Kim winning Miranda's acceptance? And Lydia winning Luke's permission to be his diabetes buddy at school, even in front of all his friends?"

Pete scratched at what had once been his beard. Seeing as now it was just his chin, he didn't do it long. "I'm not talking about that kind of fishing," he said. "Though Derek Finley and I did discuss another kind of fishing after church last Sunday. You remember how the ladies were all bunched up talking about Jessica Hansen's wedding?"

"Yes. Jennifer is going to be the maid of honor, and they plan to wear apricot and carry calla lilies. I'm doing the whole bridal party's hair and nails. We've already scheduled it in my appointment book."

"Okay, well, while you were discussing all that stuff, some of us men lingered around our cars waiting for you to finish up. That's when I asked Steve Hansen about this 'fishing for men' business. He explained it to me pretty well, and then Derek Finley went to asking questions. And before long, Steve had up and decided to start a men's Bible study at Rods-N-Ends at six o'clock every Wednesday morning."

Patsy sat up straight. "A men's Bible study? Are you going to it?"

"Of course. It's at my store, remember? And that brings me to what I wanted to tell you. Even though I don't completely understand about being 'born again'—or exactly why anyone would want to fish for men—I'm giving it a shot. Derek said he'd come to the Bible study too. We're both kind of ignorant, but we like what we see in church. Even better, we like the people we know who call themselves Christians. So, Patsy, I may not be all I should be—or could be—but I hope you know I'm trying."

"Oh, Pete!" Unable to bear it another moment, Patsy threw her arms around the man's neck and hugged him tightly while tears flowed down her cheeks. "I'm so happy I don't know what to say! I can't believe you really listened to me. And cared about what I think. And shaved off that beard. And decided to go to Bible study. And—"

"Whoa, hang on a minute!" Pete's arms tightened around Patsy. "Slow up, girl. We've got us a potential problem here. It looks like trouble—but I think Derek's got it covered."

Patsy lifted her head and tried to see through the mist of tears that covered her eyes. "What is it, Pete?"

"There's something out in the lake. Looks too big to be a carp or a catfish. I don't think it's a paddlefish either. Why is it that every time we have a barbecue we wind up with a hitch in our giddyup?"

Still folded in Pete's arms, Patsy turned around and wiped at her eyes. She could see a dark shape a little way from the shoreline. It seemed to be drifting along at a slow pace—maybe it was a log or even a large turtle. Derek had picked up a heavy stick and was walking toward the water. Parents called their children out of the swim area, and everyone gathered in clumps with their arms around each other.

Just when Patsy had decided the object was some kind of debris, it rose straight out of the water. The whole crowd cried out and stumbled backward. The thing was standing now, wading to the shore.

"Is it a deer?" Patsy asked.

"Too hairy and tall. It might be a bear. It's too big for a raccoon. What is that thing?"

At that moment, the thing lifted a hand and began waving. "Hi, I'm Cody!"

"Cody!" Patsy scrambled out of the chaise so fast that Pete found himself holding air. Kicking off her sandals, she ran for the water. "It's Cody! Cody, you came back!"

"Hey, Patsy Pringle! Hey, Pete! Hey, Brenda Hansen! Hey, Steve! Hey, Mr. and Mrs. Moore!" Dripping, Cody Goss staggered onto the beach. His hair and beard had grown scraggly, and his T-shirt was covered with grease stains. "Hey, Mrs. Finley and Officer Finley! Hey, the other Mrs. Finley! Hey, Ashley and Brad! Hey, Opal!"

Patsy rushed right up to Cody and threw her arms around his skinny, wet shoulders. A moment later, nearly every person in Deepwater Cove was making a valiant effort to hug Cody. Brenda Hansen began sobbing. Ashley Hanes started tossing necklaces over his head. Kim Finley wrapped him in beach towels as her twins danced around him. Esther and Charlie were so happy they broke into a spontaneous waltz of joy. Even Brad Hanes began to applaud Cody's arrival in the neighborhood.

"You came back to us!" Patsy said as the young man made his way onto the grass. "Oh, Cody, we've missed you so much!"

"I missed you, too." He sank onto a blanket someone had spread out, and everyone gathered around him. "I missed everyone, and let me tell you something. Deepwater Cove is not an easy place to find."

"But why did you decide to leave Kansas?" Miranda Finley asked. "We thought you would be happy with your aunt."

"I think my aunt is a very nice lady," Cody said. "She told me she liked me, and she was sorry my daddy had died. Aunt Marylou stays at her flower store pretty much all the time. She makes bouquets for weddings and funerals and birthdays and holidays and church altars and hotel lobbies."

"She's a florist!" Esther said.

"Yes, and she has a big television in her house, and she told me to watch it all the time while she was gone. When she came home, we would eat together. My aunt is a vegetablearian. We ate beans and peas and lettuce and carrots. But we never ate meat. Or eggs. Or nothing interesting but nuts. We ate lots of nuts—peanuts, walnuts, macadamias, you name it."

"Yuck!" Luke Finley announced. "That's worse than my diabetic food."

"You're right," Cody said. "Yuck. Besides that, my aunt and I didn't have too much to talk about, because she was always at her shop working on flower bouquets. She said she didn't have time to teach me reading or social skills, and she didn't want me to clean anything in her house or mow her yard. Aunt Marylou always said, 'I'm glad you came for a visit. How long do you plan to stay?' I told her I was glad to have a family and a home. Anyway, one day I decided I had watched enough television to last me for a long while, because in case you didn't know, the things they do on television are not good. So I wrote my aunt a letter to say good-bye and thank you for the vegetables and come see me in Deepwater Cove sometime, because that is my real home and my real family. And then I bought a bus ticket back to St. Louis."

"St. Louis!" Patsy exclaimed, imagining the innocent young man stranded in the middle of such a large city. "But that's miles from here."

"I know. I could not find any of your houses or even Just As I Am or Rods-N-Ends. I lived in the woods for a while, just like my daddy and I used to do. But living in the woods makes you stink. And that's why . . . well, after I found Deepwater Cove a few minutes ago, I tried to get into the lake and wash off. . . . But Brenda will tell you *I am not a fish*. So, that's how come I stink."

"I don't think you stink." The voice belonged to Jennifer Hansen, who stepped between Patsy and Pete. She was carrying a plate, and she offered it to Cody as she settled down cross-legged beside him.

"Three hot dogs!" he practically shouted. "And chocolate cake!"

"Cut into squares, not triangles," Jennifer said. "Because squares are better."

Cody stared at her for a moment as if he truly could not believe his eyes. Then he picked up a hot dog. "This is the happiest day of my life," he announced. "And here's another thing I want to say. I love you, Jennifer Hansen."

The young woman smiled. "Everyone here loves you, too, Cody," she said. "Welcome back to Deepwater Cove. Welcome home."

DISCUSSION QUESTIONS

The principles and strategies illustrated in this novel are taken from *The Four Seasons of Marriage* by Gary Chapman. In this book, Dr. Chapman discusses marriage as a journey back and forth through different "seasons."

- **Springtime** in marriage is a time of new beginnings, new patterns of life, new ways of listening, and new ways of loving.

- **Summer** couples share deep commitment, satisfaction, and security in each other's love.

- **Fall** brings a sense of unwanted change, and nagging emptiness appears.

- **Winter** means difficulty. Marriage is harder in this season of cold silence and bitter winds.

1. In *Summer Breeze*, which season of the year is it in Deepwater Cove, Missouri? Which season of marriage do you think Derek and Kim Finley are experiencing? What are the signs that let you know?

2. At the start of the book, someone has drowned near Deepwater Cove. What changes does this event bring about in Derek's life? How does the drowning affect Kim? What does the news mean to Cody? Can you think of an example in your own experience in which God has used one event to bring about change in many peoples' lives?

3. What are Luke and Lydia like at the beginning of the book? How do their personalities change through the story? How does a family's structure affect children? How does the parents' relationship affect children's behavior?

4. On the way to church, the Finley family erupts into a furious argument (pages 135–139). What is the end result for each member of the family? Do you ever find your own family engaged in disagreements on the way to church? Catherine Palmer's family refers to these quarrels as "holy wars." Why do you suppose tensions are so high at such times? Can you think of some good ways to prevent "holy wars" in your family?

5. Patsy Pringle gets angry with Pete Roberts over the lawn chair incident at the Fourth of July barbecue (page 117). How does her version of the event differ from his? What is the root cause of her anger? Twice, Patsy is challenged to forgive Pete. Why do you suppose it takes her so long to admit her wrongdoing? What does Cody say that finally propels Patsy to forgive Pete? How can we forgive others?

6. What does Miranda think of Christians? What are her own religious beliefs? How does Jennifer Hansen respond to Miranda's declarations about religion (page 183)? What do you think of Jennifer's method of stating her beliefs? Have you ever tried to share your faith with someone else? Has anyone tried to tell you about a religion different from yours? What happened?

7. In this book, Kim and Derek are dealing with Luke's diabetes. What impact can a chronic illness have on a family—financially, physically, emotionally, and in other ways? How is Kim handling the situation at the start of the book? What is Derek's attitude about Luke's problem? How has Dr. Groene chosen to deal with his diabetes?

8. In the first book in this series, *It Happens Every Spring*, Steve and Brenda Hansen's marital problems grew from within their relationship. In this book, Kim and Derek face trouble that comes from outside their marriage. They are struggling not only with Luke's illness but also with a blended family and with in-law relationships. But Kim and Derek also have trouble within their marriage. What are some of the mistakes they have made in building their relationship?

9. Strategy 3 in *The Four Seasons of Marriage* encourages couples to discover and speak each other's primary love language. The five love languages are (1) words of affirmation, (2) acts of service, (3) receiving gifts, (4) physical touch, and (5) quality time. What love language does Derek speak? How can you tell? What is Kim's response to his way of communicating love? What is Kim's love language? How does Derek feel about it?

10. In this book, Charlie Moore teaches Derek how to "fish" (pages 171–172). "Fishing" is Strategy 4—empathetic listening—in *The Four Seasons of Marriage*. What is the goal of this kind of "fishing"? Practical ways to do this include (1) listening with an attitude of understanding (not judgment); (2) withholding judgment on the other person's ideas; (3) affirming the other person, even when

you disagree with his or her ideas; and (4) sharing your own ideas only after the other person feels understood. How did Derek begin to listen empathetically to Lydia? to Kim? How was Kim's "bait" different from Derek's? Can you describe how you might listen empathetically to your spouse or loved one regarding an area of disagreement in your relationship?

11. Think about the other couples in *Summer Breeze*. Along with Kim and Derek Finley, you have met Ashley and Brad Hanes, Esther and Charlie Moore, and Brenda and Steve Hansen. Patsy Pringle, viewing her salon as a garden, describes the season she believes each woman is experiencing in marriage (pages 85–87). From what you have learned about these marriages, would you agree with Patsy? Why or why not?

12. During a meeting of the TLC, Cody quotes a Bible passage his father taught him, Isaiah 2:18-21: "Idols will completely disappear. When the Lord rises to shake the earth, his enemies will crawl into holes in the ground. They will hide in caves in the rocks from the terror of the Lord and the glory of his majesty. On that day of judgment they will abandon the gold and silver idols they made for themselves to worship. They will leave their gods to the rodents and bats, while they crawl away into caverns and hide among the jagged rocks in the cliffs. They will try to escape the terror of the Lord and the glory of his majesty as he rises to shake the earth" (NLT). What characteristics of God does this passage reveal? Do these traits fit with your concept of Him? What are idols, and why is God so angry about them? Idols made of gold, silver, brass, clay, and wood are still worshipped in many countries of the world, mostly in the East. Are there other things that people in the Western world idolize?

13. In this book, the character of Cody is childlike in his faith and understanding. Recall some of the truths he speaks and how they affect the other characters. What was your favorite "Cody moment"?

ABOUT THE AUTHORS

Catherine Palmer lives in Missouri with her husband, Tim, and sons, Geoffrey and Andrei. She is a graduate of Southwest Baptist University and holds a master's degree in English from Baylor University. Her first book was published in 1988. Since then, Catherine has published more than 40 novels and won numerous awards for her writing, including the Christy Award—the highest honor in Christian fiction—in 2001 for *A Touch of Betrayal*. In 2004 she was given the Career Achievement Award for Inspirational Romance by *Romantic Times BOOKreviews* magazine. More than 2 million copies of Catherine's novels are currently in print.

Dr. Gary Chapman is the author of *The Four Seasons of Marriage*, the perennial best seller *The Five Love Languages* (over 3.5 million copies sold), and numerous other marriage and family books. He is the director of Marriage & Family Life Consultants, Inc., an internationally known speaker, and host of *A Growing Marriage*, a syndicated radio program heard on more than 100 stations across North America. He and his wife, Karolyn, live in North Carolina.

Turn the page for an exciting preview from

FOUR SEASONS

Falling for You Again

the third book in the

FOUR SEASONS SERIES

by Catherine Palmer & Gary Chapman

Available Fall 2007

TYNDALE
FICTION

www.tyndalefiction.com

Falling for You Again

Charlie had his mind on tomatoes as he drove around the curve that led to his clapboard house with its neatly manicured lawn. Feeling a little itchy for change, he had tried some different varieties this year. In the past, Esther had wanted only beefsteak and cherry tomatoes. Beefsteaks for their sandwiches and cherries for their salads. But Charlie had put in three new bushes as an experiment—pear-shaped romas, a yellow variety, and even one that had a hint of purple to it. To his surprise, Esther thought the new tomatoes tasted delicious, and she had enjoyed showing them off at Deepwater Cove's Labor Day barbecue.

Having decided to be bold with peppers in the coming spring, Charlie was pondering the difference between sweet bells, anchos, and jalapeños when he heard a loud bang from the direction of his carport. He saw the back end of Esther's long bronze Lincoln traveling forward at ninety-to-nothing. The car had already taken down one of the wooden support posts holding up the carport's roof. Now it crashed through a second post and sailed off the four-foot-high concrete wall that divided the driveway from the backyard.

Charlie stepped on his brake, gaping in disbelief as the Lincoln flew through the air and then slammed down a good ten feet onto the lawn. The hood popped open and the horn began to blare. And the car kept going, careening across the grass as steam billowed from the engine and the hood bounced up and down like a jack-in-the-box lid. Somehow the Lincoln swerved around the purple martin house before grazing the trunk of an oak tree and mowing down a walnut sapling. Then it hurtled toward the thin strip of beach and the lake edge beyond.

His heart frozen in his chest, Charlie put his own car in park, jerked back the emergency brake, and threw open the door. Was someone stealing the Lincoln? Had it rolled down the driveway on its own? Or could that dark shape in the driver's seat be his wife?

"Esther?" Charlie took off at a dead run. The Lincoln was now barreling toward the shed. Charlie had built it a few years before to store his riding lawn mower and tools. Just as the car reached the shed door, it veered to the right.

"Mrs. Moore! Mrs. Moore, stop!" Cody Goss suddenly burst from the house, leaped off the end of the carport, and raced past Charlie. "Mrs. Moore, the post office is the other direction!"

With the Lincoln's horn still blaring, Charlie could hear little else as he watched the car miss the side of the shed by inches. It pulled around in a tight curve, swayed toward the lake again, and then rolled to a sudden stop beside a lilac bush. Smoke billowed out from under the hood, and steaming water gushed onto the ground. The unremitting horn sounded louder than ever.

Cody reached the car five steps ahead of Charlie, but as the young man grabbed the handle, the door swung open. Esther surged up from the driver's seat, shoved her way past Cody, and headed up the slope in her high heels.

"Where's the mail?" she shouted. "I've got to get to the post office before it closes."

"Mrs. Moore, you had an accident!" Cody called after her as she marched toward Charlie, arms flapping in agitation.

"Esther, what on earth?" Charlie caught her by the shoulders and forced her to stop. "Are you all right, honey? What happened?"

"I can't find the mail," she snapped. "Cody keeps moving it, and I'm late for the post office. Those bill aren't going out today unless I—"

She looked up at her husband and seemed to see him for the first time. "Charlie?"

"Esther." He wrapped his arms around her and drew her close. "Oh, sweetheart, you scared me half to death."

"I don't know . . . I'm not sure what happened, Charlie."

"You drove the Lincoln out the wrong end of the carport. You've been in an accident, honey. Let's sit you down."

"Where's my purse?"

"Here, sit on my jacket."

"On the grass?"

"Yes, right here. I'll help you." He pulled off his lightweight jacket and spread it out for her. Then he eased her down onto the lawn. "Now catch your breath, Esther."

"What did Cody do to my car?" She glared in the direction of the shed. Cody was leaning into the driver's side of the Lincoln. A sudden silence sounded loud as he somehow managed to turn off the horn.

"Look at that boy," Esther grumbled. "He's gone and wrecked my car. I knew we never should have taken him on. You think you can trust someone, and then . . . where's the mail, Charlie? I've got to hurry to the post office. And my hair. Good heavens, I'm late for my set-and-style."

As she checked her watch, Charlie noticed a discoloration on her wrist. "You're hurt! Esther, honey, let me see your other arm. Oh, for pete's sake, sweetheart, you're all bruised up."

"Esther? Charlie, what happened?"

He looked up to see their neighbor Kim Finley hurrying across the lawn with her twins in tow. "Charlie, is Esther all right?"

"We heard the crash!" Lydia sang out.

"Your carport roof is caving in, Mr. Moore," Luke added as they neared the couple seated on the grass. "You lost the two middle support posts."

Behind them, Charlie noticed Brenda Hansen and Kim's mother-in-law, Miranda Finley, moving toward the scene. Suddenly it seemed like half the neighborhood was descending on the Moores.

"I wish Derek was here," Kim cried as she knelt in the grass at Esther's feet. "He's got all that first aid training. Charlie, it looks like she might have hit her head. Her face is beginning to swell."

"Whose face?" Esther asked. She was looking from one person to another. "What's wrong? What happened?"

"You drove the wrong way out of the carport," Cody told her. "You meant to go backward, but you went forward. We need to call 911 right now, because that's what you do when someone has an accident. Even if they don't look hurt too much, they could be hurt inside, and that's why the doctor needs to check them. I saw it on TV when I was at my aunt's house and all I did was watch TV and eat vegetables. They said to call the ambulance no matter what."

"I've already called." Brenda Hansen, crouched beside Esther, took her hand. "Do you remember getting into your car?"

"Well, that's what I've been trying to tell everyone. I need to get to the post office. And Patsy's expecting me for my set-and-style."

Charlie had noticed a lump growing in his throat, and he tried to speak around it. "After you got into the car, honey, why did you put it in drive instead of reverse?"

Esther gazed at him, her blue eyes misty. "Did I do that?"

"Do you recall driving off the end of the carport?"

"I saw the birdhouse, that's all." She blinked a couple of times, and then she turned to where the car was still sending up clouds of steam. "I looked up, and the birdhouse was coming right at me, so I turned the car a little bit. And then there was a tree."

"Two trees," Cody said. "You did some fancy steering, Mrs. Moore. You missed the birdhouse, the trees, and even the shed."

"Well, what do you know. . . ."

"We know you scared us halfway to deaf!" Cody exclaimed. "I still can hardly hear. But I got the horn to quit, and here are your keys. I switched off the engine all by myself."

Charlie reached up and took the keys. The Lincoln wouldn't be going anywhere soon, if ever again, he realized. The front end looked somewhat like an accordion, and the smell from the smashed radiator still hung in the cool late-afternoon air.

"I hear the ambulance," Esther said. "Oh, goodness, I don't think that's necessary. But I guess we ought to go and thank them anyway for coming out this far."

As she moved, Charlie saw her pretty face crumple in pain. "You sit right here with me, Esther," he said, tucking her under his arm. "Just the two of us. We'll sit here together, and everything will be fine."

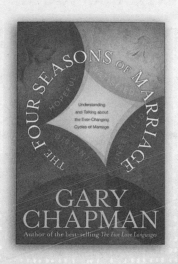

Introducing the

Chapman Guides

Simple solutions to life's most difficult problems

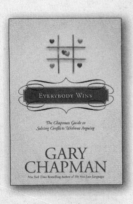

Everybody Wins

The Chapman Guide to
Solving Conflicts Without Arguing

Conflict is inevitable.
Arguing is a choice.

Relationship expert Dr. Gary Chapman provides a simple blueprint to help you and your spouse find win-win solutions to everyday disagreements and leave both of you feeling loved, listened to, and appreciated.

Home Improvements

The Chapman Guide to
Negotiating Change With Your Spouse

Is your spouse's behavior driving you crazy?

Over time, annoying little habits can wreak havoc on a relationship. After years of counseling battle-weary couples, Dr. Gary Chapman has developed a simple and effective approach that will help you and your spouse turn those irritating behaviors around once and for all.

PROFIT SHARING

The Chapman Guide to
Making Money an Asset in Your Marriage

WHEN YOURS AND MINE BECOME OURS.

Money is often listed as the number-one source of conflict in marriage. In this simple and practical guide, Dr. Gary Chapman shows couples how to work together as a team to manage their finances.

NOW WHAT?

The Chapman Guide to
Marriage After Children

AND THEN THERE WERE THREE.

In his trademark simple, direct, conversational style, relationship expert Dr. Gary Chapman answers the age-old question, "How do we keep our marriage alive now that the children have arrived?"

Available now in stores and online!

BOOKS BY BEST-SELLING AUTHOR
CATHERINE PALMER

FOUR SEASONS FICTION SERIES
(COAUTHORED WITH GARY CHAPMAN)

It Happens Every Spring
Summer Breeze
Falling for You Again (COMING SOON!)

THE MISS PICKWORTH SERIES

The Affectionate Adversary
The Bachelor's Bargain
The Courteous Cad (COMING SOON!)

ENGLISH IVY SERIES

Wild Heather
English Ivy
Sweet Violet
A Victorian Rose

TREASURES OF THE HEART SERIES

A Kiss of Adventure
A Whisper of Danger
A Touch of Betrayal
Sunrise Song

A TOWN CALLED HOPE SERIES

Prairie Rose
Prairie Fire
Prairie Storm

FINDERS KEEPERS SERIES

Finders Keepers
Hide and Seek

CHRISTMAS ANTHOLOGY SERIES

A Victorian Christmas Tea
A Victorian Christmas Quilt
A Victorian Christmas Cottage
Cowboy Christmas

STAND-ALONE SUSPENSE

A Dangerous Silence
Fatal Harvest

STAND-ALONE

The Happy Room
Love's Proof
The Loved One
(coauthored with Peggy Stoks)

Visit www.catherinepalmer.com today!

have you visited tyndalefiction.com lately?

Only there can you find:

→ books hot off the press

→ first chapter excerpts

→ inside scoops on your favorite authors

→ author interviews

→ contests

→ fun facts

→ and much more!

Sign up for your **free** newsletter!

Visit us today at: **tyndalefiction.com**

Tyndale fiction does more than entertain.

→ *It touches the heart.*

→ *It stirs the soul.*

→ *It changes lives.*

That's why Tyndale is so committed to being first in fiction!

TYNDALE FICTION